Planet Hibernia, A.D. 3153

Began May 1979 Completed October 29 1979

by

John J. Shelton

DORRANCE PUBLISHING CO., INC.
PITTSBURGH, PENNSYLVANIA 15222

First Printing
For more information or to order additional books, please contact:
Dorrance Publishing Co., Inc.
701 Smithfield Street
Third Floor
Pittsburgh, Pennsylvania 15222
U.S.A.
1-800-788-7654
www.dorrancebookstore.com

Acknowledgments and Dedication

I would like to thank the following people
for their inspiration and assistance:

To my brother Allan and his son Dale for inspiring Uncle Eugene.
To Bruce Benstein for inspiring Joe Harrigan.
To Judy Hanning for inspiring Cathal and Deirdre.
To Vivian Source for typing the story.
To Tom Lundie, who gave me a table of hyperlight speed.
To Diane Meskin, Jim Miyahara, and Mary Beth Webber for a table of
metric measurements and a list of sub-atomic particles.
To Todd Marsh for drawing my face.

This story is dedicated to those who are working to
make the island country Ireland truly a nation once again.

Prologue

The Great Migration from planet Earth to the Outer Solar System was one of the major epics of the human race. Space exploration had taken place since the twentieth century. At the dawn of the twenty-second century, science developed light-speed travel. Late in the twenty-third century, space technology invented new hyperlight transportation factors up to fifteen, which made exploration of deep space by manned vehicles possible. Alpha Centuri, fifty-one light-months distant, could now be reached in three and one-half months.

In 2349 an unmanned series of probes reached a solar system fifteen light-years from Earth. The solar system consisted of twenty-five planets of varying sizes, densities, and gravities. These planets were found to be habitable. A series of manned exploration teams reported that these planets could support colonization.

In 2387 the first interplanetary settlement squadron left Earth. It consisted of five giant transport craft, over one kilometer long and up to one-quarter kilometer in diameter, traveling at hyperlight speeds. The first five planets were settled on the basis of a certain nationality moving to one particular planet. One planet was selected to be settled by the Soviet Union, and the colonists named their planet "Sovietia." The second planet was settled by Germany, Austria, and part of Switzerland. It became the planet Deutsch.

After the inaugural flight in 2387, squadrons of the giant hyperlight transports began to leave Earth every three years. Entire populations were transferred. Planets were settled by specific Earth nations. Certain small nations were put together on a planet, although in separate quadrants. On one planet, French colonists were placed in the northern hemisphere while

Italians settled in the south. People coming from the Benelux nations colonized a habitable moon that revolved around the planet.

At first colonization was primarily by science-oriented explorers. This was followed by mining interests that began to ship gold, silver, oil tars, uranium, etc., back to Earth. As the planet Earth was plagued by overpopulation, pollution, and scarcity of mineral supplies, the movement, led by political leaders, to migrate en masse to the Outer Solar System gained momentum.

Through the twenty-fifth century, the transport squadrons left Earth once every year. Whole Earth nations were depopulated, and empty stretches of land began returning to wilderness. Only handfuls of people remained. These were led by religious or environmentalist cults opposed to technology. In the eastern hemisphere, a combination of the nations of Japan, China, Korea, and India elected to remain on Earth. The political leaders of the Combine planned an Earth-based technological development to rebuild the planet abandoned by the colonists. However, they did open diplomatic relations with a planet colonized by people from their nations. In Africa, a similar combine was formed. Its colonial settlement was on the planet Nigeria, its colonists coming from the entire African landmass. There were nation-planets settled in the Outer Solar System. The planet Transylvania was where the Romanian colonists settled in the eastern hemisphere and Hungarians in the western. The people from Poland settled a medium-sized planet which they named "Polonia." The planet Bohemia, settled by Czechs, revolved around Polonia like a habitable moon. The gravitational pull caused by their proximity caused massive tidal waves which were harnessed for electrical power.

A similar case developed for the planet Balkan, whose colonists were Yugoslavs, Bulgars, and Greeks. The Albanians inhabited the moon of Balkan.

Ironically, one nation remained totally uninvolved—indeed, opposed to the epic migration—the United States of America, which had once led in space exploration. In the twenty-first century an environmentalist-political party came to power. All nuclear plants and most coal-fired electrical plants were shut down. The new rulers proclaimed electricity would be generated by the sun itself. This proved to be a cruel hoax. Electricity became so scarce that radio and television communications collapsed. Only electrical lighting remained. The only people who had sufficient power for the conveniences associated with American life were a handful of people wealthy enough to afford windmill generators or expensive solar power cells. These privileged few were the bureaucrats or academics of the Ecology party in power and the film-industry colony that supported them.

Throughout the twenty-first century massive emigration depopulated the once powerful USA. Total numbers fell from a peak of 281 million in 2007 to only 104 million by the dawn of the twenty-second century. Millions of those who had ambitions and scientific beliefs fled to Canada or Mexico, which were rapidly industrializing. Those who remained were so sedated by drugs, legalized in 2009, that no real opposition faced the Ecol-fascists until the Scientist Revolt in 2087, resulting in a decade of rioting and an end to the drugged era. The Ecol-fascists ordered the building of a "death zone" at the 49th Parallel and the Rio Grande borders. It resembled the old wall in the two Berlins of Germany.

By the year 2118, the USA was a totalitarian state. At this time Russia—whose old militarists had died out—had achieved a high level of both personal and economic freedom. There was another bloody uprising in 2160 by an underground cadre of scientists. They had secretly taught the forbidden articles of chemistry and nuclear physics. As a concession to the people, a highly processed coal was allowed in sufficient amounts for generating plants. Steam engines again powered trains, electric turbines, and ships. For the next millenium, America's technology stood rigidly at approximately the year 1910. Alcohol and coal oil brought back the limited use of buses and motorcars. Many of these vehicles had been stored in museums, private warehouses, and even caves for over one hundred years.

When the migration began to the Outer Solar System, the U.S. government opposed the entire idea. Their claim was that "It would pollute the heavens as we polluted the Earth." American leaders refused an offer by the United Nations Space Council to build solar satellites. These space crafts, orbiting at 800 kilometers above Earth, would beam solar-generated electrical power to Earth in the form of microwaves. Ironically, back in the twenty-first century, the Ecol-fascists had claimed this power source would replace the outlawed nuclear plants. The only concession made by the U.S. government was a limited annual quota of emigration visas. This enabled nearly 35 million Americans to join in the colonization of the new planet-nations, although as citizens of other countries.

An American Cultural Preservation Society carried on the culture of that once proud land. Its music, sports, and arts were exhibited on nearly every planet in the new solar system. It held the continuing hope that someday America would again join her brethren in science and progress.

In 3107 a dozen hyperlight transports returned to Earth. They came under the auspices of the Interplanetary Federation, an outgrowth of the United Nations. The explorers landed by shuttle craft in the African and Eurasian Co-prosperity Republics. Then the teams sailed by hydro-foil and hovercraft to just off the coast of the North American continent, where they transferred to an armada of ancient steam and sail ships. The exploration team spent seven months in America, secretly contacting scientists underground while gathering entire catalogues of information on American life. A treaty was signed again allowing emigration to the Eastern republics and from there to the Outer Solar System.

Of all the signatories to the treaty, the proudest nation-planet was Hibernia, for that nation had just emerged from her own Dark Ages.

By 2500 the planet Hibernia had been completely settled by the old Earth nation of Ireland. The *auld sod* had achieved both unity and independence back in the twenty-first century. For over three hundred years, Hibernia had a "Golden Age." The use of Gaelic, the noble tongue of Gael, had been recovered by 85 percent of the populations. Her people had never achieved such a high level of prosperity. The beauty of the planet attracted settlers from other nation-planets. Soon the tongues of many peoples were added to the land. There were many refugees from the Earth-planet nation America. Hibernia had a higher percentage of members of the American Cultural Society than any other nation-planet. This was understandable, since on Earth the Irish people settled in America in the nineteenth century.

The Hibernians constructed their capital, Athlone, in their southern hemisphere. They named the four quadrants for the provinces on the old Earth: Ulster in the northeast; Connaught in the northwest, and the southern quadrants were Leinster in the east; and Munster in the west. Athlone rests on the border between the southern quadrants, on a plateau south of a massive swamp. At the very spot where the four quadrants intersect, they had constructed a subterranean railway over two kilometers deep. Their vacuum-gravity propulsion reached speeds of up to 4800 kilometers per hour. It had been, indeed, a Golden Age; but it came suddenly to a halt.

Hibernia was unfortunately to be nearest to her enemy, the planet Brittania. That planet had been settled by the Earth countries of Great Britain, Canada, Australia, and New Zealand. Her royalist-aristocratic government had never forgiven the Irish people who had broken from Britain in the twentieth century. Hibernia supported the planet Hindustan when the Brittanians threatened economic encroachments.

In 2994 Brittania attacked its Hibernian neighbors without a formal declaration of war. Thermonuclear-tipped interplanetary missiles destroyed Athlone, Dublin, and other cities of the Irish planet. Then transports, used in the migration, landed a mass of troops. Hibernia became a province, her people deported to Brittania, where they were used as slaves for twenty years.

Brittanian mining and industrial interests built a complex in the northeast quadrant. Whole families spent decades in exile. Young men were seized at the age of sixteen and not returned to their homes until the age of forty.

But the Fenian spirit has physical properties that cannot be destroyed, and gradually an Irish "underground" was formed. It received the help of idealistic volunteers from all over the solar system, even anti-royalist Brittanians. The subterranean railway, buried for thirty years, was used without detection to train guerrillas.

In 3085 the great uprising began in the southern hemisphere, then spread to Connaught and massed an assault on the Ulster quadrant. Small shuttle craft, armed with lasers, destroyed the missiles that the Brittanians fired at the planet. They wiped out an entire troop convoy and ferried through space to the northeast quadrant, but the final assault on the quadrant failed. A peace treaty came about when Brittania was paralyzed by a rebellion in the Scottish and Welsh sectors near the south pole of the royal planet. Although three quarters of Hibernia was free, the Union Jack still flew over the Ulster quadrant.

In 3124 the Brittanians launched another nuclear attack, only to have several troop convoys lost in near space eight hundred kilometers above Hibernia. Still her quadrant garrison held after an eleven-month siege.

In 3149 the Brittanians launched assaults with their laser-armed Boomerang fighter-bombers; great damage was suffered in Hibernia's major cities. The advent of Hibernian Needlecraft fighters soon ended enemy raids; however, assisted by a fleet of space tankers, they raided Brittania itself, but the Hibernians still lacked the power to overwhelm the quadrant.

In the decades between the conflicts, Brittania had employed pirate spaceships to blockade Hibernia. This only served to sharpen Hibernia's fighting skills.

Now, in the year 3153, peace talks have broken off after three years; again the clouds of war threaten.

* * *

Main unit of currency:

- 1 coin of 1.333 grams, 75% gold, 25% alloy.

Sub units:

- 1 coin of 4 grams, 75% silver, 25% alloy, 10 silver to 1 gold.
- 1 coin of 10 grams, 75% copper, 25% silver, 20 copper to 1 gram silver.

Private citizens can have coins assayed without government permission. No paper currency can be issued except during a declared war, and these are to be retired quickly afterward. Any government bonds are to be sold and redeemed for hard coins only. No connection of paper money to public bonded debt is allowed.

Preface

The History of the Third Millenium
A.D. 3000–3150

The Colonization of Deep Space

Humanity, in its long history, had experienced few epics to compare to the Great Migration to the Outer Solar System. It reached its highest level of intensity in the mid-twenty-fifth century and remained at that level until the mid-twenty-seventh century. From the twentieth century onward, man had explored space. Aero-space engineers had developed engines that could reach the speed of light by the early twenty-second century. After this the Doppler effect on navigation and communications formed a new speed barrier. It took fifty years of complex experiments before the Taurus-Astro compensatory computer was invented. Then, in the late twenty-third century, double-positive ion reactors reached fifteen times light speed. The marriage of the Taurus computer to factor 15 hyperlight drive made exploration of deep space by manned spaceships possible. Alpha Centuri, fifty-one light-months from Earth, was reached in three and a half months.

In 2349 a series of unmanned probes reached a solar system fifteen light-years from Earth. It consisted of over two dozen planets of varying sizes, densities, and gravities. There were, in addition, many moon-sized planetoids. One or more of these small spheres would revolve around a larger planet, like a moon. Finally, there were asteroids suitable for navigation stations.

Several scientific explorations determined that the planets could be habitable and that mining operations were feasible. After 2360, several such operations proved successful. Then the United Nations prepared a program of colonization. To avoid conflicts, planets of specific size were assigned to Earth nations on the basis of relative population and geographic size.

In 2387 the first interplanetary settlement squadron left Earth. It consisted of five blimp-shaped space transports over one kilometer long and up to one-half kilometer in diameter, traveling at hyperlight factor 15. The first planet settled was a Jupiter-sized planet with several planetoids orbiting around it. It was colonized by the nations of the former Soviet Union and was thus named Sovietia, as it was decided to reform this union. The major population groups, i.e., Russians, Byleo Russians, and Ukrainians were settled on the main planet. The many minority groups were colonized on the planetoids. The Baltic peoples, like the Latvians, were kept on one planetoid, while Moldavians and Armenians settled a second habitable moon. Still a third planetoid became the new home for Uzbeks, Kalmucks, Turkomen, etc.

The second planet nation to be colonized became the planet Deutsch. It was allotted to the peoples of Germany, Austria, and the largest part of Switzerland. The third planet to be colonized was divided by the French and Italians. The former took the northern hemisphere, while the latter colonized the southern half of the planet. Citizens of the Benelux countries settled one planetoid, while another became the home of the transplanted Vatican.

The fourth and fifth planets colonized were on the same orbital path around the sun of the Outer Solar System. The larger of the two was settled by the Spanish-speaking nations of Earth. The second planet was colonized by their Portuguese-speaking neighboring countries.

After the inaugural flight in 2387, a second squadron of the giant hyperlight transports left three years later. The next planets to be colonized were several of the larger ones. The planet Sino was assigned to the Earth nation of China. The tributary planetoids around it were settled by Mongolians, Tibetans, Koreans, and Indo-Chinese. The Earth nation Japan carried out a phenomenal feat of geographical engineering to develop what became the planet Nippon. It housed almost all of its colonists on the outer planetoids. The main planet was almost wholly ocean, with a series of islands forming chains of land. Coffer dams were built linking a series of islands that formed a huge chain, then the water was pumped out leaving a dried-out ocean floor. A wholly enclosed, water-tight city was constructed on the ocean floor, with tunnels running up to the islands. Then the water was slowly released back in place and the coffer dam removed. As the number of underwater cities grew, the Japanese colonists settled onto the main planet. The planetoids were given to the Korean and Ainu minorities.

The people from the sub-continent of India settled the huge planet Hindustan. The peoples of Nepal and Bhutan colonized another planetoid moon. The entire black population of Africa settled planet Nigeria. The Arab population of the northern part of that great Earth continent settled one large planetoid. A much smaller habitable moon became Afrikaanderstan, the home of the whites of South Africa.

After the year 2400, a transport squadron left Earth every year, even making round trips. Earth was badly strained by overpopulation and tight supplies of minerals. That, and man's natural wanderlust, led officials of all nations to plan the mass transfer of Earth's people into space.

More planets were colonized and developed. Peoples from Poland and Czechoslovakia made homes on what became the Planet Polonia and the planetoid Bohemia. The planet Brittania was a medium-sized planet; however, its populations came not just from Great Britain but also from Canada, Australia, and New Zealand. The mother country settled the eastern hemisphere, English people in the northeast quadrant, Scots and Welsh in the southeast. Canadians developed the northern part of the western hemisphere. The southwest quadrant became the new home for Australians and New Zealanders. The government decided to build the new city of London near the North Pole. A large area of underground springs was found, providing geothermal steam. Heating and electricity would be available, making a comfortable city in that frigid zone. From the island nation on Earth, Windsor Castle and Buckingham Palace were disassembled and sent to New London. The royal castles were reassembled inside a massive steel and glass geodesic dome that became known as the Crystal Palace.

A less-friendly engineering feat was carried out on the planet Transylvania. The Hungarians colonized an island continent in the western hemisphere. The Romanians settled a vast chain of islands in the east. The latter built a coffer dam around their hemisphere. Then they removed the water, in effect cutting the planet in two. For the next three centuries, the two nations had far more trade with other planet-nations than with each other.

After 2500 the Islamic planet nations Arabia and Turko-Persia were settled. They even received migrants from the Islamic planetoids of Sovietia and Nigeria. A planet that rotated on an east-west axis instead of a north-south axis became Scandinavia. Previously empty planetoids of Sino and Hindustan were settled by Thailand, Burma, Malaysia, Java, and other Pacific islands. The Greeks, Bulgarians, and Yugoslavians settled the planet Balkan. A planetoid was settled by Albanians.

There were two planet-nations colonized in the twenty-seventh century. Planet Abraham was settled by the Earth nation Israel and Jewish people from around Earth. It was the smallest of the planet-nations, almost a planetoid. It was located right between its ancient foes Arabia and Turko-Persia, but peace reigned between these planets.

The very last planet settled was Hibernia, colonized from the nation of Ireland. The Hibernians divided their planet into four quadrants and thirty-two sectors. These were named for the provinces and counties of the nation back on Earth. In the northeast was the Ulster quadrant, which included Donegal, Antrim, and Cavan sectors. In the southeast was Leinster quadrant, in which were Dublin, Wicklow, and other sectors. Kerry and Clare sectors were among those in Munster quadrant. Connaught quadrant included Sligo and Roscommon sectors. The Hibernians built their capital, Athlone, on a high plateau south of a massive marshland where the four quadrants intersected. Using laser drills, a subterranean railway network was built, often over two kilometers deep. Using a vacuum-gravity propulsion system, it reached speeds up to forty-eight thousand kilometers per hour.

By 2700 the massive migration from Earth had spent itself. The planet-nations began to turn inward to develop their lands. It was found that transports could efficiently operate between the planet-nations at factor 2. The only advance in hyperlight technology was an unmanned shuttle that reached factor 50. An Interplanetary Federation was formed to control space navigation and suppress space piracy. On Earth two super-national governments were formed. The first was the Eurasian People's Co-prosperity Republic, reaching, in one journalist's words, "from Paris to Peking, from the mouth of the Seine to the mouth of the Yangtse." The second co-prosperity republic was formed in Africa. By 2719 a report by professional demographers estimated that 75 percent of the population of the Eastern hemisphere had migrated to the Outer Solar System. Although far less accurate, they also reported that 90 percent of the people of the Western hemisphere had left Earth.

The Fall of America

At the dawn of the twenty-first century, the United States of America was at the twilight of its prosperity. That great nation was pouring its financial resources into one desperately needed project: national defense. Project Odin was inaugurated in 1987. Its purpose was to develop an electro-magnetic force shield to protect the North American continent from nuclear missiles. At that point in history, the U.S. and the former Soviet Union were total enemies threatening each other with destruction. In 2004 the first test of the shield was conducted; a missile with a live thermonuclear warhead was fired at Baker Island in the Pacific Ocean. A force shield projector tower had been constructed, operated by a remote control computer. The shield successfully destroyed the missile by impact at an altitude of forty kilometers. The Defense Department prepared to develop a force shield to cover the entire continent by 2013; however, a radical political change resulted in the cancellation of that project in 2011.

Back in the 1970s the U.S. and other industrial nations had begun to shift from an economical system based on fossil fuels to one based on nuclear power. Scientists were working to unlock the key to nuclear fusion. Since this form of power comes from deuterium and tritium in seawater, this would permanently solve the shortage of fuel. Tragically, this was opposed by an extreme environmentalist political party. It was a coalition of renegade scientists, neo-fascistic consumerists, and pseudo-intellectuals in the entertainment industry. They held a massive convention in San Francisco in 2002. They had held up construction of nuclear reactors used to generate electricity for two decades. Many reactors built in the 1960s and 1970s had reached the end of their operational life. Once a power plant was de-activated and disassembled, it was not replaced.

The Ecology Party also opposed the use of coal as a means of generating electricity or providing other energy needs. Mining coal, processing it into synthetic oils, even advanced magnetohydrodynamics, were considered too dangerous to the air and water. Even large hydropower dams were unacceptable because they would ruin scenic wild rivers. Their alternative to all these was a series of soft technologies. Alcohol from garbage, grains, and wood scraps was offered as automotive fuel. Solar waters were seen as a means to produce electricity. Biomass was offered as a source of gas. Windmills, "small" dams, and geothermal steam were proposed for electricity. The irony of their program was that they also favored designating much more land as wilderness. This would cut off access to geothermal steam and wood for windmills or alcohol.

Most creditable scientists warned that soft technology would not provide the electricity needed for an expanding economy. However, because the Ecology Party was backed by many celebrities, their views brain-washed public opinion. There was also a clear link between the anti-technology movement and a degenerate counter-culture. This cult promoted the use of drugs and open sexuality. This was compared to the bread and circuses of Imperial Rome.

In 2009 the Ecology Party took political power. They immediately shut down all remaining nuclear plants. They were padlocked and soon became a technological equivalent of Stonehenge. Most coal-fired electric plants were phased out. A draconian program to conserve electricity was legislated. At the same time, all recreational drugs, gambling, and commercialized sex were decriminalized or legalized. In 2011 an extreme tax was levied on the metal alloys used in firearms. A system of bounties was offered for turning in firearms. A quarter century later, in 2037, a personal property tax was levied on firearms, except ancient muzzle loaders. This was part of the anti-gun element of the counter-culture. It also curbed potential opposition to the government.

In 2029 the Environmental Trusteeship Act was passed. A person or group of persons could be entrusted with sizeable areas of land if maintained at, or restored to, a wilderness setting. Using the law of eminent domain, it became a means of taking lands from those who had put them into production.

By the dawn of the Twenty-second century, Trusteeships could be inherited. An observer from Great Britain made a profound comment: "When

William the Norman conquered England in 1066, his retainers obtained title to lands occupied by masses of Saxon peasants. Villages and cropland reverted to forest. Although its objective is allegedly different, the Trusteeship program has the exact same result. Ownership of land is to be concentrated in what amounts to a form of aristocracy."

Two other tools were used by the government to implement its policy. One was the expansion of regional administrators who overrode local elected officials. This program was based on a presidential executive order from 1969 that drew ten governmental regions in the country. Region 5, for example, consisted of six north central states, with Chicago, Illinois, as the capitol. Illinois, in turn, was subdivided into seven subregions. As the years passed, the representative, republican form of government disappeared. The other tool was the Environmental Regulatory Enforcement Bureau. At the beginning of 2034, the bureau consisted of civilian inspectors; however, as the century passed, the bureau began to wear green paramilitary uniforms. A visitor from France compared their outfits to the gendarmes, i.e., French police. The title soon became official. They began to carry firearms, and to use them.

By 2030 it was clear that the nation was in decline. Electrical brownouts and blackouts became very frequent. The government blamed the utilities and levied penalty taxes, which made conditions worse. Only the wealthy could afford windmill generators or solar cells. Radio, television, and computers, the basis for an advanced economy, disappeared. Only government officials and their film colony supporters still had the good life.

Even electric lighting was discontinued in rural areas. Automotive traffic declined, and the extensive network of highways fell into ruin. All air traffic ended. Cities lost population and soon the skyscrapers were closed and torn down. A few important exceptions, like Chicago's Hancock Center, were converted into historic sites. Wild animal populations increased, and rabies became a widespread problem.

Through the century a massive emigration took place. Most of the people fled over the borders into Canada or Mexico. The nation's population dropped from 281 million in 2007 to 104 million in 2099. The people who remained were in three groups. The first accepted the government policies, using drugs and sex to forget their hardships. A second group reverted to an extremely simple way of life. Many adopted the methods of the Mennonites and Amish. Horsepulled wagons and plows replaced the auto. Candles and oil lamps were used instead of electric lights. Other people converted to Mormonism or copied that church's communal social order and system of assistance.

A third portion of the people of the nation decided to oppose the government. These included scientists and industrialists. They had seen their countrymen lied to, deceived, and robbed of their birthright. They were watching the rest of the world prepare to reach into space. They were determined to end the decay of America. The Association for the Rebirth of

Science was chartered in 2078. Their basic demand was repeal of the ban on nuclear power. They had a comprehensive program for the re-building of the stricken nation. The supporters of the program began pamphleteering, demonstrating, and speech-making. The Gendarmes responded by trying to suppress the science movement. Offices of the Rebirth Group, as the science advocates were called, were ransacked and their members beatened and imprisoned. In 2087 the Rebirth group held a number of outdoor rallies coast-to-coast. The Gendarmes attacked those demonstrations, touching off what became a decade of rioting.

The Gendarmes began a severe program of repression. Members of Rebirth were jailed, exiled, driven underground, or executed. Electrical power disappeared except for in government offices. Government personnel carriers, i.e., armored trucks, were the only automotive vehicles left in the nation. The few remaining theaters, now using handcranked cameras, became propaganda outlets. The livestock industry disappeared. The only way many people could obtain meat was by hunting, trapping, or fishing. Unemployment was so widespread that by 2100 the government began an extreme make-work program. Without telling its real purpose, the government set people to work digging a deep ditch along the 49th parallel. A similar ditch was dug along the Rio Grande River and the Mexican border. After a section of ditch was completed, barbed wire was set in place. Land mines, some a century old, others imported, were added. Watch towers were erected, equipped with automatic weapons. In effect, death walls sealed the borders. They resembled the Berlin Wall of the twentieth century.

People continued to escape, however, often by fishing boats. Many citizens felt the walls were to keep people out, i.e., those who would help the Rebirth Group. The scientists went underground, to set up the organizational structure that would endure a millenium. At the top was the High Council, men and women highly educated. Many would slip out of the country for years of study in advanced science. Then they would be smuggled back in, often with money raised by sympathizers overseas. A number of schools were established to teach what they had learned. The schools, called "university centers," were in secluded areas. These were shifted at varying intervals for security reasons. At the second level were the activists, the point men, who passed out leaflets and made speeches. They were the ones who risked life and limb. Ambitious plans were formed to infiltrate the government but had to be abandoned. At the third level were the supporters, people with little knowledge of science but desiring a better life. Supporters included businessmen tired of being harassed by officials, farmers trying to save their land from the Trusteeships, and even municipal policemen who disliked the corrupt and brutal Gendarmes.

The supporters supplied the movement with money and often food. They provided apparent employment for activists and safehouses while in hiding. The police, who supported the movement, would give intelligence reports of the Gendarmes' operations. Many businesses were, in effect, fronts for the movement.

Rotation was a risky but necessary part of the operation. Scientists who had spent several years teaching in the university centers would take a working furlough. Men who had taught advanced bio-chemistry worked in quarries, cranberry bogs, or cotton fields. Women who had taught nuclear physics worked in millinery shops or as waitresses. Often they worked right under the noses of the Gendarmes. Conversely, activists who had had one too many run-ins with the Gerdarmarie would flee to the underground schools.

By the year 2118, the U.S. was a totalitarian state. Ironically, its ancient foe—the nations of the former Soviet Union—had achieved a high level of political and personal freedom. The old militarists had died out and had been replaced by officials who preferred consumer goods.

The government instigated two more measures to erase public memory of past history. The faces of the founding fathers—George Washington, Thomas Jefferson, Abraham Lincoln, Alexander Hamilton, etc.—disappeared from paper money bills. Faces of various twentieth century environmentalists were printed into the paper, i.e., Brown, Commoner, Nader, and others. The faces of the celebrities who had supported the government were engraved into stamps. The second decision the environmentalist party carried out was symbolic. The old American flag of red and white stripes and stars on a blue ensign was officially banned. The banners were thrown into a public bonfire. The new flag had green and white stripes with an ensign with a Greek letter meaning death. The ensign became armbands worn by the Gendarmerie.

The science Underground responded with an information blitz. The writings of Alexander Hamilton, particularly his 1791 "Report on Manufacturers," were distributed. The works of nineteenth century economists Friedrich List and Henry Carey were also presented to a confused public. For several decades the science activists would carry a hidden stripe of red, white, and blue bunting. Presented behind closed doors, it became a recognition sign. Another means of identity was foreign translations of the word "ODIN." This was, of course, for the ODIN Project, America's last achievement of advanced science. The top officials of the science movement could recite the details of that project almost by heart. Eventually other identity codes were adopted, but Project ODIN was taught in the Underground's universities, so great was its symbolism of America's past.

High Council scientists met in secret in 2147 to formulate plans to launch another rebellion. A number of activists crossed the border into Canada near Detroit. Guns and money were smuggled in by the Great Lakes. Contacts were made with Canadian officials. Hopes were raised that the Canadian Army would breach the wall along the 49th parallel. In 2160 the Rebirth Group launched a huge rally outside what was left of Detroit.

Police units acted as guards. When the local garrison of Gendarmes arrived to suppress the rally, gunfire opened up.

In one month most of Michigan and Wisconsin were liberated. Activists spread south into Illinois and Indiana, then west through Minnesota toward Montana. In vain the scientists waited for the Canadians to breach the death zone. Instead the northern neighbors moved troops into the state of Alaska. The 49th state had resented governmental repression of economic development for two hundred years. Gradually the Gendarmerie were mobilized into large combat groups and counterattacked. After three months of brutal fighting, the science supporters were pushed back into Michigan and Wisconsin. The Gendarme groups were posed to launch the final attack. Suddenly from Washington officials proposed a negotiated peace. A quarter of a century later documents would be released proving that the Canadians had threatened to invade. The ambassador from Mexico offered to act as a mediator.

The Environmentalist government flatly refused to legalize nuclear power plants. They also frowned on the use of coal. After three years of arbitration, two ways to use coal for electrical power were found acceptable.

In one process coal would be burned in a specially designed boiler with a bed of crushed limestone. The limestone would trap impurities; however, there were no plants in the country to manufacture the boilers. The boilers would have to be imported under extremely expensive licenses. The second process involved crushing the coal into a fine powder, then treating it with hydrogen and steam. This produced a solid gel of almost pure carbon. As with the boilers, processed coal had to be imported under licensure. Licenses were also issued to permit domestic mining of coal, under the most rigid regulations. The coal could be used in the limestone boilers or sent overseas to be processed and returned. In addition, import licenses were issued for gasoline, kerosene, and alcohol. For the government, it meant a huge windfall of money, which partly assuaged the Gendarmerie; however, for the science movement and the people of America, it meant the hope for a better life.

During the remainder of the twenty-second century, America awoke like an animal coming out of hibernation. Electrical power returned to the larger cities, bringing telephones and lights. In New York a streetcar system reopened. Television receivers reappeared in theaters; however, the bill of fare was fake newsreels from overseas. The government inaugurated a program to repair the railroad beds and also the nation's highways. Automobiles and trucks, which had been preserved on cement blocks for years, were prepared for new use. Many required spare parts, and a cottage industry was set up to meet the need. The parts were manufactured overseas, imported, and assembled by small firms. It made more revenue for the government, but it meant new business fronts for the science movement. Soon automobiles reappeared on the highways. They had to share the roads with horses and buggies, pushcarts, bicycles, pedestrians, even roller skates.

The speed limits, even one expressways, were a fraction of the limits the road had been designed for.

A similar cottage industry assembled steam machines for locomotives and farm equipment. By the year 2200 the standard of living had returned to the level of the year 1900.

For the next three centuries, the balance of political siege war shifted back and forth. Through the twenty-third century, the science movement pressured the government for more concessions. Electricity appeared in more cities and more traffic appeared on the roads and rails. Progress was measured in years and decades instead of months and years. In many rural areas there had been little progress or change from the last century.

Environmentalist officials soon discovered they could use the improved communications to their advantage. Unethical cinemagraphic firms overseas created fabricated newsreels featuring oil spills, dam ruptures, exploding nuclear reactors, and other disasters. These films were shown in theaters owned by relatives of government officials. One newsreel reporting a nuclear reactor disaster in Paris was shown five times in less than two years. The dateline was updated in the first fifty frames each time. This propaganda program was to convince a gullible public to believe the equation of science with witchcraft.

The science movement found that as conditions improved many businessfront supporters dropped out of the movement. The Underground's school network was expanded. It was then found that many young people used the schools for a rudimentary education and then emigrated, although some later returned.

The men of the Environmental Regulatory Enforcement Bureau (EREB) watched the changes in the country with seething dissatisfaction. The Gendarmerie saw that their only allies were the holders of Environmental Trusteeships. The Bureau of Land Management had been gently asking Trustees to lease land to farmers. The men of the EREB began to regard themselves as the retainers of the Trustees, not as officials of government. In return the Trustees saw the Gendarmerie guarding their economic privileges. The third part of the cabal was the purveyors of commercialized vice. The government had set them up in business in the twenty-first century to divert people's attention from their economic hardships. Later their payoffs kept the government in operation. By the twenty-third century they primarily served as recreation for the idle Gendarmerie.

Toward the end of the century the population had returned to a level outpacing food production, creating shortages. The underlying cause was the fact that so much fertile, available land was locked into Trusteeships.

Farmers began to encroach into these lands. Gunfights resulted; the farmers armed only with muzzle-loaders against Gendarmes armed with automatic weapons. The government announced a study program on the feasibility of revoking some of the Trusteeships. The Gendarmerie responded immediately, and a number of high-level government officials vanished.

Their replacements were hand-picked by the Gendarmes, and it was the import licenses that were revoked. Electrical power was gradually withdrawn from the smaller cities. Automotive traffic and rail activity declined and the general economy fell off. Another massive illegal wave of emigration took place. It was not until after 2370 that the science Underground was able to reorganize its operational structure. The political tide turned, although with considerable violence. By the year 2450 the economy had returned to the level of 2300.

This political cycle would have continued indefinitely but for the migration into space. The United States government voiced its total opposition to the United Nations. After extreme arguing for a decade, they relented. The government even consented to allow legal emigration through a quota of visas. Over 35 million Americans left their hapless land and emigrated to the Outer Solar System. Many more simply emigrated to Canada, South America, or the Eastern Hemisphere.

As the migration to the Outer Solar System continued, Canada and Mexico were emptied of population. The death zones along the 49th parallel and the Rio Grande were finally dismantled. The excess population moved as far north as Hudson's Bay and as far south as the Yucatan. Many people in the north reached Alaska, independent since the twenty-second century. Then, as the Eastern Hemisphere became almost depopulated, the Environmentalists launched an attempted political coup. If they were successful, Earth could cut itself off from its children and stagnate forever.

Rebirth, the scientist group, had been conserving its resources for one final attempt to liberate America. It transferred most of its first- and second-level operatives to the Old World. Between 2600 and 2700 the scientists battled the Environmentalists for the soul of Eurasia and Africa. The Eurasian and African Co-prosperity Republics were formulated, and treaties with colonized planets were ratified. The scientists had won the war; however, the Underground had exhausted itself. Many of their activists had given their lives to save Earth from tyranny.

During the next two centuries America sank further and further. New York City, a showcase for a few tourists and diplomats, was the only city with electricity. The railroads and highways were abandoned. The few remaining scientists withdrew into their secluded schools. These became like medieval monasteries. People dissatisfied with the poverty and repression simply emigrated. One family took thirteen years to move from Cincinnati to Alaska. They worked for four years in Chicago, then they moved to Des Moines. After five years there, they trekked to Winnipeg and then to Dawson three years later. In the cold of winter, they took dog sleds into Alaska, a protectorate of Eurasia.

In every planet-nation of the Outer Solar System American emigrants settled. They took with them the folklore, the books, the legends, and archives of that ancient land.

The American Culture Preservation Society was chartered by the Interplanetary Federation. Occasional exhibits of twentieth century American films and demonstrations of sports were held. The ancient country became like Camelot or Shangrila. George Washington became a King Arthur figure; history mixed with myth.

In the early thirty-first century tourists from the Eastern Hemisphere began to visit America en masse. The primitive conditions were considered quaint. Eventually a few tourists reached the deepest hinterlands, stumbling onto the science monasteries. The comatose movement stirred itself awake. Some of the tourists made return visits to America. Money began to fill long-empty coffers. A second-level network of activists was recruited. By 3080 activists were again demonstrating against government policy. The Gendarmerie had been deactivated for over one hundred years. This gave the scientists a head start. Several councilmen slipped out of the north country into Alaska, then to Eurasia. To the chagrin of the scientists, the Eurasians offered neither arms for an uprising nor an invasion; however, one council member reached the embassy complex of the Interplanetary Federation. The embassy transmitted his grievance to the Outer Solar System by ultra-hyperlight mail shuttle.

The Interplanetary Federation decided to make a formal visit to America on Earth. In 3107 a hyperlight transport carrying several thousand officials achieved stationary orbit over eastern Eurasia. Shuttle craft landed in Shanghai, and diplomatic letters were presented to Eurasian government officers. Then an American embassy official began the processing of visas. The teams of diplomatic explorers took several hyper-sonic airliners to Paris. From there hydro-foils and hovercraft sped the visitors down the Seine, out of LeHavre, and across the Atlantic. Off the Bermuda isles the diplomats transferred to a motley armada of ancient sailing ships. The antique fleet entered New York harbor and the visitors were surprised by the primitive conditions.

The landing party was formally escorted to the few major cities by government officials. Still, a number of the visitors spread into primitive rural areas and contacted Underground scientists. For seven months the visitors from the Outer Solar System catalogued information on American life. A new treaty was signed allowing emigration to the Eastern Republics and then into space.

The science councilman who had arranged the visit from the Outer Solar System soon became governor-general of the Council. On the wanted list of the Gendarmerie for two decades, he now went on a death list. Over the next forty years he led the science movement forward—one year teaching nuclear physics on Long Island, the next year harvesting wheat in Nebraska, and on educational furlough in Paris the next. As the decades passed, electricity returned to Chicago, Detroit, San Francisco, Salt Lake City, etc. Highways were again rebuilt and bus lines made coast-to-coast travel possible.

This progress came at a high price, and many activists were in and out of prison and faced many beatings. The Gendarmerie decided the only way to discover the identity and location of the High Council would be to plant a double agent into the movement. Unlike previous spies, he would remain inactive until needed.

In 3146 the High Council decided to directly contact the planet-nations of the Outer Solar System. The object would be to enlist one or more of those nations to send direct military assistance for an uprising. Two years later a carefully selected team of over a dozen activists trekked north into Alaska. From Juneau they sailed by hydrofoil to Shanghai, and the following year they obtained visas. In 3150 a transport took them into space. The first planet they landed on was Nippon. At Tokyo they were greeted with all proper courtesy. A generous offer of financial assistance was made, but no directly military pact was considered. In each following planet it was the same case. What none of the science activists knew was that one of them was a spy planted as a double agent in the High Council.

In January 3153 the team of scientists surveyed the results of their efforts. They had sent a considerable amount of money to Earth but received no offer of arms. There were only a few planets left, so the team broke up into groups of only two or three activists. In April a three-man team reached the last planet-nation—Hibernia.

The Hibernia-Brittania Wars

"Tragic; an unfortunate consequence that the planet nations Brittania and Hibernia were adjacent to each other," read the comments of an Interplanetary Federation historian. The scholar added, "If the two planet-nations were in different parts of the solar system, or separated by one or more larger planets, the wars fought between them would have been avoided." Proximity was not the only cause of the conflict; rather it was their stormy history on Earth carried with them into space.

Ireland did not achieve full nationhood until the early twenty-first century. For over eight hundred years it was a colony of the English. England had conquered the neighboring island in 1171 and ruled through retainers for four hundred years. At the dawn of the seventeenth century, a plantation of settlers was established in the far northeastern part of Ulster. This colony was a mixture of Lowland Scottish Presbyterians and Anglicans from the north of England such as Yorkshire. The colony was concentrated in Antrim and Down countries. In time they eventually spread through the entire province.

During England's Glorious Revolution of 1690, the settlers sided with William of Orange. They became known as the Orangemen and were steadfastly loyal to the crown. Strict Calvinism ruled their private lives, making them distinct from the native Irish. In the nineteenth century the native

Celtic, Catholic, "Green" Irish demanded home rule, i.e., an autonomous parliament—which Orangemen opposed. Then, in the twentieth century, the Irish civil war was fought from 1916 to 1923 to create a united Ireland. A peace treaty kept six of the nine counties of Ulster province under British rule. In the last third of the century a bloody guerrilla war was fought to complete unification.

At the end of the century, the British government had agreed to surrender Ulster to the legal government of Ireland. The Orangemen declared their own independence. While British soldiers were bivouacked awaiting evacuation, an atrocity brought the conflict to an end in 2002.

An active service unit of provisionals, i.e., Irish Nationalist guerrillas, entered the Shankill, an Orange community in east Belfast. Two hundred men, women, and children were deliberately murdered. Entire families were put against a wall and machine gunned or herded into their brick homes and blown to bits. In the midst of this barbarianism an adolescent girl was forced to witness the murder of her parents. Then she was repeatedly ravished, three men at a time, and shot in both kneecaps.

This act of savage cruelty broke the back of Orange resistance. A number of the vanquished departed to England. Most of the Orangemen remained and clung to their cultural traditions. In the face of a government program of Gaelicization, the English language continued to be used in homes in communities in East Belfast and other Orange areas. The Twelfth of July, the anniversary of the Battle of the Boyne, was still celebrated, though in private. As the years passed, many former guerrillas, the provisionals, rose to government offices.

The young girl who was so brutalized in the Shankill massacre survived. On every anniversary of that horrid act, she hobbled on crutches across the length of Belfast. She braved epithets, threats, and rotten fruit walking through the Falls, the Short Strand, and other nationalist neighborhoods. In 2017 an officer of the Foreign Ministry died. He left a diary implicating three members of the Dail Eireann in the Shankill massacre. The government refused to prosecute. The "maiden of Shankill," as the young woman was now known, was beaten up during her annual walk. This was the final breaking point of the patience of the Orangemen. A car-bomb assassinated one of the ex-provo gunmen. A second ex-gunman was found floating in the Shannon River. The last ex-provo died of heart failure when he mistook a backfiring car for a gunshot.

When Ireland began to participate in the colonization of the Outer Solar System, many Orangemen first thought of remaining on Earth; however, as colonization continued, they joined in with increasing enthusiasm. As the four quadrants were named for Ireland's four provinces, the Orangemen settled in Ulster quadrant. While they were settled in each sector, the main concentrations were in Antrim, Down, and Armagh sectors; saltwater lakes, a source of deuterium and tritium, were scattered in the three main sectors. As the result, the Orangemen were exporting fuel for nuclear fusion reactors and became among the wealthiest people in the planet. Many other Hibernians became jealous, and social ostracism resulted. The severe division in the society would render the planet unable to meet its most dangerous challenge.

Across a corridor of space, sixteen light-hours away, was Brittania. The British Commonwealth had settled their planet-nation a century before their Irish neighbors. The two planets negotiated a plan to transfer Celtic Britons, the Scots, and Welsh to Hibernia. The plan was culturally related to the Orangemen.

After the twenty-eighth century, the various planet-nations turned inward; commercial and diplomatic relations declined. During that splendid isolation, Brittania's government degenerated from a parliamentary democracy to an autocracy similar to the age of the Tudors and Stuarts. The monarchy and the aristocracy regained old prerogatives, while the commercial, democratic elements were strangled. Revival of the imperialistic instinct took place, hack authors turning out reams of romanticized descriptions of the nineteenth century Empire. Royal extravagance overtaxed the masses of ordinary folk.

By 2980 relations between Brittania and the other planet-nations deteriorated as interspace trade was being interdicted.

Hindustan, a planet with a large population and resources, was being blockaded. Letters of Marque had been issued by Brittania to pirate space freighters. At the 2983 session of the Interplanetary Federation, Hibernia openly supported the Hindustani's claims against the Sassenach. Diplomatic relations between Brittania and Hibernia were broken off. H.M.S. *Coventry*, a passenger transport carrying Brittania's diplomatic staff, exploded just twenty miles short of landing outside London. King Edward XXII and Queen Catherine were at the launch port waiting for the freighter to land. Arthur Gordon, the Prince of Wales, was the pilot of the ill-fated craft. M-I-6, Brittania's intelligence service, uncovered evidence that an underground cabal had planned an anti-royalist rebellion. The freighter was to explode on landing. One of the conspirators was captured and a Hibernian passport was discovered on his person.

Brittania did not declare war or present its case to the Federation. It quietly prepared its plans for war. Privateers were given formal military rank. A land army was conscripted, trained, and equipped. Space freighters were prepared for landing troops on Hibernian soil. M-I-6 ascertained that no planet-nation had any military defenses, so twentieth century technology would be sufficient for the war. Radio beacons were designed to guide missiles with thermonuclear warheads. The Shetland and Orkney asteroid chains became vast military complexes. The Hibernians were apparently unaware of the mounting danger.

In 2994 the Brittanians put the finishing touches to their war plans. Two dozen transports were assembled into a vast armada. Each carried thirty thousand men and equipment and moved two apiece to the Shetland asteroids, then toward Hindustan. From there the armada was turned into deep space, then countermarched to near Hibernia's Aran asteroids.

Brittania's ambassador to the Interplanetary Federation presented a proposal for a return to normal relations with Hibernia. The unsuspecting government assembled most of its officials in Athlone to await Brittanic representatives. The missiles were fired and came across the space corridor of the two planets. Athlone, Dublin, Belfast, Killarney, Derry, and other smaller cities vanished. The transports encircled the stricken planet and troops were landed by shuttle craft. The planet was conquered in a week. Those Hibernian government officials who did not die in the missile attack were tried as criminals and hanged. Many of the surviving Hibernia citizens were seized and exiled to Brittania as conscript labor. Men as young as age sixteen were seized and did not return until far past the age of forty.

The Brittanians understood the value of Ulster quadrant. As the decades passed, a considerable mining and industrial complex arose in the quadrant. Brittanic citizens were brought in to work in the complex on ten-year contracts. Brittanic army units built a line of field fortifications on the borders of the quadrant. Other army units were garrisoned throughout the planet-nation.

Hibernia's remaining citizens were now impoverished peasants working for Brittanic overlords. The entire population of Ulster quadrant was exiled into the rest of the planet. The Orangemen were crowned into Louth and Meath sectors of Leinster quadrant just south of the equator. To everybody's surprise, they flatly declined a Brittanic offer of reparation to their quadrant in exchange for an oath of loyalty. The deaths of relatives in the thermonuclear obliteration of Belfast could not be erased by appealing to memories of William of Orange. In Shankill, a refugee village in Louth sector, a sign was painted on a stone wall that read, "King William forever but King Edward never!"

If Brittania had quickly mobilized the resources of the new colony and itself, it would have easily conquered Hindustan. And with the far larger resources of that planet, it might have subjugated most of the solar system. Other planet-nations began attempts to build defenses. The Interplanetary Federation unanimously censured Brittania after its ambassador gave an incredible rationalization for his planet's actions. Everybody throughout the solar system expected the juggernaut to roll on to its next victim; however, like a predator that swallowed its victim whole, then went to sleep, Brittania was content with its conquest. In a few years the crisis passed and an uneasy peace returned to the solar system.

The Hibernian diplomats who had been stationed on other planet-nations formed a government in exile. Joining the diplomats were the pilots and crews of space freighters that had been on voyage during the holocaust. A rudimentary underground was prepared, although several decades would pass before active resistance could begin. Contacts were established with the now factionized anti-Brittanic revolutionary committees.

Forty years passed, and the Babylonian captivity of the Hibernians ended with a mass reparation to their planet. The Brit troops garrisoned in the planet had become apathetic and complacent. In each village a cell of the "Fenian" underground was formed, just a dozen agents or less. The leader of a village cell would report to an intermediary. In turn, the intermediary would communicate to both the next village cell and his superiors. Thus, compartmentalized, no one cell would endanger another. Above the village cells were the district units and then sector units. The lower-level cells primarily engaged in surveillance. They even took employment in the Brittanic-owned businesses or as the servants of Brit officers.

In the year 3060, the major Fenian leaders met on the Aran asteroids. The government in exile reported a small number of idealistic volunteers from other planets were offering to aid the Fenians. The fundamental question of strategy was discussed: Should a low-intensity guerrilla war be instigated, gradually building up to a full unit battle? It was noted that the Brittanic soldiers were becoming quite careless in their duties. Any guerrilla raid, however small, would cause the authorities to go on alert, losing the element of surprise. The Fenians would have to build their strength for a single mass revolt.

A discouraging report came from the Brittanic anti-royalists: There were still a number of thermonuclear missiles ready to launch from Brittanic bases. The bases were too heavily guarded to be overrun before the missiles would be launched. The problem of the missiles held up the Fenian rebels for two years. Then a team of Interplanetary technicians developed a laser weapon. It was a modification of the lasers used by surgeons and mining firms. Tests conducted on the Aran asteroids proved it could destroy small shuttle craft. With miniaturization, hand weapons could be produced. An ever-increasing number of shuttle and freighter pilots prepared to arm their craft with the new lasers. Under the battle strategy, the enemy missiles would be intercepted in space.

The following twenty years saw the Fenian rebels build a mass force. The deep tunnels of the abandoned subterranean railroad system were used for training, hiding, and quartering guerrilla units.

On Brittania the anti-royalists had planted its spies throughout the Defense Ministry. Military bases, munition plants, even the Crystal Palace were wiretapped. Anti-royalist agents were searching for the perfect time to launch a revolt. It would keep Brittania's military occupied, even causing the government to pull troops off garrison duty on Hibernia. Then the Hibernians would unleash their own uprising. It was recognized that the fortified Ulster quadrant would be the Brittanian's last redoubt. It would be necessary to completely win the other three quadrants before the final assault could be successfully launched. Sadly, the Orangemen in Louth and Meath sectors were totally excluded from the plans of the Fenian rebels. It was still assumed that when the uprising took place they would side with the Crown.

An extremely elaborate communication code was prepared to link the Hibernians with their allied units. First, an ignorant-sounding jargon language was formed. It was a blend of Gaelic, English, Welsh, French, German, even Greek and Arabic. This was converted into a version of the interplanetary radio code; parts of ancient Morse Codes were safeguards. Finally, the dots and dashes became electromagnetic impulses of ever-varying frequencies and amplitudes. The code could be shifted into different tables, at intervals, as another guard. The standard procedure for broadcasting would be to relay through the asteroid chains. A Brittannic rebel unit would radio to the corresponding station in the Orkney asteroids. It would relay the transmission to the Shetland asteroids, which in turn sent it to the Aran asteroids, then to Hibernia. The Hibernian reply would return by the same chain, in reverse. A special emergency code was perfected for direct planet-to-planet messages. A linguist specializing in extinct languages formed a jargon of Slavonic, Manx, and Aramaic.

After 3080 the finishing touches to the uprising were put in place. Dozens of laser-armed shuttles with trained crews were stationed along the asteroid chains. Anti-royalist agents were now planeted even on the missile bases to put out an alert if the missiles were to be fired. In every sector in Hibernia, outside Ulster quadrant, the Fenian rebels awaited the signal to jump the British garrisons.

The Brittanic royalty had unintentionally handed the opportunity to the awaiting rebels. When Arthur Gordon, Prince of Wales, perished in 2983, his dissolute brother Harold was the next in line of succession to the throne. Infant princess Theresa was the third in line. King Edward XXII died in 3009, and Queen Catherine died early in the following year. The new king was not on the planet during the two months lapping the funerals. Princess Theresa had been in the hospital at the same time. The sickening details were revealed by a chambermaid at the Crystal Palace, who was also in the Underground. The royal brother and sister had an incestuous relationship, the princess dying in childbirth. The uncrowned King Harold drank himself to death on Planet Sovietia. The infant, Prince Phillip, grew up in total seclusion while a military regency ruled the country for thirty-five years. The secret little king married Baroness Von Tromp of the royal house of Benelux. In 3032 a beautiful daughter, Amanda, was born. In short time she won the hearts of Brittanians to whom the royal scandal was a bitter memory. As Princess Amanda grew, she visited the length and breadth of both planets. Her warmth and cheerful, active life were in great contrast to her almost hermit-like parents. Still no crowned head sat on Brittania's throne. When Princess Amanda wed Count Konig of Scandinavia, the people gasped with anticipation. Prince George was born in 3058. It was apparent by age ten he intended to rule like Edward. With deliberate arrogance he declared that he would be crowned at the age of twenty-seven; that it would coincide with the arbitrary pension age of the Regency-General was forgotten.

As the royal authorities prepared for a festive coronation, the anti-royalists planned their own festivities. Back on Hibernia, a provisional government had already been established. The vast complex of Brittanic-owned industrial firms was to be nationalized in the name of the Hibernian people. The rigidly socialist constitution would produce ill feelings from those Hibernians whose ancestors had been of the business classes. This fact was ignored while the rebel government finalized its plans for the uprising.

Huge crowds had gathered in London in early June 3085. Two space freighters had transported fifty thousand troops from the Hibernian garrison duty to act as honor guards. Elaborate horse-drawn carriages were readied to carry the royal family at the site of the coronation. Massive tents were set up around the Crystal Palace for the members of the nobility.

June 10th of 3085, Prince George mounted a golden carriage. Escorted by the household cavalry, he led a procession to St. Paul's Cathedral. Amidst the crowds of cheering people, tightlipped men and women awaited a signal.

As soon as the jeweled crown was set upon the head of George XXX, the Cathedral was struck by a mass of rotted fruit. Ancient catapults had been built by the rebels. The absurdity of the act was to create panic. In the cities in the south, huge demonstrations appeared and a list of demands was made. Restoration of power to the impotent Parliament, reduction of taxes, and negotiated autonomy for Hibernia were among the demands. The political rallies turned into riots. Within two weeks the royalty was on the verge of collapse. Five transports of troops were pulled out of Hibernia. It was the personal courage of King George that prevented the government from being swept away.

By early July martial law had caused the riots to cease. The special branch of Scotland Yard began to round up anti-royalist rebels. Like a century before, a rebel was tortured into revealing the links with the Hibernians. In just twenty-four hours an attack order came down from the Crown. The thermonuclear missiles were targeted for Hibernian cities and fired. The remaining troops in these cities (all outside Ulster quadrant) were not radioed an order to evacuate. They were deliberately sacrificed to destroy the Hibernian rebels. It was a matter of pure luck that one of the fire control technicians at a Brittanic missile base was also an anti-royalist. He radioed a secret rebel base, and it was relayed to the armed shuttle fleet.

The laser-armed shuttles intercepted the incoming missiles a few hundred kilometers in space from the planet. Portlaois and Killarney were the only cities hit by the missiles. Then throughout the entire southern hemisphere the Hibernian rebels struck the Brittanic garrisons. Several of the garrisons surrendered without a shot. The soldiers had mutinied when they realized the royal authorities considered them expendable. Other garrisons put up varying levels of resistance. In Ulster quadrant Governor-General Smith-Dorian pulled many of the units back from the quadrant frontier fortifications. He had plans to form a mobile field army then launch a counter offensive into Connaught quadrant. From there he would drive into the southern hemisphere. He had to await a transport convoy to bring additional men and equipment. The Brittanians massed a convoy of nine space transports. The convey carried a total of seventy-eight thousand men, two thousand tanks and personnel carriers, and a half million tons of ammunition. Halfway across the space corridor the convoy was annihilated by the shuttle squadron. Only one transport, which had been diverted to the Shetland asteroids for repairs, reached the quadrant.

Lord Smith-Dorian decided to launch a pre-emptive offense. He would set up a defense line right across Connaught quadrant. Brittanic troops entered Leitrim sector, at the North Pole, and Mayo and Sligo sectors farther south. Before they could set up the new "Trafalgar" line, a new danger to Ulster quadrant caused a withdrawal.

Throughout August and September the Orangemen watched the uprising sweep northward to Connaught. They had not been asked to join the revolt, which was an affront. In their Calvinistic chapels they debated on the question if they should aid the rebellion. The few royalists were expelled from their villages. Finally, in mid-September, a torch-lite rally was held in Shankill Village that straddled Louth and Meath sectors. A mass of Orangemen drove into Dublin, seized a supply of arms from a dazed "Green" rebel unit, then drove back north. They marched through a part of the Brittanic defense wall where the troops had been removed. They penetrated into Armagh and Monoghan sectors, reaching Carrickmacross and Newry. Then a Brittanic counterattack hit on their exposed flanks. Outgunned and undisciplined, the Orangemen were routed. One unfortunate unit recruited from the village of Waterside was surrounded and captured. The young men were cut to pieces, some staked to the ground and run over with tanks. Others were machine-gunned, their "officers" hanged, all buried in a mass grave. When the news of the massacre spread, the Hibernian government sent a work unit to Shankill. "The Bowler boyes," as the Orange units were named, trained with enthusiasm. "Remember the Waterside Boys" became a war cry. While they trained with laser rifles, the Orangemen brought out a double-edged sword as a sidearm.

Although the Orange offensive had been repulsed, it had caused Lord Smith-Dorian to pull out of Connaught. Before he realized the danger had passed and he could resume his plans, it was too late. The Hibernians had streamed deep into Connaught.

Back on Brittania, the anti-royalists harassed the Brittanic forces by any means possible. Bombs wrecked defense plants, railyards, and other facilities. The Brit forces were being tied down and could not be transported to Hibernia. Finally, in early November, a convoy of ten space freighters rocketed across the space corridor. A quarter of the way the convoy split in two. Half of the transports continued across the corridor on automatic pilot, their crews being shuttled to the other freighters. These other freighters pulled out of line, turning to a course straight to planet Hindustan. Afterward they turned toward deep space, out of the solar system. They pulled around and reached Hibernia from deep space. They succeeded in transferring most of the cargoes of men and weapons to the surface before detection. Lord Smith-Dorian used the reinforcements to launch his long-delayed attack.

The Hibernian ground forces had put up an improvised defense wall along the Ulster-Connaught frontier. Masses of Brittanic tanks punched through it and the mechanized infantry followed. The rebels were able to escape envelopment, and small village cell units harassed the Brit rear guards.

By December, Brittanians entered Galway and Roscommon sectors, where a secondary rebel line was readied. The Hibernians radioed for assistance to the entire solar system. Help was not long in coming. The squadrons of laser-armed shuttles had doubled in number with crews of what became known as the Interplanetary Volunteers. The shuttle force massed at the Aran asteroids, then attacked the advancing Brittanians. Over a thousand tanks and other vehicles were literally melted by strafing laser fire. The infantry groups behind the armor were hastily withdrawn. Before the year ended, all of Connaught sector was cleared of Brittanic forces.

Meanwhile, in northeast Leinster, the Orangemen avenged their earlier loss. They drove back into Monaghan sector, seizing a huge new ammunition depot. Then at Carrickmacross they surrounded the very Brittanic units involved in the Waterside massacre. Using laser cannon, they cut down the Brit troops before they could even surrender. Their Claymore swords hacked most of the remaining Brit soldiers to pieces. Scalps were even taken and bodies burned in a huge bonfire. Then, after a reconnaissance unit reported enemy reinforcements, the Orange militia dropped back south into Leinster.

In early February the combined Hibernian units launched attacks on the Ulster quadrant frontier defenses. This time the field fortifications were fully manned and the lines held. The shuttle squadrons were still too few in number to provide air support for the ground attack and also blockade the quadrant. The Brittanians started running the blockade, one freighter at a time. King George himself thought of building a squadron of attack shuttles. The Royalists were still harassed by the rebels on their home planet. After a siege of six months with small battles, sector by sector, a truce was called. The Interplanetary Federation drew up a temporary armistice. The Hibernians had won three-fourths of their planet back. Still, Brittanic-occupied Ulster was an unclaimed prize; however, for the next four decades the solar system savored the sweet stillness of peace.

With the end of hostilities, the rebel government proclaimed the Second Republic; the pre-2994 government was now referred to as the "First." The self-styled Worker's Republic took the name Sinn Fein from the twentieth century. The Sinn Fein government nationalized all heavy industry taken from the Brittanians. In addition, heavy taxes and severe regulation were levied upon the small middle class of farmers and shopkeepers. The new

Sinn Fein party paper *An Phoblacht* began a propaganda campaign against this class.

After establishing their philosophical motives, the government tackled the task of military demobilization. Most of the Interplanetary Volunteers (IPVs) returned to their home planets but promised to return to Hibernia if needed. Other IPVs settled and eventually obtained Hibernian citizenship. This was related to the second problem the government faced—language division.

Prior to the holocaust of 2994, nearly 90 percent of the Hibernian population used Gaelic, the ancient Irish language. English was the tongue of the fiercely stubborn Orangemen. A generous number of people were bilingual, permitting the two groups of work together in government or commerce. A post-rebellion census revealed that less than a third of the population still retained a working knowledge of Gaelic.

The government inaugurated construction of schools and formulated a program of educational services in Gaelic. As radio and viewscreen broadcasting was restored to urban areas, most programming was in the ancient tongue. After several years, a battery of written and oral examinations were constructed. The examinations were to be held in the last year of secondary educations. Any person who passed these exams was registered in an order of part-time para-professional bilingual instructors. They would be expected to teach one day a week, or several days a month, rotating from school to school.

When the military demobilization was complete, the re-industrialization of Hibernia began in earnest. Electricity was non-existent, except at the industrial sites seized during the rebellion. The Robert Emmet Dam was constructed on the Shannon River at the point where it flowed from Tipperary into Limerick sector. A second dam, the Padraic Pearse, was built on the Shannon in southwest Limerick sector. The two dams produced hydro-electric power for most of Munster quadrant and the capital, Athlone.

To provide fuel for transportation and chemicals for industry, a massive coal gasification plant arose in Offaly sector east of the capital. Dummy facilities were built on the surface, while the real refineries were constructed in deep underground galleries. The re-activated Hibernian postal offices doubled as retail outlets for synthetic gasoline and oils. A pipeline was constructed across Leinster quadrant to a municipal-run oil-fired electrical plant in Dublin.

These extensive projects were financed by a government-operated industrial bank. The bank had floated issues of small bonds for its source of capital. As most of the planet's workers were in government unions, their pension funds were invested in the bonds.

Athlone, which had been reduced to a small farm village, grew by almost exponential progression. The city straddled the Prime Meridian between Offaly sector of Leinster quadrant and Tipperary sector of Munster quadrant. A wide boulevard contained the new city core. The streets inside were in a radial pattern, where the government's new building was to be constructed. There was great concern that another war would soon take place. It was mandated that no building would be built above two stories; instead, the structures were to be built downward. Despite the restriction, a rich variety of architectural forms was used. Old photographs were found of the original Earth buildings that had been transplanted to Hibernia. The Dail Eireann building was a glass steel building, a duplicate of the pre-war Dail except the underground feature. The buildings for the various ministries were of hewn stone in the twelfth century Irish Romanesque style. The office and residence of the Taoiseach was a red brick structure, similar to eighteenth century Georgian mansions.

Outside of the core area, a linear gridiron of streets was constructed. Here the commercial and residential areas arose. North of the circle, stores, restaurants, banks, and other businesses opened up, and also some expensive penthouse apartments and hotels. A number of schools, both public and church-operated, were built south of the core area, and churches were constructed later. Residential neighbors were developed farther north and south of the business districts. In general, the southern neighborhoods housed the families of employees of the various municipal services and the lower levels of national government ministries. In short, they were white-collar clerical workers. To the north of the core city, the neighborhoods housed a more blue-collar population, mainly the employees of the huge synthetic gas plants east of the city. On the western edge of the city, cultural facilities were built, museums and theaters. Later, sizable mansions were constructed, the homes of top-level government officials, like members of the Dail. An encircled residential area was constructed. Here the new embassies were constructed; the buildings were arranged in a circle. As with any other major structure, the embassy buildings went down into the ground instead of skyward.

On the other side of the planet, Dublin grew in similar fashion. Many smaller cities grew as well.

As soon as the post-rebellion demobilization was completed, the Defense Ministry began preparation for the next conflict. The Hibernian Aerospace Defense Force was a nebulous compromise between a volunteer army and a conscript force. The ground forces were formally established as separate units distinct from the shuttle craft forces. Military academies were constructed and a War College planned to coordinate air and ground tactics. The remaining IPVs either formed their own units or were integrated into Hibernian units. The Orangemen had formed their own militia. Once the formal military infrastructure was completed, the actual military bases were developed. A line of fortified positions was developed along the Ulster quadrant frontier. Aerospace bases for launching and landing the armed shuttle craft were constructed. One each was built at Dublin, Athlone, and both Arctic poles.

Military technology was gradually improved, for another war was expected soon. Aerospace engineers were projecting a new generation of laser-armed fighter craft to replace the shuttle craft used in the rebellion. Tanks and personnel carriers were designed to carry lasers and a surface laser anti-aircraft gun came into production. Wartime analysis revealed the one major shortcoming of laser weapons. Lasers could only be used for line-of-sight targets. During ground fighting, the weapons were hampered in hilly or mountainous country. To overcome this tactical handicap, a high-trajectory, recoilless, rocket cannon was successfully tested. In time the rocket cannons were integrated with the laser weapons.

The year 3100 heralded the new century, and the planet-nation bubbled over with celebrations. Predictions were made that Ulster quadrant would be recovered and that the Celtic Brittanians, i.e., the Scots and Welsh, would immigrate to Hibernia. Negotiations with planet Franco-Italia were begun for the transfer of the Celtic Bretons from that planet to Hibernia. However, under the surface of apparent harmony was building one conflict that would throw the nation into chaos.

The Sinn Fein Party had held a near monopoly of power in the Second Republic. The only opposition in the Dail were a few independents elected in northeast Leinster. They were elected with the votes of the Orangemen, who were unable to represent themselves directly. *An Phoblacht*, the Sinn Fein party organ, propagated a steady barrage of insults against "the Brit-loving bowler boys and their petty bourgeois cohorts." The latter term referred to the small farmers and store keepers who, despite heavy restrictions, had prospered. Farms as small as one hectare had expanded up to five hundred hectares. Small family-run stores had become large merchandizing centers. With their almost congenial financial acumen, the Orangemen defended the men of small property. Samuel Clarke O'Hara, proprietor of a Dublin-based department store chain, organized a committee of correspondence to represent the merchants and farmers.

A far more serious social fracture was an ideological division in the trade unions. The unions had been the base of what *An Phoblacht* called the "Workers' Republic." There were two basic union structures. One was the industrial unions, consisting of the less educated and unskilled workers of production line manufacturers and mines. They began to demand a revision of the socio-economic order on an anarcho-syndicalist basis. Specifically, a federation of unions and co-operatives would replace the socialist bureaucracy in running the economy. The syndicalists prepared to elect their own members to the Dail, with the aim of dissolving the Dail.

The other union structure was narrow craft unions. These unions represented skilled artisans, administrative and supervisory personnel, and even the professions. These unions and their individual members had purchased large numbers of government bonds and had begun to consider themselves the real owners of the nation's industries. The craft union members soon felt a common interest with the petty bourgeois, their heretofore class enemy. Union officials joined the Samuel O'Hara Committee of Correspondence. In the autumn of 3105, a convention was held in Kilkenny. The assembly of farmers, merchants, and skilled artisans organized the Liberal Party. Their platform called for immediate denationalization of all manufacturing and mining facilities, lower taxes, and future denationalization of the utilities that had been state-run since the First Republic.

The Sinn Fein government responded with a number of repressive measures; arson attacks on stores owned by Liberals; a call for a boycott of such stores; and finally by canceling the general election of 3106. By-elections were held in 3108, 3111, and 3113 to fill vacancies in the Dail. Most were won by the Liberals and the rest by the Syndicalists. In 3115 the Liberals delivered a petition for a constitutional convention. The government reacted by arresting Sam O'Hara and other Liberal officials on a falsified charge of espionage. A Bill of Attainder was presented to the Dail. It was intended to bypass the centuries-old abstention from capital punishment.

In one decade Hibernia had slid to the edge of the abyss of tyranny, not unlike the Brittanic occupation. Before the mock trial could begin, the Syndicalists ordered a general strike. Then the Hibernian military seized power in a *coup d' etat*. Without running any candidates of their own, the military ran a general election for the Dail and a constituent assembly. The Liberals won a near total monopoly of power and declared the Third Republic. Samuel O'Hara became Taoiseach, and under his leadership the denationalization of mines and manufacturers took place. The proposals of the Syndicalists for a system of cooperatives were ignored. New plans for denationalizing the utilities were brought up for consideration; however, these plans had to be put aside as the nation turned to face outside danger again.

King George XXX had spent nearly two decades fighting to secure his throne. Although the riots and sabotage by the anti-royalists were curbed, they continued to keep the government under surveillance. A steady stream of information was relayed to the Hibernians. After the turn of the century, the exhausted monarch put aside plans of a war of revenge. His marriage to Lady Helga Wallenburg of Planet Scandinavia, who was twenty years his junior, began a placid period of his rule. An amnesty was declared for almost all political prisoners, and the following year half of the taxes were suspended. An infant girl, Princess Elizabeth, came into the world in 3108. Her face soon appeared on stamps, dishware, ashtrays, towels, and in art works. Her parents, meanwhile, began to live a fairytale life of royal balls, steeple chases, and yacht races. They visited hospitals and foundling homes and conducted ceremonial investitures of bishops and professors. Some of the erstwhile rebels pledged loyalty to the Crown. King George hinted his consent to the emigration of the Scots and Welsh to Hibernia. Many believed a formal peace treaty would be signed that would end the strife between the two planets.

Suddenly and sadly in 3116, the placid decade, the "time of bliss," ended in a rapid trio of royal funerals. The Queen Mother Amanda and her consort, Count Konig, passed away of old age, as had been expected. Then beloved Queen Helga died in a miscarriage; the child was stillborn. The King seemed to go mad, turning against everybody, even his weeping daughter, Elizabeth. He exiled her to an exclusive finishing school on Planet Benelux. It was operated by relatives of his maternal grandmother, the late Baroness Von Tromp. Then, as if he imagined that the anti-royalists and the Hibernians were responsible for his wife's death, he prepared for a new war.

Letters of Marque were issued to privateers authorizing raids on Hibernian space transports. This, of course, lead to general space piracy, and that fact did not win Brittania any support among Interplanetary opinion. Along the Ulster defense lines, military activities like trench raids and mortar barrages were stepped up. Transports carrying additional troops and equipment were sent to the quadrant. Counter-intelligence efforts were instituted to confuse the anti-royalists. The most elaborate scheme was constructing new missile bases with dummy missiles on the old sites. The real thermonuclear missiles were moved by transports to the Shetland asteroids. The war mobilization was stretched over a seven-year period to achieve stealth and subtlety. By the end of 3123, the preparations were completed.

In mid-January 3124, a Brittanic freighter was en route across the length of the solar system. It carried the dregs of the Brittanic penal system—hardened criminals and some political prisoners. Also on board were some minor diplomatic officials and some trade representatives of other planets. One-half day's travel from Sovietia, it radioed that it was under attack, identifying its attacker as a Hibernian craft. The freighter vanished and later fragments of debris were found in deep space. The Brittanic government accused Hibernia of a deliberate attack on a "diplomatic courier-vessel of His Majesty's Service." Months later the crew and passengers reappeared, safe on a Soviet asteroid. They had abandoned the ship by a number of shuttles, then detonated a remote-control self-destruct program built into the ship's computer system.

Brittania withdrew its truce negotiators from Athlone, and in early February its all-out offense was launched. The missiles were launched in a full salvo from the Shetland asteroids. The missiles were intercepted by Hibernian armed shuttles almost immediately after launch. The anti-royalist intelligence network had kept Hibernia completely informed of the Brittanic plans and full mobilization soon took place. Then the armed shuttles raided the Shetland asteroid missile bases, destroying them totally.

The Brittanic ground forces launched a general offensive against Connaught quadrant. First an artillery barrage hammered the Hibernian positions for nearly twenty-four hours. Then the armored units and infantry swept over the frontier. At the Arctic pole, the shuttle base at Manor Hamilton in Leitrim sector was overrun after three days of fighting. Two days later the Brittanians were repulsed. Hibernian infantry units were thrown into battle using electro-mechanical dog sleds as personnel carriers. The shuttle squadron assigned to the Leitrim base returned from the Shetland raid to give air support for the counterattack.

Farther south, the Brittanic army pressed into Sligo and Mayo sectors. Teenage schoolboys and members of the Retired Veterans Reserve Legion, "the men of '85," joined Hibernian regulars and IPVs in stopping "the hired thugs of the Sassenach Monarchic Monster," as one officer proclaimed. In Roscommon, three Gaelic church schools—St. Basil's, St. Agnes, and St. Benedict's—in the village of Boyle were literally defended by boys as young as fourteen. Across the other side of the quadrant, IPV ski troops held Galway sector. The sector's mountains were snow-capped, belying its equatorial latitude. Here the new rocket cannons proved their value in an area where lasers were hobbled by lack of line-of-sight targets. The Brittanians had developed lasers but of an obsolete design. They had almost abandoned all ballistic weapons and had no tactical training for using laser artillery.

In the massive marshland where the four quadrants intersected, a kind of naval war took place. Flat-boats and barges carried infantry units from the opposing sides and the units collided. A correspondent of Dublin's *National Journal Gazetteer* wrote of "sea battles in an ocean only a meter deep. Boats sunk and raised up by their crews to float again. Boats run aground and pulled free under fire. Marsh water mixed with oil and blood. Fish floating dead from concussions. Little furry mulquix blown to shreds."

It took many weeks to push the enemy out of Connaught and back into their own lines. It cost a great loss of life. Then the frontier fighting declined to the level of trench raids, as before the war had begun.

While the tide of battle rose and fell along the Ulster-Connaught frontier, a different kind of war was fought along the Ulster-Leinster line. The frontier was a tropical rainforest from the quadrant marshland eastward to Meath sector. The higher altitudes in that sector produced grasslands, running all through Louth sector. In early February, a week of rainstorms pelted both Longford and West Meath sectors. When the sun broke through the clouds, the jungle was blanketed in thick fog. Clearings, where the forest had been cut away, were seas of red mud. The Brittanic tank columns sank in the mire. The infantry coming behind the trapped vehicles had to pull their helpless comrades out with ropes and block-and-tackles. The Hibernians brought a new weapon, the autogiro gunships, to the jungle. Flying just above treetops, it strafed the unlucky Brittanians with laser and rocket-cannon fire. The frontier became a continuous series of small battles after the initial tank fiasco. The Brittanians, long accustomed to their dry, hardened fortresses, suffered from the heat and humidity. A special problem was the spoilage of much of their provisions. The Hibernians had it easier outdoors, having long ago learned to bivouac outside. They were acclimated to the conditions, and in addition they had cultivated tropical vegetables and fruits and thus were well fed.

By the end of the month, the offensives were repulsed along both the Connaught and Leinster lines. Only along the Meath-Louth area had there been an absence of fighting. At Carrickmacross, in Monaghan sector, the local Brittanic garrisons were used as a rest area. Here many battered units were replenished with freshly trained recruits, transported in the very last month before the war.

In early March a convoy of ten transports left Brittania for Ulster quadrant. The on-board shuttles were laser-armed and became the convoy's escorts. The Hibernian shuttle command sent two squadrons to intercept the convoy. One of the squadrons did not consist of shuttles but prototypes of an actual fighter craft. They were faster and more maneuverable than shuttles. Also, they were equipped with a new laser-targeting system of extreme accuracy.

Only two of the transports survived to reach Ulster quadrant. On board one of the freighters was the new governor-general of the quadrant, Viscount Cromwell of Huntingdon. He shared his king's murderous hatred for Hibernians and all who supported them. He directed the special branch in ferreting out anti-royalists in the past decade. Promoted to M-I-6, he had masterminded the faked attack on a Brittanic freighter in January.

Viscount Cromwell set up his new headquarters at Carrickmacross. In the following weeks he directed the build-up of units in the adjacent Monaghan and Armagh sectors. His intelligence sources reported that Meath and Louth sectors were defended by the Orange militia. The militia lacked armor, air support, or fortified positions. Cromwell formulated an ambitious plan: He would smash through the Orangemen and capture Dublin, Hibernia's major industrial center. He was certain his enemy would deploy both their armed shuttles to block the attack and their ground forces to defend Dublin. The diversion would permit a large transport convoy to land in the quadrant. The reinforcements were to launch an offensive in another sector. The second offensive might capture Athlone; then the two columns would converge and take all of Leinster sector. Or, it could sweep down from the Arctic to take all of Connaught.

Operation Nightstorm began in mid-April, with a laser barrage that illuminated the starless night-skies and charred fresh grasslands. Then Brittanic tanks swept over the equator in the direction of Orange villages like Shankill, Waterside, and Lisburn. The militiamen abandoned the forward lines and set up pillboxes along the southward roads. The Orange militia units dug into their villages after evacuating the women and children. The advancing enemy tanks and foot soldiers by-passed the villages. The support units followed: the Quartermaster Corps, the Signal Corps, Medical Supplies, Paymaster, the Provost Marshal, and finally, Siege Artillery. Raiding parties from the villages and the pillboxes northward sortied out to hit the supporting units. Soon a number of the advancing troops were counter-marched and sent to attack the villages.

The siege of Shankill, Waterside, Lisburn, and the other Orange villages began with a barrage that smashed many homes. In their basements and root cellars, the Orangemen waited for the fire to end. When the Brit tanks and infantry approached, the militia answered with petrol bombs and laser-rifle fire. Autogiro gunships from Dublin began to provide support, dropping off supplies and picking up wounded men. A village newspaper was still being printed during the siege. A copy was picked up by a giro pilot and taken to Dublin. The paper's editorial proclaimed, "The siege of Shankill will be down in history with the 1689 siege of Londonderry. Until the last drop of Ulster-Scots blood is shed, the Shankill will not fall!" A correspondent of the *National Journal Gazetteer*, who had just covered the battle of the marshlands, picked up the editorial. "Shankill will not fall," became a battlecry throughout the planet.

In the second week of May another convoy left Brittania, ten transports in all. Before they reached the Orkney asteroids, two of the transports exploded, apparently due to bombs planted by anti-royalists. Two more freighters were so heavily damaged they had to return to their launch base. The remaining ships stopped at the Shetland asteroids and had to carefully inspect their cargo holds for bombs. On the last day of the month, the convoy left the asteroids. The Hibernian shuttle fleet intercepted the convoy, and only one freighter reached the quadrant. The disaster finally made the Brittanic command understand the folly of unescorted convoys. The Brittanic Defense Ministry tried to order their privateers to assemble into one fleet; however, the pirates were too widely scattered through the solar system to be contacted.

By early June, Operation Nightstorm had ground to a halt fifty kilometers north of Dublin. The Hibernian ground forces had been deployed in two parallel lines running south from the equator. The enemy was crowded into a deep salient. Then the counteroffensive began with armed shuttles, autogiros, light armor and IPV commandos all thrown into the battle. Gliders, escorted by gunships, dropped an IPV unit into Lisburn and they were nearly fired upon by the militia. From Lisburn they spread out east and west and lifted the siege of Shankill and Waterside. In one week the main Hibernian units reached the villages. On the last day of June, the last Brit units withdrew into Ulster. After a two-week hiatus, the Hibernians launched a general assault on the quadrant. It was halted in three days and fighting returned to the level of trench raids and barrages.

In Brittania the anti-royalists had engaged in a wide range of sabotage. Munition plants, generating stations, and bridges were destroyed, key military officials ambushed, and riots started. The Brittanic monarch was informed that if the war continued, the throne might be lost. An armistice was called for through the Interplanetary Federation. The fighting ceased, except for isolated raids. Soon negotiating teams began the same charades as before the war.

The Hibernian economy had been overheated before the war, and afterward it went out of control. The cost of living rose rapidly when demobilization caused some unemployment. Taoiseach Samuel O'Hara, who had spent the months of war convalescing from a stroke, retired to private life. He returned to Dublin to run his department store chain and to play with his grandchildren. His son, Colm, rose from the back bench of the Liberal Party to party whip. He soon revealed that while he inherited his father's intellectual brilliance, he lacked his father's backbone. In 3126 the general elections resulted in gains for the Sinn Fein and the Syndicalists. Soon each party developed a militia branch, recruited from recent war veterans. Fistfights broke out in Dublin, Athlone, and Kilkenny at veterans' lodges and union halls.

Another conflict that disrupted the society was that many native Hibernians began to resent the presence of the IPVs and their families. The various objections included the loss of jobs; strange languages, music, and foods; refusal to learn Gaelic; sympathy for Orangemen; even bad smells. The more devout natives, including Catholic clerics, were appalled by such imported entertainment forms as music halls, i.e., burlesque theaters, and erotic books. Reports that off-duty servicemen were going to girlie shows and even rumors of marriages of servicemen to dancers were denounced from the pulpit. The slur "Peevee" was spat out at all foreigners.

By late summer fights were even taking place in the chamber of the Dail. Colm O'Hara, after months of indecision, made an impassioned speech to the restless chamber. Trembling violently he warned, "If we are divided by a civil war, we could be threatened by outside violence. Brittania could trap us like rats in this condition. We cannot defend ourselves by fighting among ourselves."

At noon on the last day of August, over a thousand IPVs seized the major government buildings in Athlone. The Hibernian regular military command gave their implicit approval. Under house arrest, with armed guards inside the chamber, the Dail rewrote the constitution. Colm O'Hara was the chief architect. The Fourth Republic was to become an economic triad of private, government, and co-operative sectors. In addition, to assure stability, there would be no general election until the Ulster quadrant was recovered.

Athlone soon became the showcase of the triad economy. The western side of the city received electrical power from the government hydro plants on the Shannon River. A new private electric company built a complex of nuclear and coal-fired generators at Portlaoise that transmitted power to Athlone's east side. In some neighborhoods people could hook up to one service in the front yard and the other service in the back yard.

The new private textile companies in northwest Athlone used electricity from the municipal branch of the state power authority. They sold most of their production wholesale to a number of consumer co-operatives, including one run by the textile workers' union. Over on the east side, the state-owned coal-gasification plant bought much of its coal from private mining interests. It used electricity from the new private utility at Portlaoise.

People in Athlone were receiving mail twice a day—their morning mail by the state postmen and evening mail from private postal services. A cooperative brewery was built and operated by a number of families originally from Fermanagh sector. Soon Enniskillen Ale became the popular potable in the city.

After the war of 3124 ended, the Defense Ministry immediately began to plan for the inevitable next conflict. One of their foremost desires was to carry the war to the enemy planet. Also, the space pirates were crippling Hibernia's commerce. It was assumed the pirates were acting under Brittanic orders.

Technical analysis of the shuttles proved they could not make the round trip between the two planets without refueling. It was also clear that if the shuttle fleet was sent out to escort Hibernian merchant craft, refueling ships would be needed. Finally, it was discovered that when shuttles were used for air support for the ground forces, fuel consumption was even greater. This was due to gravity and atmospheric friction. A shuttle traveling below the speed of sound, at an altitude of less than one kilometer, consumed fuel faster than if it were in deep space traveling at light factor 2.

Another problem developed in the new prototype fighter craft. They were much smaller than the shuttle craft. The ancient shuttles had an electrical generating system capable of independently powering their lasers. The fighters, because of their size, carried a photon battery to power the laser. The battery would have to be recharged after a limited period of combat use.

In 3127 a squadron of shuttles and a modified freighter left Hibernia for a tour of escort duty. A complicated system of hoses, manned by crewmen in pressure suits, carried out the refueling operations. After the first tour the shuttle was joined by a flight of the prototype fighters. A system of cables was used for recharging the batteries. There were collisions resulting in loss of space craft and men.

From the experiences of that prototype operation of just less than a year, designs were drawn up for the first space tanker. The ship would be propelled by a modified factor 15 engine. It was to carry two huge armored spheres filled with double ion plasma fuel. On the underside of the ship were nozzles for the fuel and cables for recharging lasers. The nozzles and cables were paired together in rows spaced for the length of the expected fighter craft. A pair of compartments were placed amidships between the fuel spheres for future defensive armament. The ship would be constructed and launched from the shuttle base at Killarney in Antarctic Kerry sector. The launching platform would then be prepared for when the ship would be landed for repairs or refueling the huge tanks.

In 3131 the tanker was launched and named the *Arthur Griffith*. In two and one half years, three larger space tankers were constructed, the *John*

Redmond, the *Michael Collins*, and the *Daniel O'Connell*. By 3135 the tanker fleet was patrolling the entire solar system. One squadron of shuttles or fighters could be towed underneath a tanker while several other squadrons acted as escort. A repair freighter, the *Edward Carson*, was launched at the same time as the *O'Connell*. It was shaped like a number of shuttles boxed together and carried several extendable and retractable docking bays for repair operations.

While the tanker fleet was constructed, the new fighter craft they would service were brought into operation. The Needlehead fighter was a single-seat double-delta wing craft. Its thin fuselage blended into the wings. The pilot's seat could be adjusted to a sleeping position for when the craft was in tow. The nose of the fighter carried a new, highly accurate dual-action laser. The gun could fire pencil beams for ground targets or short bursts for combat with enemy craft.

After the first squadron carried out a six-month tour of duty, additional equipment was designed for the newer craft. A cockpit pod with life-support equipment enabled a pilot to eject from a fatally damaged fighter. A small laser was placed in the tail to shake off pursuers.

By the year 3140, the Hibernian military foresaw other potential dangers. There was a possibility that most of the first-line fighters could be spread through the solar system. The cities of the home planet would be defended by the now obsolete shuttles. A large number of anti-aircraft lasers were deployed in the major cities. The next problem was the need for gunners to man these batteries. Manpower could not be diverted from the fighter fleet or the ground forces. After two years of heated debate, the Women's Auxiliary Service was formed. The women were trained to operate the surface guns. Like volunteer firemen, they were to be on standby alert. Regardless of their regular occupation, each had a one-piece gunner's suit in a duffel bag. At the first alarm they were to leave their jobs to man their batteries.

In Athlone the first class of trainees included the wives, sisters, daughters, and mothers of fighter pilots. They included teachers, women from the textile mills and the coal gasification plant, music hall dancers, even relatives of members of the Dail. In Dublin and other cities, a similar cross-section of the women of the planet responded to the call of patriotism.

While the Defense Ministry prepared for the next war, the Foreign Ministry made a futile attempt to prevent it. In 3139 the new minister, Colm O'Hara, began a series of diplomatic missions to every planet nation in the system. Although he obtained several generous commercial and cultural treaties, he failed to obtain a military alliance.

Brittania was itself girding for war. It continued to subsidize the space privateers, despite their now-increasing ineffectiveness. The first prototypes of the Boomerang fighter-bomber were constructed. It was shaped like a flying wing with twin lasers, one firing pencil beams and the other firing bursts. What was not known was that several of her designers were secretly in the anti-royalist Underground. They had designed deficiencies in the fighters. Also, the Brittanians had no coherent fighter pilot training program. It would soon be clear that the strategy of mass numbers would be used instead of finesse.

Opposition to the Crown was rising, although factionized. The Underground included socialists, Scotch-Welsh separatists, the isolationist English National Front, and simple over-taxed common folk. The new legal branch of the opposition was the Freedom Party in the House of Commons. It was led by W.E. Gladstone, a latter-day Jeremiah. He risked threats of arrest for treason and assassination to call for withdrawal from Ulster quadrant. He had earned the hostility of King George and Princess Elizabeth, who had returned from schooling wed to her father's hatred of Hibernia. Accompanying the princess was her handsome confidant, Lord Churchill of Marlborough. Although their relationship was platonic, the dilettante was soon promoted to the office of defense minister. He also used his influence to obtain posts for his friends, some of whom were secretly involved in the Underground. This enraged the far more capable Lord Cromwell, who threatened to resign from the government.

In 3144 Colm O'Hara visited London in a direct diplomatic mission to the royal family. He was accompanied by a military aide, fighter squadron Captain Seamus O'Rourke. While the foreign minister attempted to negotiate a withdrawal from Ulster, his aide contacted the anti-royalist Underground. Maps of military facilities throughout Brittania were delivered to the Hibernian officer. The last negotiating session was held at the Crystal Palace. Lord Cromwell made a series of abusive remarks about Hibernians and the foreign minister personally. Captain O'Rourke responded, and the two men came to blows. Afterward, Minister O'Hara had to persuade his military aide against challenging Cromwell to a duel.

With the diplomatic gestures past, the Defense Ministry continued its war plans. Near Kilkenny, a cruise missile base was constructed for the purpose of bombarding the industrial facilities in the enemy quadrant. Built and manned largely by Deutscher IPVs, it was soon nicknamed Peenemude after a famous twentieth century rocket base. Another unit of Deutschers were developing the Brunnehilde artillery carrier. It was to carry a laser and a rocket cannon in a tandem mount. Its integrated computer system could fire both guns simultaneously at separate targets. A second-generation fighter craft was reaching the prototype stage. The two-seater Bullethead fighter would carry an ion plasma cannon. The weapon was to produce a fireball of anti-matter that could disintegrate more than one enemy craft at a time.

The most secret and ambitious project was code-named Alpa-X-10. At Cashel in Tipperary sector, a nuclear linear accelerator was constructed for separating subatomic particles. The particles were to go through amphilication boosters then into a laser-like projector. The resulting particle beam would be tracked up a radio-like transmitting tower, then up to a special shuttle craft. The shuttle was to broadcast the beam outward on a 360-

degree horizontal plane in near space. A network of the projectors would be built around the planet. The object would be a force shield to seal off the entire planet from the enemy and permit retaking Ulster quadrant. As a counter-intelligence measure, disinformation was leaked to the press about a particle beam cannon.

The Alpha project was derided by several major Hibernian military officials. One of their alternatives was a proposed attack ship. It was to be able to carry, launch, and land fighter craft and also carry heavy armament. The planned warship was shelved because they could not perfect a fighter launch tube. However, the new tanker *Charles Stewart Parnell*, launched in 3147, did carry defensive lasers.

In late 3147, Colm O'Hara became Taoiseach and soon faced a political crisis that threatened the Fourth Republic. There had been no general election since 3126, only by-elections to fill vacancies in the Dail. Some of the new members of the Dail were impatient with their back-bench status. They seized the first opportunity to disrupt the political status quo. It happened right in Athlone.

Unlike the well-oiled machine that ran the nation from the same city, the municipal governor of Athlone was a social climber whose main interest was self-aggrandizement. The local school system was noted for waste and the local district of the An Garda Siochana was staffed by men as old as members of the Dail. The city had surprisingly few outlets for young women, and several all-girl delinquent gangs had been formed. In early 3148 the local Garda finally launched a number of raids, arresting a large number of young women involved in the various gangs. By summer, six of these women were to be tried as adults. The most shocking feature of the trial was that many of the girl gang members, including those on trial, were from prominent families. One was Shelley O'Rourke, the daughter of Seamus O'Rourke, who by then was in charge of the fighter base of Athlone.

When the trial began, the defendants were wearing special black uniforms and in handcuffs and leglocks. During the trial the girls were gagged several times.

The charges included vandalism, drug use, accusations of robberies, assaults, arson, and, most ridiculous of all, charges of espionage. The main charge was contributing to the delinquency of minors, stemming from their initiation of girls under age eighteen. The most shocking aspect of the state's case was the rituals of initiation, which involved lesbian acts. One after another each of the girls defended the rituals. Shelley O'Rourke stood straight up in her chains and stated, "The ritual of lovemaking between the members of the Tigeress gang is the symbol of our unity, our devotion to the idea that the young women of our nation should be given a far greater opportunity to participate in and serve in the development and defense of our motherland Hibernia."

The trial attracted nationwide attention and began to divide the country. Demonstrations between groups calling for the release of the defendants and those groups demanding prison or death sentences began to take place and soon became fistfights. Universities held debates, student groups passing resolutions pro or con. The *National Journal Gazetteer* commented, "The entire nation is at the edge of a nervous breakdown." Several Sinn Fein back-benchers introduced a bill for a vote of no confidence in the government. It was voted down with laughter, even from the Sinn Fein leaders. Then an independent from Dublin, a minister, introduced a Bill of attainder that would send the young girls to the gallows. Colm O'Hara addressed the Dail to oppose the bill. He pleaded for the life of "these young girls, one of whom might someday give birth to a hero who will save the nation." In an hour the entire assembly was in tears and the Bill of Attainder was defeated.

After the guilty verdict came from the jury, the three-judge bench remanded five of the girls to their parents until the date of sentencing. Shelley O'Rourke, however, was put in solitary confinement for contempt of court. Two months later the girls were sentenced to an indeterminate number of years in the women's prison in Limerick. Shelley O'Rourke, in chains, answered, "You have destroyed the moral band between the state and society. Your action will result in the destruction of the nation."

The O'Rourke family, which was the only family to attend the trial, wept openly. In a few weeks the trial was forgotten and the crisis ended. The scandal had almost cost Seamus O'Rourke his command, and as he was a supporter of the Alpha project, it nearly faced cancellation.

A couple of months later, the minister-cum-member of the Dail who had introduced the proposed Bill of Attainder was beaten half to death. He survived, but his mind was too badly injured; he became a resident of a home for the retarded. It was believed girl gang members had inflicted the injuries as punishment for demanding the death penalty for the girls who were on trial.

All through 3148 Brittanic transports were arriving in Ulster quadrant at the rate of one a month. The freighters were carrying the new Boomerang fighters and the pilots and support crews. Fighter bases were constructed in the quadrant; most of them were close to the border. Through diplomatic channels the space privateers were bribed for one last mass attack on the Hibernian merchant craft. The hidden objective would be to draw the tanker fleet and the fighter craft deep into the solar system. After this was accomplished, the Brittanic fighter craft would be launched in a full air offensive. First they were to raid the cities of Athlone and Dublin to try to force a quick surrender. If this did not succeed, the fighter craft would destroy the Hibernian border defenses and support a ground offense. King George had conceived of the plan with the aid of Lord Cromwell, who had been promoted to the level of air marshal in the Defense Ministry. As a final step to insure success, the privateers were to assemble into an armada to intercept and destroy the tanker fleet. This would require an exact timetable for their operations. Anti-royalists in the foreign ministry altered the schedule to delay the rendezvous of the privateer fleet.

The operation, Nightstorm II, began January 30, 3149. Several Hibernian space freighters were ambushed at various points in the solar system. This sudden flare-up of piracy after a half decade of inactivity resulted in the complete mobilization of the Hibernian fleet. Within four days, the entire force of five tankers, one repair ship, and fifteen squadrons of fighters had fanned out as far as planet Nigeria. The diversion had apparently succeeded. On February 10, Lord Paisley of Inverness, the new governor-general of Ulster quadrant, ordered the initial aerial attack. Nearly three hundred fighters took off from the new bases. After a prefatory strafing of Hibernian positions on the equator, the force split into two groups. One headed for Dublin, where the sun had just set; the other air group steered to Athlone's bright dawn.

The Brittanic pilots were barely trained and some of the fighters collided with each other. As they approached their target cities, the green pilots received an unwelcome surprise. Whole squadrons of aged shuttle craft intercepted the Brittanians. The Boomerang fighter-bombers shot down a considerable number of the old ships, then continued southward. When they reached cities, another surprise came in the form of laser surface fire from the Women's Auxiliary Service. The Brit fighter-bombers strafed everything in sight—the surface guns, homes, schools, textile mills, buses of people fleeing. Not since the holocaust of 2994 were Hibernia's two main cities subjected to such heavy attack. Children who had been playing outside the school buildings were burned alive. Had it not been for the elaborate underground design of the major buildings, the loss of life would have been even worse. The Brit attack did not get off without loss, as a number of fighter craft were brought down by surface fire. Then, as they withdrew to return to the quadrant, the Brittanic fighters were again intercepted by the shuttle craft. The Hibernian pilots used their experience and skill to overcome the technical inferiority of their vintage craft. They paired off in twos and threes and singled out individual Brit craft and destroyed them.

That evening a factor 50 mail shuttle delivered a full report of the offensive to London. At first King George was elated at the results of the attack. He would have then ordered the operation to continue as planned; however, when he was informed of the combined resistance of the shuttles and surface guns, he countermanded the order. A mail shuttle was sent back with a new order: destroy Athlone and Dublin.

During that same night, the Hibernians recovered from the shock of the surprise attack. The Women's Auxiliary Service was carefully redeployed, the surface guns arranged in patterns that would create a tight crossfire. A factor 50 mail shuttle was launched from the Killarney base to contact the tanker fleet. An evacuation program was activated to move civilians to safe quarters. Taoiseach O'Hara made a radio broadcast calling on the people to remain calm. He did this only after heavy sedation for shock.

The following day the Brittanic fighters again attacked Athlone and Dublin. This time the Hibernian shuttle pilots had perfected the pick-off tactics they had crudely attempted the day before. They also coordinated their operations with the ground forces, drawing the enemy into a trap of laser fire. The loss ratio shifted from three to one in Brittania's favor to dead even. In the next three days the ratio slowly shifted to Hibernia's favor. The damage caused by the continuous raids dropped off as the Brittanic craft had to defend themselves. Along the border the ground offensive had been launched without air support and was stopped in two days. A salvo of cruise missiles from Peenemude hit a Brittanic base in Cavan sector, vaporizing a mass of armored vehicles.

On the eighteenth, the Brittanic fighter command had begun to copy the Hibernian pick-off tactics and the loss ratio shifted in their favor. By the twentieth the Hibernian shuttle forces were almost driven from the sky. In the next three days, the cities of Athlone and Dublin suffered increasing damage and the surface gunners suffered high casualties. Then on the twenty-fourth, after the Boomerang fighter-bombers were returning to their quadrant bases, they were intercepted. The tanker fleet had arrived in time to save the cities from total destruction. The year before the engines of each tanker had been modified to reach speeds of up to factor 4 for limited periods. Over 220 Needlehead fighters hit the Brittanic craft. The Boomerang pilots were exhausted, their craft low on fuel, and their laser photon batteries were out. The Brit craft were shot down by the dozens, few of them ever reaching their bases. The particular facts of this air battle hid the clear technical inferiority of the Brittanic craft.

The Hibernian fighters landed at their assigned bases to repair and refuel their craft and to rest the pilots. Many of these pilots and other crewmen of the tanker fleet had lost friends and relatives during the attack upon Athlone and Dublin. Pilots whose wives had entered the auxiliary service were now widowers. Others had lost their mothers or daughters. The loss of so many women in action was a greater shock than the civilian casualties. Among the losses in Athlone were the daughters of three top members of the Dail; a cousin of the Taoiseach; two music hall dancers; and the mother of a newborn infant, her husband having died in a shuttle crash. The wives of several senior Hibernian officers also died in action, including the wife of tanker fleet Commander Seamus O'Rourke.

On March 2, the tanker fleet left their orbital stations to attack Brittania itself. For the first time in the extended conflict, the war would be carried to the King's home realm. Commander O'Rourke had left the bridge of the *Parnell* and was at the controls of a prototype of the new Bullethead fighter-bomber. He had clear knowledge of major Brittanic targets dating from his 3144 contacts with anti-royalists. He would lead the attack himself. Among the pilots in the attack force was his eldest son, Lieutenant Eamon O'Rourke.

When they reached the enemy planet, the tankers and their assigned squadrons were deployed. The *Parnell* and the *Griffith* moved toward the English quadrant in the northeast. The *O'Connell* transported its fighter squadrons to the Scots-Welsh quadrant to the southeast. Canada quadrant, in the northwest, was the target of the *Redmond*. The Australian and New Zealand quadrant of the southwest was to be attacked by the fighters assigned to the *Collins*. The repair ship *Carson* acted as a communications ship.

The Hibernian pilots had ambivalent feelings as their sleek fighters approached the Brit cities. They were distressed by the thought of attacking what they knew were undefended cities. This could not overcome their desire for revenge to punish the Brittanic warlords who had brought so much suffering to Hibernia. Their first targets were military bases, munitions plants, rail yards, ball-bearing plants, smelters, and refineries. Residential areas were hit; it was unavoidable. Birmingham, Leeds, Manchester, Cardiff, Glasgow, Wellington, Sydney, Toronto, Edmonton, etc., all came under fire. In all, thirty-five cities were hit in thirty-six hours. As a *coup de grace*, all five tankers moved toward the North Pole—to London.

The force of over two hundred Hibernian fighter craft struck London like a swarm of fire locusts. Many government and commercial buildings were shattered by laser fire. Fire storms leveled whole city blocks, homes were flattened, and bridges were cut in two. People fleeing in panic were hit by falling debris. Then the fighter force headed for the Crystal Palace, where King George and Lord Cromwell were holding a strategy conference. The steel and glass geodesic dome cracked and crumbled, and inside Windsor Castle received heavy damage. The rescue teams would find the King critically injured; Lord Cromwell would be disfigured for life.

As the tanker fleet pulled about to return to Hibernia, a distress signal came from the *Carson*. The privateers had belatedly arrived. Over twenty small freighters and some shuttles with various armament attacked the repair ship. Most of the Hibernian fighters were being refueled and could not respond immediately. The *Carson* exploded with incandescent brilliance as the tankers arrived. A savage running battle took place as the Hibernian fleet ran the gauntlet of the privateers. The *O'Connell* was destroyed before the fleet passed the Orkney asteroids. The *Collins* vanished amidst the Shetland chain. The enormous explosion took several pirate ships with it. The Hibernian pilots, although exhausted, began to gain the upper hand as the pirate craft proved clumsy. The *Parnell*, with its defensive armament, shook off its attackers. The *Griffith* used an erratic zig-zag tactic to evade the pirate craft. As the battered fleet approached the home planet, the last privateer freighter rammed the *Redmond* amidships. The night sky over Dublin became as light as day from the brilliance of the resulting fireball. The two remaining tankers limped home. Aside from the loss of three tankers and one repair ship, the equivalent of three fighter squadrons was gone. It had been a Pyrrhic victory.

On March 14, the Hibernian fighter craft began to bombard the Brittanian's fortified Ulster-Leinster line. On the eighteenth the Hibernian ground forces launched an offensive on a fifteen hundred kilometer front. The columns advanced nearly one hundred kilometers by the twenty-fifth, then a huge counter-offensive drove the Hibernians back to the equatorial line. Only the arrival of over a hundred of the new Brunnehilde artillery carriers prevented further retreat.

At an emergency meeting of the Interplanetary Federation, the deceitful Princess Elizabeth and Lord Churchill proposed a cease fire. They were so successful in denouncing the March raid on Brittania that it was forgotten that King George had started the war. Taoiseach O'Hara, vacillating as usual, accepted the truce. On April 15, the war ended just as a new Hibernian offensive was being prepared. The military command was appalled. Rumors developed of a *coup détat*, but nothing happened.

In 3150 king George died of both old age and his injuries. Princess Elizabeth was crowned Queen Elizabeth XVII. She was no longer the angelic child of years past. She was now heavy set, vain, and seething with hatred for those whom she believed had killed her father. Lord Churchill and Lord Cromwell now battled for her personal favor. The former desired to merely conquer Hibernia, while the latter advocated extermination of the entire population of Hibernia. The supporters of the Crown in the House of Commons began talking of turning the solar system into a Brittanic empire. They were calling for punishing the other planet-nations that were aiding Hibernia.

As years passed the two planets began to enlarge their fighter fleets. The Hibernians had two major advantages: one, most of their fighter squadrons had survived the war. Even more important was the fact they had a long-established program to train pilots, the veterans pilots being capable instructors.

The Brittanians' offsetting advantage was their much larger industrial capacity, although delayed by wartime damage. In a short time they were building twice as many fighter craft; however, the Brittanian pilot training program was still in a rudimentary stage.

The anti-royalist Underground continued to provide intelligence service for Hibernia. As the Brittanic quadrant fleet was rebuilt, their future strategy became obvious. The Ulster quadrant fleet would engage the Hibernian force in an all-out aerial battle to the finish. The home fleet would be sent across the corridor between the two planets. They were to attack the Hibernian craft that remained at the point at which the craft were out of fuel and photon charges. They would overwhelm the exhausted Hibernians by sheer weight of numbers. This fact caused the Hibernian Defense Ministry to deadlock over the Alpha project.

By the spring of 3153, peace talks were suspended. Again the clouds of war darkened Hibernia's skies.

Part 1

Defense of Hibernia

Chapter 1

It is the dawn of a spring day in Athlone, mid-May by an Earth calendar. People are rising to go to work or school. At 9:00 the Viewscreen network broadcasts the morning news. The Viewscreen broadcast was on two different channels, one in English and one in Gaelic. The national population was divided almost evenly as to which tongue was used in everyday conversation. (The number of people who were totally bilingual were so few and important that they had formed a special caste of society.) A small golden medallion was awarded to those who passed examinations in both tongues. Those in this caste gave their time teaching in the schools, often one day a week, regardless of their regular vocation. In return, a bilingual of any class could go anywhere.

"This is the Hibernian State Viewscreen transmission network news. It is Friday, May 8, 3153. At the top of news, all diplomatic negotiations with the Royal Brittanic government have been broken off. The Hibernian ambassador is returning to Athlone by hyperlight spaceshuttle. This morning the Taoiseach, Colm O'Hara declared "Hibernians will not compromise their national honor. . . ."

At the office of the Taoiseach, in the main government building in Athlone, a discussion was reaching its climax. A thin, gray-haired, nervous man sat at a massive desk, puffing on a clay pipe. In front of him two men (one uniformed) were trying to sway his opinion on a vital matter of state.

"Mr. Prime Minister," said the imposing military officer, "the Brittanians' strategy is an open secret. They are building a large fleet of fighter-bombers and reinforcing the squadrons in their quadrant steadily. They will launch a two-pronged attack. The quadrant force will battle our air defense until our laser guns are out of charges, then their home squadrons will simply overwhelm us. If Lord Churchill is the head of government, we will be slaves; if Cromwell is their leader, we are to be exterminated. The only way to save our people is to begin work on Project Alpha-X-10."

Immediately the second man, in civilian dress but of no less martial bearing, answered, "Commander O'Rourke, the force field project is an impractical scheme that will divert resources from building up the fighter and ground battery forces. I believe, Mr. Prime Minister, our defenses can be strengthened to meet the threatened attack. Does the Commander doubt the ability of his own men?"

Commander O'Rourke replied, "As a former fighter pilot, I am the first to believe in the superior abilities of our fighters and pilots. But against odds of up to 10-to-1 or more, even our best fighters will be crushed by might of numbers."

The man at the desk stood and answered, "Defense Minister Flynn, Commander O'Rourke, I will report your views to the Dail Eireann."

The two gentlemen each gave a sign of resignation. Then another man entered the room. He approached the desk. After a sharp click of his heels, he handed a report to the Taoiseach. "Herr Taoiseach, a report of increased activity in the Brittanic quadrant. They may be planning an assault by the fighter-bomber squadrons in their bases," announced the stiffly erect gentleman.

The Prime Minister read the report, then handed it to the other two men. He said, "Thank you, Colonel Becker."

The colonel turned in a military fashion and marched to the door.

Commander O'Rourke spoke. "I am returning by Shuttle craft to my tanker, the *Parnell*. I will order that the fighter patrols for Athlone be tripled. All leaves for pilots and full-time base gunners will be cancelled; auxiliary base gunners will receive notice to be on standby alert. I will recommend Commanders Donahue and MacMullen to make similar arrangements. I'll report back to Athlone in seventy-two hours or after the first engagement with the enemy." The Commander walked through the door, following the colonel.

The latter stopped and, in a near whisper, said, "I agree with you, Herr Commandant, but it is not my place to make these decisions. Unfortunately, Mr. O'Hara cannot make any kind of decision at all."

The two gentlemen left the main government building and walked separate ways.

❖ ❖ ❖

On a street in a neighborhood at the edge of the city, two young people discussed the friendship they felt for each other. One was a small, thin boy, his dishwater-blond hair combed neatly and his eyes shielded by thick glasses. He wore a white linsey-woolsey jacket reading *Corbett Flower Shop* and sat on a pedicab. In the open truck were bouquets of flowers. The young girl standing on the sidewalk was also small and thin, her red hair tied in braids.

"Deirdre," the young boy said, "I heard from a friend at school that you're going to join the Tigeress gang."

The girl answered, "Yes, and why not? To be a Tigeress girl is the one way that I can be part of something, not a nobody in this town where girls are ignored."

The young man pleaded, "Please, Deirdre, listen to me. My sister joined that gang five years ago. She is still in jail! They make you do unnatural acts. Perverted acts!"

"Cathal O'Rourke, you're jealous! Being initiated won't hurt at all."

"Deirdre, you're the only girl in school who has treated me like a human being. I don't want to lose you. My mother is dead; my sister is in jail. Father and Eamon are in the service. Please, don't leave me!"

Suddenly two older girls appeared, wearing yellow linsey-woolsey sweaters with black stripes. One, a brunette carrying a pail full of what appeared to be greaseballs, spoke. "She isn't going to marry another guy; she's just becoming a woman, dedicated to protecting her fellow girls against the ginks who run this town."

The second girl, raven-haired, paused to light a cigarette and added, "A Tigeress girl can get any man she wants—and gives him what he needs."

"Hi, Clara," Deirdre greeted the first girl. The girl set down the bucket and shook hands.

"Deirdre will be the first wire-mouth to join the Tigeress. You should be proud of her, you're a wire-mouth yourself." She pointed to the braces that both Deirdre and Cathal wore on their teeth.

The second girl now walked up to Deirdre. She took the cigarette from her mouth and handed it to the small girl facing her. Deirdre coughed slightly after taking a deep drag, and said, "Thanks, Karen."

Being ignored, Cathal thought to himself, *I am alone now. They will corrupt her just like they corrupted Shelley, my dearest sister.* Cathal turned around on his pedicab and pedaled slowly away. *Maybe Eamon is right. If it weren't for my thick glasses, I could be a Needlehead pilot like him.*

✦ ✦ ✦

Several blocks from the government buildings is located the Athlone Inner Space Defense Base. Here the Needlehead fighters, the Delta-winger craft with double-purpose laser guns, await the alarm. The pilots were quartered in a row of underground barracks. In the ward room, the pilots assembled at attention.

A stern-faced young man with a fleet captain's insignia on his cap entered the room. Eamon O'Rourke prepared to deliver the orders of the day.

"Gentlemen, of as today, all leaves are cancelled; all pilots and full-time ground gunners are on alert. We believe the quadrant forces will attack within seventy-two hours. The part-time women auxiliary gunners are ordered to be on standby alert.

"The enemy will probably attack in three waves. Flight Lieutenant Cosgrave will direct his Bullethead fighter-bombers to meet the second wave; we are to hit the first wave. Keep clear of the Bullethead craft or you'll be hit by plasma bursts. I will lead squadrons 1 and 3 on the right. Lieutenant O'Connell will lead the squadrons 2 and 4 on the left. The reserve squadron 5 will wait near the city to face the third wave.

"Commander O'Rourke sends one more instruction. If we must engage the enemy over the city, take care not to hit our own ground facilities. He says, 'Good luck, good hunting.'"

✦ ✦ ✦

The Interplanetary Volunteers had been a major factor in Hibernia's war effort. The IPVs, as they were known, came from almost every planet: Transylvania, Polonia, Franco-Italia, Espanol, Hindustan, Nippon, etc. Many volunteers settled and became citizens. Of all the volunteers, the most aggressive were those from the planet Deutsch. The most famous volunteer was the aide to the Taoiseach, Colonel Dietrich Helmut Becker. He became a decorated fighter pilot, strategist, and tactician. His address to the people of his home planet rallied many young men and women to the cause. His bearing was martial, a revival of the spirit of the ancient Prussians of Earth.

After Colonel Becker had left the main government building, he was joined by Lieutenant Colonel Victor Kalminsky of Polonia. Kalminsky was staff aide to Commander O'Rourke of Athlone's defense system and the immediate supervisor of Flight Captain O'Rourke.

"Victor," said Colonel Becker, "as I was telling the Commandant, the Taoiseach is a man incapable of making a decision."

"Yes, but don't forget, he is from the diplomatic service. Euphemism is the very soul of that professional. He is a sensitive man," answered Kalminsky.

As they continued to walk westward, they approached what appeared to be a group of young people fighting.

✦ ✦ ✦

As Cathal pedaled away, his heart broken, the three girls ran after him. Clara and Karen literally pulled him off of his pedicab.

"Look, wire-mouth, if you say one word about this initiation to anyone, our boyfriends will take you to the brickyard and shove you up a kiln. Even if you are our leader's brother, your ass will be grass, and we will mow the lawn."

"What?" the now crying delivery boy asked. "You mean my sister is the leader of the Tigeress gang?"

"Yes, suckwad, the founder," Clara boasted. "She went to jail just because she was eighteen and was accused of contributing to the delinquency of minors. I was only seventeen; I got off with a beating by my old man. When Shelley gets out, she'll fix whoever squealed."

Cathal, mustering what little courage he had, answered, "On my mother's grave, I swear I'll never say anything! I don't want to ever see any one of you ever again!" He remounted his bike and quickly left.

Clara, turning to Deirdre, said, "Forget that one, he is a baby!"

Two minutes passed; Cathal vanished from sight. Then two girls in red sweaters approached.

Clara yelled, "You Imperials don't belong on this street."

"Try and stop us," the two answered.

Clara pulled a greaseball from the bucket she carried and threw it. The two girls retreated and a volley of greaseballs followed.

Then a greaseball fell and splattered a polished military jackboot.

"*Achtung*, halt," barked an angry Colonel Becker. In a doggerel of English and Gaelic the two officers berated the girls as though they were cadet pilots who had failed in laser gunnery practice. "This city could be under attack any moment, and you hoodlums throw mudballs. You should be considering becoming auxiliaries."

Clara answered with her arms folded defiantly. "Listen you Peevees, before the last war, you ginks trained two hundred women as pilots then cancelled their commissions. When the Brits attacked, you complained you lacked trained fighter pilots. Don't tell us about serving on the ground. You get medals, commissions, money, glory. We get nothing."

The two officers relented. Becker answered, "That was not our decision. We are carrying out the wishes of the Dail. If you object, demand that they call an election."

Karen answered, "There has not been a general election in twenty years. Only by-elections, when one of those ginks dies."

The officers left, muttering about the lack of discipline in the society.

✦ ✦ ✦

In space, hours away by hyperlight speed, lay the planet Brittania. The capital city, London, was set near the North Pole, around the Crystal Palace.

In a chamber in that edifice to Brittania royalism, one regal woman and two men were locked in discussion. It was the chamber of her Brittanic majesty, Elizabeth XVII. Before her throne stood two men barely less elegantly attired.

"Lord Churchill, we should build a fighter fleet of at least three thousand total craft before an all-out attack." The man who spoke was stocky with a scarred face, the result of hot metal hit from a conflict in the past.

"Your majesty," a handsome but vain gentleman answered, "Interior Minister Cromwell forgets we must test the enemy's defenses. A successful raid on the Hibernian cities could panic them, perhaps into surrender."

"You fail to understand that I am proposing the only means to end the Fenian obstacle to a Brittanic Imperial Solar System: extermination of Hibernia! Any premature attack will only alert their defense abilities. It could even create allies for them."

Then a bearded man, very plainly dressed, entered the chamber room. "Lord Cromwell, your attempt to build an empire will result in disaster. As leader of the opposition, I respectfully suggest we immediately announce our intent to leave the quadrant of Hibernia we unjustly control."

Cromwell answered, "The only disaster that will happen will be the noose around your neck when I prove you a traitor, W.E. Gladstone!"

Then the woman sitting on the throne rose and declared, "Mr. Gladstone, you were not summoned here and your presence displeases us. Lord Churchill, you may plan what immediate measures against the Hibernians you believe necessary. Lord Cromwell, you will prepare the follow-up actions to what will undoubtably be a first of the blows against the ancient enemy. You are all dismissed."

✦ ✦ ✦

Back on Hibernia, at Athlone's air defense center, Lieutenant Colonel Kalminsky was in his office. Flight Captain O'Rourke entered and saluted. "Colonel, I propose we send one of our patrols northward to the quadrant swamp and another east to Portlaoise. They should meet the patrols from Dublin and the Connaught Gaeltacht."

"What are the Captain's reasons? We have a total of 185 fighters to face at least 300 in an arc from Roscommon to Dublin."

"Athlone's electrical power could be knocked out before a direct attack on the city," he replied, pointing to a map. "West of the city are the Robert Emmet and Padraic Pearse Dams on the Enniskillen. To the east in Portloaise is a complex of generators. If either gets hit, panic would result."

"I can see an attack on Portlaoise," the Colonel answered, "but the dams? How?"

"Straight through the quadrant swamp, northeast to southwest."

"You are right, Captain. I will radio the Commander, your father, and the other Commanders. Also, the atomic reactors of Portlaoise should be shut down at the first sighting of the enemy."

The Captain then brought up another matter. "While all of our pilots are on base, some ground personnel have not reported. I will take a security detail into town to bring them in. I suspect some will be at those tasteless music halls."

"Yes, Captain, but wait until evening. Most of those men will be back. Also, don't judge those music halls too harshly—or the men who watch the shows there. I have been on this planet nearly thirty years. I remember your father, when he was a pilot like you, before he met your mother. All of us spent many an off-duty hour trying to catch a garter suggestively thrown from a chorus line runway."

"Must you remind me, sir?"

"Your father always says you take life too seriously. From the time you could walk, you marched. Your father was a Gaelic footballer as a youth, an architect in peacetime. When we finally end this war, you will have to start your life all over again."

"I am just trying to perform the duties assigned to me. I request to be dismissed, sir."

"Dismissed, Captain."

Athlone's music halls were a cultural import from the other planet-nations. Some were simply restaurants with waitresses who sang and danced. Others were burlesque houses, featuring the ancient art forms from Earth: belly dancers, strippers, tassel twirlers, girls who performed gymnastics in clear plastic outfits. The girls had scores of admirers. A widowed shirt-factory owner once named over a dozen of these performers in his will, leaving each 12,000 grams of gold. Many of the girls would eventually marry and settle down to raise a family. Often the daughter of an ex-chorine would follow in her mother's footsteps.

One of the most famous music halls was the Golden Peacock. Once a month they held a carefully chaperoned charity dance. The girls were auctioned off for an evening of dancing; proceeds went to the orphanages and other benefits. On that night the girls were fully dressed, but the rest of the time, the Golden Peacock had the most over-developed, underdressed girls in Athlone. The girls were constantly receiving flowers, candy, and gifts from pilots, factory hands, salesmen, and others.

In the dressing room the performers relaxed after rehearsal, talking about their favorite subject, men. The girls were all paying close attention to a statuesque blonde standing in the middle of the room. She was the star, Miss Brigid Hallohan, queen of Athlone. She pulled a green jade cigarette holder from her mouth and addressed the other girls.

"My mother worked at this very hall over twenty-five years ago. Of all of her male friends, the man who is my father was the only one who had never slept with her. One night he proposed and she turned him down. Then she propositioned him, she seduced him. For over a year this went on. He would propose, and she would seduce. Finally one night he proposed when they were already in bed. To this day my father is a very shy, gentle man."

Then a door leading to the backstage opened and a voice called, "Delivery boy, floral shop." An obviously timid boy entered carrying several bouquets. As his eyes fell upon Brigid, his mouth fell open in shock and his face turned red. The blonde walked toward him, followed by the others.

Cathal said meekly, "I must have receipts from each of you." Then in Gaelic he said, "Miss Hallohan, this one is for you."

Brigid smiled and answered "You know me" in purest Gaelic.

"I saw you lecturing twice at my school," he replied. "Once you addressed us on Gaelic authors. Then, in an auxiliaries jacket, you encouraged the class to be ready to serve the nation. I could have never guessed that a Gaelic instructor and auxiliary could be a. . . ."

"An exotic dancer of a music hall? I am a bilingual." She pointed to her gold medallion. "I have been an auxiliary as long as I have danced here. What is your name?"

"Cathal O'Rourke." He attempted to stand straight at attention.

"You're Shelley's little brother. I just got a letter from her. She is healthy and wishes her family would write!"

"You know Shelley?"

"Yes, she left me in charge of the Tigeress."

"The Tigeress? Deirdre, she is—"

"Going to be initiated tonight!"

"Eamon will not believe this at all!"

"Eamon? Yes, he is your older brother. Girls," Brigid pointed straight at Cathal and said in English, "this is old stone-face's brother!"

A massive collective groan went through the room.

"My brother is a good pilot and officer; he tries to keep his men in order."

Brigid shot back, "Of all the pilots in Athlone, he is the only one who has never honored us by his presence in the audience. Instead he has security police round his men up. He stands outside with his arms folded, scowling at us like we were just so much dirt. What is wrong with him? Doesn't he like girls? Is he afraid of girls?"

Brigid walked up close to Cathal, who by now was pale with fear.

"You must sign these receipts. I am sorry to intrude." He handed the bouquets to the girls as they came up.

Brigid blew a massive cloud of smoke in the face of the paralyzed boy. "You are really a cute boy; I hope you don't grow up to be as narrow-minded as your brother."

Cathal picked up the receipts and bowed, almost falling over. He stumbled out the door.

A slim girl in a black kimono spoke. "He is just like a boy I met back in school once. I had him on a blind date. He almost fainted when I took out a cigarette. I handed him a matchbook and promised to neck with him if he gave me a light, then threatened to brand him if he refused."

"What happened?" asked a redhead with tassels hanging from her pasties.

"By the time we got home his face was smeared all over with my lipstick and his hair was covered with ashes."

The girl's green eyes contrasted with her black hair and olive skin. This betrayed a Hibernian father and Nipponese mother. "He is such a cute, frightened little boy. Wouldn't you just want to wrap your legs around him and never let go?"

Brigid replied, "Yes, Pam, but I want that brother of his first."

"You mean to set him up?"

"Maybe. But I suspect if a girl gets hold of him and screws the hell out of him once, he will become a human being."

Cathal, gasping for breath, reached his cab, pulled a paper bag out, and stuck his head in it until he resumed normal breathing.

In the pilots' day room at the Athlone base, the pilots attempted to break the tension of waiting for the alarm. Most of their attention was centered on one corner of the room. The uniforms they wore were a drab green, with rank insignia on one shoulder and the tricolor stripes of the Hibernian Republic on the other. A thin white stripe down the pant legs indicated a Needlehead fighter pilot, while a blue stripe was for the Bullethead crews. Two of the blue-stripe men had everyone else watching. One, a burley red-head, played an accordion, his grin curling his mustache. This was Ensign Liam O'Brien, the best musician on the base. His musical talent was exceeded in fame only by his manners at the dinner table, which could shock a six-year-old. The short, wiry man with raven black hair was his pilot, Conor Evans Cosgrave. His voice carried the "Beer Barrel Polka" to the accordion. Stone mugs were raised even though they were only filled with hot spiced tea.

A couple of women auxiliary ground gunners had reported to the base, and were dancing with the pilots. One dance team was actually husband and wife, IPVs from Portuguese planet Oporto. Colonel Becker, who had just delivered an attaché to Kalminsky, started stomping his foot to the music.

"If there was a beer barrel, it would be like a Hofbrau back on my home planet," he quipped.

"What we need to make it like a Dublin pub is a barrel of stout and a dart board, complete with a picture of her Brittanic degeneracy herself, Elizabeth the Seventeenth," was O'Brien's reply. This triggered Cosgrave to sing out:

> Lizzy's sanitary napkins are her hankies every day,
> Lord Churchill never changes shorts,
> Lord Cromwell never bathes.

Then everyone in the room opened up:

I want no more of army life,
Gee Mom, I want to go home.

O'Brien opened a new verse:

Colonel Becker and his Teutons,
a brave and virile race,
they'd walk right up to Lizzy,
and rasspp (tongue out) right into her face.

They all joined in:

I want no more of army life,
Gee Mom, I want to go home.

Then Cosgrave stepped forward. "As member of the American Culture Society, I had a virtual library of audio-visual tapes of old plays the Yankees made in the twentieth century. Here is my rendition of a song from *West Side Story* with Hibs and Brits instead of Jets and Sharks. Of course, the Hibs are us.

The Hibs are going to have their day, tonight,
The Hibs are going to have their way, tonight,
The Brits say that they tell us, fair fight,
But if they try to rumble, we'll rumble them right, tonight."

Everyone in the room applauded. Then a handsome flight lieutenant entered accompanied by an auxiliary nurse. "Lieutenant Sean O'Connell, this half-Welsh vocalist yields the floor to you." Cosgrave winked as he referred to his mother's family, who had fled Brittania. He pointed to the pilot, whose grey eyes and thick curly brown hair had made him the most popular serviceman in Athlone.

The lieutenant, in turn, pointed to the woman beside him. "Ladies and gentlemen, we have a celebrity here. This is Constance Fitzgibbon, captain of Athlone's camogie team. Her team has broken a five-year string of losses to Dublin by defeating the Dubs three goals eleven points to two goals nine points."

Again the entire room applauded. Then Cosgrave asked, "Where is her team?"

Constance answered, "At the Golden Peacock."

"You mean those young camogie players, those sweet girls, are watching the sexiest show in town?"

"I'd be there myself if it weren't for the alert. Isn't Brigid Hallohan a knockout? And she is an auxiliary gunner on top of it."

"Boy, if she got wounded, wouldn't the medic be lucky examining that frame?"

Lieutenant O'Connell asked, "Where is our captain?"

Cosgrave replied, "O'Rourke is taking a security patrol into town to bring in a few overdue ground crew, cooks, and orderlies."

"That is overkill," O'Brien exclaimed. "Lieutenant O'Connell, you knew the Captain in your boyhood days; why is he so maniacally against girls, shows, or any other way to have a good time?"

O'Connell, sitting down in a chair at the end of a long table, began his story.

"Eamon wasn't so serious back when we were boys. He even played Hurling almost as good as me. Then as we began pre-military courses, he overly imitated his father. His sense of humor began to fade. Two things happened that changed his personality entirely. First his sister, Shelley, was arrested as the leader of the Tigeress gang. I was shocked, I had dated her for a year and was on the edge of proposing. I got over it though, and now I want her back, out of jail. I have dated many girls in five years, but Shelley is the one I want."

Cosgrave interrupted, "What about Eamon?"

O'Connell continued, "Eamon's father, the Commander himself, ordered his son to visit his sister in gaol. It is over in the forest area in Munster. His anger at Shelley subsided, but he redirected it at girls in general. Then the next war broke out. His mother was an auxiliary gunner. Her battery was destroyed by a Brit fighter bomber. She was buried with three other auxiliary gunners. A nurse, a shirt factory girl, and a showgirl from the Golden Peacock. They were laid in their coffins wearing the civilian dress that was under their flak suits. The showgirl was almost nude. This was offensive to him, that a stripper could be buried right alongside his mother. His father reminded Eamon that he, Seamus O'Rourke, when a young pilot, had visited the Golden Peacock. He ordered all of us to walk up to each of the open coffins and salute each one separately before they were closed. Well, Eamon turned pale while saluting that showgirl. From that day on he has nurtured an aversion to showgirls—all girls, for that matter."

The men and women in the room began to depart toward their barracks.

❖ ❖ ❖

Thousands of kilometers southwest of Athlone, in a timezone six hours behind the city, was the Limerick sector in Munster quadrant. Unlike the capital city, which rests on a plateau, Limerick sector had a sub-tropical climate. An area of lush, green hills, small lakes, and streams, it had attracted many tourists from other areas during peace. Its warm weather made it possible to raise vegetables and citrus fruits all year long. In addition to those crops brought originally from Earth during the Migrations, the Canapec plant was also cultivated. The plant had important medical uses. The leaves, when used in a vapor inhaler or smoker, relieved asthma. The juice of the Canapec root was found to be such a strong sedative, three drops in a glass of water could sedate a patient facing surgery. Later a less acceptable use was found. Tobacco soaked in the juice became a strong intoxicant. As the result, the cultivation of Canapec was under government licensing.

The region was an island of prosperity. Farm families and small towns dotted the countryside. The only blight to this paradise was a large island in the James Connolly lake. There was the Hibernian National Gaol for Women, constructed 3103.

The island had an autogiro landing strip at one end. The prison was at the other end. It was fortress-like, four walls of granite and ferro-concrete. Machine gun towers stood at each corner. The wall, spreading wider as it reached each house, had all the necessary apparatus. The center mall of the square edifice had only an enclosed wallway from the north to south sides of the outer infrastructure. In 3141, on the east side of the wallway, a brick building was constructed. It housed a dining hall for the guards and staff. There was no kitchen as those facilities were in the bowels of the surrounding complex. Here over 80 percent of the staff could feed at once while the remainder received their meals by trays brought by honor prisoners.

In 3151, on the opposite side of the wallway, a two-story building was erected. A day room was on the ground floor, the night facilities above. Part of the inner courtyard was enclosed by a barbed wire fence. All this construction served to incarcerate six young women now called the "Athlone Six."

The girls' gang scandal was the type of social problem that was bound to afflict the nation eventually. Any nation that for sixty-eight years had drifted through alternating tides of war and peace could not help but suffer breakdown. That it happened in Athlone only sharpened its painful effect.

All over Hibernia the young men of the country knew their destiny as early as age twelve. At that age pre-military training began, directing them into air defense service by age eighteen. The best physical specimens became pilots, the less able ground gunners and support crew. In the civilian fields, all trade was open. The Gaelic sports, football and hurling, produced opportunities for fame, though not fortune.

In contrast, girls in Hibernia had far fewer options. Their schooling was not directed at all in most places. In Dublin and the Gaeltacht, careers in education were stressed. The academic centers in Dublin also allowed women into scholarship and classical arts and sciences. The Gaeltacht offered training in bilingual programs. Camogie, the girls' counterpart to hurling, was available to the athletic-minded with scores of teams.

But in Athlone there were almost no activities available for girls and young women from the age twelve to the early twenties. One Camogie team, whose losing streak to Dublin had been a local joke, was the only athletic outlet. The schools had no programs for targeting women into professions. Almost all the girls of Athlone eventually became wives, mothers, and homemakers. The most beautiful girls had a chance for gold and glory in music halls, but the rest worked in the many shirt factories around the city.

As with so many other aspects of life in Hibernia and other planet-nations, the girl gangs were based on the Earth nation America. The forms came from the middle of the twentieth century. The gang wore distinct uniforms, sweaters of specific colors. Streets and neighborhoods marked off as a "turf" were defended with fists or balls of coal dust, machine oil, and shirt factory lint. Pranks such as putting "For Sale" signs on public buildings, drunkenness, use of Canapec juice in tobacco, all shocked the officialdom.

The one feature of the girls gangs that most unnerved society was the apparent display of "unnatural" behaviors—girls kissing each other, dancing, walking with legs rubbing together. Finally one spring night the police raided gang headquarters in the middle of initiation rites. They found naked girls, intoxicated, drunk on poteen liquor, stout, and "loaded" cigars. The raids took place in the spring of 3148, the trial in early fall.

After a preliminary hearing, all the girls under eighteen years were released to parents with charges dropped. The tacit understanding was that the parents would apply a "board of education" to the "seat of the matter," in the words of the judge.

Among those released was a girl one month under eighteen who, when her record cleared, eventually became the "Queen of Athlone." Her name was Brigid Hallohan. Brigid, unknown to officials, had been named the leader of the Tigeress gang until the founder was released.

Six girls were left to be tried as adults. The charges were "contributing to the delinquency of minors" and "taking indecent liberties with minors." The six were a varied lot. Kate MacBride of the Imperials was raven-haired, buxom, quiet, and the head of the second largest gang. The leaders of two small gangs, each with two co-founders, included, from The Green Devils, Caroline Quinn and Mairead McNutt, with their red hair greased with rosewater and glycerin. Caroline had a dimple on her chin, Mairead freckles. The Girl Knights were led by Jamie Feeny, a blond with no front teeth, and Mary Plunkett Concannon, tall, flat-chested, her brown hair bound in blue ribbons. The most impressive of all was the leader of Tigeress, the largest gang of all. She was a strawberry blonde whose blue eyes fired with defiance of her captors. The daughter of the famous commander of Athlone's Air Defense System, her name was Shelley O'Rourke. Her family, including her father Seamus, the commander himself, was the only family to attend the trial that followed. It was a trial where, as one newsman commented, "The verdict and sentence were in before the opening gavel." Bail had been refused.

The farce began on the opening day of the trial. Unlike the defendants in any other trial, the six girls were brought into the courtroom chained hand and foot. Special uniforms, totally black, were worn. In addition, an armband with an old Earth symbol was worn. The computer memory banks covering Earth history had failed to include the particularly genocidal meaning of the emblem, the swastika. Then an uproar from outraged IPVs took place. The armbands were removed, but the poisoned atmosphere remained.

At first a great deal of hearsay was introduced linking the girls with scores of unsolved robberies, beatings, and acts of arson. Even espionage was suggested. The accusations were stricken from the record, but not before mobs outside the judicial building demanded death.

As the trial dragged on Shelley O'Rourke, the "Blond Firebrand" as she was labeled, became the central figure in the case. Although bound and gagged several times, she defended not only herself but all other girls. She pointed out the social conditions that had prompted her to start the Tigeress outfit. She even defended the very rituals of initiation that were the basis of the state's case. In her own words, "The ritual of lovemaking between the members of the Tigeress and other gangs is the symbol of our unity, our devotion to the idea that the young women of our nation should be given a far greater opportunity to participate in and serve in the development and defense of our motherland, Hibernia."

As the trial progressed, the news reverberated through the county. In Athlone the mobs called for instating a death penalty for the young women. Elsewhere the girls were becoming martyrs for the cause of social justice. Debates at the universities between factions on both sides of the question led to fights. An important journal of opinion, the *Dublin National Journal Gazetteer*, commented, "The entire nation is at the edge of a nervous breakdown."

The socialist Sinn Fein party, forced into a coalition government for over twenty-one years, saw an opportunity for a *coup d'etat*. Civil war threatened for the first time since 3127. Then suddenly the crises ended with the trial itself.

After the guilty verdict was pronounced by the jury, the three-judge bench released five of the girls to their parents until the date of sentencing. Shelley O'Rourke was found in contempt of Court and returned to her cell. When the court reconvened two months later, it sentenced the young girls to an interminate sentence of years. Shelley O'Rourke, manacles on hands and feet answered, "You have destroyed the moral bond between the state and society. Your action will ultimately result in the destruction of the nation."

Her family, the only one that attended the proceedings at all, wept openly.

At first the girls were placed in the general prison population; however, they immediately began to organize prisoners for better conditions. As a result of this, they were segregated in a special annex.

The building housing the girls was a two-story brick structure. There were six cots in the sleeping room, two pushed together into three of the four corners. The stairwell was at the fourth. As the mattresses had been pushed together, the occupants had an opportunity for physical contact. This was tolerated by the staff as inevitable.

In one corner lay a double cot where two of the girls lay nude under a thin sheet. They were rubbing their thighs, kissing, and tightly hugging each other. As they kissed, they talked of the men they loved and missed. One was the strawberry blonde, the other was the raven-haired girl.

"Kate, I miss him so much it hurts all over. He's a Needlehead fighter pilot, Sean O'Connell. If I was out of here I'd go right to him. If he wants to ball me, I'd have his baby, I would!"

"Shelley, my man works in a state synthetic gas plant. He takes me in the ass. He'll drop his trousers, put petrocream on his log, bend me over, and goose me real slow so I'll enjoy it. I wish he was on top of me now."

In the other two corners similar occurrences were taking place, Quinn and McNutt in one bed, Feeny and Concannon in the other. Concannon's leg hung out over the edge of the bed.

None of the girls noticed that a short, fat, ugly woman in a guard's uniform walked into the room. She held a riding crop and hit Concannon's foot on the arch with it. "Up and out, you dykes."

As the girls tumbled out of their cots, the guard continued her harangues. "Get your asses movin' or I'll use this cropstick like a doctor's proctoscope." The girls were herded downstairs and then legirons were placed on one foot each. They were marched out the wallway, turning southward to the doorway. Through the door they turned east to a small alcove-like room. There, on a serving cart, was their breakfast. Glue-like porridge, stewed prunes, and greasy sausage all in one large covered bowl. Six small bowls with spoons served this mess, washed down with cups of weak tea from a teapot. The girls were mostly separated from contact from any other prisoners or people. Separate work details, visiting privileges only once a month instead of once a week, and the deliberate poor quality of food was used, implying that they were less than human. Only on the Saturday afternoons in the alcove were they granted smoking privileges. Since they could only visit the prison commissary once a month, this made it necessary to share what little tobacco they could obtain. In contrast, the other prisoners could visit the commissary daily and smoke anywhere, anytime, outside their cells. The few male guards extorted sex from the prison population and occasionally harassed the six girls in the annex. The only pleasant factor of the annex was that, even with six girls, they had far more room.

After the girls returned to the dayroom and the guard had departed, M.P. Concannon muttered, "I could kill Sowface."

Shelley O'Rourke answered, "M.P., that is just what they want us to attempt, then they will put us at the bottom of the lake." After ten minutes by the clock hanging on the ceiling in the dayroom, Sowface returned.

"I have news that will make you scumbags thank us for our hospitality. The peace talks have broken down and Athlone is on alert. As for me, if the Brits take over, they'll probably leave me in charge of you whippers." Then she departed, slamming the door.

Shelley yelled: "That traitor! You're right, M.P., I could kill her. That does it. I have got to get out of this goat's nest."

Kate MacBride answered, "Shelley, there is no way we can get off this island, and even if we could, every yokel in the sector will be ready to kill us on sight."

"How do you know that?"

"When we first got here, they split us up. They put me in a cell with a twenty-goldgram-a-night hooker. She told me that even before we got here, our pictures and descriptions were all over the sector. One month ago, while I was in the sick ward, I met her again, and she said that her contacts on the outside told her those signs are still up. I have no desire to face a farmer armed with a shotgun full of ball bearings or his wife armed with an iron skillet."

Shelley sank into a chair. Over five years of incarceration had failed to break her spirit. Now in a few minutes her spirits were crushed. Then Sowface returned with a rolled-up paper that she pinned to the board on the north wall of the dayroom. The guard quipped, "Here is a way to get out of here; all you need is a desire for suicide."

Shelley walked up to the board and read:

CHILDREN OF HIBERNIA

AGAIN THE HAND OF BRITTANIC IMPERIALISM THREATENS THE MOTHER-LAND. AGAIN HIBERNIA CALLS ITS YOUTH AND ITS ELDERLY, MEN AND WOMEN, ALL OF ITS CHILDREN. ANY OF THOSE INCARCERATED IN THE PENAL INSTITUTIONS WHO WILL VOLUNTEER TO SERVE AS FULL-TIME AUX-ILIARY SERVICEMEN WILL RECEIVE CONSIDERATIONS FROM REDUCTION OF SENTENCES TO COMPLETE AMNESTY.

COLM O'HARA, TAOISEACH

Shelley screamed, "This is my way out! Guard, I want a pencil." She signed with gusto, then turned to her fellow inmates.

"Well, what are you waiting for?" When no other girl moved, she opened up. "I know that I am not a model citizen, but I am Hibernian and I am proud of it. My father is the commander of Athlone's defenses. He told me that the Brit leader, Lord Cromwell, intends to exterminate our entire people. My mother died manning a surface laser gun. I don't know about your gangs, but the first vow of a Tigeress is loyalty to Hibernia to death. If I must die, I intend to die like my mother. I will not wait for a Brit squad to walk in here, take me out to one of the prison walls, and shoot me. I am going to do this even if by myself."

One minute passed, then Kate MacBridge signed. Another two minutes, M.P. Concannon and Jamie Feeny wrote their names. Another five, then Caroline Quinn and Mairead McNutt signed the letter.

"Guard!" Shelley yelled as she tore the paper off the wall. "When Sowface came in, she took the paper saying, "It's your funeral, dykes!"

The guard took the paper and walked out the door leading to the walk-way. She walked north to the end, then unlocked and opened a metal fire door. This immediately led to an elevator that went two floors down. Then, getting out on the same side she got in, she walked straight west in an aisle to a room of cubby-hole office spaces. She handed the paper to a secretary.

"Photo transmit this to Athlone, priority one," was her command. The paper was slipped into the chute of a transmission scanner, its light beam rod moving across the sheet picking the figures off. The scanner's comput-er's predetermined coordinates were matched with those of the recipient terminal in Athlone. At the capital, a scanner rod across the blank paper printed the characters received in transmission.

The induction non-commissioned officer in the terminal room of Athlone Defense Center picked the printed letter off the scanner. After reading it, he simply typed the names into the keyboard of a computer terminal. The computer's memory bank printed out all available data on the six names mentioned. The sheets of the readout were placed on a file marked "inductee." An orderly was summoned to pick up the sheets and take them to the panel that ultimately decided induction of "unusual cases."

The answer came in the form of an audio-transmission telegram to the prison. The very guard who sent the original paper received the message and took it directly to the annex.

"You misfits are now in the auxiliary service, out of my hair for good. You will all leave in thirty minutes; God help the instructors who will be in charge of you," the guard muttered.

After the girls' initial joy, the guard answered, "You'll be back, all of you."

Shelley shot back, "Don't make book on it."

The guards reacted by swiping her cropstick across the buttocks of the impudent prisoner, and then she stormed out.

The girls packed the few belongings they had into small handbags. Shelley whispered to Kate, "I got to have some way to get even with that creep, and I have it." She led Kate upstairs to the nightroom and into a clos-et on the south side. Shelley closed the door, while the second turned on a light. Shelley jimmied open a ventilation grating on the floor and pulled out a small wrapped bundle. She opened it and inside was a large cigar, one match, and an eyedropper bottle. It was labeled "Canapec juice, 120 milli-liters." Shelley noted, "I put twenty drops of juice on this cigar, enough to make us all float away. I was saving it for something to celebrate. If they put us in a sealed railcar there'll be no guard, and we can have it then."

Kate, in shock, asked, "How do you get that?"

Shelley answered, "First I saved some of the coppergrams that my father gave me for the commissary, then I gave the bundle to that old guard, you know, that fool that dropped dead last month. He got me the juice, and I let him eat me out. If I had let him ball me, I'd have twice as much."

"What now?"

"Slip the cigar and match into your blouse; I'll take this bottle." Shelley put back the grating, opened the door, switched the lights off, then slammed the closet shut. "Follow me, Kate. Cover me," she asked.

The two girls hurried down to the dayroom, the other girls nodding willingness to cover for the two. Dropping to waist-height, Shelley opened the door then walked across to the door of the staff dining room, Kate following. Slowly a crack was opened, then she peeked in. "Keep down, keep the door open, cover me." As Kate watched in puzzlement, Shelley walked into the empty room to a cafeteria line. She got up to the eighty liter urn that served hot water for tea, then pulled the top off the urn. She took out the bottle of juice from her pocket, opened it, then poured the contents in. Then she put the top of the urn back on and put the bottle in her pocket. She used a red wiperag to wipe any fingerprints away. Stooping low, they slipped out of the dining room, wiping the doorlatch. Shelley took the bottle out, wrapped it in the wiperag, then shoved it into a full trash.

As they returned to the room Kate noted, "Today they will dump that bin, but why did you do that?"

Shelley replied, "It will knock the whole staff out cold, and maybe the others can get off this rock. They are not marked for death like us; at least they can take over this goat nest."

Five minutes later Sowface and three male guards came in. The girls were handcuffed and leglocked. Their handbags were clipped to their backs like soldiers' knapsacks.

"Actually, we have built a gallows for all of you," Sowface quipped.

The girls marched north through the door to the elevator. Down two floors, then east to another elevator, and down three levels the girls were headed. From the second elevator they walked for what seemed half a kilometer to a third elevator. After five floors they emerged outside the massive structure. An autogiro faced them, and they were herded in like baggage. In ten minutes, after a flight in darkness, they emerged outside a small village.

The sight of the six girls in black uniforms panicked the local population. A young mother, clutching her child, begged, "Please don't hurt us."

Jamie Feeny answered, "Lady, we are handcuffed and leglocked, what can we do?" The footpath from town led to a downramp to the tunnel from where the subterranean railway would emerge. On the loading ramp, a farm family stood waiting. Shelley, eyeing the sunburned farmer, said, "Hi, handsome. Want to take me out tonight? I could please you, your wife, and your darling children." The farmer turned pale and his wife red. The guard ran his knee into Shelley right at the hips. When the rail-tram arrived, the girls were herded into a car with no seats. The leglock chains were hooked at both ends of the cab. Then the girls' handcuffs were released.

"Guard, is that the correct time?" Shelley pointed to the device in the car.

"No, it's 3:40, Limerick, 9:40 in Athlone. Goodbye and good riddance." He turned on the cabin lights and pushed the door close latch. In just seconds, the train began moving. First it rolled slowly under electric coasting motors. Then, as it descended into the gravity vacuum lock, it moved faster even faster until it was roaring along at 1200 kilometers per hour. The train's speed was set at one-quarter of maximum as a power saving measure during the alerts.

Kate MacBride opened her blouse and took out the cigar and match. She bent over to light the match by hitting it on the legiron. Puffing a dozen times, she lit the stogie, then handed it to Shelley. The strawberry blonde remarked, "This is like being hit with a load of bricks. I'm floating." The cigar was passed backward to Caroline, Mairead, Jamie, and Mary Plunkett. After an hour the butt was crushed out, put in the first aid box on the wall, and then the girls fell fast asleep. The train would reach Athlone at dawn.

✦ ✦ ✦

The Golden Peacock was holding its last performance until the alert was over. Every star, every major act was available. There was Pamela Fuchida O'Reilly, the gymnast in the transparent plastic leotard, and Maureen Kelley, the girl with the jetprop tassels, the Interplanetary chorus line and the Queen of Athlone, Brigid Hallohan.

Brigid stepped out on the stage in a black merry widow gown, long white gloves, high heels, and a white beaded necklace. She started off by singing in both English and Gaelic, a torchy love song, while twirling the necklace. Then, as the drum roll began, she went into the main part of her act. First she pulled one long glove slowly off, then the other. In several steps the gown and then her bra and panties followed. As the crowd was whistling, cheering, and applauding, she fired her garter like a slingshot. It was caught, not by one of the leering service men or workers, but by one of the women on Athlone's camogie team. They were sitting in their team jackets in the front row. The girl who caught it dropped her camogie stick. Then Brigid gently removed her fishnet stockings, her pasties, and g-string. The only items remaining were the necklace and her bilingual medallion. After she left the stage, the curtain dropped and stage hands began to move in the apparatus for the gymnast's act. In two minutes boos and catcalls could be heard from the audiences. Through the side door Brigid could see the brown-shirted security patrols round up AWOL servicemen.

"Stoneface has struck again," Brigid said while putting a long black leather overcoat on her tasty body. "I am going to give Captain Eamon O'Rourke a piece of my mind."

The stern-faced captain, whose brown hair was thinning early for his age, left the cab of the security patrol wagon. "You send your men inside and I will go around to the backstage exit to cut off escapees," he ordered, adding, "If a raid had already taken place, they would be court-martialed."

As he approached the stepway to the exit, he came upon a bland-faced man who resembled his brother, Cathal. The man was pushing a baby buggy and leading a small boy by the arm.

"What are you doing out at this time of night, and here, of all places?" the Captain asked.

"I am going to meet my wife. She finishes her last performance about now."

"Your wife works in there! How long have you been married, and with those children?"

"Two months, and the children are hers, not mine. They were hers before we met."

"Oh, I am sorry to hear about a widow."

"No, she wasn't widowed."

"Divorced or deserted?"

"No, not either at all."

"What do you mean?"

"They are illegitimate."

"You mean to say you married a woman with two children before wedlock? I can see how it could happen to a woman in this place. And what do you do for a living while she performs?"

"Nothing, except take care of the house and the children."

"What kind of man are you! Living off the earnings of a woman and an obviously immoral one at that. You are disgusting!"

Then the young man lunged at the Captain, yelling, "Don't you dare talk about my wife that way. She is the best thing to happen to me in thirteen years. I don't care if you are one of those fighter pilots, you can't insult my wife that way."

"If you were in my squadron, I'd have you in the stockade as a disgrace to the service."

Then out of the stage door emerged two women in black leather coats. One was a redhead, the top of whose coat was open, revealing the tassels on her outfit. The second, a blonde, had her coat buttoned completely tight. The redhead yelled, "Don't you talk about my man that way, I finally got lucky. I hooked a man who didn't get himself killed like your pilots."

"What are you talking about?"

"First a couple of introductions, Captain, and then the facts of the matter you should know before condemning people. I am Brigid Hallohan," the blonde bowed, "and I want a word with you after you hear what they will say."

The Captain, arms folded, said, "What is there to talk about?"

The redhead shot back, while lifting a baby girl from the carriage, "My boy is Barry Lynch, age three. My girl is Esther Sennech, age one. My man is Theobald Wolfe Tone McLaughlin, and I'm Maureen Kelley."

"Barry Lynch? Esther Sennech? You mean Captain Garrett Lynch and Lieutenant Issac Sennech were their fathers?"

"Yes. I used to work at a music hall where girls were expected to mingle with the customers. You know, hustling drinks, arranging off-stage performances in bed. In both cases, I found I was carrying a child two days after I learned they had crashed; and as you see, they do have their father's features."

"My God, Garret Lynch was my old squadron leader, my immediate superior when I was a lieutenant. Issac Sennech was an IPV from Planet Abraham. He had the Star of David on his fighter. I was the one who wrote the death notice to his parents."

"Your pilots couldn't fly their planes right, but they sure knew how to use their man-guns. They scored two direct hits on me."

"But surely your husband can't stay home and. . . ."

"Why not? Housework is all he did since he was ten. He had to quit school to take care of his crippled parents. His father was injured at work, and his mother had a nervous disease. With no schooling he can't get a job. He stays home, cleans, cooks, tends our little garden, and takes care of my precious little bastards. We met in the cemetery where my pilots and his parents are all buried. When we get enough money to get him some schooling, Theobald will find work. I'll retire from the stage, keep the home, and my next baby will resemble him."

"I am sorry for misjudging the two of you. I do, however, request a small photo of each of the two children to send to their paternal grandparents. It is the least we can do for those who have lost their sons."

Theobald answered, "We will be honored to do that. Could you tell a pilot at your base, Conor Cosgrave, that Ted McLaughlin of the old neighborhood says hello?"

"Yes, I will," the now shakened Captain answered.

The Captain had started to leave the alley when Brigid came up to him and asked to speak.

"Captain, why is it that you treat Maureen or me or the other showgirls in this area like we are so much dirt?"

"I am just enforcing military discipline."

"I understand that part of it. I have my gunner's jacket inside the dressing room."

"You? An Auxiliary?'

"Auxiliary Ensign Hallohan, ready on standby alert, sir."

"What is Hibernia coming to?"

"Don't give me that snobbish, prudish drivel. At least twenty girls in this area operated surface batteries. Remember, a girl from this very music hall was buried with honor alongside your mother."

"Must you remind me?"

"As I asked your little brother, Cathal—"

"Cathal? Here? At this place? Doing what?"

"Delivering flowers. As I asked him, what is wrong with you? Don't you like girls, or are you afraid?"

"I . . . it's . . . just . . . that you . . . don't understand!"

"You are trembling underneath your uniform. You are just a frightened boy like your brother, " said Brigid as she walked forward. The Captain stepped backward, step by step until his back was against the wall of the blind alley at the end of the building.

Brigid unbuttoned her coat, then threw it open to reveal the frame that had inspired cheers a few minutes earlier. She asked, "Ever see a woman's body before? Take a real good look, because some night we will be alone and I will have my way with you."

The Captain's voice broke as tears formed in his eyes, "You don't understand. I am an idealist . . . I don't believe in the double standard other men have. If a man wants to meet a proper lady, he should remain clean himself."

"That sound so noble, but it is so naïve."

"You are trying to hurt me." His voice was now that of a child.

Brigid looked into eyes that revealed both his fear of intimacy as well as his need for it. Her voice softened, "I am not going to hurt you. I wanted to ravish you, but now I want to make love to you." Then she reached out and touched his cheek with her hand.

"I am only trying to be a good soldier," the Captain answered.

"Your father was a good soldier, but as a young pilot he came to the Golden Peacock. My mother remembered because she worked here. Eamon, right now you look just like my father. I am going to bed you some night. I'll be real gentle to you."

"You aren't going to hurt me?"

"No, I would take you home tonight if it weren't for the alert. Goodbye, Eamon." She buttoned her coat.

Eamon smiled shyly, bowed, and walked out of the alley.

Brigid walked back to the stairwell where the McLaughlins were. Maureen said, "That was rather forward, even for you."

"All I did was tell him I planned to perform surgery on him—removal of his virginity," was Brigid's reply.

"That is something Theobald can understand." Maureen pinched her man right on the rump.

"You know, Maureen, I had planned to humiliate him, but now I could love the socks off him, he is so innocent."

"Brigid, on our wedding night Theo blushed purple. He had never seen me perform or touched me during courtship."

"Well, Maureen, I must go now." She returned inside the building. The McLaughlins departed out the alley.

✤ ✤ ✤

At the eastern edge of the city was a street where closed, abandoned factories and warehouses stood. They were the remains of firms closed during the last war. One had been a printshop, and one entire sidewall was missing, the workrooms and office exposed. A brick fence two meters high shielded the open side from the street. Sitting atop the fence the Quinncannon sisters, Clara, and Karen, and Deirdre O'Toole acted as lookouts. Here, Tigeress gang initiated new members.

Karen had just lit one of what would be by midnight a chain of cigarettes, then handed it to Clara. After a deep drag Clara passed it to Deirdre, who then said, "If my mother saw me with this, she'd slap my face off."

Karen answered, "The thrill, the trick, is never getting caught." Clara noted, "Remember our first smoke? We were thirteen and our father had set up a dinner party to get a promotion from his boss. Well, the boss had an obnoxious brother-in-law who came drunk and made suggestions to everybody's wives. Then, in front of Dad, he lit a cigarette and gave it to me and Karen to smoke. We waited for Dad to take it from us as Rob-Roy, as the twerp was called, hinted that we were over-developed for our age. Finally he came over and whispered, "Go out to the garden, then finish it. I'll forget all about it, but if I see either of you smoking again, I'll smoke your rumps good."

"Well, when we returned to the house, both a little queasy, Rob-Roy pinched me on the butt. Dad decked him with one punch in front of the boss, then stood waiting to be fired, but his boss fired Rob-Roy and promoted Dad in his place."

Just then Brigid Hallohan walked up to the fence through a doorless gateway and to the open building. With her were the two Imperial girls from the morning. "Quinncannons, I've a short word with the two of you," was Brigid's command. The three on the fence jumped down and walked up to her. "You must make an apology to these two that you threw greaseballs at to keep the truce between our two gangs intact. In return, they will stand as lookouts during the proceedings." Brigid took Clara's hand and extended to one of the red-sweater girls.

Karen answered, "We are sorry. We didn't hit either girl, but one greaseball splattered a Peevee's jackboot. He had walked up to us and talked real mad at us, him and another Peevee."

"Cut the prejudice. Two of my best friends at work are IP girls," was Brigid's reply, adding, "Without the IPVs the Brits would have crushed us long ago."

Clara shot back, "It was those goosesteppers Becker and Kalminsky."

Then Brigid said, "Oh, if I had been there, they would have recognized me and summoned a security patrol."

Then the four girls, Brigid, Clara, Karen, and Deirdre, walked into the large open workroom. At one end was an electro-victrola with a stack of indestructible but tin-sounding brass records. At the other end stood a large galvanized steel tub full of ice. Resting in the ice was a ring of stone mugs surrounding a twenty-liter stainless steel beer bucket. It had a right-fitting lid and wire handle and was filled with Enniskillen Ale from the Athlone Cooperative Brewery.

Brigid gave the command, "First form two rows facing each other, members in one row, novices the other. We will count off to six, then two pairs of six will form a circle of twelve." After a few moments two circles formed, a total of twenty-four girls, twelve members and twelve novices. There were four extra members. Brigid extended her right palm down to the center of her circle. Clara, Karen, and three other members followed, then Deirdre and five other novices. The right hands overlapped, one on top of the other. The same sequence took place in the other circle.

Brigid spoke, "All repeat, in Gaelic if you speak it. I solemnly pledge my life to Hibernia till death. I vow to work for the sisterhood of the Tigeress. I vow to keep our secrets and to work toward the day when women can take their place alongside their men to defend the motherland. I vow personal revenge against the Brittanic tyrant, Elizabeth the Seventeenth, to help me God."

Then one of the extra went to the victrola and placed the top record in. As its scratchy tones blared out, each girl's voice was lifted in unison to the ancient Hibernian anthem, "The Soldier's Song."

We'll sing a song, a soldier's song
With cheering, rousing chorus
As round our blazing fires we throng,
The starry heavens o'er us;
Impatient for the coming fight,
And as we await the morning's light
Here in the silence of the night
We'll chant a soldier's song.
Soldiers are we, whose lives are pledged to Ireland
Some have come from a land beyond the waves.
Sworn to be free, no more our ancient sireland
Shall shelter the despot or the slave;
Tonight we man the bearna baoghal
In Erin's cause, come woe or weal;
'Mid cannon's roar and rifle's peal
We'll chant a soldier's song.

In valley green or towering crag
Our fathers fought before us,
And conquered 'neath the same old flag
That's proudly floating o'er us,
We're children of a fighting race
That never yet has known disgrace,
And as we march the foe to face,
We'll chant a soldier's song.

Sons of the Gael! Men of the Pale!

The long watched day is breaking;
The serried ranks of Innisfail
Shall set the tyrant quaking.
Our camp fires now are burning low;
See in the east a silv'ry glow,
Out yonder waits the Saxon foe,
So chant a soldier's song.

After the anthem, other patriotic songs were played. "Kevin Barry," "The Patriot Game," "The Boys of the Old Brigade," the songs that their ancestors on Earth had sung over a millenium before. Then, at Brigid's signal, the girls formed a double-file line. Brigid took Deirdre's arm at the head of the line, and each member took a novice. They walked to the steel tub, the beer bucket was opened, and stone mugs were dipped, filled with ale, and passed out until each girl had one.

In unison the member raised their mugs to shout "To Hibernia!" and the novices repeated the toast. Then Brigid, who had walked in carrying a knapsack on her back, removed it and opened it.

"Here are six good-sized cigars. Sorry they are not loaded with Canepec, but there is an alert. If that siren goes off, I must head for my battery sober; I have my gunner's jacket in the sack."

She lit the stogie then gave it to Deirdre. Deirdre choked on her first draw, then handed it to Clara, who in turned passed it to her novice. After the cigars and beer were finished, the double-file line formed again, except two girls at the victrola.

Another record was put on, but this was a drum roll, bump and grind number. Brigid ordered, "Just follow my every move," as she began to remove her yellow and black sweater. She repeated every move she had ever performed on the stage. Each girl disrobed to the music, but none could even approach her smooth professional moves. When the record ended, all twenty-eight girls stood in suggestive nudity. Then a series of records were played. They came from the archives of the Earth planet-nation America, circa 1950 to 1970; the music form was known as "rock." Each gang member danced with a novice. At the end of the last record, each member picked her novice partner off the floor. Brigid, who carried Deirdre, walked into a hallway to the next workroom. There over a dozen double-bed mattresses with blankets were placed. Brigid set Deirdre onto a bed and laid down beside her, pulling a heavy wool sheet atop them both. As she began to kiss, caress, and fondle her young novice, she said, "I met your boy Cathal today."

Deirdre replied, "The Quinncannons say I should forget him."

Brigid answered, "Dee, listen to me, Cathal is a shy, sweet, frightened, and lonely little boy; find him and love him all you can."

✦ ✦ ✦

"Eamon," Cathal would often say, "there are times I feel like I am in a world where everybody is as tall as a street lamp, but I am only as tall as a fireplug." The day that had just passed was one of those days. Never sine he was eleven had his life been so badly jarred. In 3148 his sister had gone to jail, and then the following year, his mother died. Now, in one day, he had lost his girlfriend to the gang his sister was in and learned that his sister had founded the gang. On top of that, he discovered that a teacher he admired, a bilingual instructor and auxiliary gunner, was also not only a stripper but a gang member too.

He pedaled his delivery cart to the florist shop. He took from the bin in the back his concertina, rosary, and missal. He walked to an isolated part of the huge Memorial Park. He sat down by a large oak tree brought from Earth and planted centuries earlier. He began to play his concertina. It was a gift from his Uncle Eugene, who lived in a houseboat in the marshland where the four quadrants of the nation-planet came together. Eugene O'Rourke, like Seamus, Cathal's father, was an architect in peacetime. But whereas Seamus also had a military career during intermittent conflicts, Eugene had never been in service. He had a pancreas disorder that on Earth was named diabetes. He lived in the marshland with Beth, his wife, a refugee from Brittania's Yorkshire sector. He had taught Cathal how to fish; how to set traplines for the Mulquix, an animal valued for flesh and fur; and how to play the concertina. Cathal played in secret, never before his father or older brother.

He played an old folk song from Earth's America, twelve hundred years old, by a now-forgotten man:

> Boilin' Cabbage down, down
> Turn the hall gates round, round
> The only song that I can sing
> Is Boilin' Cabbage down
> Boilin' Cabbage down, round.

Cathal played old Hibernian rebel songs of Earth, American theatrical numbers, and "Edelweiss," which Colonel Becker taught him in secret.

Long after dark, Cathal got up from the tree and walked to the far north edge of town. He reached a residential area, with many vacant lots where homes had once stood, and followed one street to a dead end. It had sidewalks and low stone fences on both sides. On the north side of the street, the brick bungalow of Mr. and Mrs. Joseph O'Toole stood. Cathal climbed over the stone fence on the opposite side of the street. He peeked through a hole where a stone had fallen. He would wait all night until morning, when Deirdre returned home, for one last look at her. If she wore a Tigeress sweater he would leave Athlone by subterranean railtrain and never see her again. As the night wore on he opened his missal and began the rosary. "Hail Mary, full of grace, Hail Mary, full of grace." He was the most religious member the O'Rourke family. Finally, feeling like he cared not whether he lived or died, he lay down beside the stone fence. Soon a deep sleep ended his day of pain.

Chapter 2

Eight hundred kilometers above Hibernia's south pole, the armed space tanker *Charles Stewart Parnell* circled at its battle station. Like a sentinel the *Parnell* awaited the enemy assault, her crew on full alert. Her elongated hull was a study in asymmetrical form. The bow was like a mushroom's cap and the four armored spheres filled with double-positive ion plasma fuel combined beauty and purpose. On both sides of the hull, three double-barrel laser gun turrets were mounted. On her underside, retractable muzzles and cables were ready for the inflight refueling of Hibernian fighters.

Although the wars of 3124 and 3149 proper were of short duration, actual fighting had been almost constant. Privateers under Brittanic subsidiaries, border raids, and other incidents kept Hibernia's pilots in the air for long periods. The one weakness of the Needlehead fighters was their lack of interplanetary range. This necessitated inflight refueling. The first tanker launched was the small *Arthur Griffith*, in 3131. In the years that followed a series of tankers were launched, the *John Redmond*, the *Michael Collins*, the *Daniel O'Connell*, the repair ship *Edward Carson*, and finally the *Parnell*. Actually, the *Parnell* was to be constructed as an attack ship. It was to have carried fighter launch tubes and landing bays and over twenty laser batteries; however, the financial limits of Hibernia's government and the fact that Brittania still held the Ulster quadrant kept the craft a tanker.

The fact that it was an armed tanker was decisive in her survival during the previous war. The Hibernian fighter force was ferried by the tankers across space to the enemy planet. Over a twenty-four-hour period, the fighter force struck the Brittanic capital city and destroyed a convoy of troop transports as well. During their return to Hibernia, however, the tanker force was ambushed by an armada of privateers. Over 90 percent of those were destroyed by Hibernia's fighters, but the tankers *Collins*, *Redmond*, and *O'Connell* and the repair ship *Carson* were lost. Only the *Parnell* and the older *Griffith* remained. The *Griffith*, less than half the size of the *Parnell*, rode over the South Pole, four hundred kilometers below the larger ship.

Aft of the bridge, there was a private walkroom. There, a single man collected his thoughts on the approaching battle. A veteran with decades of service, his age was indicated only by his silver hair. His nimble moves belied his size. This was the captain of the *Parnell* and Commander of Air-Space Defense Force for Athlone, Seamus O'Rourke.

As he paced about the sanctuary, he thought of his scattered family and how their safety was at stake. He thought about his late wife, Bernadette, who had died manning a surface battery in the previous war. He missed his wife at all times, all the more when an alert was called. He thought of his firstborn, Eamon, his feelings of pride at his abilities as a pilot and officer. But he also felt disappointment at his son's inflexible personality, his intolerance.

He thought about his daughter, Shelley. He had shared his wife's shock at the arrest and trials and disbelief at the charges, but as the trial progressed, he not only forgave his daughter's errors but came to admire her courage. Finally he thought of his youngest, Cathal, and a feeling of shame overcame him as he felt he had neglected the timid child. He then exited the walkway and headed for the bridge. Putting feelings aside, he regenerated energy from within. As he approached the bridge, he confronted his orderly, Corporal Alexis Kamzov.

The Kamzov family had settled from the planet Sovietia over fifteen years earlier. The young man was between Eamon and Cathal in appearance. Saluting, the orderly handed a dispatch to the Commander, saying, "Commander, this is a report from the recruitment personnel center addressed to you, sir."

Seamus read the outside of the envelope, then put the dispatch in his uniform belt pocket. He noticed the look of terror and worry on the young man's face. "It is perfectly all right to be scared, corporal, this is not a diplomatic reception we are awaiting," was the Commander's instinctive reaction.

"It isn't for myself, sir," he replied in Slavic-accented English. "My younger brother and sister are in a Gaelic school, St. Columba's in Roscommon."

"I understand. In fact, I am also scared for others. Eamon, of course, is a pilot; he can take care of himself. Shelley, well, Limerick Gaol is safer than Athlone. It is Cathal . . . I gave him five goldgrams for a southbound train from Athlone, but I just know he is pedaling his little florist wagon about the town."

"Your youngest sounds like a busy individual, a bright child."

"He has been by himself practically since he was twelve. When this is over I am going to take him up to the marshes. You know, I was considering retirement before the truce broke down. My brother Eugene and I, we've had this dream since we were children. We would dredge out part of the marshlands and build a small city. It would be like the old Earth city of Venice, with canals instead of roads. Last month he was negotiating with an Islamic bank. . . ."

"An Islamic bank, sir?"

"Immigrants from the planets Arabia and Turko-Persia set it up. They charge no interest on loans; instead fees are levied for services and they commission a percentage of profits from successful ventures, very favorable. Now my brother's dreams, my dreams, go back into a night fog."

The two men were walking together toward the bridge. As he entered, the Commander's eyes fell on the wide viewscreen scanner that gave a panoramic view of the southern hemisphere of the planet. Seamus immediately ordered the scanner to be concentrated on the area from Athlone to Dublin. In two seconds he told the radio operator to call to Athlone's Defense Base. "Colonel Kalminsky, I have noticed our patrols are spread far north and east of the Capital; what is the explanation?"

The reply: "Captain O'Rourke here suggested that the enemy might hit the Portlaoise and the Enniskillen power plants."

"That is the instinctive reaction of a flight captain, not a staff strategist, which is precisely why he may be right. Even if there is no attack there, no major risk is involved. It is the Gaeltacht, however, that is my major concern. I hope Commander MacMullen has received reinforcements," Seamus commented. Then he turned away from the viewscreen. He told the navigator, "Chart us a due north course toward Portlaoise." Then to the ship's helmsman: "Pull us out of latitudinal orbit; forward at cruising speed."

The two subordinates obeyed the directions, then the Commander returned to the viewscreen. The Colonel said, "Congratulations on the news about your daughter, Shelley."

This brought a puzzled reaction from Seamus, then he took the envelope that was in his pocket out and read it.

"Yes, she is arriving in Athlone to be inducted into the auxiliary service." The Commander hid his actual tension. "Good luck, Colonel. Tell the pilots to watch themselves over the city. Over and out."

✦ ✦ ✦

The Athlone underground railway terminal was jammed with crowds of people. The children of the city were being evacuated for their safety to the far south. At one departure ramp, Theobald and Maureen McLaughlin were instructing an elderly woman on caring for Barry and Esther.

"Miss MacDevitt, my parents are in Kilkenny," Maureen said. "This letter will introduce you."

Theobald added, "They are two very wonderful people; they accepted me like a son."

The woman turned to push the baby buggy on board the railcar and Barry tried to help her, then the car's wide doors closed and the train pulled away. As the two adults walked up a long stair, Theobald asked, "I didn't quite get the details on how you met her."

Maureen answered, "Do you remember in the papers reading about a widowed shirt factory exec who left twelve thousand grams of gold each to a dozen music hall showgirls?" Theobald nodded his knowledge. "Well, Brigid and Pam were two of the girls in the will; they were among those who had become his   paramours in his last days. Brigid found out that old rascal had left his kid sister only fifty grams of silver, and she's a pensioner from the same company as the old man." Maureen threw her hands up in disgust.

Her male companion asked, "Then what happened?"

"She talked all the other girls into setting that sweet little spinster up in a nice little apartment, better than the run-down place she was in," replied Maureen. Then she placed her arm tightly around her husband's waist, saying, "Theo, that root cellar of yours will be the place to hide if the Brits hit the city. Why don't we get ourselves comfortable in there? It could be like our wedding night."

"Fine, Mo, it sounds beautiful," was his reply.

The incoming train came to a jarring halt. The doors opened and light fell upon the six girls still asleep inside. Two guards in military police brown shirts entered and handcuffed the young women before they awoke. "Up and at 'em," was the order of a guard-sergeant. The hooks locking the leglock chain to the car wall were released, then the six girls in black emerged onto the arrival ramp. Immediately a crowd of people who had been slowly moving toward exits began to stampede. The strawberry blonde who was in the lead asked, "Sergeant, why are they panicking that way? What do they think we could do, chained up like this?"

The sergeant answered, "I followed your trial out of curiosity. You are still the stuff of which mad rumors are made, but I, for one, think they are overreacting. Oh yes, these chains are procedural. I know you are to be inducted."

The young women walked to a truck and climbed into the flatbed in the back. In just fifteen minutes they had crossed town into the Athlone Defense Base.

A flight sergeant approached and announced there was a change in plans. "We need only one replacement as a surface gunner. The rest will go to the base hospital at Kilkenny to become nurses." Turning to the girls he asked, "Have any of you even so much as fired a laser rifle?"

"Cadet O'Rourke. I won a marksmen's medal in school," was the reply of the leading girl. A guard removed the irons from her limbs and led her down from the truck. "Sergeant, I beg just a minute to say goodbye to them. I spent five years with these girls, they're almost family."

"That will be acceptable; also, you are still to be wearing your black outfits despite induction," was the flight sergeant's reply.

Shelley climbed back onto the flatbed, saying, "Kate, Carol, M.P., Jamie, Mairead, I, I can't believe it. I'm going to miss all of you."

The five other girls crowded around her, "Shelley, did you have to volunteer for that? You'll be killed," was their response.

"If we lose this war, we all will be in heaven." Shelley kissed each girl squarely on the mouth, as if kissing a man. Then, her face sparkling with tears, she climbed off the truck. She waved, then walked away with the flight sergeant.

"Cadet O'Rourke," the sergeant opened, "I know you must be puzzled at having to continue in that prison outfit. It puzzles me, too, but orders are orders."

"My father might object to it, but he would accept what the state commands," was her answer.

"Your father? Are you . . . the Commander's daughter? What made you do the things you did, a beautiful child like you? Were you a man-hater?" The sergeant's shock was total.

"I am looking forward to meeting three men on this base; my father, my brother Eamon, and Lieutenant O'Connell," was Shelley's reply.

"Now, don't expect special favors, young lady."

"On the contrary, I suspect they'll push me especially hard."

In the servicemen's dining room, Defense Minister Joseph Flynn was talking with Colonel Becker. "I understand there is a Bullethead fighter gunner who has over seven years of service but no full commission. What is the reason for this?"

"Ensign O'Brien is the gunner in question. If he was promoted we would then have to court martial him for conduct unbecoming an officer. We would lose a competent co-pilot. That is him over there."

At a long dinner table, the pilots were sitting down to breakfast, even before a chinaware plate and silverware. The exception was the barrel-shaped redhead who lifted a large wooden spoon from a wooden bowl. The spoon held a much of scrambled eggs and porridge. The ensign steered the spoon to his mouth like a man shoveling coal and then began to chew in a slow, circular motion like a cow chewing cud.

The Minister of Defense muttered, "Gawd, a child would have better manners."

Colonel Becker replied, "In the first six months of his time in service, he broke more plats and bent more silverware than any twenty children. He is brave and loyal, however, so we overlook his one major gaucherie. He is also the best accordion player I have ever met, excepting myself. I have sat in on his performances in the servicemen's club room. His pilot, Lieutenant Cosgrave, is the vocalist."

✦ ✦ ✦

Captain O'Rourke had eaten a hasty early breakfast before joining Colonel Kalminsky in addressing the auxiliaries in front of the barracks. Some women surface gunners arrived in their flak suits. Others had their suits in a duffel bag to slip on right over civilian garb. The women came from every stratum of Athlone. Many were housewives and mothers with children either on the southbound evacuation trains or in Gaeltacht schools. Others were from the shirt factories, dressed in the linsey-woolsey workshirts. Some were girls barely out of secondary school. Finally the Captain's eyes fell upon the blond auxiliary in the front row. The drab green uniform barely diminished the ripe body underneath that had been brandished as a weapon the night before.

Colonel Kalminsky announced, "We have a new cadet coming here this morning, a parolee from the Limerick gaol. She is to be regarded as one of your comrades, regardless of her past. We have a vacancy amount scanner operators. Which gun is without a full crew?"

Auxiliary Hallohan spoke. "Shiralee Rankin is in a maternity hospital; I am the one in need of a scanner operator."

Colonel Kalminsky then announced, "Auxiliary Hallohan is to remain here; the rest of you are to report to your perspective batteries. Dismissed."

In a minute all the other auxiliaries had departed. Then, escorted by a flight sergeant, the recruit arrived. Captain O'Rourke's mouth opened in surprise, then he attempted to regain a military posture. The woman dressed in black attempted as correct a salute as possible. "Cadet O'Rourke, reporting for duty, sir."

After regaining his official dignity, he said, "You are to operate the range scanner on Auxiliary Hallohan's gun, report immediately. Dismissed." As the two girls started to head to their post, again the Captain spoke. "Attention, Auxiliary Hallohan. After your display of insubordination yesterday, I considered charges against you of threatening an officer with a weapon; however, I realize in the resulting trial I would become the laughing stock of the service. We will discuss this later. Dismissed."

After Hallohan had left he turned to address the new cadet. "Cadet O'Rourke, at ease. Cadet, er . . . Shelley." He seemed pained.

Shelley asked, "Eamon, why did you never visit me? Why did you write so rarely? Father visited whenever possible, and Sean O'Connell wrote often."

"I was ashamed . . . of myself. After Father ordered me to make the one visit, I could not stand myself."

After a minute the Cadet buried herself in her brother's arms. "Where is Sean, I want to see him. Where's father, Cathal? Also, what is this thing about Brigid? What do you mean, threatening an officer with a weapon? What weapon?"

"Her weapon was her . . . her body."

"Her body? Brigid? You? She has better taste than you."

"Attention, Cadet! At ease. . . ." He threw his captain's cap to the ground. "I don't know whether to treat you as an insubordinate Cadet or a sassy kid sister."

"I still don't understand you and Brigid."

"She reacted to my rounding up overdue servicemen that were attending her performance."

"You always were a stickler for discipline."

"As I told her, I am just doing my job. Father is on board the *Parnell*, and Cathal is supposed to be on a train evacuating town, but he's probably in town delivering flowers. I must report to the Colonel. So now, you better catch up with Auxiliary Hallohan." He departed.

Shelley turned and ran up to Brigid. Their arms encased each other.

"Brigid, have you taken care of the store?" was Shelley's line.

"Yes, we just initiated a dozen girls, including a kid named Deirdre O'Toole who likes your little Cathal."

"Brigid, what did you do to Eamon? Surely you are not so lonely he would begin to look good?"

"It's because of his heavy-handed treatment of servicemen who visit the music hall and his disdain for me and other showgirls. I wanted to seduce him, to humiliate him, but now I feel I could really do him good. I see his loneliness and fear. Underneath his military exterior, he is like Cathal."

By then, the two girls had reached the laser battery they were to man. Brigid said, "It takes two to operate the gun, one to operate the joystick that raises and lowers and turns the gun turrets. Here, it is just like the joystick of a fighter. Push forward, it lowers the gun; backwards raises it; moving it side to side turns the turret." Pointing the two viewscreens at the right side, Brigid continued. "The top screen will give you a profile of the enemy target. The crosshair will light up when you direct the gun in line for a direct hit. The bottom screen will flash red, and I will fire the gun. It takes two hands to pull the trigger. That's why the seats are diagonal with you three steps up." The two girls sat down to the gun and waited.

✧ ✧ ✧

In the Defense Military building, five floors below the surface was the war room. A pair of massive 360-degree viewscreens showed the entire southern hemisphere and almost half the northern hemisphere of the planet. The South Pole was at the top of one ceiling dome. On this screen the minute-by-minute changes in the location of air-space craft were available. Minister Joe Flynn and Colonel Becker entered the room, followed by Colonel Kalminsky. Then the Taoiseach entered with his wife, Margaret, a petite woman with raven hair. She leaned against her husband, saying, "Colm, it will be all right. I know it will."

His voice trembled. "Margaret, I am worried. Our two wee wanes are at St. Columba's."

"Colm, I know, but we must have faith." So often it was this small woman who steadied the Hibernian head of state. Because of her, he continued to drink strong black tea instead of poteen and stout.

✦ ✦ ✦

The main weapon of the Hibernia Air-Space Defense System was the Needlehead single-seater fighter. The craft was so named because its pencil thin fuselage seemed to bend into the double-delta wings. Its pointed noise carried a powerful double-action laser gun. The gun could fire pencil beams for strafing surface targets or bursts for dogfights with enemy craft. A small gun was carried at the tailfin for shaking pursuing enemy fighters. Fast, highly maneuverable, and manned by pilots whose skills were honed to a razor sharpness, the Needlehead fighters were superior to those of the enemy. The fighters and pilots awaited the attack alarm in their ferro-concrete hangers. These were below the surface, and the craft would go out and up a gentle incline to the launching strips.

Behind the flight hangars, three underground silos stood. Inside were the Bullethead fighter-bombers. These crafts, shaped like an old-fashioned gun bullet, carried a crew of two. They were equipped with a projector that fired Proton-Positron Plasma. The plasma would explode into an ion fireball that could disintegrate several enemy craft at once. This necessitated always attacking the second or third wave of craft to avoid hitting friendly pilots.

As they awaited the alarm, the pilots talked, joked, and sang to relieve their tension. Ensign O'Brien played "Off to Dublin in the Green" on a mouth organ. Then Lieutenant Cosgrave led the other pilots in a chorus of an old camp song

> Sweet Ivory Soap
> You are the dope
> You clean me so
> Like Sapolio
> In all my dreams
> Your square face beams
> You're the flower of my bath
> Sweet Ivory Soap.

Then Lieutenant O'Connell took his mind away from the racing form he was reading to quip, "Cosgrave, keep that up and it won't be the service that will court martial you, it will be every lover of good music on the planet."

After everyone had a good laugh, Cosgrave opened up a new tune:

> Queen Lizzy is so ugly
> She is a big disgrace
> Someone should walk up to her
> and white wash her whole face
> I want no more of Army life
> Gee, Mom, I want to go
> But they won't let me go
> Gee, Mom, I want to go home.

The pilot of one of the Bullethead craft came up to Cosgrave. He asked, "Sir, I have checked out my equipment, and I detected some faulty maintenance on the plasma gun. If it breaks down, I request permission to pull out of the battle, take her up to one thousand kilometers, and attempt a repair. I'll have my downward scanners on to check if the enemy tries to punch at the Connaught area."

Cosgrave answered, "Try to get back in action as quick as possible, and if your scanners pick up the enemy, radio Athlone or the *Parnell*."

"Thank you, sir. I bet the Captain's father, Commander Seamus, is cricking his guts out over the thought of what could happen up there. They have only three squadrons to guard an area as wide as the Dublin to Athlone sector covered by nine squadrons," the young officer noted.

"What is this that you are saying about our commanding officer, Ensign?" came the intimidating voice of Captain O'Rourke.

"No disrespect intended, sir. I was reflecting on those children in the Gaeltacht schools," was the reply.

"I understand that. In fact, my father and I should both be cricking our guts out over Cathal. If only I could be sure he was on an evacuation train instead of in town delivering flowers," was Eamon's comment. Then he turned to Cosgrave. "Lieutenant, do you remember a man from your boyhood named Theobald McLaughlin? He sent his regards."

"Yes, sir. We used to kid him saying he'd make someone a great little wife, and look at who he marries? That couldn't happen to a nicer guy. Never got past the fourth year of primary school, but I bet he got a real graduation present on his wedding night," was Cosgrave's joyful remark.

"Do you know those two children and their alleged fathers?"

"Yes, I know Mo Kelley had flings with late pilots Lynch and Sennech. I pass no judgments on her. In fact, I wish I could have sampled her charms myself. Oh, yes, Captain, is it true that the Queen of Athlone, Brigid Hallohan, has got you in the crosshairs of her range finders? Get set for some real action."

"You're out of line, soldier." The Captain first blushed red, then turned a shade of green. Then he walked away.

Lieutenant O'Connell remarked, "If Brigid does to the Captain what she is capable of doing, he might become just one of the boys yet, in spite of himself."

✦ ✦ ✦

South of the quadrant marshes, the range scanner of a Needlehead fighter on patrol picked up trackings of enemy craft. The pilot radioed the Athlone base. The surface range scanners dropped their altitude range from the 100 to 500 kilometer span to below 100 kilometers. In the war room the tracking appeared on the massive viewscreen. An auxiliary scanner operator, a colleen with red hair and blue eyes, watched the tracings on a smaller scanner. Then, in the most perfect Gaelic outside the Connaught area, she said, "The enemy is coming into the Leinster air space in two groups of about one hundred. The first is coming out just east of the marshland, in three waves, thirty, forty, and thirty. They are coming in due south. The computer readout indicates their target is . . . Athlone. The second group in apparently one wave. They are 250 kilometers east of the marshlands heading southeast. Readout of target . . . Dublin. They are both coming in at twelve thousand kilometers per hour, altitude eighty kilometers and declining."

Immediately Defense Minister Flynn turned to Becker and Kalminsky. "Get the Athlone and Dublin wings into the air at once. Also, radio the *Parnell* and the *Griffith*; tell them to leave their polar stations and come north and communicate to the power generating centers at Portlaoise and the Enniskillen to initiate all emergency procedures." Colonel Becker answered, "At once, sir; however, the *Parnell* is already coming north at flank speed."

At the Athlone base, the siren sent the pilots of squadron 1 jumping into their craft. In barely a minute, the Needlehead fighters wheeled out of the hangar, up the ramp. The squadron was into the air in two minutes. Then squadrons 2, 3, and 4. The reserve squadron 5 remained on standby for five minutes. Then each ship in double file reared off the launching strips. Behind the hangars, the three Bullethead fighters were fired straight out of the silos.

✦ ✦ ✦

During the Golden era of 2600 to 2994, over 75 percent of Hibernia's electrical power came from nuclear fusion reactors using deuterium from the Ulster quadrant. The remainder came from solar satellites beaming power in the form of microwaves. This had been entirely destroyed, and Hibernia had had to rebuild its electrical systems from scratch with windmills, photoelectric cells, and water wheels. The government itself built the Padraic Pearse and Robert Emmet Dams on the Enniskillen. The Athlone Municipal Service Commission brought power to the western half of the city from those hydroelectric plants.

East of Athlone and south of Portlaoise, mining operations discovered thick seams of coal and deposits of uranium. In 3127 a complex of four power plants was built by the North Leinster Electric Illuminating Corporation, comprised of two coal-fired and two nuclear fission reactors. In 3145 six more plants were constructed. Three were nuclear breeder reactors producing plutonium. The other three were coal-fired thermo-magnetic generators that converted heat directly to electricity with no moving parts. Leinster Electric provided power to Athlone's east side.

When the sirens rang throughout the valley of the Enniskillen, a carefully planned evacuation plan was put into action. The people living below the dams were moved to shelters on the highground. At Portlaoise, another careful program went into action. The nuclear reactors went immediately into a cold shutdown. The coal-fired generators increased their power production. A large part of the work crews went into air raid shelters. At both Enniskillen and Portlaoise, the defensive batteries of laser guns were manned in part by the workcrews.

✦ ✦ ✦

The enemy craft approaching were Boomerang fighter-bombers, so named because of the shape of their fuselage. In front each carried a tandem pair of lasers. One fired pencil beams for ground targets, the other fired bursts for aerial combats. Designed primarily to attack surface targets, their abilities as fighters were inferior to the Hibernian craft. Slower and with a wide turning radius, this was aggravated by their inferior pilots.

The Brittanic pilots were recruited by a combination of cash bonuses and ethnic propaganda against the Hibernians. The turnover of pilots reflected the great losses they suffered. Prior to the breakdown to truce talks, a number of their pilots had deserted to the Hibernians.

✦ ✦ ✦

In the war room in Athlone, the scanners picked up more enemy craft. The young girl operating the scanner said, "There are two more flights of enemy craft. There are about 25 fighters in formation. One is coming into the quadrant marshes. It is heading due southwest in the direction of Enniskillen. The other is headed southeast toward Portlaoise." Then Colonel Kalminsky radioed the Athlone flight wing. "Captain O'Rourke, detach two of your squadrons; one is to intercept the enemy before the Enniskillen River; the other will defend Portlaoise. Reserve squadron 5 will be sent up to reinforce you." Captain O'Rourke answered, "I will take squadron 1 to the west; Lieutenant O'Connell will take squadron 2 east. We have to use our secondary afterburners, and we will need to refuel before we return to action."

✦ ✦ ✦

It was one of the strange effects of atmospheric friction and gravity that shortened the fuel range of the opposing fighters. A fighter traveling at hypersonic speed, at an altitude of under twenty kilometers, consumed fuel many times faster than traveling at hyperlight speed in deep space.

The tricolor triangle insignia of the Needlehead fighters gleamed in the midmorning sun, an inverted white triangle between upright green and orange triangles. IPV pilots also had their insignia, two globes speared by an arrow, and specific planet emblems. The Iron Cross of Planet Deutsch, the Crescent of Arabia and Turko-Persia, the Hammer and Sickle of Sovietia, and the rest were carried with honor in battle.

✦ ✦ ✦

Reserve squadron 5 caught up with squadrons 3 and 4. The squadron approached the enemy in a wide formation. Then, as they came into visual contact, they converged together in a fight phalanx. Lieutenant Jacque Ranier radioed, "We are going to work now. *Viva la Republique*." The fighters opened up with pencil beams. Firing in unison, they formed a wall of fire. It cut through the first wave of enemy craft, destroying a half dozen fighters at once. Then they broke off into one-on-one combat. They had not only out-numbered the enemy's first wave three to two, but they had gotten into the crucial first blow.

The three Bullethead fighter-bombers reached one thousand kilometers in altitude before beginning their descent. They centered their range find-ers on the second wave of enemy heading toward Athlone. The three craft fired their plasma guns as one. Nearly a dozen Boomerang fighters flew into a massive ion fireball and disintegrated.

To the east, toward Dublin, another battle raged. The enemy came in one massive wave of one hundred craft. The squadrons of Needlehead fight-ers hit the enemy on its right flank, while the two Bullethead craft struck on the left.

When Athlone squadron 1 intercepted the enemy heading to Enniskillen, it was already being pursued by squadron 1 from Connaught. A crossfire of laser-bursts brought down one enemy fighter after another. The last Boomerang craft crashed into the reservoir behind the Robert Emmet Dam, shot down by a surface gun.

✦ ✦ ✦

At the war room, the reports of the airspace craft destroyed began to come in. Minister Flynn commented, "We are inflicting a loss ratio of five to one on the enemy."

Colonel Becker answered, "However, Herr Flynn, the enemy has another one hundred fighters not committed to battle; and there are now only two squadrons to guard the Roscommon Gaeltacht. We may have another battle even before this one is over." Then Colonel Kalminsky noted, "One of our Bullethead pilots asked to be allowed to pull out of the battle if his gun malfunctioned. At one thousand kilometers, their downward scanners could pick up everything below the North Pole. If the enemy strikes at the Gaeltacht, we will know it."

Becker replied, "If the enemy strikes too far north they could return to their own bases before our forces could intercept them."

The radio operator in the war room was an IPV. Her dark hair and skin declared her to be from Planet Nigeria. The woman turned off the loudspeaker and carefully began to take down messages through the earphones: "Squadron 2 is returning from Portlaoise; they have suffered the loss of two fighters. The Dublin squadron lost four fighters; Lieutenant O'Connell says he may have to make an emergency landing; his ship is damaged. Also, the other fighters must refuel."

Defense Minister Flynn turned to Colonel Becker. "On this map on the enemy quadrant, here are the three bases where a strike at the Gaeltacht could be launched. They are bases 1-4, 1-5, and 1-6. Our intelligence indicates Lord Paisley is in command of those bases."

Becker answered, "He is the only competent wing commander they have. He'll probably launch his attack at a very low altitude, after the other attacks are pulled back."

Then Flynn asked, "Are the Werewolf rockets at your countrymen's Peenemude launching base ready?"

The Colonel answered, "They are ready and targeted to hit the massive industrial complex at the center of the Ulster quadrant."

Minister Flynn ordered, "Retarget those rockets to the coordinates of these bases. Keep them on hold until my command to fire."

Then the radio operator reported, "The enemy is breaking off their attack on Dublin. The squadrons report losing eleven fighters but they destroyed forty-seven. Four others were seen making forced landings. The squadron leader believes the enemy is out of laser photon charges."

Minister Flynn answered, "Radio Commander Donahue. He is to instruct his squadron to pursue the enemy. Force them to land or bring them down." After delivering the communication, another message was received. "Lieutenant Ranier has reported that the enemy's first wave is destroyed and the second wave is breaking off and withdrawing. At least fifty-two confirmed kills of enemy craft, while seven of ours were lost; but the pilots are parachuting to the surface in ejection pads."

The radio operator turned the loudspeaker back on. The voice of Captain O'Rourke announced, "Our fighter's getting low on fuel. Our squadron lost three fighters in battle, but four have made forced landings already. The Gaeltacht squadron lost two fighters during the fight, five of their other craft had to ditch. We need fuel now."

Colonel Becker answered, "The *Parnell* is approaching the Athlone area."

The scanner operator reported, "Thirty more fighters are approaching Athlone, speed eight thousand kilometers per hour, altitude five kilometers and declining. They apparently dived below our fighter defenses and our scanners."

Colonel Kalminsky immediately walked to a panel beside the scanner and pushed two buttons at the bottom of the console. The final red alert alarm rang through the city.

✦ ✦ ✦

Most of the major buildings in Athlone had their most vital components underground. The six-floor Athlone Labor Congress Credit Union building had only two floors above ground level. The state-run coal-gasification plants on the east side had their storage tanks in a cavern-like vault half a kilometer below the surface. Therefore, synthetic gasoline was safe from attack, while dummy storage tanks were on the surface; however, other buildings were exposed to attack. The Brewery Co-op, stores, music halls, and residential areas were all in danger. The masses of people were already in air-raid shelters built around the city.

The surface laser batteries were manned by the women's auxiliaries. Many had husbands who were pilots. Many had children in Gaeltacht schools, and the safety of those children was in the back of the minds of their mothers.

As the enemy came over the city, they were met by a sky criss-crossed with laser fire. Not only would the auxiliaries bring down enemy craft, but also their fire would cause the enemy to take evasive action. Thus, they would not be able to strafe the city.

The Boomerang fighters came in low, firing pencil beans, attempting to destroy anything in sight. Houses, the fountains of DeValera Park, the yet to be opened First Islamic Bank Building all were shattered. A shirt factory warehouse filled with cotton, wool, and flax began to burn. When firefighting vehicles came out to extinguish the conflagrations, the enemy fired at firetrucks and men. A pencil beam struck the north wall of the Athlone Brewery Co-op. The vats of Enniskillen Ale ruptured and thousands of liters of nectar flooded out. The brewery workers had to flee from their air-raid ditches to avoid drowning.

✦ ✦ ✦

A Boomerang fighter, after strafing the length of the city, turned north-ward again. The pilot approached an area of vacant lots and rubble of destroyed homes. At the end of one long street, a single brick home sat. The pilot closed in to attack.

Cathal O'Rourke had awoken and waited behind the stone fence. He was still waiting for his girl, Deirdre, to see her one last time. He looked across the street into the large picture window and he saw Deirdre's parents wait-ing for their daughter. Then he saw the young girl approaching from down the street. Deirdre moved in short rushes from shelter to shelter toward her home. She reached a wooden gate leading to the walk to her house. Her par-ents were waving to her. Deirdre was wearing the Tigeress sweater, and her red hair was combed out straight. Cathal prepared to walk away. Then he hear the ominous roar of an incoming ship and saw the Boomerang ship approach. Deirdre dived to the pavement. Then Cathal watched in horror as the red tongue of a laser gun hit the brick bungalow. The house exploded and two bodies were thrown into the air. Without thinking, he was up and over the fence almost instantly. There was no sign of his girl, and he leaped over the fence on the other side of the street.

He found Deirdre on her knees before the charred remains of her moth-er and father. He heard the returning enemy fighter. Cathal simply scooped the girl up in his arms. He carried her back across the street to where he had sat through the night. He held her tightly, as she cried, "It's all my fault; they were waiting for me. If I had stayed home last night. . . ."

"You would be dead alongside them. It's not your fault; it's the Brits, those murderous Brits who killed my mother," replied Cathal. "Let's stay here. If we're going to die, let's die together." Then they both saw the enemy craft fleeing a Needlehead fighter. A laser shot exploded the Brit craft. The pilot's body fell into the street. Deirdre tore herself away from Cathal and ran to the body. She began to claw and bite the pilot screaming, "Murderer! You disgusting, vile, murderous swine!" Then she broke down in tears.

Cathal carried her in his arms back to where he sat. He opened his missal to prayers for the dead and then took out his rosary. The two young people knelt and began to chant: "Hail Mary, full of grace; Hail Mary, full of grace."

✦ ✦ ✦

"Damnit, Brigid, this range finder isn't working or I just can't use it," Shelley muttered. Their surface gun had not even shot near the enemy. Shelley then turned off the scanner, and said, "I am going to aim this like a hand rifle, fire when I shout." An enemy craft appeared in the distance. Shelley pushed the joystick forward, lowering the gun barrel to a near hori-zontal level. Then she pulled the joystick back, raising the barrel's elevation. She realized she was raising the barrel too quickly, so she jerked it back once more then stopped. Then she said, "Fire now!" The first two laser bursts shot up far affront of the Boomerang craft. The third intercepted the fighter. As the Brittanic craft nosed down to crash, Brigid shouted, "Eat my twat, Brit!"

"That was for my mother," Shelley said.

✦ ✦ ✦

Lieutenant O'Connell's fighter was badly damaged and the pilot looked for a place to land. He dropped his landing wheels. Entering the airspace on Athlone's north side, he found a street in an area of vacant lots. He fired retro rockets and slid down the street. His craft fishtailed and tipped halfway over before righting itself. Thinking to himself, "I am alive," he opened the cockpit and climbed out. He walked back up the street to get his bearings. He then saw the burning remains of a house. As he came closer, he heard a familiar voice. Walking up to the wall across the street, he found Cathal and a young girl. Sean asked, "What are you doing here, Cathal. Why didn't you take an evacuation train?"

The boy answered, "This is my friend Deirdre O'Toole, and what's left of her parents are over there. He pointed to the burning house. Then, gathering themselves together, the three walked back to the fighter down the street. The Lieutenant radioed his position to the Athlone base. Then, keeping low against the stone fence, the three began to move south toward the center of the city.

✦ ✦ ✦

The enemy fighters converged south of the city, then turned about for a last strafing attack. They headed to the center of the city in a tight pattern. As they dived in low, they were caught in the crossfire of the surface guns. Several of the enemy craft were hit. One fighter made a forced landing. As soon as he left his cockpit, he was seized by a crowd of civilians, who beat him severely before ground troops took him away to prison. The enemy craft, taking a number of losses, broke off their attack and departed northward. In the war room, the radio operator relayed the report. "Nine enemy fighters destroyed, one forced to land."

Colonel Becker noted, "By the reports of our pilots and auxiliaries, 158 of 250 enemy fighters have been destroyed. This is a tribute to the superiority of our pilots and fighters."

The radio operator reported, "The Connaught quadrant reports a small enemy force has entered our air space. They are about twenty craft. Connaught squadrons 2 and 3 are intercepting now, directly north of the quadrant marshlands."

Minister Flynn noted, "That leaves eighty enemy fighters unaccounted for." Then he turned to the scanner operator, "You are to use the data banks to compute the time for round trip operation from the enemy bases 1-4, 1-

5, and 1-6, to the Gaeltacht area. Then compute the time for a strike at the bases by the Werewolf rockets at the Peenemude base." In a few minutes the computer readout came.

"The time for a round trip attack at the Gaeltacht, 90 minutes. The time for a strike from Peenemude, 150 to 180 minutes," the scanner operator reported.

"Becker!" the Minister commanded, "What is the time needed to launch the entire rocket force from the base?"

"One hour, sir!" the Teuton replied. Then after thinking for several minutes, the Minister answered to Colonel Becker, "Allowing a thirty-minute period of the enemy's strafing attacks, your rockets will hit thirty minutes to an hour after their return. How many rockets and how many launchers are at the base?" Becker replied, "Fifty rockets, sir, and five launchers. We can fire a salvo every six minutes."

"Then, Becker, open fire the very minute they break into the sector," Flynn answered.

"Ya, Mein Herr," the Colonel answered, saluting sharply.

✦ ✦ ✦

On board the *Parnell*, Commander O'Rourke was listening in on every transmission to and from Athlone.

The radio operator, an Arabian girl IPV, interrupted. "Sir, Captain O'Dwyer is reporting from the *Griffith*; he is following the *Parnell*'s course toward Athlone. He requests to directly report to you."

The Captain appeared on the viewscreen. "Commander, I am suggesting that our courses diverge. I could steer my ship toward Portlaoise and Athlone Squadron 2. Your ship could head west to Athlone and Squadron 1."

The Commander answered, "Captain, proceed with utmost speed. Your plan is quite good. Also, check for any fighters from Dublin that may need assistance."

"Good luck, sir." The Captain's face faded out. A minute later, squadron leader 1 from Athlone radioed the *Parnell*; "This is Captain O'Rourke with squadron 1. We are five kilometers below you and twenty kilometers northwest. It's going to be a close one, but we can make it."

The Commander answered, "A very good job guarding those hydropower dams, Captain."

"Sir, I have picked up squadron 2 leader's position. He forced landed at the edge of Athlone. He reports two young people are safe near his craft, a girl and a boy named Cathal O'Rourke."

"I heard that report myself, Eamon."

"He was described as a bit of a hero by Lieutenant O'Connell, Father, ah, sir."

"If he was a serviceman, he could be given a court-martial or a medal."

"But he is a delivery boy. What could they do, take away his flowers or his pedicab?"

"Have you heard about Shelley?"

"Yes, father, she's manning a gun in Athlone now."

"We will have a little reunion after this alert is over, assuming we are all in one piece."

"I've heard the concern for the Gaeltacht area. Commander, I request permission to return to action when refueled."

"Affirmative. Good luck, Captain."

The Needlehead fighters passed directly under the tanker. Making a wide 180-degree turn, the fighters pulled up her underbelly. They slowed their speed to equal that of the mother vessel. From the underside of the ship, fuel hoses and electro-cables were lowered to the fighters below. The cable for recharging the laser went in just behind the nose. The fuel hose entered behind the cockpit. In a matter of minutes Athlone Squadron 1 was entirely under the *Parnell*, like piglets feeding under a huge sow. Then fighters from Gaeltacht Squadron 1 that assisted the Athlone fighters over the Enniskillen joined in the refueling process. To the east, the *Griffith* had intercepted the fighters of Athlone Squadron 2 and Dublin Squadron 1. Being smaller than the *Parnell* it could not refuel the two squadrons together. Each pilot reported the amount of fuel remaining. Those craft with the least amount of fuel were serviced first. Then, as the first craft finished refueling, the less thirsty fighters were refueled.

✦ ✦ ✦

Far to the south near Kilkenny, a secret base had been built. The base was manned by almost entirely IPVs, mostly from planet Deutsch. There, a secret weapon had been developed: an air-breathing, ultra-low altitude, radio-guided rocket. It was armed with a warhead consisting of a solidified version of the ion plasma used on the Bullethead fighters. They fired in a horizontal launch on rubber wheel axles, down a concrete monorail launch ramp. The craft were raised from an underground hangar by an elevator. Then a crane lifted the rocket up and lowered it onto the ramp. An electro-impulse battery fired up the engine, and when it reached sufficient thrust, it shot down the launch ramp. When the rocket reached the end of the ramp, the axles dropped off for reuse. A light beam passing directly across the ramp activated a radio beam that guided the rocket to its target.

The Deutscher IPVs named the base Peenemude, after a base during the major war of twentieth century Earth. The rockets were named Werewolves, after a character in Teutonic mythology. The rockets, in fact, resembled the famous V-1 Buzzbombs of that very Earth war. The Deutschers tended to run the base as if it were on their home planet. The Hibernian and IPV symbols were removed, leaving the Iron Cross. Also, some of the workers painted unauthorized symbols on the craft, the *Totenkopf*, the death-head insignia, and an ancient slogan, *"Gott mit uns."*

The base workers were singing war songs of over one thousand years ago. To battle England, as was Brittania's ancient name, was a mission as much as a war. A tall robust Teuton, a sergeant standing on guard at one of the launchers, noticed one of the few Hibernian servicemen. The serviceman was writing in chalk on the side of a Werewolf rocket. In broken English he asked, "What is that you are writing, soldier?"

The native answered, "In Gaelic, sir, it reads: 'To Lizzy, who sucks.'" The sergeant turned away in disbelief.

✦ ✦ ✦

In the war room in Athlone, the radio operator reported, "The enemy fighters are leaving the southeast Connaught area. Seven of the enemy fighters were brought down with no losses to ourselves." A few minutes later another radio message came in: "From Peenemude, their first rocket salvo is targeted at base 1-4. The second salvo will be aimed at base 1-5 and the third salvo will hit base 1-6. The remaining salvos will be targeted in that sequence."

After a long nerve-wracking wait, a transmission came in and was put on the loudspeaker. "This is Athlone Bullethead Number 2 reporting to Athlone or the *Parnell*. We are over the marshlands at nine hundred kilometers. Our downward scanner detects seventy-five to eighty enemy craft entering the north Connaught Gaeltacht area. They are coming in low, under two kilometers, and at a low speed. They are spread out wide in small groups. We are returning to base, sir. We are low on fuel," the pilot reported. Minister Flynn turned to Colonel Becker and the radio operator, "Signal Peenemude, commence firing!"

✦ ✦ ✦

The radio and scanner operators were relieved by replacements. The two young women entered the lounge part of a woman's washroom and sat down. After fumbling and breaking several matches, they lit up cigarettes and began a difficult conversation. Both had very heavily accented English. One colleen said, "My parents teach at St. Columba's. I am worried sick." The IPV answered, "My sister's children are at St. Basil's, near your parents' school. This war is so, so obscene."

✦ ✦ ✦

A messenger from the cablegram office entered the warroom and handed an envelope into the hands of the Taoiseach. His face paled as he read the message inside. As he neared collapse, he turned to the radio console.

"Turn to open channel, all frequencies, civilian and military," he said as he reached for the hand microphone. Summoning his remaining strength he spoke, "This is the Taoiseach. It is my sad duty to report that the following Gaeltacht schools have been destroyed by the enemy attack: St. Columba's, St. Basil's, St. Agnes, St. Athanasius, St. Benedict's. The children were burned alive by laser fire while hiding in air raid trenches. Villages in the area have suffered a great loss of life . . . I . . . I can barely go on . . . this . . . . this will go down in history . . . with the massacres our people suffered on Earth . . . Drogheda in 1649, Croak Park, Dublin 1920, Derry 1972. I am declaring a ten-day period of . . . of mourning for our country's children."

The premier's wife, Margaret, collapsed in tears. The screams of the two women in the women's lounge could be heard down the hallway from the war room. Colonel Becker, his fist pounding a desk, muttered, "Lord Cromwell is the spiritual reincarnation of the most infamous ancestor of my countrymen when they were still on Earth. In the twentieth century he started a war that killed 50 million people. We are ashamed to even say his name . . . Adolph Hitler!"

✦ ✦ ✦

Across the vast vacuum of space lay the enemy planet. At the Crystal Palace, in the chamberoom, Elizabeth XVII was in discussion with her two top ministers. "Test the enemy's defenses you said. Perhaps a successful raid would panic the Hibernians into surrender, you said, Lord Churchill. Look at what your stupidity has brought about! Half of the fighters of the quadrant fleet are gone!" The Brittanic monarch roared in fury.

"Lord Churchill, I told you we should wait until your fleet has reached sufficient numbers for an all-out attack. Now, thanks to your blunder, we will have to detach part of our home fleet in order to replace the quadrant ships lost," said Minister Cromwell.

"Your Majesty, I am afraid that I, I have miscalculated," was Churchill's apologetic reply.

"Lord Churchill, you are dismissed from the Prime Ministry. Lord Cromwell will be your replacement," the Queen answered.

Then M.P. Gladstone entered the chamberoom. Looking straight at Cromwell, he shouted, "In the name of God, I must protest this insanity!"

Cromwell's retort: "Shut up! Traitor!"

"If you call me a traitor again, I will forget that I am a gentlemen!" threatened the opposition leader whose beard lent to his countenance a resemblance to Moses.

"Traitors are not gentlemen, they—" Cromwell fell as the other man swung his angry fist right on the Minister's nose.

"Enough of this! Guards, put both of these men under restraints! Gladstone! You are not to enter this palace again under threat of immediate ejection!" The monarch was red-faced now.

Then a young orderly entered and said, "A communication from Lord Paisley in the quadrant is coming to the viewscreen, your most gracious Majesty."

The monarch turned and by a hand signal commanded the screen to be turned on. "Lord Paisley reporting from quadrant base 1-4, Your Grace. My fighters have annihilated the Gaeltacht area of the enemy's Connaught section without the loss of a single finger. I am sorry to report the other wing commanders lacked my luck," was the reporting officer's announcement.

"I am elevating you to the level of commander for all attack operations by the quadrant fleet, Lord Paisley," was the monarch's reply. "You will still be under the command of Governor General Byng, however."

"You're most considerate and regal, Monarch. I will serve in—what was that?" Paisley started as an explosion took place.

An orderly ran up behind him, screaming, "Enemy missiles are coming into the bases."

Lord Paisley turned to look out of a window of his office as three loud explosions followed. "It's some sort of missile. My God, it's headed right for me—no!" The viewscreen went silent.

"Lord Paisley is dead! Churchill, you will replace Lord Paisley and you will leave with the next convoy of replacement ships. You are all dismissed!" The now pale monarch fell back onto her throne, totally defeated.

✦ ✦ ✦

Colonel Kalminsky disliked the task he had to perform. No sooner did he announce to the assembled pilots and auxiliaries of the news of the Gaeltacht massacre, than an outpouring of moans and sobs rose up. Pilots and auxiliaries alike mourned the death of the children. Lieutenant Antonio Soares, a pilot, and his wife, Maria, an auxiliary collapsed into each other's arms. Other pilots and two auxiliaries Hallohan and O'Rourke, cursed the enemy monarch. Hallohan brandished a weapon of several metal knitting needles fused into one, "I'll plunge this into Lizzy's black heart!"

The Colonel finished his address, noting, "The rockets from the Pennemude base have already avenged the barbarous act that took place today. We will avenge those innocent children a thousand times over. Dismissed."

Captain O'Rourke approached his sister, saying, "Father will arrive in a few minutes."

Then Lieutenant O'Connell came up, with Cathal and Deirdre behind. When the older O'Rourkes saw their younger brother, they threw their arms around him. Shelley kissed the boy fiercely and then, without thinking, turned and kissed the Lieutenant.

"Attention," was the order of the veteran commander as he approached his family. "Front and center. Good work, Captain. A classic job of landing, Lieutenant."

"Cadet, it has been reported that you were firing your gun without the benefit of a range finder. What is your explanation?" The Commander eyed the subordinates as if they were all cadets.

Cadet O'Rourke answered, "Sir, I had never used a range finder before, but still our gun brought down two enemy craft by manual aiming."

"At ease, all of you." The Commander eyed Lieutenant O'Connell and his daughter and continued. "Since you two were friends in school, I will overlook that indiscreet display. Lieutenant, report to Colonel Kalminsky. Dismissed." Then he turned to his youngest son, "Cathal, why did you remain in this city?"

"Father, I had a problem involving my friend, Deirdre," was the son's answer.

The Lieutenant, who had not yet walked away, added, "Commander, he saved this girl's life after her parents died in the attack."

The father threw his arm around the boy, asking, "Who is this pretty young thing?"

"She is my closest friend, Deirdre O'Toole."

"She will have to become a ward of the state authorities."

Auxiliary Hallohan, who had watched this discussion, came up. "Commander, sir," she saluted. "I have two friends, the Quinncannon sisters. They can care for Dee, at least for tonight."

Seamus replied, "If the girl accepts that, she can go with you. Dismissed."

Before Brigid and Deirdre left, Cathal went up to Deirdre and kissed her right on the mouth. The two girls walked away with Brigid saying, "It has been a lousy day."

The Commander turned to his daughter, "Shelley, kitten," then he embraced his young girl. Summoning her brothers, he said, "Let's go home." The four walked out the gate of the Athlone base.

Seamus said to his firstborn, "Eamon, we will have to get to bed early. We will have a long staff meeting tomorrow." The four walked until they came upon a large motorcycle with a sidecar on both sides.

Eamon said, "It's an experimental model. It has an alcohol-fired thermo-magnetic generator and motor. It purrs like a kitten, but runs like a gazelle." The firstborn mounted the saddle behind the handlebars. His sister, hugging his waist, sat behind him. The youngest opened a sidecar door for his father, then climbed into the sidecar on the other side. A moment later the vehicle sped away.

Chapter 3

The evacuation trains arrived in Kilkenny after dusk, their speed slowed greatly by the crush of traffic. The trains pulled into the underground station, and the doors opened to an inclined ramp. Miss MacDevitt emerged from one of the cars pushing Esther's baby carriage and leading little Barry. As they walked up the ramp, the boy saw the gray-haired couple awaiting them at the top of the ramp.

"Gramma! Grampy!" the little boy ran up to his grandparents and threw his arms around their legs.

Michael Kelley lifted his grandson up in the air, saying, "Little man, we have to go start the motorcar."

Ann Kelley greeted Jan MacDevitt with a handshake and a kiss, then lifted the baby girl out of the buggy, "Got a phone call from my daughter about an hour ago. She and her man Theo are safe and sound. The raid was over, but did you hear about the horrible thing in the Gaeltacht! Those poor children! How could anyone be so cruel?"

The governess answered, "Yes, and to think that monarch of the Brits is a woman! Ya'hd think a female would be against war and killings, but she's worse than fifty menfolk."

After leaving the station, the women walked up to an ancient open-top vehicle. At the back of the after-seat a tapered cylinder stood up like a smoke stack. Michael was shoveling charcoal chips into the chamber through a grate. Then he took a cord from a huge storage battery and plugged it into a socket on the side of the stack.

"Ya see, grandson, when the light there above the socket turns on red, it means that the heat coil is partly burning the chips inside. The methane gas formed will go out this copper tube to the engine. Then we start 'er up with this crank."

Several minutes passed before the light came on. Then Mike grabbed the crankwheel atop the engine hood and with his hand cranked the engine up. Ann had placed the baby back into the buggy, settled into the driver's seat, and switched on the ignition. When the engine roared to life she slid over to the other side of the fore-seat. Her husband and the governess locked the baby buggy between the seats. Barry climbed in upon Jan's lap. The father took the steering wheel. The ancient car started forward, lurching at first, then accelerating smoothly.

"She is a real antique; she's alike the motor-car me Dad brought in the year thirty and ninety, right after we kicked the Brits out o' Leinster. They'd not had any petroleum gas fur cars or nonesuch things, so the coal-gas generators were all we had. She is still cheaper than gasoline or alcohol in the area, I think."

Ann tapped her husband's thigh, saying, "Let's use our nation's tongue, all the better to teach our grandchildren." A beautiful dialogue of Gaelic followed.

"I have a very good dinner for all of us tonight, a fresh ham shoulder with onions, tomatoes, and mushrooms. A potato spice-pie will be the dessert, and a strawberry preserve will be the topping," announced Grandmother Kelley.

Jan MacDevitt answered, "Do you use both white and sweet potatoes in a spice-pie? With the yellow yams you do need only half the molasses."

"I use honey instead of molasses, and I bake the outer crust first, and a rye-flour crust at that."

Mike then noted, "Ann here is well without a possible challenge, the most highly proficient craftswoman of the culinary arts! Her ability to make even wild game taste like aged beef or mutton would provoke jealous envy in the finest chefs in the better restaurants in Dublin or Athlone. And, I can point out, that includes the gourmet chefs from the planet Franco-Italia!"

After twenty minutes had passed, the motor car pulled up the driveway road to the red brick farmhouse of the Kelley farm. In the starlight the barn still glowed with a recent coat of red and white paint. After the engine had stopped and the passengers unloaded and headed for the house, Michael pulled the plug off the storage battery. Then he walked over to the barn to the windmill and generator aside the structure. A three-pronged safety cord and two-pronged adapter extension cord were coiled by the generator. He plugged the safety cord into the generator and plugged the extension cord at one end to the safety cord. He carried the unwinding cord to the motor-car and plugged it into the storage battery. He then turned about and walked to his house for supper.

✦ ✦ ✦

It was just before midnight when the last evacuation train reached Kilkenny. The five girls from Limerick prison disembarked with a flight sergeant as escort. They were still wearing the black denim prison outfits and would have panicked anybody remaining at the station. The sergeant said, "You will probably remain in those jail suits for a while, but if we remove the shoulder patch and put an Auxiliary armband on, you'll not scare these country folk out of their wits! Kilkenny is a good-sized city, but she ain't Athlone or Dublin for sure."

They reached a waiting military truck and climbed on the flat car behind the cab. After a half-hour bouncing along a slate road, they reached the Kilkenny Paramilitary Hospital and Nursing School. The facility was a non-profit civilian operation in peacetime but was automatically "drafted" in time of war. Any fully registered nurse was a commissioned officer, as were the doctors on staff. Student nurses, interns, and orderlies were non-coms. After being allowed entrance by the posted guards, the truck was parked outside a barracks building. The top floor, which stood at ground level, was the nineteenth floor. The other floors were underground. The sergeant and the five girls entered an elevator that went straight to the very bottom floor, over fifty meters below ground level. Leaving the elevator, they climbed aboard a three-wheeled tram and whisked down a slotted runway to a ten-story structure set below the roofed surface. This was the hospital itself. Then the girls got off and the sergeant drove away. A woman with graying hair and a stern face in a uniform with officer's insignia approached.

"Attention!"

As the five girls stood in rigid form, the officer continued, "I am Colonel Patricia McCracken, head nurse and instructor at this hospital and your commanding officer! At the very start of this, let me say that I didn't want you coming here as you will probably disrupt my nurses and the patients, regardless of your behavior, good, bad, or indifferent. Also, I checked your educational backgrounds. None of you have any qualifications to become nurses; therefore, you are to be orderlies. I have read the reports of your unfeminine behavior. You will keep that behavior to yourselves. You will keep your hands off my nurses, or I'll have all of you in the stockade. I have arranged for you to share a night room for six, with a student nurse who will probably be demoted to orderly. If any of you have any feelings on this situation, you had better air them out now before they go on the record."

Kate MacBride spoke for the five. "Sir? Or is it Ma'am?"

The colonel answered, "Use the female term, but only when there are no male superior officers present; otherwise address me as sir."

"Ma'am, we all signed up to be auxiliary gunners in Athlone. Shelley O'Rourke is probably ducking Brits' fire up there. Our families and *boyfriends* are there, and we had hoped to be with them now."

"So you are not entirely abnormal?" was the officer's reply.

"When a girl in prison can't see her man for months on end, another girl can be a warm bed partner."

"In any other kind of planet-nation your kind of unnatural acts would bar you from any military service, but Hibernia can't afford the luxury of a service of priests and nuns. But hands off my nurses or I'll kick your butts right into a cell," the nurse answered, then signaled the group to follow.

The five girls were led into the hospital building, then into another elevator. They shot up to the tenth floor. Colonel McCracken led the girls into a nightroom. It looked disturbingly similar to the one they had left at Limerick, with six cot beds, two each on three sides of the room. One bed, nearest the door, had a nightstand and the furnishings indicating a young woman's occupation of the bed.

The Colonel said, "Your roommate has a ten-minute break from your work shift in a couple minutes. Introductions will take place then." The colonel departed.

Immediately Caroline Quinn and Mairead McNutt walked to the back wall. They lifted one bed, moving it to the other. They lapped the mattresses together. Jamie Feeny and Mary Concannon likewise moved two beds together on the wall across from the bed with the nightstand.

A few minutes later, the colonel returned with a student nurse, who looked barely older than a schoolgirl. The colonel saw Jamie and M.P. standing by one bed, Caroline and Mairead by another. She muttered, "So, you are pairing off like you did in gaol." Then, turning to the girl behind her, "This is Private Teresa Lynch, student nurse. Hands off!" The colonel departed.

The girl was slightly shorter than the girls facing her. Her chest was almost as flat as M.P. Concannon's. Her hair, a dark wheat blond, had been tied into two braided pigtails, then looped up and tied back at the top. The braided hair loops were like handles. Her slightly crooked teeth and short-skirted nurse's dress made her appearance like that of a child.

"Call me Terri, please, everyone else calls my 'clumsy' or 'dummy.' I have been teased all day about being roommates with you. Why?"

After the girls introduced themselves, Kate explained, "We are just out of prison. I hope you aren't afraid of us."

"Why? Did you kill someone?" was the girl's reply.

Kate answered, "Jamie and M.P. are going to sleep in each other's arms. Caroline and Mairead are going to lock limbs. And if Shelley O'Rourke was here, I'd be sleeping with her tonight. You're sure you're not afraid?"

Terri blushed red and then turned pale. "You're not going to hurt me?"

Kate answered, "If I was in Athlone, my boyfriend would be screwing me in the ass right now. I haven't been butt-balled in months and I'm in heat, and you do have nice legs."

The young girl answered, "I must get back on duty soon," then walked to her table. She looked at the two photos on her table, one of an elderly couple, the other a young pilot. Crossing herself, she winced. "If only my family were alive. I was born here in Kilkenny, but we moved to Dublin when I was three; my brother was ten already. That's him, Garrett. He was a pilot.

I wanted to become a service nurse. I dreamed of my day graduating from nursing school; my parents and brother would be so proud. Then back in the last war, Garrett was killed. Mother dropped dead two days after the memorial service. I never thought the first patient I'd nurse would be father. He, he wasted away. I sold everything I inherited to pay my tuition at nursing school. It wasn't enough, so I enlisted. I must return to duty. Goodbye for now."

After Terri departed, Kate was asked by the other four girls, "She is kind of cute. You gonna rape her?"

"No, dammit, at least not for now. Hell, I couldn't force myself on that poor kid. Her life is worse than ours—we can't hurt her. Besides, that ramrod colonel might send us back to the goat's nest," was Kate's angry reply.

"Let's get to bed, I am tired," was Jamie Feeny's motion.

Kate answered, "I am staying up for a bit."

✦ ✦ ✦

When Terri Lynch returned to the nightroom at shift's end, she walked into the clothes closet on the sidewall on the side of the door across from her bed. As she modestly undressed, Kate's voice interrupted. "You are cute from the back. Turn around."

The nurse turned to face the buxom raven-haired girl who was twenty-five centimeters taller. Kate removed her denim top jacket and gray blouse and bra. Her massive firm breasts contrasted with the tiny form of the nurse across from her. In the pale light of a single bulb, the two faced each other.

Kate closed and locked the door behind her, then walked straight up to Terri. "You are lonely, like me, and I'm in heat. I need a bed mate. I can be your man; I am my boyfriend's woman, and I can be any woman's man."

The nurse protested, "Please, the colonel will . . . have both of us for breakfast. Please."

Kate's passion turned to anger. "Don't make me beat you into submission."

"Please don't." Tears began to flow down the nurse's eyes. Kate propped one of her legs behind Terri's, then struck her with the full force of her fist right in the sternum. Little Terri collapsed flat out on the floor. Kate threw herself atop her, one hand at the girl's throat, the other raised into a fist. Terri sobbed, "Don't hurt me, please."

Kate stopped. "Terri, forgive me. I didn't want to hurt you. It's just that I need a man or someone tonight. I could be so tender to you. Please, Terri, be my friend, be my lover."

Kate lowered herself prone atop the little nurse and kissed her on the mouth. She rubbed her breasts against Terri's chest and began to shove one hand into the nurse's panties.

Terri flayed her weak fists against Kate's back at first. Then her hands went limp, and then squeezed Kate warmly. Terri kissed the larger woman's cheeks, "Kate, we better stay in here. If the colonel sees our beds together, we will both be court martialed."

The big woman replied, "If you had refused me, I would have had to wait until my first time on leave. Then, either I'd go up to Athlone to find my boyfriend, or I'd have to go to a bar and pick up a streetwalker." Terri looked up at Kate in disbelief. "Yes, Terri, a working girl will take a dyke's money as quickly as she'd take a stud's."

"Kate, I'm feeling like I am wetting my pants, but it ain't that."

"Let's get up and strip totally nude." In a minute they eyed each other's juices dripping from the hairs between their legs. Kate laid back down on her back and pulled Terri atop her. As the big girl spread the organ below her waist, she guided Terri's mouth on to it. Then she pulled the nurse's legs wide, spread the inner cheeks, and put her lips against them. "Shove your tongue right into the slit and suck with your lips, just follow everything I do."

Minutes became ten minutes, then tens of minutes. The love juices flowed and were happily swallowed. Kate lifted up, taking Terri off of her, and turned until their faces met and kissed. "We must clean the juices from the floor."

"We have a mop against the other end of the closet," Terri replied.

After they cleaned the mess from the floor, they dressed in night clothes. Kate said, "Let's keep our beds separate for a couple of months." As the two girls headed to their beds, the other four awoke and applauded Kate's conquest and Terri's initiation to sisterhood.

"Goodnight, Kate," Terri said.

Kate replied, "Goodnight, lover."

✦ ✦ ✦

Dawn had barely begun to break on Athlone when the city began to stir. Priests and ministers of the old religions of Hibernians back on Earth gathered in DeValera Park. Amid the rubble of yesterday's attack, folding chairs were set up. People from all over the city gathered. Native Hiberians, IPVs, settlers, every sort of personnel entered the park. In addition to the Catholic and Protestant clerics, those of other faiths were present. Orthodox priests from planets like Sovietia, Transylvania, and Balkan; rabbis from planet Abraham; Islamic Imans from Turko-Persia and Arabia. Even Hindu, Shinto, and Buddhist clerics of the planets Hindustan, Sino, and Nippon.

The Taoiseach, Colm O'Hara entered the park, followed by his wife Margaret. A grandstand had been built overnight. The Taoiseach reached a crude podium. Then, summoning all his courage, he began:

"Ladies and gentlemen, today we are gathered to commemorate the memory of our innocent children. Our dear wee wanes, so unjustly taken. I have personally dispatched an emissary to the Interplanetary Federation to ask that the enemy planet be censured for murder. The Brittanians must be told they cannot slaughter children and brag of it."

Then the head of state left the podium and the clergymen began the memorial service according to ancient traditions.

The O'Rourke family was among the many well-known people attending the service. Young Cathal, the most religious of the family, led the family's participation. Seamus had taken his children when they were young to early Catholic mass, then to a Protestant chapel in the afternoon. This was the pragmatic nonsectarianism that the O'Rourkes practiced. Cathal held a missal in one hand, a King James Bible in the other.

For over an hour the service continued. Shelley got up from her seat and walked out and around to another side of the park. Beside a smashed fountain, Brigid Hallohan, Deirdre O'Toole, and the Quinncannon sisters were taking part in the service.

"Brigid," Shelley whispered, "we got trouble. They'll try to put Deirdre in a crummy orphanage, make a gink out of her."

"I know, but we can hide all over town. The Quinncannons took her last night; I'll take her to my place tonight," was the reply.

"I am going to pass the word to the other Tigeress girls and the other gangs too. We have a truce now."

"Yes, we can shift Dee around town until she's eighteen and can fend for herself."

"If only I could con Father into taking her in as a foster child. Or my Uncle Eugene, who lives in the marshlands."

As the services ended and the people began to leave the park, Brigid said, "I guess old man O'Hara took losing his two little ones badly."

Shelley answered, "Yes, he is kind of a spineless gink, but he saved my life and the lives of Kate, Caroline, Mairead, Jamie, and M.P. when half the people in the town wanted to hang us."

✦ ✦ ✦

Hibernia's ability to raise and equip its defenses would have been much easier had the nation been spared decades of political turmoil. The present government was called the Fourth Republic. The First Republic had ruled from the settling of the planet during the Great Migration to the Brittanic invasion of 2994. The provisional government of the uprising of 3085 became the Second Republic.

During the occupation of the planet by the invaders, practically all industry and mining was Brittanic owned. Except for a small number of shopkeepers and farmers, Hibernian people were impoverished workers. Taking the name Sinn Fein from the party of Earth history, the provisional government proclaimed a "Worker's Republic." A rigidly socialist constitution nationalized all industry. The tiny class of small store owners and farmers, the petty bourgeois, was subject to stern regulations, high taxes, and a drumfire of insult. *An Phoblacht*, the Sinn Fein party organ, propagated accusations that the propertied class was pro-Brittanic. A reverse class order was formed.

For twenty years the socialists ruled without challenge. The Sinn Fein party organization became the bureaucracy of the state industrial system. Then cracks began to appear in the social order. The workers in the various industries formed unions. They ranged from narrow craft unions of highly skilled technicians and artisans to wide-based industrial unions of the unskilled work force in the mass production industries. There were even unions to organize the supervisory and office personnel. They were all originally under Sinn Fein control. As time went on, however, they broke away. An ideological schism began.

The industrial unions began to demand reform of the socio-economic system on a syndicalist basis. An autonomous alliance of trade-union owned and operated producers and consumers cooperatives would replace the centralized socialist state. A federation of unions would become the government.

The craft unions consisted of the better-paid workers, the more highly educated workforce. Many of these workers brought state industrial bonds and considered themselves to be the real owners of the factories and mines. At the same time, despite every barrier they faced, the petty bourgeois merchants and landowners managed to grow. Small farms had increased from as tiny as one hectare to as large as five hundred hectares. Small stores grew to large merchandising centers.

Among the "merchant princes" of Hibernia was Samuel Clarke O'Hara. He had built a tiny one-floor dry goods shop into the largest department store in Dublin. He incorporated his business and sold shares to many of his employees. His speeches before church groups and letters to the editors of Dublin newspapers won him the undying loyalty of his employees. Even the union shop steward praised his advocacy of economic opportunity and freedom. He also won the wrath of the Sinn Fein party, which called for a boycott of his store.

In 3105 in Kilkenny, a convention of farmers, merchants, and skilled workers organized the Liberal Party of Hibernia. Sam O'Hara was the keynote speaker. As the audience roared with approval, he called:

"For a constitutional convention to set up a new government based on the fundamental right to own productive property, the right to use that property in commercial activity for a profit motive . . . based on a system of unfettered free market private enterprise, in short, capitalism!"

The convention adopted resolutions that called for re-privatization of all industrial activity not state run prior to 2994. Specifically, the mining and manufacturing facilities were to be sold off by either unit sales of plants or by stock capitalized to value of facilities. They even called for a study group to explore the feasibility of selling off activities that were state monopolies even during the First Republic. These were the postal service, cabalgram, electrophones, radio and viewscreen transmission, and electrical power.

The Sinn Fein party's response was a cry of "Treason!" Arsonists damaged the O'Hara department store in Dublin. The founding members of the new party received death threats. *An Phoblacht* called for a general strike and boycott to break the Brittanic-run interests that threatened the working classes. The general election of 3106 was cancelled. In 3108 elections were held to replace vacancies in Dail. The Liberals won every seat. In 3111 and 3113 the new party gained despite open violence against them. Sam O'Hara put his wife and family into hiding. A splinter faction of Sinn Fein formed by syndicalist unions held the balance in the Dail. In 3115 a petition for a constitutional convention was presented to the assembly. The government's response was to arrest Sam O'Hara on a fake charge of spying for Brittania. A Bill of Attainder was introduced to the Dail. It was to bypass the centuries-old abstention from capital punishment. Sam O'Hara was to hang. Then two sudden events took place. The syndicalist unions announced a general strike, declaring, "If the Sinn Fein can destroy the Liberal party, it can destroy us afterwards." Then the Hibernian military forces seized power. They surrounded the Dail. While not running or supporting any slate of candidates, the military ran the general elections for the Dail and the constituent assembly. The Liberals won handily.

Beginning in 3116, taxes were cut, state industries sold off, regulations eased. The unions were put under regulations. The cooperative plans of the syndicalists were ignored. The economy took off like a rocket all the way to the mid 3120s. The war only greased the boom farther. For the first time in years, real millionaires existed. Inflation caused by temporary printing of paper currency created economic hardship among workers. Sinn Fein gained enough seats in the 3126 election to bring the Third Republic to a crisis. Armed party militias fought with fists and rocks in Athlone and Dublin. Fights were even taking place in the Dail.

Sam O'Hara had retired from the Dail the previous year. His son, Colm, was Liberal Party whip and was pleading to save the country from civil war. He warned, "Brittania could trap us like a rat in this condition." Then, from an unexpected source, the crisis ended.

For over twenty years, Interplanetary volunteers had aided the Hibernian war effort. While most of the natives greeted and thanked their guests, some chauvinistic Hibernians began to use the derogatory term "Peevee." The IPVs in return became distressed and disgusted with the squabbling natives.

On a hot summer day, a thousand IPVs seized the Dail. Two young officers, Dietrich Becker and Victor Kalminsky, put the Taoiseach under house arrest.

With guards in the aisles of the Dail chamber room, the debate for a new constitution began. Colm O'Hara crafted a compromise constitution allowing a "competitive economic triad" between private, public, and cooperative sectors. Both nationalization of private industry and re-privatization of state industry was forbidden. For the first time in Hibernian history, private businesses competed with state electrical, postal, and communications services. On the other hand, the state again competed with private business in manufacturing industries. The cooperative movement also entered the economy.

As the economy settled down to steady growth, political activity declined. *An Phoblacht* and its Liberal rival, the *National Journal Gazetteer* continued editorial vitriol, but the masses ignored politics. No general election was held for over twenty years, but by-elections every two years caused the government to drift left to right to left again.

Nowhere in Hibernia did the term "triad economy" apply more completely than in Athlone. A municipal service provided electrical power on the west side, while the east side received power by a private company. In neighborhoods in the core of the city, people could hook up to one service in the front yard or the other service in the back yard. On the west side, the private companies running the shirt factories bought their electricity from the municipal service. They sold much of their product wholesale to a number of consumer cooperatives, including one run by the union representing the workers. On the east side, the state-run coal gasification plant bought coal from private mining firms and electricity from the N. Leinster Electric Co. People got their morning mail by the state postal service and afternoon and evening mail by private services. Almost everyone drank Enniskillen Ale, brewed by the Brewery Cooperative.

The Hibernian economic boom was further fueled by three factors. One, oil and natural gas, was found by a consortium of private companies in Munster quadrant in 3138. Two, a series of trade treaties with other planets between 3139 and 3147 increased exports and imports. Finally, settlers from the planets Turko-Persia and Arabia incorporated Islamic banks providing easy credit.

Colm O'Hara became the speaker of the Dail in 3137. Two years later he was appointed to an interplanetary trade mission. It was his diplomacy that led to the trade treaties.

In 3148 he became Taoiseach. Then the girls' gang trial began. The nation again teetered on the brink of civil war. Sinn Fein saw a chance to seize power. They even backed a Bill of Attainder proposed by a fanatic minister. It would have sent the six girls to the gallows. The Taoiseach lacked the will to grant a total pardon to the girls on trial; however, he addressed the Dail, opposing the Bill of Attainder. In one hour, nearly everyone in the chamber, including himself, was in tears. He pleaded for the life of "these young girls who might someday mother a hero who will save the nation." Only the minister voted for the Bill of Attainder, and it was rejected. The six girls went to prison, but the Taoiseach received only one letter of thanks. It was signed by the entire family of Commander Seamus O'Rourke.

A month after the trial ended, the minister who introduced the Bill of Attainder was found beaten severely and covered with greased lint balls. His mind was so damaged he became a flowershop boy in Dublin. It was rumored the girl gang members had assaulted him as punishment for demand the death penalty.

✦ ✦ ✦

North of Dublin, just below the Leinster-Ulster quadrant border, was the area nicknamed the Orangeland. It was so named for its inhabitants, the descendants of a painful part of Hibernia's Earth history.

At the dawn of the seventeenth century on Earth, English and Scottish settlers colonized the Ulster province in the northeastern corner of Ireland. This became known as the Orangemen after King William of Orange, a Protestant monarch of the late seventeenth century. They were steadfastly British in culture and loyal to the crown. In the nineteenth century, they found Home Rule. During the twentieth century, the six northern counties of Ireland remained British to appease this group of people. Even after Ireland was unified and totally free of Britain, the Orangemen remained distinct from the native Irish, the "Green" Irish. Somber, solemn Protestants noted for abstinence from drink or dance and stubbornly clinging to the English language, they formed an alien minority.

During the Great Migration and the colonization of planet Hibernia, they settled in Ulster quadrant named for the province on Earth.

Despite their Anglophile tendencies, they were as cruelly treated during the Brittanic occupation of 2994–3085 as the Green Hibernians. During the two previous wars of 3124 and 3149, the Orangemen had launched heroic assaults on the enemy quadrant, but their attempts to recover their homes failed. Now, again, this unusual people offered their services to the Hiberian nation in which they were an alien race.

Dr. Joseph McIntire was an Orangeman. Always dressed in a black suit and bowler, with orange tie, his appearance accented his serious mind. A nuclear physicist, he was in charge of the Alpha-X-10 project. At Cashel, in the Tipperary sector, be directed the operation to construct a force field around the planet.

When the peace talks broke off, he received a summons to report to Athlone. His mission, an up-to-date report to the Taoiseach on the Alpha project.

Dr. McIntire reached the Athlone in the afternoon following the memorial services. Entering the central building of the Defense Ministry, he was escorted to the war room. He met Colm O'Hara with an introduction.

"I am Joe McIntire of the Cashel research base. Let me say first, Mr. Premier, you have my deep sympathy in your hour of sorrow and the condolences of my people in the border country."

"Thank you, Doctor," Colm answered. "My wife is still taking it hard. Let me introduce you to Defense Minister Joe Flynn, my military advisor, Colonel Becker and the Athlone area Commander, Seamus O'Rourke. The other base commanders, Donahue, MacMullen, and the rest, will receive transcripts of your report."

The doctor immediately began his report. "Here are copies of the report for each of you. Here is a general outline. The Alpha project began in 3146 with an initial funding of 250 million grams of gold. The object is to create a force field of subatomic particles, such as photons and mesons. At our research base at Cashel, four hills form a box-like valley perfect for the first level test.

"Into one hill we have built a nuclear accelerator for separating sub-atomic particles. The particles will go through several amphilication boast-er, then into a projector-like laser. The beam released from the projector will strike a parabolic mirror on the hill across from the gun. The beam will deflect and spread a cone-like double shield across the valley back to the first hill on an east-west axis. The third hill, on the south end of the valley, has a laser surface gun. It will fire across the valley at an attempt to go through the shield. Its target, solidified plasma warheads on the fourth hill to the north."

The Taoiseach then asked, "If the first-level test is successful, what is the second-level test?"

"In Connemara, in the Galway sector, we have a radio to be built under it. The beam will broadcast a shield one kilometer above and around the tower. Needlehead fighters will attempt to destroy the tower with lasers. Then a radio-guided fighter will attempt to crash into the tower. The sec-ond-level tests will indicate if the force field can last ten seconds, minutes, hours, days, or years."

Commander O'Rourke then questioned the doctor as to how the opera-tional version of the field would work.

"We will use twelve viewscreen transmission station towers, all set at the frequency at channel 150. As you all know, there are no viewscreen stations between channels 145 to 155. That is to prevent interference. The beams will transmit up to specially designed shuttle craft, with volunteer crews, at eight hundred kilometers above the surface. The shuttles will broadcast the beams outward on a 360-degree horizontal plane."

"But the enemy controls the Ulster quadrant," was O'Rourke's answer.

"That is where your ship, the *Parnell*, comes into the operation. It will release the three shuttle craft for that quadrant. Three transmitting towers, one each in Dublin, Roscommon, and Galway, will beam their projections to them. Your fighter force will, no doubt, engage the enemy's quadrant at the lower altitude."

"Dr. McIntire," the defense minister asked, "what are the potential problems with this project?"

"The first problem is simply that we don't know if the damn thing will work. We could turn on the projector and it could blow up, or the particle beam could be a weapon like a laser. Second, if it does create a force field, we might need the entire electrical output of our planet to operate the field for as little as a few seconds. This could alter any plans you have to attack the enemy quadrant. If the force field lasts only a few minutes, you will have to turn it on just before the enemy's home fleet reaches eight hundred kilometers. This will give the force field the maximum time to destroy the enemy, then your fighters will have to finish the rest."

The Taoiseach then asked, "How much money will it take for the first-level test, and if it fails, what do we do next?"

"Fifty million gold grams for the first-level test. If it fails, we will be grouping in the dark. We are trying photons this time, but afterward we will have to try anything."

Minister Flynn repeated his objections. "This is a wild goose chase! Since 3146, 700 million grams that could have been spent to build two hundred Needlehead fighters, or fifty Bullethead fighters, or three hundred Werewolf rockets, have been thrown away. Mind you, it's not that the force field isn't a desirable defense system, but I don't believe it is possible."

Just then a messenger brought in a sealed envelope. The Taoiseach opened it. "According to our friends in the Underground in Brittania, Churchill is out as premier and Cromwell is in. Churchill will be sent to the Ulster quadrant with the next reinforcement convoy."

Colonel Becker, in shock, exclaimed, *"Ach! Mein Gott in Himmel, nein!* Now we are in more danger than ever. Cromwell will not stop with the destruction of this planet. He intends to build a Brittanic empire across the Outer Solar System. If he attempts this, the other planet-nations will have to form an alliance to stop him. It will be like the twentieth century World Wars. The civilization we have built here could be destroyed."

"Herr Taoiseach, I cannot remain silent. We must go ahead with this project. Cromwell must be stopped. And we must stop him, here and now."

With that, Minister Flynn gave in, saying, "I have argued with Seamus and Colm, but I can't argue with you, Becker. We apparently have no choice. Let's go for it."

The formal meeting broke up. Colm O'Hara said, "I have a bottle of poteen in my office, hid from my wife. You can all join me in a taste."

Dr. McIntire replied, "Myself, I'll have good strong tea, but the rest can indulge, I don't mind."

Then Seamus asked the doctor, "Is there any historical information in the Earth archives of anyone trying this before?"

"No, but it might be worth checking into," the doctor answered.

❖ ❖ ❖

The O'Rourke family sat down to dinner that evening, and after Cathal led them in saying grace, the four began. Seamus noticed the tube loaf sitting in the meat plate and asked, "What is it?"

His daughter answered, "A hog sausage, one kilogram. Cathal picked it up this very noon after the services were over. It was the last one in the meat shop. It has everything in it, smoked ham and bacon, tenderloin and chops, feet, nose, liver, kidneys, brain, and guts for its casing."

Eamon was the first to ladle up a bowl of hot soup. "Turnips, onions, radishes, rutabagas, carrots, and barley? What kind of soup is this?"

"They were the only vegetables left in the root cellar," Shelley replied. "And for bread we have some corn-rye rolls, three days old and kind of stale, but they'll make good dunking."

"Here is a fresh cheese I bought today, Father," Cathal announced as he presented a pale yellow cylinder of aged milk.

"And a pot of tea for all," Shelley added.

The family engaged in conversation, switching from English to Gaelic and subject to subject as they feasted.

After dinner they retired to the parlor. For half an hour they quietly listened to a radio news report. Seamus and his son Eamon noting every serious item. The announcer reported, "The uprising at the Limerick gaol for women was finally ended with the release of all guards and staff. Surprisingly, only one woman guard suffered serious injury during the time the prisoners controlled the island prison. The major question is, how did the entire prison staff become drugged?"

When Shelley began to laugh, her father immediately turned to her and asked, "You know anything about this taking place?"

His daughter answered with the same serious tone, "I might, but do I have your word of honor as an officer and gentleman you will not say anything to anyone else?"

"Shelley, that kind of infraction of law could land you right back there. Someone could have been killed." Her father's voice carried not just his paternal weight but the full authority of his military rank.

"They say thirty milliliters of canapec in a twenty-liter water urn could knock out one hundred people." Shelley rubbed her fingernails against her black denim top-jacket.

"You didn't." Her father was now totally shocked.

"I did. It was the only way to avenge all the abuses women suffer there— poor food, threats of beating, sexual extortion. I once saw three male guards poking one girl, all at the same time. One man's log was in her mouth, the second up her ass, and the third in her box. She let those pigs poke her just so her whole family could visit for ten minutes.

"One bitch of a guard threatened to use a riding crop on me and the other girls. She'd use it like a doctor's proctoscope. I hope she was poked with it herself a hundred times," Shelley answered, expecting the back of her father's hand at any moment.

Seamus was now completely disoriented. "If what you say is true, the staff there is guilty of criminal abuses. My God, how could such things be permitted to happen?"

His daughter quipped, "We had a saying in that goat's nest: They're in the right place, but on the wrong side of the key. I only got the C. P. juice by saving some of the money you gave me to use at the prisoner commissary and by letting a senile guard lick up my box like it was a bowl of gravy. All those five years during which I was sleeping with Kate MacBride, I was thinking of Lieutenant O'Connell. If it weren't for this crummy war, you would have a son-in-law and grandchildren. I want to have Sean's children, I do."

Seamus threw his arms around her. "Kitten, you are as brave as any pilot in the fleet. You're a hood, but you're my baby. If only your mother were alive, I. . . ."

Shelley answered, "Father, that is why I can't let them put Deirdre O'Toole in an orphanage. That's almost as much a prison. If you can't do anything about it, the Tigeress will hide her for the next two years if need be."

Cathal added, "Please, Father, Dee is my only friend in school. I don't want her to leave, to go far away."

Their father answered calmly but firmly, "The Athlone school for orphans is only a few blocks from here, Cathal's school, and the flower shop. She won't disappear. It's a safe, clean school. Underground, it's safer than this house. She'll be taken care of."

Shelley protested, "They'll try to make a gink out of her, but if she is a true Tigeress, they'll throw her out—if they take her in the first place."

Cathal asked, "There are three weeks of school left before summer. Couldn't she go to Uncle Eugene's?"

Seamus answered his children, "Gene and Beth would be good stewards for her. In fact, my young son, you could spend summer up there. Mulquix are caught summer and winter and he needs assistance with that trapline of his. Maybe your girl might sport a Mulquix skin coat. However, this will have to be discussed a few days from now. Eamon and I are headed to Cashel tomorrow."

"The Alpha project?" Shelley asked.

"How did you know that?" her father demanded.

"It is such an open secret, I wouldn't be surprised if the Brits try to muck it up," Shelley replied to her father. "I even heard of it back in Limerick gaol," she added.

The four sat down for a few minutes in almost total silence, each pondering the momentous events of the last seventy-two hours. Then Eamon spoke, "Father, here in the mail pouch are two photographs. The boy is Barry Lynch Kelley McLaughlin, age three, and the girl is Ester Sennech Kelley McLaughlin, age one."

Seamus, after studying the photos asked, "Captain Lynch and Lieutenant Sennech are the fathers of these children?"

His son answered, "The mother is a dancer at the Golden Peacock. She formerly worked at a very disreputable place. She had liaisons with the two pilots and bore the children after their deaths, both out of wedlock. She is married to what might be called a house-husband and has as close to a normal environment for the children as possible."

"What does that matter to you?" Seamus asked.

"I have considered sending these photos to the family of the late pilots. I am worried that they might be as prejudiced in their initial opinion as I was when I first met the couple," said Eamon.

"My son," Seamus replied, "for the first time in years you are showing the compassion that your late mother and I tried to instill in all of you. Look not to military regulations but into your heart; it will tell you what to do."

"I'll send these photos in the morning mail," Eamon answered.

Seamus then walked into an air-pipe-organ and sat down to the keyboard. Cathal surprised everyone by showing his concertina. While Eamon and Shelley handled the bellows, the father played the keyboard. With Cathal on the concertina, the family began a *ceili* of song.

✦ ✦ ✦

The following morning Commander O'Rourke and his son Captain O'Rourke reported to the Athlone base. They entered the office of Colonel Kalminsky. The base officer greeted them. "Good morning, gentlemen. I have just received a radio report from Cashel. Dr. McIntire arrived there by train and is already preparing the projector. I suggest that the two of you use a Bullethead craft; you'll be there in time."

The Commander answered, "That is an excellent idea. It will be a personal pleasure to get back at the controls of a fighter. The last time I flew myself was during our great raid on the enemy's capital city. Eamon here was my navigator and gunner. With a hundred Bulletheads we could win total victory."

As the three officers headed to the vertical launcher, the Commander continued his reminiscence. "If only those other tankers had not been lost, we could have battered Brittania into total surrender. If the *Parnell* was the attack ship that it was meant to be, it could win us the war single-handedly."

The two officers walked onto the gangplank, into the side door atop the Bullethead. The launch tube was opened on top. The engines roared awake. Then the manned rocket lifted up, straight out of the tube. In minutes it was one thousand kilometers up, then it leveled off to glide downward as it headed south to Cashel.

The rocket's retro-jets slowed the craft until it was able to turn itself back upward. Using its engines to slow its final descent, it landed vertically on a Cashel airstrip.

The two officers were greeted by Dr. McIntire. Without an initial report to Cashel's base officer, they took a motorcar to the four hills test. The three officials stood beside the laser on the south side. An electrophone kept them in direct contact with the projector on the east hill.

"This is Dr. McIntire. You have the power up to a maximum wattage?" After the man on the other end confirmed, he continued, "Turn the projector on as soon as the accelerator reaches maximum velocity."

Two minutes passed, and then the voice from the phone called, "We are firing the projector."

A pencil-thin beam hit the parabola, then reflected back out. A whitish aura, like a fog, covered the valley. The two men manning the laser fired. Just a second passed, then an ungodly flash and roar shattered the quiet valley.

"My God!" the Commander exclaimed. Dr. McIntire pounded his fists into the ground. Eamon stood silent, like a man who had witnessed creation come to pass before him. The laser beam had shot through the aura of force field and struck the plasma ammo dump on the northside hill. When the smoke cleared, half the hill had been blown away, leaving a ragged plateau.

The phone rang. The officer in the projector shouted, "The circuit panels are shorting out. I said we'd need a refrigeration system to cool them down. Now the whole control is going. We'll have to shut off the electricity in this room or a super fire will blow the whole hill to bits."

As the whitish aura vanished, Dr. McIntire called back into the phone, "Shut it down, and get out of there. We just blew the north side hill to kingdom come."

Commander O'Rourke muttered, "Those boys in the Earth archives had better find something on a force field; otherwise, we're dead."

Part 2
Flight to Earth

Chapter 4

A short distance from the Crystal Palace, the Brittanic parliament was the scene of a violent debate. The new Prime Minister Cromwell was attempting to appropriate funds to continue the war with Hibernia. Dressed in an ancient robe and powdered wing, the minister spoke:

"Gentlemen of the Lords and Commons. For nearly two thousand years we have attempted to raise the Irish race above its level of savagery. We tried to introduce them to our glorious language, our Anglo-Saxon culture, even our old religion back in those days when faith mattered. All this, and what was their thanks? Treason, disloyalty, alliances with enemy nations, rebellion, separation from the twenty-first to thirtieth centuries. Even now, with the assistance of the heathen Soviets, Nigerians, Nipponese, and Deutschers, they seek to violate our divine rights as master and overlord. I tell you, Brittania cannot build the empire of greatness that is her destiny until the Irish race, that obstruction known as Hibernia, is eliminated from the solar system."

After the Prime Minister accepted a roar of applause from the back-benchers in his party, he sat down. Cries of "Kill the micks! Wipe out Hibernia! Death to the Irish race! and the stamping of feet and hands created a din that threatened to shatter windows and break plaster. The building, dismantled brick by brick from Earth and brought to the planet during the Great Migration, seemed ready to collapse.

After the noise died down, the opposition leader rose to his feet. Gladstone was dressed in a very plain grey suit, only his beard giving him any distinguishing appearance. "On behalf of the loyal Opposition, I must reply to this distortion of history. Two thousand years ago we illegally seized the Irish nation, robbing those people of their identity and livelihood. We reduced them to the level of animals. When my namesake in the nineteenth century attempted to give those people back the right of self-determination that we had stolen from them, this very body prevented it. The war that spanned the entire twentieth century could have been avoided. Now we are making that same mistake again. We did not, do not, and shall not ever have the right to rule over the Hibernian people. Back in the early twentieth century, the Soviet politico Lenin predicted that we would expand our empire until we paralyzed ourselves. Our total economic collapse by the end of the twentieth century proved that forecast to be correct. Let us not make the same error again. Pull out of the quadrant! Leave Hibernia before we destroy ourselves."

While Gladstone's supporters clapped, members of Cromwell's bloc rose, shouting, "Treason!"

Cromwell then declared, "Her Majesty is behind the government entirely in our holy cause. More correctly, the government is behind Her Majesty, for she was the one who predetermined the truce talks to fail."

Gladstone led his party members in a walkout. He could not yet believe what he had just heard. He had felt that Cromwell had misled what once he believed to be a fair and noble queen. Now it appeared that she, not the prime minister, was the instigator of the conflict. In the back of his mind was the realization that the monarchy might have to be overthrown to end the war and save the planet from ruin. He considered attempting to contact the Underground.

❖ ❖ ❖

Several days after he returned to Athlone, Seamus O'Rourke reported to the war room of the Defense Ministry building. Dawn had barely shattered the night's darkness outside. In the war room the Taoiseach, the defense minister, and Dr. McIntire all were waiting. The Taoiseach opened the conversation:

"It looks like we've been handed a poor set of cards. Over 700 million grams of gold spent just to destroy a hilltop. Is there any chance we can attempt another test at another test site?"

Joe McIntire answered, "We can test again at Connemara using the second-level test method. We could use mesons instead of photons; however, we have no more assurance of success than before. If subparticles can't work, we would consider the higher-level particles, protons or electrons, or a combination of both particles and subparticles. Perhaps the beam might have to be delivered by a medium such as microwaves or gamma wave radiation."

Defense Minister Flynn asked, "Wouldn't that cost several billion to attempt that series of tests? I believe we should stop and consider alternatives."

Seamus O'Rourke answered, "I feel we should still wait for the Earth archives report."

✦ ✦ ✦

Above the night rooms of the pilots' barracks of the Athlone Defense Base, a large shower and locker was available. There pilots could change from flight jacket to work uniforms to formal dress uniforms and even civilian garb.

Sean O'Connell, Liam O'Brien, Conor Cosgrave, and several other pilots were reading a racing form. O'Connell read, "In the first race at Dublin this very afternoon, Kennie's Pride is favored to win at 10 to 1. Willy's Key is 7 to 1 to place, and Eggnest 8 to 5 to show. Gents, me thinks we should go for it and now!"

Cosgrave held a hat filled with coins. "Well, Sean, with the money from you, your girl Shelley, and the rest of us, she comes to thirteen gold, twenty-one silver, and twenty copper grams."

O'Connell walked to a pay electrophone, dialed a number, then began, "Sammy's Record and Music Shop? I have an order for sheet music. It's the Dublin Record Co. songbook, Volume No. 1 and the songs on pages 4, 3, and 7. We will pay the balance due on the thirteenth, the twenty-first, and then the twentieth of next month. O'Connell and Co. Glee Club, Athlone Defense Base."

Just then Lieutenant Colonel Kalminsky entered the locker room, "Attention! Did I hear correctly? Pilots, officers gambling, phoning bets to a barely disguised bookmaker? Do you know, Lieutenant O'Connell, what is a far more serious infraction than betting on a race horse?"

The nervous junior officer answered, "No, sir?"

"It is betting on a race horse whose mount will charge him out of the starting gate so hard that poor steed will collapse before the far turn. On the radio this morning, I heard Kennie's Pride will have a new and very poor jockey. These goes your trifecta, gentlemen. I hope none of you fools are married. Your wives will brain you. I know when I was a pilot of your age and rank, our whole squadron, including Seamus O'Rourke, bet a total of forty grams of gold on a steed that broke its leg and was destroyed. We spent our next furlough not with the wives cuddling, but attempting to ice fish near the South Pole. Good luck, gentlemen, you are going to need it." The colonel walked away from the demoralized pilots.

Cosgrave muttered, "I guess there is no such thing as a sure bet."

O'Connell replied, "Except for one. What will happen to the captain if Brigid Hallohan corners him so he can't escape her sweet body?"

O'Brien added, "Well, she'd better hurry, else his rod will dry up and away from lack of use."

Cosgrave added, "He'll go blind or crazy for sure if he doesn't get action soon."

O'Connell replied, "When we were in school Shelley and I were already loving good. I told him I'd pay a million just to see him in bed with a woman.

118

He answered saying I'd get a laugh when she plunged a knife into his back. What kind of man is he? He'll fight the whole Brittanic fleet single-handedly, but he is afraid of a soft, warm, cuddly sex-kitten of a girl."

Lieutenant Ranier said, "On my planet any male over twenty who has never had a girl is not considered a man, just a mere boy. Not even the women respect them."

The pilots were all having a good laugh, not realizing the flight captain who was the butt of the joking was right behind them.

"Attention!" Captain O'Rourke barked out. He walked past the pilots with the close eyeing of any out-of-order part of a uniform like in an inspection. He stopped in front of Lieutenant Ranier, nose to nose, "Lieutenant, have you seen any shortcomings in my performance as a pilot or officer, even taking into consideration that I am a mere boy?"

"None, Captain," was the reply.

"Cosgrave, have you ever heard of a priest of nun going blind or crazy because of their holy vows?"

"No, sir," was the answer.

"Ensign, has a physician told you that the male gland will atrophy from non-use?"

"I can't say I ever heard of it, sir," O'Brien replied.

"Then where do you get this candy-ass crap! They call this discussion a bull session, and do you know why? Because ninety percent of all of the 'conquests' you meatballs boast of are bull, lies. Some of you pilots are just as virgin as myself. But while you are ashamed, I am damn proud of my virtue. I will never throw my virginity away, or my heart, simply to live up to the phony idea of manhood passed down from bull session to bull session for five thousand years. I've heard this phony he-man idea since my first shaving days. It makes me want to puke!"

Then he walked behind a paving dividing line in the cement floor.

"If any of you don't believe that a man has the God-given right to retain his virginity until he decides when he has found the woman he loves, just step across this line. We will meet in the boxing ring in the servicemen's gymnasium. I do warn you, I was my academy class boxing champion for my weight class."

Five minutes passed without a single pilot crossing the line on the floor. The captain then declared, "I knew you so-called he-men were a bunch of candy-asses. A priest is more of a man than any of you meatballs. I am leaving this locker room. You will remain at attention for five minutes afterwards, and if I catch any of you not at attention before those five minutes are up, you will all be on report!" He departed.

Five minutes passed, then two minutes for good measure. Then the pilots sighed with relief. "My God," Cosgrave exclaimed, "he could have killed all of us. I've never seen him even go into battle so angry, even after his mother died in the last war."

O'Connell answered, "We hurt his feelings. I now realize that he is just like an uncle of mine. He married at age forty-three and never had a woman before. His wife was a spinster, the same age. Their two kids are six and two. Eamon does not have to make love to any woman, but he must soon fall in love with a woman. The goofy, painful kind of love that most men go through during their school days. It isn't his virginity that will drive him insane. It is that all-consuming hatred that will destroy him. If a woman, any woman, breaks his heart, he'll be stomping our butts until we are all out of the service or dead."

✦ ✦ ✦

The war room meeting continued into midmorning. Taoiseach O'Hara ordered a teapot brought in and the bottle of poteen he hid from his wife. Dr. McIntire deferred spiking his tea but gladly took a can of Multi-Veg-All, a canned juice of a dozen vegetables with a dash of spice. It was the cocktail the Orange border people toasted with.

"We will have to use the coolant system my aide at Cashel suggested," the doctor noted.

"It will at least prevent fires burning out the system before it works," Commander O'Rourke replied.

The Taoiseach then gave a somber warning. "The Dail Eirenann is unhappy at the thought of more money going into a project that so far has only succeeded in breaking windows."

✦ ✦ ✦

Just south of the heart of Athlone stood the No. 1 Secondary School. Its intake hall, administrative offices, and lunchroom were on the surface. Below there were five floors of academic facilities, classrooms, laboratories, and a library. The basement held the heating equipment and supplies and offside a bomb shelter.

The No. 1 Secondary School was called Thomas Ashe High School after one of Hibernia's ancestors on twentieth century Earth. The school's reputation as a center of learning had been overshadowed by a half decade of problems. The members of the girl gangs had created an atmosphere that terrorized teachers and won the hearts of the student body. A door would open to a girl's washroom and clouds of cigarette smoke rolled out. A teacher would open his top desk drawer and find the dumpings of ashtrays from the teachers' lunchroom. A physical education instructor berates a frail young boy for not doing 100 sit ups in a limited time period. He slaps the lad and casts aspersions on the boy's masculinity. That afternoon after the school closes the instructor tries to start his motorcar. He will find sugar had been poured into the gas tank. A shy freshman girl is snubbed and cruelly teased by two senior girls whose father is on the school commission.

Before classes begin the following day, they are standing outside of the building. A motorcycle runs down the street past the school. A series of greased lintballs pelts the girls, staining their dresses.

The gangs were identified by the color of the sweater they wore, the yellow and black of the Tigeress, the red of Imperials, the blue of Girl Knights, and the emerald of Green Devils. The girls of the different gangs did not fight each other on school grounds. They would walk to a meadow part of DeValera park. Then the two opposing girls would duel with their fists. While in school, the four gangs acted as one against their common enemies. The enemies were teachers, the principal, the school commission, and the snobbish girls of Athlone's social elite. Occasionally some tough boys who bullied other students came in conflict with the girl gangs.

The 8:30 bell rang in the administrative office. Sharrey Fitzgibbon a slim brunette student office aide, stepped outside the office to meet a library aide. "Hi, Deirdre," she said in a near whisper. "Miss Keane will stand outside the girl's john by the library at 9:00 A.M. Ten minutes later she will go into the teacher's john."

"You mean she'll sneak a smoke herself."

"Not only that, but they say a couple other woman teachers come in and play bridge for up to five grams silver."

Sharrey stooped down to the floor, like she was going to pick up a pencil. The two girls reached the floor. Deirdre reached down into the knee-high cotton socks she wore and pulled out a pair of cigarettes. Sharrey took them and put them into her sock. "We'll meet at lunch across the street in the park, Sharrey."

"Bye, Dee."

At 9:08 Deirdre O'Toole walked from the service desk at the front end of the library. She walked to the glass and wood side door, where she saw Miss Keane as she entered the teacher washroom. She turned around and walked back to the service desk, her hands behind her back. The teachers assigned to the library that period were in the office behind the service desk. This gave six girls, from the various gangs, the chance to slip out the side door, into the hall, and then into the girls' john. They found no one in the washroom but did find a cafeteria serving wagon. They propped it against the door so no one else could get in.

Two of the girls had large handbags, one containing a beer bucket, the other small tin cups. Another girl brought matches in one of her socks, a fourth had cigarettes in her blouse between the cups of her bra. In a couple of minutes they all toasted with beer, then lit up. One Imperial girl asked, "Will Deirdre join our party?"

"No," a Tigeress answered. "If she gets into trouble they will learn that her parents are dead and she will be transferred to the orphan's school."

The first girl shot back, "Why not let the orphans come to school here but live in their home?"

A Girl Knight replied, "That way they'll not become ginks."

121

A Green Devil asked, "Will Sharrey Fitz join us?"

"No, but she admires us and will help us just like most of the other girls here," the Imperial girl stated. "You know Dee has quite a boyfriend. Cathal O'Rourke saved her life, or so they say."

At ten minutes to ten the girls slipped out of the washroom, moving quickly before the smoke clouds could roll into the hall. They bunched up by the side door to the library. Deirdre had walked back to the near door. When the teachers were busy, she gave the signal. The girls slipped back into the library. The Imperial girl walked Deirdre to a shelf. The two stooped low, and a pair of cigarettes were handed to the library aide. She put them into her sock.

At the noon bell, Deirdre met Sharrey just outside the building, then they crossed the street. Deirdre carried a lunch bucket containing a long boiled sausage, a few bread rolls, cheese, and apples. Sharrey brought a tin bottle of tea and tin cups. After their lunch, they took out the cigarettes.

"You know what I heard?" Sharrey said. "They caught Miss Keane and Mrs. Winter and Miss Jones shooting dice."

Deirdre, exhaling smoke, replied, "If you could discover the teachers gambling operations, we could blackmail them. Say the principal was taking bets for all the teachers to a bookmaker. Or they are playing poker in the teacher lounges. We could get anything."

Sharrey's reply: "They would have to put ashtrays in our washroom. It would be our smoking room, and they would let us gamble too."

Just then Cathal pedaled by on his way to the florist shop. He started school ninety minutes before others, as was the case of student workers. He said, "Hi, Dee, and hello, Sharrey. I have a little good news. Mr. Corbett is adding mushrooms in the basement to the flowers we sell. Perhaps, Dee, you could get work there."

"Fine, honey," Deirdre kissed her boy on the cheek. "Do you mind?" she asked as she was about to take another drag.

"No, that doesn't matter to me," her boy answered.

"Want a pull?" She offered the fag to Cathal, who politely declined. Then he kissed her on the forehead.

Just then his sister Shelley and Brigid Hallohan came up, followed by the Quinncannon sisters. The two were fraternal twins. Clara was larger, though not disproportionately thick, with dry, mousy brown hair. Karen, who had wavy black hair, was slender. The raven-head lit a long thin black cigar. It was passed around to the other girls. As earlier, Cathal politely declined an offer.

Clara said, "We were wrong about you. You showed guts when that attack took out Dee's family."

Deirdre added, "I'd do the same for him."

Suddenly a scream filled the air. The girls and the florist shop boy ran to the center of the park in the direction of the cries for help.

They stopped just before the remains of a fountain. They saw a woman being harassed by three tough boys. The woman was wearing a black bonnet and a dress that covered her frame. The sleeves went to the wrist, the skirt down to the ankle. Gray, it looked like the dress that a grandmother would wear. On the ground lay a broken jar of orange marmalade. An orange meringue pie had been splattered on her dress. Two of the boys held her arms and the third began to hit her in the face.

Deirdre and Cathal ran up to the fight first. Deirdre yelled, "Let her alone!" When the boy punching the woman turned, she bent over and threw her shoulder hard into the boy's midsection, so hard he fell over to the ground. Cathal charged on the two boys who were holding their victim. When the thug swung a fist to the delivery boy, Cathal dived and grabbed one of the bigger man's legs. He lifted up, throwing his enemy on his back. Then, using gym-class wrestling skills half forgotten, Cathal rolled the thug up until his shoulders were pinned to the ground. The others arrived to throttle the third boy. In a minute the three were fleeing.

"Thank you all. I was afraid for my life," said the woman. Her hands covered her face. When she put her hands down, a pale face appeared. Sad dark eyes, the face pinched at the mouth, thin lips, and tears flowing down her cheeks. She removed the bonnet. Her hair was a dark reddish brown, like clotting blood with two orange ribbons.

"I am Agnes McKerr," she curtsied. "I live in the Shankill village near the border." The girls around her introduced themselves.

"What is an Orange girl doing in Athlone?" was Shelley's question.

"These preserves and the pie were to be a gift for Dr. Joseph McIntire. He is in town. My father and my brother, Billy King, are trying to meet him at the government building. He is to address our Twelfth Night celebration in July. We are going to hold our celebration here if your city fathers allow it."

Shelley asked, "Why, after fifteen thousand years, do you celebrate a Brit king? We are Hibernians, or have you forgotten?"

"King William of Orange was the founder of our people. Back on Earth, the twelfth of July was a symbol of loyalty to Britain, but now he is revered as our father. I know my people aren't liked or wanted by your people. On Earth you made a war with Britain until you controlled the whole island. In the twenty-first century you subjugated us. All we want now is to return to our homes in the Ulster quadrant. My family lives on a farm of only twenty hectares. Back in the quadrant, we have a deed for a thousand hectare lot."

She was nervous, but when Karen offered a pull on her black cigarette, she declined in horror. "My father'd pound knots on my head."

Shelley watched the tears running down Agnes's cheeks. She had read the history of the alien race, as the Orangemen were called. The sober religion controlling their lives, they lived near the border area, alone and isolated. Here before the Athlone girl gang leader and her followers was a girl who was worse off than any of them.

The girl finished, "We buy citrus fruits from the southland and sell the preserves to raise money for our English-language schools, but we will offer part of our money to help you rebuild your schools that were wrecked just a week ago."

Karen blurted out, "You will become real Hibernians despite yourselves."

After giving Karen an icy glare, Shelley said, "Forgive her. Karen often speaks without thinking. As the Tigeress leader, I pledge we will prevent anyone from harming you again." Then, turning to Deirdre and Sharrey, she added, "When you get back into school, contact the other gangs. This'll take all of us."

Just then two men, one much older, came up. Both were dressed in black suits. The older man spoke with anger, "What are you doing with these . . . heathens?"

"Father, please don't be mad at them. Forgive me, they protected me from three boys who—" The girl was cut short by a slap across the face.

Shelley, Brigid, and the Quinncannons threw the man down, while Cathal, Deirdre, and Sharrey throttled the younger, boyish man behind him. Shelley screamed into his face, "You dumb gink, three thugs beat her up and we saved her. Now you treat her as if she is in the wrong? What are you, creep?"

The girl tried to pull Shelley off the man, crying, "Don't hurt my father or my brother, Billy King!"

After the men got back up and introductions were exchanged, the older man apologized, saying, "Perhaps I jumped to conclusions. If your people intend to protect us, you have my gratitude." Then, with their daughter-sister, the two men left.

Cathal looked at his watch, saying, "I'd better hurry. The floral store will open soon."

As he pedaled off, Shelley said to him, "I am going to the Golden Peacock. Afterward I am going to Brigid's apartment. Father and Eamon are remaining on base." Then Shelley and Brigid departed.

The Quinncannons walked off saying, "Lunch break is near over."

All that remained were Deirdre and Sharrey. The 12:55 bell rang. The two girls ran across the street and ducked below a low walk wall. Then, after opening the door leading to the administrative offices of their school, they slipped in. As they were about to go to separate classes, Deirdre said, "Thanks for helping the girls have a party. Want to be a Tigeress?"

Sharrey replied, "My sister Connie would brain me with a camogie stick if I joined, but I'll help you in any way possible. Thanks for the cigs."

❖ ❖ ❖

A week had passed. Another meeting was held in the war room at dawn. The Taoiseach, the defense minister, Commanders O'Rourke, Donahue, and MacMullen were there. The Taoiseach was cheerful:

"I have good news. Our search of the Earth archives paid off. We have discovered that a force field was successfully operated on Earth at the dawn of the twenty-first century. The Americans were the ones who created it."

Dr. McIntire entered the meeting room, followed by two men and a girl. The first man looked like a Nigerian with wooly black hair and brown skin. The other man had a badly scarred face and grey hair. The girl was petite with brown hair. She followed close behind the second man.

The colored man spoke. "I am Sammy King. This is Roger Steck and his daughter, Betty Ann. We are all refugees from America. We arrived on your planet just five months ago. We are part of the scientist Underground, trying to liberate our country from the environmentalist dictatorship that has vexed our people for one thousand years."

The second man, who walked with the limp resulting from many beatings, spoke. "Our country's population is now about 130 million, spread from Hudson Bay to the Yucatan peninsula. Our economy is beginning to revive a bit. Electrical power is now in a supply sufficient to allow radio and television transmission. We have cleared enough debris from our highways to use motorcars, but at speeds the equal to forty kilometers per hour, only one-third of the speed for which the roads were designed. A four-lane divided highway has only two lanes used for motorcars. The other two lanes are used for pushcarts, horsedrawn wagons, people on foot, even people on roller skates. On the farms, horses or steam-driven equipment are used. The cities are mere shadows of their once proud glory. I and my family lived in Chicago. In the twentieth century, 5 million people lived in the radius equaling eighty kilometers. Only a half million live there now."

The young girl then spoke. "When Dad was a boy, back forty years ago, anyone passing a petition to reactivate the nuclear reactors was arrested as an environmental saboteur, jailed for years without trial and beaten cruelly. Now, at least, if we petition and a fight takes place between our workers and the enemy, the arrest is for disturbing the peace and we do get bailed out. The scientist Underground has cells throughout the country. We have even some of our supporters in government positions. But some of their spies have infiltrated. One and a half years ago a number of teams were sent to the Outer Solar System. They were to try to enlist the support of one or more of the nation-planets to assist us in a revolt. We understand that you are trying to build a force field. The Odin project was begun in 1987 and the force field was first tested successfully in 2004. The entire North American continent was to be shielded from Soviet nuclear-tipped missiles by 2013. But the project was cancelled in 2011 by the environmentalist government. I am sure the technical information is available in one of our secretly located Underground centers."

Taoiseach Colm O'Hara then spoke, "I believe that our government could make an offer. We will help you overthrow the Ecolo-facists ruling America in return for the plans for a force field."

Roger Steck answered, "We can radio our colleagues on the other nation-planets. An ultra-hyperlight-factor mail shuttle could have a message there in less than two and a half months. They could even send back a computer printout of all available technical data."

Sam King answered pessimistically, "But you might need a whole team of technicians to actually put it into operation. We might have to bring one of our entire cells to your planet."

The defense minister then asked, "Do we have a hyperlight transport? If not, we will have to send the *Parnell*."

Commander O'Rourke arose from his seat in shock. "This is impossible. The *Parnell*'s hyperlight capability is only factor 2. Even if we tooled the engines up to factor 8, it would take two and a half years to reach Earth. We will have to study this carefully. The *Parnell* will have to reach a hyperlight factor of at least 50, or we will be too late."

Defense Minister Flynn then made a suggestion. "We could remove the two aft fuel tanks. Then we could put up on-board engines we have built for the tanker *Henry Joy McCracken*. It could increase the speed to factor 15, even factor 20. We have not even begun building the *McCracken*, and the engines are available."

Then Seamus, regaining his confidence, remembered, "My orderly's father, Leon Kamzov, was an engineering specialist for the Ministry of Transportation of Planet Sovietia before he settled here. Corporal Kamzov, my orderly, mentioned that they were working on an advanced engine that could propel a transport at speeds up to factor 60. Because we have a trade treaty with planet Sovietia, we could request borrowing their engine design. We could use it as an operational experiment, then report the results."

The Taoiseach answered, "An embassy meeting could be arranged to propose borrowing that kind of technology."

Dr. McIntire added, "If we can go to Earth, I want to go along. I want to see the material first-hand."

The other base commanders, Donahue and MacMullen, had been silent until then. Then Donahue spoke. "I believe we should have a contingency plan in case the enemy launches an all-out attack while you are gone."

Commander MacMullen added, "Can the *Arthur Griffith* handle the refuel jobs by itself?"

Commander O'Rourke answered, "Captain O'Dwyer and his crew are highly competent. I propose the *Griffith* rise to the station of the *Parnell* as the *Parnell* leaves latitudinal orbit."

The Taoiseach then stood up again. "Gentlemen, I believe we now know exactly what must be done. It is simply a matter of doing it."

By the evening of the same day, Commander O'Rourke had returned to the *Parnell*. He entered the bridge and immediately instructed the radio operator to signal the *Griffith*. In a minute, Captain O'Dwyer reported, "Commander, sir, I have received the instructions from the Defense Ministry for receiving the fuel load from the *Parnell*."

The commander answered, "Captain, you are to immediately pull your craft from your orbiting altitude and pull up along my ship."

The captain replied to his superior officer, "We are ready to go at once, sir. My crew has a number of welding technicians and extra pressurized suits for work outside the ship. We can transfer the crew members and equipment when we reach you."

The commander answered, "Excellent. Work crews are going to be sent up by shuttle craft from Dublin and Athlone, as well as the South Pole. After studying the blueprints for those engines, we may need to dismantle only one fuel tank. The Taoiseach is right now attempting to contact the Soviet Embassy."

In half an hour, the two tankers were side by side. From vacuum hatches, workmen in spacesuits emerged. They carefully walked out a magnetized footpath along a safety chain. As a further assurance against drifting off, each man had a guidance jetpack built into his spacesuit. The worker walked to the stern ends of the ships. The men on the *Griffith* had brought out a special hose. The line was connected to the aft fuel tank, then a hand jet was attached to the hoses, which shot across to the *Parnell*. The hose was plugged into the aft tank of the larger ship. Pumps began to operate on both ships, drawing in on the *Griffith*, pumping out on the *Parnell*.

Captain O'Dwyer radioed to the bridge of the *Parnell*. "Commander, at the rate we are pumping the transfer will be completed by midnight."

"Good," the commander answered. "The second step of operations will begin tomorrow. I hope that Taoiseach can succeed in the diplomatic side of this operation. Embassy affairs are a trial to my patience."

At the embassy of the planet Sovietia, the Taoiseach had been received with courtesy despite the short notice. The ambassador was Her Excellency, Ludmilla Samsanov. A veteran diplomat, she had been the official who represented her planet's government in the negotiations leading to the trade treaty of 3142. She admired Hibernia's courage in its fight to gain independence; however, her government had been neutral in the conflict—as neutral as any planet that allowed its citizens to become IPVs. The arrival of Leon Kamzov, late of the Soviet Transportation Ministry, further divided her feelings.

Former Colonel Kamzov was a tall man whose black hair was just beginning to gray. His eyes were a blue-gray. His face was still handsome, and he would have been a very available bachelor if he were not a husband and father. The ambassador was small and flaxen-haired. She was in a very plain outfit as the meeting was on short notice. The ex-colonel was in a civilian outfit, as he was now in neither Soviet or Hibernian service.

The Taoiseach addressed the envoy. "Your Excellency, as you know, there is a treaty between our two planets, a treaty providing for the exchange of commercial and scientific information. I am here to make a very special request based on that treaty—a request upon which the survival of my nation-planet may hinge."

The ambassador answered politely. "Mr. Premier, I have been informed of the nature of your request. I can tell you only that the communiqué is being sent to my planet's capital. The colonel here has explained the details of the technology you are seeking. He believes it might be necessary to have our technicians on board the craft. This might prevent any kind of accident deep in space."

Then Leon Kamzov addressed the Ambassador Samsonov in the familiar title of their homeland, "Comrade, as you may know, the Supreme Soviet passed a resolution declaring our support for the Hibernian struggle for freedom from Brittanic colonialism."

The ambassador replied, "Colonel, my personal concern is to prevent your spacetanker from literally blowing up. My official position is to maintain at least the appearance of our neutrality in the war that has commenced between Brittania and Hibernia. If I could be the one to make the decision, the craft would have to come to our planet to receive the necessary engines and modifications. If we were to send a transport of equipment here, it could directly involve us in this war. May I remind both the colonel and you, Mr. Premier, our planet has no war-making capacity."

The Taoiseach then removed the niceties of diplomacy. "Madame Ambassador, if Brittania succeeds in destroying our planet-nation, their next step will be to conquer Hindustan. Then Nigeria, Arabia, Turko-Persia. With each conquest they will have more resources to build a war machine. They mean to turn the entire solar system into a Brittanic empire. We must have factor 50 hyperlight capacity. We much reach Earth and learn how to copy the American's force field of 2004. We must defeat Brittania, or you will someday have to fight them yourselves. It would be like the disastrous World Wars of the twentieth century. In the simple name of humanity. . . ."

"Mr. Premier, you have my personal support, and I will try to influence my government. However, we must be discreet," Ludmilla Samsonov replied.

The three had sat in a small, almost insignificant side office off of the main entrance to the embassy building. Inside the room where stationery was stored, no one could imagine the physical beauty of the red brick building. It had no gate as the relations of the country had been excellent. The ambassador led the Taoiseach and ex-Colonel Kamzov into the hallway from the entrance up a stairway to a formal dining room. A samovar held water for tea and a decanter of vodka sat in an ice bucket. The ambassador then said, "Gentlemen, I propose we toast the success of our efforts."

✦ ✦ ✦

The following three weeks were marked by tremendous activity. The first crews came up by shuttle from the South Pole base. The crews worked four thirteen-hour days before returning to the surface. Then, in successive order, crews from Dublin, Athlone, and the Roscommon area followed. The after fuel tank was removed, followed by the aft-mid-section tank. When the first tank was removed, there was sufficient space for the engines to be brought up. The second tank was removed for the room for the equipment expected from planet Sovietia.

For Commander Seamus O'Rourke, the operation was a more heady intoxicant than the best poteen and stout. He went forty-eight hours a stretch without sleep, mulling over blueprints, radioing the Quartermaster Corps for adequate supplies. His only relaxation during this period was an evening game of chess. When the work crews came from Athlone, he brought his son, Eamon, into his private quarters for the evening's match.

"How is the morale of our pilots working on the outer hull?" he asked.

"Some of the married pilots are complaining, and Lieutenant O'Connell was crabbing a bit. I guess his plans involved Shelley," his son replied.

"Yes. When this war is over, you may have a brother-in-law. In fact, you may even have a sister-in-law. That girl of Cathal's is as mischievous as your baby sister was at that age. If your dear mother was alive, she'd already be selecting white silk and satin for the wedding gown. It's just thinking of it that makes me miss her all the more and wish I could end this damn war. I'll tell you one thing, they won't marry until after this war is over. There are already too many war widows and widowers."

"Father, I think pink would be more appropriate for Shelley instead of white. I've heard of showgirls wearing scarlet red when they wed."

"Eamon, must you always pass judgment on people's human frailties?" Seamus answered, shaking his head.

✦ ✦ ✦

After three weeks the major work was completed. Commander O'Rourke returned to the surface for another pre-dawn meeting in the war room. The Taoiseach, Defense Minister Flynn, Dr. McIntire, Sammy King, ex-Colonel Kamzov, and Colonels Becker and Kalminsky were all present. Also present were Commanders Donahue and MacMullen.

Taoiseach Colm O'Hara spoke first. "We have good news and bad news. The good news is, first, we will get those new engines the Soviets have. Also, we know the next move the enemy is going to make. Now the bad news. First, we have to go to Sovietia to pick up those advance engines, and their technicians will be on board. Second, we don't know exactly when they will make their next move. The others present will explain the details."

Dr. McIntire and Leon Kamzov together spoke. "These advanced engines require a modification of the plasma used as fuel. It is dangerously unstable in the hyperlight range of between factor 40 and factor 50. Soviet technicians are going to be on board. Otherwise the ship could be scattered across deep space."

Commander O'Rourke asked how long would it take to modify the engines and received an estimate of two days to two weeks.

Then Sammy King, the American refugee, spoke. "Our operatives in the other planet-nations are all converging on planet Sovietia. They will come on board the *Parnell* with the technicians. However, when we reach Earth, the Soviet personnel should remain on the ship. The Americans could be panicked by the appearance of 'Rooskies.' No offense intended to Colonel Kamzov, but there is an atmosphere of xenophobia back home."

The defense minister decided to inject a note of humor. "If Commander O'Rourke had not called back to the quartermaster corps a dozen times, he'd have ship full of turnips with no meat for the gallery or ale for the servicemen's recreation room. Also, he would have a large supply of women's bras for the auxiliaries."

After a good five minutes of laughter, Colonel Kalminsky then addressed the meeting. "Gentlemen. From the last war and the attack last May, we have almost two squadrons of enemy fighters. By removing the Union Jack insignias, they could become a phantom squadron, flown by our own pilots. When the Brits bring down their next convoy, they could be the perfect ambush. They could get a first strike, maybe five minutes, then break off, and our own fighters could finish them off. I have discussed this with the commander's son."

Commander O'Rourke replied, "That is exactly the kind of operation my son can really excel in. His subordinate, Lieutenant O'Connell, is a natural-born gambler. It would appeal to him as well."

Finally the defense minister announced, "Our friends in the Underground report the enemy will send a replacement convoy in the next month or so, three hundred fighters and several transports. A curious note to this says the transports will be carrying old-fashioned aerial bombs, the kind to be carried on a fighter's wings and dropped at low altitudes and speeds. It is a throwback to twentieth century warfare. What could be the purpose of this?"

Colonel Becker read the report and, after a few minutes, answered, "They might send a flight of craft just over our frontier to knock off our forward scanners. A second wave could hit Athlone or Dublin undetected. Or it is to be a terror weapon to hit the border villages."

Commander MacMullen then shot back, "If that is their plan, I say we should ambush the transports. Go right past the fighters and hit those freighters. My God, enough innocents were slaughtered in the last attack. We can't let it happen again."

Commander Donahue then said, "The convoy will come in by the North Pole, the perfect place to ambush the convoy, and it would be the perfect time for the *Parnell* to break away."

The defense minister ended the discussion. "Gentlemen, we have the rumor that Gladstone will contact the Underground. He might have the exact date of when the convoy will come in."

✦ ✦ ✦

Like Hibernia, the planet Brittania was divided into four quadrants. The northeast quadrant was the English sector. The southeast quadrant was populated by the Celtic minorities of Brittania, the Scots, and the Welsh. This was the reverse of the Earth island Britain. Canada was the northwest quadrant, and the southwest quadrant was Australia and New Zealand.

Liverpool sector was straight south of London, the capital city. The eastern edge of the city was a zone of sleazy theaters, porn shops, and massage parlors. One flight up the available women awaited male clients.

It was past midnight. The gentleman who walked alone up the stairway from a broken down pub looked uneasy. Sweat rolled down from his brow to his beard and down his neck. His palms soaked the plain brown envelope he carried. He reached an apartment marked 14 and knocked. In a minute, the door opened. "Hi, love. What's your pleasure?" came from the woman inside the door. Brown hair, blue eyes, and a face ghastly with make-up. A bra and panties with clear vinyl boots were all she wore.

"Call me Candy, love," she said as five ounces of silver were dropped into her palm. "Want a drink? You seem kind of nervous. Worried about your old lady?"

"No," the man answered. "My wife is gone five years now." The nervous man sat down on a silken sofa, and then the girl sat right down on his lap.

"You want me to rub your back? Why don't you remove your outer garments for a start?" the girl asked. After several minutes of inaction, the girl became impatient. "What's the matter with ya?" Don't insult me by paying me for nothing. It's against me ethics. I do have to think of what me peers think. Are you one of those odd ducks who just talk?"

The man finally answered. "I actually do little before talking a bit. I do little indeed."

The girl rose off his lap in shock. "You, you are the man I am to receive papers from? You are Gladstone. I, I—it's an honor to have you here whether we do anything or not."

The man was in shock. The girl then teased him, "You're surprised. I'm just a good-time girl, but I am a patriot. I want our planet freed from that monster Cromwell and his sow queen. Her most Brittanic Majesty, my ass. I'd be a better queen than that old witch. And Cromwell—they sez that the bastard's pleasure is beating little children. I'd never beat a child. Ball a child, yes, but not beat 'em. I'd never take Cromwell to bed, even for a whole ounce o' gold."

Gladstone handed her the envelope, "This is a timetable for the next convoy to the Ulster quadrant. It is a code, but I believe you have the decipher. I can go now."

"Oh, stay, love," Candy answered. "It would be the height of my career to please you. You are a kind and decent man. Let's to bed now."

Gladstone looked up and down at the girl, whose profession was men's pleasure. "Miss Candy, it's been so long since my dear wife died. I've forgot what a woman's body feels like."

"I can show you how to do it all over again, love. Please stay. If any man deserves good lovin', it's you," was Candy's answer.

With that, Gladstone yielded and undressed. As the two slipped into a large bed, Candy said, "I'm going to knock your socks off."

The afternoon following the dawn war room meeting, Commander O'Rourke and his son returned to their home. Daughter Shelley and the youngest Cathal were waiting. For Seamus O'Rourke, it was one of the most painful moments of his life. The failure of the Alpha project at Cashel had depressed him deeply. The weeks of working and preparing the *Parnell* for its flight to Earth had been an intoxicant. Now the hangover arrived, the realization he might never see his children or the people of his planet again.

"Shelley, Cathal, I have something very serious to tell you. Your brother Eamon already knows," he began.

"What is it, Father?" his youngest asked with the look of fright he had often had as a boy of less than ten.

"I am leaving for planet Earth and may be gone for up to a year, my children," the father answered.

"Is it something to do with the Alpha project?" Shelley asked, understanding the sadness in her father's face.

"Yes." He turned to Cathal, still too young to fully understand. "If I get back here in time, we will have a means to whip the Brits once and for all. But if I don't get back, or I am too late, it will mean. . . ." The words couldn't come out of his mouth, only pain showed on his face.

"Does it mean we will all die, Father?" the boy asked as a tear rolled down his cheek. The father nodded, then his arms pulled his children close to him as the family all began to cry. Seamus could hardly control his voice.

"Cathal, you obey your older sister and treat that girlfriend of yours like a lady. Shelley, you act like a lady around Lieutenant O'Connell and obey your brother Eamon. Eamon, you are to take care of them. Oh, if only Bernadette, your mother, were alive."

The four walked as one to Seamus's room. There, on a mirrored dresser, in faded black crepe, was a picture of the woman who had been wife and mother for twenty-two years. Through eyes dimmed by tears, Seamus looked at the picture of the girl he had courted as a young pilot, wed as a captain, raised a family with as base officer.

"Bernadette, wait for me. Wait for all of us. I know you're watching over us. I'll join you, maybe in a few months, maybe in a few years, but please, my wife, wait for me."

✦ ✦ ✦

If the time and place was Athlone 3153, the atmosphere was Vienna, 1900. The Golden Peacock music hall was holding its monthly dance auction for charity. This time the proceeds would go to the Gaeltacht School rebuilding fund. The showgirls were on hand in black evening gowns. Each girl would be auctioned off for a dance ticket. This on top of a three-gram gold invitation ticket and cash bar would raise a great deal of money. The event was always chaperoned as the Golden Peacock had a respectable reputation. The only showgirl not up for auction was Mo Kelley. She was sitting in the audience with her dance partner for life, Theo McLaughlin.

This was a very special dance. The elite of Athlone society were present, including those who ordinarily would never come near a music hall, the Taoiseach and his wife, the mayor, members of the school commission, Colonels Becker and Kalminsky and their wives.

Also present were Commander Seamus O'Rourke, his less-than-willing son, Eamon, and his daughter, Shelley, whose escort and dance partner was Sean O'Connell.

A slick-haired announcer stood center stage. "Ladies and Gentlemen, the Golden Peacock is proud to hold its monthly charity dance for the Gaeltacht School fund. In just two minutes, the first dancer will come up center-stage and the bidding will begin."

The first dancer was an ebony delight from the planet Nigeria, almost as dark as the gown she wore. Three IPV pilots, all of her own homeland, bid up to twenty grams gold. When the auctioneer announced, "Sold," the man with the winning bid paid a man running an electric cash register and took his ticket. He met the girl at the first row of seats, then they walked arm in arm to an improvised dance floor. There, a full orchestra was preparing a "Night with the Strauss Family," the music matching the décor.

In the next ten minutes three other girls passed. Then Pamela Fuchida O'Reilly came to center stage. After two men—obviously paunchy businessmen—had bid against each other up to twenty grams gold, the audience all turned around in surprise. "Twenty-three grams gold and fifteen grams silver!" The voice was that of a Hibernian legend. The other two men decided to beg off. The auctioneer yelled, "Sold to the gallant defender of Athlone, Commander O'Rourke."

Shelley and Sean both clapped with approval as Seamus went up to hand his dance ticket to Pam O'Reilly. Eamon, however, got up and slowly walked out of the auditorium in shock. He walked to an alcove outside a pair of washrooms. He thought, "How could Father do such a thing? It was not enough to get me to come here, but. . . ."

A voice from his recent past came up behind him. "What's wrong, Ace? Your father more of a man than you think an officer should be?"

Eamon turned around and, through a jet of smoke, he faced a smiling Brigid Hallohan. "I, I don't understand it," he muttered.

"Remember, I told you that when my mother worked at this very same music hall, your father often sat in the front row, and he did catch a couple of garters," Brigid answered. "Eamon, this is only a charity dance. It's not like Pam is going to take your father to her apartment. But I wouldn't blame them if they did plan to meet later. Your father is a man," she added, delighted by Eamon's suffering.

He replied, "Miss Hallohan, the last time we talked I told you only half the reason why I don't chase women like most guys. It's that I don't want to get my feelings hurt, or worse, hurt some poor young girl's feelings. Treating a girl like a lady is the only way I know how."

"You really sound like my father, Eamon. Remember, I can be gentle to you if you aren't afraid. I will have to go now. I will be up in a few minutes."

As she started away, Eamon thought to himself, "Am I really afraid of life?" He found himself attracted to the woman who had threatened him with seduction. He walked back up to the auditorium.

In five minutes the announced blared out, "And now, ladies and gentlemen, it is my pleasure to announce the Queen of Athlone, Miss Brigid Hallohan." Several business types soon bid up to twenty grams gold. One, a balding man, then bid twenty-three grams of gold. The auctioneer raised his gavel, "Do I hear twenty-five grams gold? Twenty-three grams once, twice—"

"Twenty-seven grams gold!" The whole audience again turned in shock. Eamon O'Rourke had made the bid. The businessman declined the challenge. When the auctioneer announced, "Sold," Pam O'Reilly elbowed Seamus, saying, "Your son is asking for it. Brigid has had plans for Eamon for some time."

"My son is an officer and a gentleman. He can take care of himself," the father answered.

"I am talking about Brigid Hallohan. When she wants to bed a man, he doesn't have a chance," was Pam's answer.

"Perhaps a romantic affair in my son's life could do him some good," Seamus replied.

When Eamon handed his dance ticket to Brigid, she kidded him, "Hey, big spender. That is just a dance, but we can arrange to meet later too." As they walked past Shelley and Sean, Shelley raised her thumb and forefingers of one hand in a circle of approval.

When the last girl was auctioned off, the orchestra began, "The Blue Danube Waltz." As they danced, Eamon whispered to Brigid, "I think I would like to see you again."

"We can meet in a couple of days," she answered.

"I don't know exactly what to do," Eamon replied.

"I'll lead," Brigid answered.

After two hours there was an intermission, a rest period for the orchestra. As Seamus headed for the men's room, he met Brigid.

"Miss O'Reilly says you have some intentions toward my son," Seamus said.

"My intentions were originally strictly dishonorable, but I have decided to be nice to him. He is lonely. I can be a very comfortable friend for him," was the dancer's answer.

Seamus replied, "I just want to remind you, he is really very sensitive underneath that ramrod exterior, and he is a gentleman."

"Commander, breaking a man's heart is not my idea of a good time. Deflowering his innocence is. In fact, if your youngest boy didn't have a girlfriend already, he would be the next boy I'd go after." Brigid smiled wickedly.

Seamus answered, "Please, just don't destroy him." He finally entered the men's washroom.

When the band started again, Shelley and Sean talked while dancing. "Sean, Father said he's going to Earth. I'm scared. We might never see him again."

"Shelley, if he doesn't return, we'll all meet in Valhalla."

"You know, Sean, we better control ourselves. If Father returns and I am in a maternity hospital, we'd both land in gaol."

"Shelley, I know how to fix myself if we decide to play house. I'd never hurt you."

It was two in the morning when the last dance couple broke up and left. The O'Rourke family returned home together.

✦ ✦ ✦

"Good cricking galls," Lieutenant O'Connell muttered. "This craft is so bad, no wonder we bring down five for every one we lose." Twenty-five captured Brittanic fighter-bombers took off from Athlone at midnight two days after the charity dance. Flying low at night, they headed north to a small base at the North Pole. There they would wait for the enemy's reinforcement convoy.

It was bitterly cold at the base where they landed. The pilots ran to an above-ground barrack while crews taxied the fighters into hangars. They were met by the base commander, Colonel Peer Neils, IPV from planet

Scandinavia. The colonel led the pilots into a conference room. After they warmed up on hot tea, he addressed them.

"Gentlemen, two important electrical improvements are going to be made. One, the two separate laser guns will be wired together so they will fire as one. Two, an electronic signal beacon will be mounted on board the cockpit. You will turn the beacon on as you pull away from your ambush; we don't want you show down by our own pilots."

✦ ✦ ✦

For the next two days every fighter base was on full alert—Athlone, Dublin, and the Gaeltacht in Roscommon sector, Connemara in Galway, and at the North Pole. The pilots of the South Pole were shifted north. Over three hundred fighters were ready. In the war room the Taoiseach, the defense minister, and Colonel Becker waited, and on the *Parnell* Commander O'Rourke maintained the vigil.

It was Wednesday, June 17, in mid-morning when the scanners picked up the mass of enemy craft. The young colleen operating the scanner said, "We have sighted a large number of craft. The computer readout says Brittanic Boomerang fighters, about three hundred. Also several large transports, at least three, maybe five, all headed to the quadrant."

The alert alarm sounded, and in minutes the entire Hibernian air fleet and the phantom squadron was in the air. The phantom approached its unsuspecting prey.

Captain O'Rourke ordered, "Keep radio silence until we get to attack range. At my signal we will tighten into an attack phalanx. We will drive through their two waves of fighters without firing unless fired upon. Then we'll hit the first transport. We'll use our afterburners to charge."

The minutes passed. A wave of one hundred Brit craft appeared. The crisp, accented voice of an enemy officer was heard. "This is Brittanic reinforcement convoy. Please give proper recognition signal." A minute passed. The officer repeated, "Please give the proper signal."

Captain O'Rourke replied on an open frequency. "To hell with Lizzy, charge!" The phantom squadron kicked in their afterburners and ran right over the first wave of fighters. Then the second wave of fighters began to fire. Captain O'Rourke yelled, "Open fire!" as the phantom craft opened up. Enemy craft exploded as one as a concentrated stream of laser fire hit them. In seconds the phantom fleet was strafing the first transport. They roared past it, then strafed the second freighter. Then they turned around and headed back.

The enemy was so shocked that a number of pilots started to turn back out into space. Others ejected from their craft by the safety pods. Lieutenant O'Connell joked over his radio, "We can even out-fight them in their own craft." A minute later he watched with horror as one of the phantom craft coming too close crashed into the side of the first transport.

Almost immediately it exploded, the shock wave shaking pilots in their cockpits. Then the second transport was destroyed. Then they swarmed on a third freighter.

Captain O'Rourke suddenly saw a button light up, "Rats, my laser batteries are out."

Lieutenant O'Connell answered, "I'm out too."

In a minute, the other pilots reported the same. Captain O'Rourke then ordered, "Let's return to Peer Neils' arctic resort." The phantom squadron flew straight down and their beacons began to sound. In a minute they saw Hibernian fighters coming up. Captain O'Rourke radioed, "We have bloodied their nose. Finish 'em off."

The familiar voice of Lieutenant Jacque Ranier replied, "*Oui, mon captaine.*"

As the Hibernian fighters came up to the enemy convoy, more of the Boomerang fighters were turning back into deep space. The remaining transports were sitting ducks.

✦ ✦ ✦

On board the *Parnell*, Commander O'Rourke told the radio operator, "Radio the *Griffith* to pull up to eight hundred kilometers." Then he turned to the new helmsman. "Lieutenant Cosgrave, pull out of Antarctic orbit and begin acceleration to maximum hyperlight speed." Then to the new navigator, "Ensign O'Brien, plot a course for Sovietia."

In a few minutes the helmsman called out, "We have reached factor 3, factor 4, factor 6, 8 . . . 10 . . . 12 . . . 14 . . . 16 . . . factor 18 . . . 20, we have reached factor 25. Congratulations, Commander, your ship is making Hibernian history."

The commander picked up his intercom. "To the galley. Bring out some heavy cream for the dinner's tea. Honey, too!"

Then he arose from his console and left the bridge. Entering the aisle, he met Colonel Kamzov. "Colonel, I have a chess set in my quarters. An after-dinner match is my main relaxation."

"Comrade Commander, you play chess?" the colonel asked.

"Yes. I understand it's a highly revered mental discipline among your countrymen. And I really need a real competitor. Most servicemen prefer poker," said the Commander.

The colonel replied, "It's a match, comrade."

In three days the *Parnell* went the length of the solar system. Past Brittania, the enemy planet, the giant planet Hindustan, then Turko-Persia, Arabia, and the tiny planet Abraham. Around the planets Sino and Nippon and huge Nigeria. The freighter went right between the enormous planet Espanol and its small twin, Oporto. Planets Transylvania, Deutsch, Scandinavia, Franco-Italia, Polonia, and Balkan. The tiny inhabitable moons, Benelux, Bohemia, and Albania. On the afternoon of Saturday, June 20, the *Parnell* signaled its approach to the planet Sovietia. The massive ship slowed to a stationary orbit above Moscow, the capital. The radio received the salutation:

"Greetings to our countryman, Comrade Kamzov, and our gallant Hibernian comrades. While our technicians begin to convert your ship to our new propulsion systems, we invite Commander O'Rourke and Comrade Kamzov to a personal audience with the brave and noble leader of our mother planet, Premier Georgi Alexis Petrov."

That evening the commander and the colonel landed by shuttle right outside the Kremlin. The ancient building had been brought brick by brick from Earth during the Great Migrations. Premier Petrov was a massive, burly Slav. At the signal of his hand, the ceremony began. The flags of the two planets were raised, followed by the national anthems. The premier gave both his guests a bear hug and a handshake.

"Comrades, it will be a few days before you can be off again. The process, I understand, requires a hazardous fuel additive. We insist on our science officials being on board. We are also sending up all the American refugees. But for now, let us toast with good chilled vodka: To the victory of Hibernian freedom fighters over Brittanic imperialism!"

Three days later, it was Tuesday, June 23. Commander O'Rourke again told his helmsman to pull out of orbit and accelerate. Lieutenant Cosgrave called out, "Factor 4, 8, 10, 14, 18, 20, 25, 30, 36, 42. . . ."

Then the red alert lights came on from the engine monitor console.

"Commander," a frantic officer yelled, "she is approaching critical pressure. She'll blow in thirty seconds."

The commander ordered, "Helmsman, dead stop!" The ship shook violently before coming to rest. "Now, accelerate again, but slowly after factor 35," the commander's voice was almost deathly.

The helmsman again began. "Factor 5, factor 10, 15, 20, 25, 30, 35. . . ."

A whole minute passed, then Helmsman Cosgrave again spoke. "We are reaching factor 40, 41 . . . 42 . . . 43 . . . 44 . . . 45." Another minute, then, "Factor 50, 52, 55." And then, "Factor 60, 61, 62, and 63." Cosgrave turned to the commander. "We have reached factor 63. It is the greatest moment in my life, Commander. I am proud to serve under you."

O'Rourke answered, "Thank you. Navigator O'Brien, plot a course to Earth." Then he switched to his intercom. "This is Commander O'Rourke. We are traveling at sixty-three times the speed of light. The serviceman's lounge will open until 2200 to celebrate. June 23, 3153, will go down in the annals of our people."

✤ ✤ ✤

Chapter 5

The planet Abraham was one of the smallest planets of the Outer Solar System. It had been settled by people from the Earth nation Israel and related peoples. For the first time in thousands of years, the chosen people had found peace. Free from threats to their survival, they developed many services for their people. Their special educational systems for handicapped children became famous throughout the solar system. The Herzl Institute of Haifa sector and the Weizmann School of Bethlehem were schools for the deaf. Their rivalry stemmed from the controversy over how to teach deaf children. The Herzl Institute taught its wards to read lips and how to speak, while the Weizmann School taught hand sign language.

It was morning at the Herzl Institute. The Star of David flag was raised in front of the administrative management center. Two men stood on the walkway from the flagpole to the building. One wore a gray suit, mustache, and felt hat. The other a black suit and beard with a yamulka and phylacteries.

The first man spoke. "Rabbi Kurtz, of all our students, Naomi Sennech is no doubt the most intelligent. Her parents sent her here at age five. At twelve they transferred her to the Weizmann School, and she returned here at age sixteen."

The Rabbi answered, "What for did they do such a thing? Were they trying to confuse the child's mind? Dr. Jankowsky, how could you allow such a thing?"

"It did not hurt one bit. She can use hand signs and speak as well. She is so bright, she is trying to learn English," was the doctor's answer.

The rabbi answered, "Her father, rest his memory, was a Talmudic scholar, and her late mother a musician. Her brother, Isaac, would have been a Talmudic scholar, but do you know what the boy went and did? He went to the planet Hibernia, became a pilot, and got himself killed. He was her last next of kin. You say she is trying to learn English? You think she is thinking to go there? And for what?"

The doctor answered, "She might want to go see his grave. Have the remains been brought here? Certainly she is not fool enough to settle there."

Jus then a tiny, slender girl, with smiling blue-green eyes, came running up. The wind went through her dark brown hair. Her hand waved an envelope. When she reached the two men, she yelled, "I have a letter. A letter!" She handed the letter to the doctor. He opened it and began to read.

"The address is Hibernia, part of it is in Gaelic. It is from a Captain Eamon O'Rourke."

Naomi took the letter back and saw the photo of a baby girl. Using her small knowledge of English, she read, "It says that before my brother died, he was involved with a Hibernian woman, a professional dancer. She gave birth to a girl eight months after he died. Esther Sennech Kelley McLaughlin, age one. The mother is now married to a Hibernian man. She also had another child, a boy, two years earlier." Then, turning to the two men, with voice and hands: "I have a niece, a niece. I am no longer alone. Please help me, I want to go see my niece."

Dr. Jankowski looked at her face. "But, my child, Hibernia is at war. You could be killed!"

The rabbi added, "We cannot be sure that the girl is the daughter of your brother." After reading the letter he added, "It appears she was a Jezebel, and not proper company for a nice Abrahamite girl."

Her hands and voice answered in rage. "She is married, what more do you want? Her blood? I want to see my niece, please." She started to cry.

Dr. Jankowsky then put his hands on the young girl. "Naomi, I have a friend at the Foreign Ministry. I'll try to talk him into getting you a passport and travel visa." Then he winked at the rabbi. "He pledged a donation of fifty shekels of silver to the school six months ago. This will square the unfulfilled pledge."

❖ ❖ ❖

Two days after his father told him of the trip to Earth, Cathal O'Rourke climbed on board a land tram to the quadrant marshlands. Deirdre O'Toole came along. After a six-hour trip down the Athlone plateau, the bus stopped at a small village. The two left the bus, and Cathal led his girlfriend to a dock at the edge of the marshland. There a middle-aged couple waited beside a flat-bottomed, big fin swamp boat. The man resembled Seamus O'Rourke except his hair was still dark and he had a sagging waistline. The woman beside him was a big farm girl whose age was only shown by her silver hair.

140

"Auntie Beth, Uncle Gene," Cathal threw his arms around the two. "Here is my friend, Deirdre." The girl kissed the two adults.

"Let us be off. Beth here plans a good old-fashioned dinner," Eugene said. As they boarded the boat and roared off past houseboats, Eugene added, "She'll make eighty kilometers per hour. We'll be home in twenty minutes."

Beth O'Rourke said, "I'm gonna make fricasseed mulquix, biscuits, gravy, a vegetable soup, and a good strong black tea."

Cathal whispered to Deirdre. "Uncle doesn't drink, his pancreas, but their tea is strong enough to walk on. I like it."

When they reached the floating home, Deirdre was surprised. It was three times bigger than the houseboats they had passed. At one end was a windmill attached to a generator. Beside it stood a biomass methane still and gas tank. At the center, to the other end, was a two-story house.

Eugene said, "Cathal will use the room of my two sons; they're in the service. Miss O'Toole will use the guest room."

"Call me Deirdre, or Dee, Mr. O'Rourke."

"You can call me Uncle Gene."

The four walked across a plank on board to the houseboat. Beth pointed at the glass boat on the other side. "That's our floating greenhouse. We dredge dirt from all about the marshlands to fill it. You can't grow good garden vegetables in a swamp."

Early in the evening they sat down to dinner, Cathal saying the grace. As the meal went on, Deirdre said, "This is mulquix? It's like good chicken."

Beth answered, "It's a versatile animal, caught for fur in winter and for meat in summer."

"Yes, and we will teach you, Dee, the art of setting traplines for mulquix. But first, we must cure them."

Beth added, "I will also teach you how to pick berries, which are used for preserves and which are used for dye, and you must not mistake one for the other, else you'll crick you guts out."

The following morning Gene led Cathal and Deirdre to an upmound where a stewing pot sat. It was big enough to set a man into. They build a fire after filling the pot with swamp water. "We'll boil 'em in strong lye soap for three hours. Then we'll put 'em in this pile of leaves to rust. Then, in a couple of days, we'll boil 'em in the husks of Darklewood nuts to cure 'em," Gene instructed.

"How do you catch mulquix?" Deirdre asked. Eugene took one of his traps and opened its jaws, setting them by the lock. "The trap is staked. The mulquix is attracted to the scent juice we put on it. It hits this trip, and the jaws close on its leg. The trap pulls it under and the animal drowns quickly with no pain."

"Does the little animal suffer?" the city girl asked.

Gene answered, "No! That is because you set the trap in the water, not on dry land. And you must have the brains to check your trapline twice daily.

Anyone who sets a line and don't check 'em is asking to lose his catch and his traps. And the lowest form of scum in the marshlands is a thief who raids other man's lines. My best friend is a game warden and a trapper too. Anyone foolish enough to raid his lines will be broken in half."

In the afternoon Aunt Beth took Cathal and Deirdre out picking berries. Later they brought the berries into the kitchen in a big copper pot. The berries were separated carefully. Those for dye were dropped into a wooden tub. Then the juice berries were washed and put in a cloth bag hanging on the bail handle of the copper pot.

"Now squeeze the bag gently, so the juice will begin to drip. Tomorrow we'll boil the juice in the pot. While it's cooking we'll sterilize these glass jars, boiling them in my pressure cooker. Then we add sugar and pectin to the juice. When she thickens, we pour 'er into the jars. We'll have this seal wax melted and ready to pour atop of hot jelly juice. When the wax hardens, it's a perfect seal."

Deirdre asked, "You do this each summer? I only saw my maw do it once, and she had to buy the fruit from a store. I guess I'm just a city girl."

Beth replied, "I have made jelly every year since we settled in the marshlands. I have to go to Athlone if I want citrus fruit for jelly."

After dinner that evening, Gene took the two children into his den. At a draftsman's table stood a half finished picture of what looked like a city of canals. "Cathal's dad, my brother Seamus, drew the rough sketch in charcoal. I am using heated wax crayons."

He lit a candle and put a crayon over it until it got soft. "We will build a small city at the south end of the marsh, just a small one. It'll have canals like Venice, an Earth city." His crayons brought a bright flow of color.

"Father was an architect too," Cathal said.

"Yes, he was, and between 3130 and 3137 he was my business partner after his term in service was up. In 3131 we designed a school for the Orange people in Shankill. It was to have red brick, not no new brick but to be found. We scoured Leinster for used bricks, big round rocks like cranite and kilnstone, and bottles, milk bottles, wine bottles, even medicine bottles. Bricks on one wall, rocks on two, and bottle on the fourth."

"What happened to your business?" Deirdre asked.

"Well, in 3137 he went back to service. I ran things myself. Then in 3145 he took a six-month furlong. Together we designed a building for the Hibernia Petroleum Institute. In 3149 she was nearly done when the war hit. The building was a total loss and all of the equipment. Our business insurance just covered the losses. Seamus was back in the service, and I closed the firm and Beth and I settled here. We had had the floating home for vacations for fifteen years, so we just settled here to live. When the Brits are beaten finally, Seamus and I will start up again."

Beth said bitterly, "That's why I hate the queen—and she has the same name as me. Besides, her father George the Thirtieth had my mother and father murdered."

"Murdered?" both Cathal and Deirdre asked in shock.

"Yes, my dear nephew. The last you saw them was 3144; they were both in their seventies. Back in 3102 they came to this planet. We lived in Athlone, where I met Eugene. In 3148 they returned to Brittania to visit friends. When the war began, they were put in jail. When it was learned I had wed into the family of Commander O'Rourke, the king ordered them hanged."

Beth sat down into a soft chair and wept as her husband, nephew, and Deirdre tried to comfort her.

❖ ❖ ❖

It was near midnight. Eugene stepped out to the windmill at the end of the floating home. He took out a clay pipe and tobacco pouch. He filled the pipe and was about to strike a match when a girl's voice came from behind him. "I use to light my dad's pipe when maw wasn't around," was Deirdre's line. He handed the pipe and match to her. She lit the pipe and took a couple deep puffs before giving it back.

"Is that all the weed you've sucked on?" Gene looked at her with a suspicious smile.

"Well, I am a Tigeress girl. I've had fags and even sweet black cigars," was Deirdre's reply. He handed the pipe back to her and she inhaled a deep pull.

"Does Cathal know?"

"Yes, and he doesn't mind."

"Maybe he is too much of a gentleman to complain."

Deirdre took out the last cigarette she had. She had kept it for a week. "Could I take a light? Please, Uncle Gene?" she asked.

Eugene bent over slightly, puffing on his pipe to heat up the bowl. Deirdre lit the cigarette by touching the end into the pipe bowl. She exhaled through her nose. "I get nervous, and it calms me. I'd try to quit if Cathal asked. I love him so, but he says he don't mind."

Eugene answered, "Maybe he loves you too much to mind. Just don't walk into the house with a cig. Beth gets upset if I go in with my pipe. She hates ashes dropping on the furniture and floor. God love her, she keeps house cleaner and better than any woman in the marshland."

Deirdre blew a smoke ring, then said, "I am sorry to hear how Auntie Beth lost her parents. I lost mine in May during the attack on Athlone. Cathal lost his maw in the last war."

Eugene said finally, "Bernadette O'Rourke was a damn good woman. Beautiful and intelligent and kind. Her death was just as much murder as Beth's parents or yours."

❖ ❖ ❖

Two days after the *Parnell* left Hibernia, another meeting was held in the war room. Colonel Kalminsky was present in the absence of Commander O'Rourke. Commanders Donahue from Dublin, MacMullen of Roscommon, and Rafferty of Galway also were present, as were Colonel Neils of the North Pole, Colonel Murphy of the South Pole, and Colonel Becker.

Defense Minister Flynn addressed the base officers. "Gentlemen, the *Parnell* has left for Earth, and we do not know if or when she will return. We, therefore, must have an alternative set of actions available if we don't have a force shield."

Colonel Becker then gave a report. "In one month we have destroyed 400 enemy craft. They now have 250 fighters in the quadrant and 600 in their home planet. A total of 850 fighters to just half that number for us. By the end of the year we could double the number of fighters, but they might triple theirs. The attrition by weight of numbers would gradually be to our disadvantage."

Commander MacMullen, rising from the table, answered Becker. "One of the weak spots of our fighters is that the photon batteries for the lasers run out too quickly. I propose two extra batteries be mounted on board each fighter. The empty space under the pilot's seat would be the spot to seal them in. We never developed the survival kits that the empty space was intended for anyway."

Colonel Peer Neils then asked, "Can the phantom squadron be used in another ambush?"

"I don't know," Joe Flynn answered. "The next time the Brits send down a reinforcement convoy, they'll probably throw their current quadrant force against one of our bases to draw off our fighters. I have in mind, gentlemen, an extreme measure involving the *Arthur Griffith*. Like all of our tankers before, it has a computer-activated self-destruct sequence. I propose that the sequence be reprogrammed for destruction on impact. If our planet is apparently being overwhelmed by the enemy, the bridge of the *Griffith* will steer the craft across the space corridor to Brittania and crash into the capital city. At least Queen Lizzy won't live to brag of her victory."

Commander Donahue protested, "That would not prevent Brittania from beginning her conquest of the solar system."

Joe Flynn answered, "It would delay it, maybe long enough for the other planets to set up some kind of defense. Anyway, gentlemen, the war is now in a wait-for-the-next-move stage. I suggest that the rocket crews of *Peenemude* be transferred to fighter bases. The retired reserves, even men in their nineties, should be issued laser hand rifles. If worse comes to worse, we may have to fight on the ground."

✦ ✦ ✦

Two weeks after the attack on Athlone, Jan MacDevitt brought Barry and Esther McLaughlin back to their parents' home. Life for Theo and

Maureen was like it was before the war. Theo fixed a large dinner at noon. After Jan and Mo did dishes, they'd sit back at the dinner table and tutor Theo. Baby Esther slept in her crib, Barry in his little bed. Jan MacDevitt treated Theo like the son she never had and taught history and math to him. Mo Kelley taught her husband penmanship and Gaelic.

"You know, Theo, if I had studied a bit harder in school, I'd be a bilingual instructor, a registered teacher like Brigid Hallohan. But wanting to dance and chasing boys was all that mattered to me."

Her husband answered, "My father had a huge library of books. He read to me when I was small. Then I read to him as his disabilities worsened."

"Now Theo," Jan lectured, "let's keep to today's lessons. Maybe in a year you could take the secondary school equivalency examination."

After "school" was over, the parents sat and played with their children. "Mo," Theo questioned, "you think we could let our neighbor's goats graze in the backyard? I've set a fence around the garden so they won't get in. It'll end needing a lawnmower as ours is rusted. The neighbors will pay us with goat's milk butter."

"Fine, that's a good idea. I was raised on the finest farm in Kilkenny," Mo answered.

At half-past four Theo and Mo took a city tram to the street where the Golden Peacock stood. Jan MacDevitt stayed with the children. Theobald returned home, and Miss MacDevitt would take another tram across town to her apartment. Near midnight Theo would walk with his step-children to pick up his wife at the backstage door of the Golden Peacock. Then, all together, they would walk home. On Sunday and alternate Mondays, Mo was off work. Sunday mass and a trip to DeValera Park or the race track were their diversions.

❖ ❖ ❖

It was the first day of July. The Athlone orderlies, as the five girls were known, performed quite well at the Kilkenny Paramilitary Hospital. They were always under the eye of Colonel McCracken, who was concerned by the unusual closeness that developed between Nurse Terri Lynch and Kate MacBride. She became suspicious when she learned the ex-con orderly was helping the student nurse cram for the academic courses that were part of her training. However, since there was no hard proof of misconduct, she did not attempt to discipline them. Then transfer orders arrived for all five of the girls. Upon reading the first paragraph, Kate cheered, "We're going home. God, it is great! I can almost feel my boyfriend's pink poker up my butt hole. We'll meet up with Shelley O'Rourke and have an orgy that will level every building in Athlone."

Mary Plunkett Concannon read the whole transfer order. "Hey, Kate, it says we will be at Athlone's base hospital for one month. Then we are all going to the Connemara hospital in Galway sector."

Kate was discouraged, but Caroline, Mairead, and Jamie reminded her, "We will be home for a month."

Just then Terri Lynch walked in. "Kate, I heard you're going back to Athlone. I'm going to miss you. I go on duty in five minutes. It's my first time assisting a surgeon. You'll be gone by the time I get off duty."

The two girls walked into the closet. They embraced tightly and kissed. "Terri, I'll write you when I get situated. If you get lonely, just remember what I told you our first night in here. A streetwalker will take a girl's money just like a man's." Terri kissed Kate goodbye and left the nightroom.

The operation Terri assisted in took ten hours, hours of painful delicate surgical action. Twice, they nearly lost the patient. After the operation and a dinner eaten absentmindedly, Terri returned to the nightroom. It looked so very empty. She walked into the closet and undressed for bed. She remembered Kate's first advance, first brutality, then tenderness. Those meetings were always in the closet before sleep. She slipped out of the closet and into her bed. She turned on her stomach and cried herself to sleep.

❖ ❖ ❖

When the five girls arrived at the Athlone railway station and got off the train, they were met by over a hundred girls. Shelley O'Rourke was at the head. Kate, Caroline, Mairead, Jamie, and M.P. were raised up and carried on the shoulders of the girls. The mass of sweater-clad girl gang members were joined by another hundred girls. They marched in four columns to the center of town, right to the residence of Taoiseach Colm O'Hara. Without any threatening gestures on their part, their numbers panicked almost everyone in their path. When an elderly woman began to cry for help, they picked her up and carried her on their shoulders until she calmed down. A group of girls broke away temporarily and surrounded a family in the process of moving. After a casual mass introduction, they helped the family load their moving van. Then, at a run, they caught up with the rest. The six gang leaders, Shelley, Kate, Caroline, Mairead, Jamie, and M.P., fell upon an elderly man. They each took turns kissing him right to the tongue. First they loaded their lips with a thick coat of lipstick, then began kissing him. Then Brigid Hallohan walked up and slipped off her black leather overcoat, revealing only a G-string and pasties on her body. "Hi, handsome. Want to dance and neck?" she said to the old man.

When they reached the Taoiseach's official home, they surrounded it. Some of the girls began to flatter the few guards. With Shelley O'Rourke leading, the six gang leaders confronted the Taoiseach, who stepped out of his building to meet the strong confrontation.

"Miss O'Rourke, I recognize you. What are you doing in Athlone? Oh, I see your auxiliary armband. What is your request?"

Shelley's answer was immediate. "The Orangies, the border people, are going to hold their twelfth of July celebration in Athlone. We are going to guard their rally. My five comrades just got in from Kilkenny, and they have agreed to join in. Over two hundred girls are ready to break heads of anyone who molests those poor folks."

"Aren't the police prepared to protect them?" was Colm O'Hara's disbelieving reply.

"Half the coppers in this town are as young as my little kid brother, Cathal, and the other half as old as you. Against some off the creeps in town, they'd have no chance," was Shelley's retort.

"What is your price for your act of public service?" Colm asked nervously.

"First, you are to direct the Justice and Finance Ministries to audit and investigate the Athlone school system. Second, you are to propose a constitutional amendment outlawing capital punishment. Third, after the war is over, you are to dissolve the Dail Eireann and call a general election."

The Taoiseach almost fainted. "But that will wreck the Compromise of 3127."

"We are not asking for a constitutional assembly, just a general election for the Dail. You haven't had a general election in a quarter century, only by-elections. Have you ever slipped into the guest galleries above the Dail chamber? Most of those clowns are asleep or drunk. Most are not just older than you, they are older than your father was when he retired—up to twenty years older."

The Taoiseach sighed, "I guess I have no choice. Maybe an election could help bring some new blood in. Most of those who won by-elections in the past decade are independents, so my party and the opposition Sinn Fein won't benefit. The Compromise will survive."

"Thank you," Shelley answered. Then the six girls each kissed the head of state.

Slowly the mass of girls departed, leaving a disoriented Colm O'Hara.

✦ ✦ ✦

That very evening after the march on the Taoiseach's residence, Shelley O'Rourke had Sean O'Connell over at the O'Rourke home for dinner. "Eamon is at the South Pole for a week. We can really get acquainted again," Sean said.

After dinner they sat on the sofa in the parlor. Sean lit a thin black cigar, then lit Shelley's cigarette.

"You know, Sean, at the gaol the six of us had smoking privileges only once a week. All the other women in the gaol could smoke all the time. It was a deliberate means to imply we were scum."

Sean opened a bottle of wine. "It's Wicklow Rose Hip and Dandelion wine."

Shelley got a pair of stemmed glasses. "To my father, may he return quickly." Shelley raised her glass.

147

Sean raised his glass in reply. "To Brigid Hallohan, may she bed your brother Eamon and soon."

After emptying their glasses and finishing their smokes, they lay back on the sofa and kissed and embraced.

"Shelley, I love you. I want you to become Mrs. Sean O'Connell."

"Yes, I want to bear your children, but not until Father approves."

Soon they were half undressed, their hands rubbing down each other's chests. Shelley felt Sean's manly budge against her thigh.

"You want to drain your balls into me, Sean?"

"I'd like to, but I don't want to knock you up."

"You won't if I turn over on my stomach." She then whispered the taboo word.

"That will tear your insides up. You'll bleed."

"Not if you do exactly as I say." Shelley got off the sofa and reached into her purse. "First, put a dab of this petroleum cream on your finger, stick it in my hole, and rub around it for a couple of minutes. When I tell you the hole wall is relaxed, put a massive glob on your poker. Push it in slow until I say stop. Then you can start pumping. Let's go into father's room and his double bed."

"Shelley, who told you about this?"

"Kate MacBride, my bed partner in gaol."

Shelley stripped totally naked and lay across the bed. In a few minutes Sean began to steadily stroke in and out of her. "Whew, this is great. You are a girl who is a good piece of real ass."

Shelley answered Sean as he approached explosion, "Yes, I like it deeper, Sean. Reach around and squeeze my breasts."

A couple of minutes later: "Good cricking galls, it's so good it hurts." Sean collapsed on top of Shelley and his legs began to sag. Finally, he pulled out.

The two walked into the bathroom. Sean washed the nightsoil from his tool while Shelley washed her underside. They showered, then returned to the bed, sitting up. Shelley had picked up her purse and took out two cigarettes.

They lit up, then Sean said, "If Brigid gets Eamon, we could go on a carnal picnic for four at Big Boy Lake. And if your little brother Cathal gets together with Deirdre, it would be a picnic for six."

Shelley replied, "Cathal is even less likely to try it than Eamon, and Deirdre won't make the first move. After all, they are both just sixteen."

✦ ✦ ✦

As the sun broke on Athlone, a crowd of strangers gathered. Men in black suits and bowlers with orange ties; the women in full length dresses, black bonnets, and orange ribbons. Ulster quadrant flags, fifes, Lambeg drums, and memorial banners. The banners commemorated the past sufferings of the Orange people: Red Lion Inn 1972, LaMons Restaurant 1976, and the largest, Shankill 2002. The Shankill village on the border was named for a neighborhood in the Earth city of Belfast on the Earth island. In 2002, at the end of the decades long war to unify Ireland, an atrocity of unbelievable proportion took place. The Republican guerillas called the Provisionals deliberately murdered two hundred men, women, and children. It broke the Northern resistance to unification, but at the cost of undying bitterness. The fact that a number of the very men and women identified as responsible received medals and government offices added to the hatred. Finally, in 2017, a small measure of revenge came. The three top officers of the Provisional Active Service Unit responsible for the massacre were assassinated by a car bomb.

As their band played, "On the Banks of the Boyne," the border people marched past jeering residents. The Orange people were still an alien race to many "real" Hibernians. Some rocks and bottles were thrown and cat calls, "Brit lovers," "Get out of Hibernia," came. Then they reached the wide main boulevard leading to DeValera Park. Standing in the middle of the street in their black denim jackets were Shelley, Kate, Caroline, Mairead, Jamie, and Mary Plunket, waiting.

Shelley spoke. "Is the McKerr family present?"

The elderly man came forth. "I am James King McKerr. This is my wife, Ann; my son, William King, and daughter, Agnes. You are the girl who saved Agnes?"

"Yes. I and my comrades will fulfill our pledge to protect your march. The Tigeress and the Girl Knights are on one side of the street. Imperials and Green Devils on the other. Each has a club ready for anything."

James McKerr looked at the girls in red or green sweaters on one sidewalk, girls in yellow and black or blue on the other. The crowd began to slowly file between the rows of girl gang members. When they reached the end of the two lines, they began to march along side by side.

When they entered a residential neighborhood, the girls began to tap their clubs in the palms of their hands. Suddenly a handful of thugs charged the escorting girls. They stood their ground using their clubs. Then some of the Orange marchers joined the battle, women as well as men. The McKerrs were the first. After five minutes the thugs broke and ran. There were bruises, some bloody noses, and a few cuts, but no great damage. The march continued, a band playing "The Sash My Father Wore" until they reached DeValera Park, an unlikely setting for an Orangeman's day march. The gang girls formed a circle around the rally. Hymns were sung, Bibles read, and speeches evoked Orange heritage. In the afternoon the crowd moved to a line of tables that were set up. The wicker baskets were opened, and pies and jars of juices and jams were brought out. Friendly people began to come into the park to buy their wares.

The gang girls rotated between standing on guard duty and taking lunch from buckets. They also bought some of the pieces that were on sale.

As the day wore on toward dusk, not a single incident took place. The people who came into the park were as impressed by the orderly, disciplined behavior of the guards as the behavior of the Orange people. Many of the women got praise for their pies and jellies.

When the rally and sale ended, the gang girls escorted the Orange people back to the edge of town. The visitors boarded chartered land trams to return to their little villages. The gang girls then returned to their own homes.

✦ ✦ ✦

In the war room of the *Parnell*, Commander O'Rourke held a meeting of the American Underground leaders, Soviet technicians, and his own crew. Colonel Kamzov opened the discussion. "Comrade Commander, I have a detailed report of the technician who worked on the engines when we were in stationary orbit over our mother planet. The fuel additives and engine modifications were performed only on the engines of the *McCracken* that were mounted on board in place of the two after tanks. If we had three more days over Sovietia, we could have converted the *Parnell*'s own engines, and we would be traveling 50 percent faster."

The commander was at first shocked. "This is an awful, most awful oversight."

The Soviet officer replied, "It is imperative that my technicians be allowed to work the *Parnell*'s engines while you are on the surface of the Earth." The commander agreed and regained his confidence.

The matter of the *Parnell*'s speed settled, the discussion turned to their destination. Sammy King, the American refugee leader, spoke. "Shanghai is where the U.S. Embassy for the Eurasian People's Co-Prosperity Republic is. One of the officials of the embassy will be our contact. Each of the Hibernian landing crew should carry a deck of playing cards. The spades and clubs should be in one pocket, hearts and diamonds in the other. When the contact meets, he will suggest a card game but will produce only half a deck of cards. You wait for the offer for a game and the presentation of the half deck. Then you present the other half of the deck. We will probably take a hydrofoil from the Chinese coast to the Hawaiian islands. There we will be transferred to an old-fashioned steam boat, which will take us to San Francisco. A bus will take us to Chicago. In all, several weeks will go by before we meet our operatives."

The commander's answer was direct. "Colonel Kamzov, I am going to leave the bridge to you when I go to the surface. Each of our ship's crewmen on the surface, myself included, will have a hidden radio. As soon as we reach Chicago, we will radio the *Parnell*, and you will move immediately from stationary orbit over Shanghai to a new stationary orbit over Chicago on the North American continent. You are to have all shuttle crew ready on full alert. We will want to get on the way as quickly as possible."

In the Crystal Palace of the enemy planet, a heated discussion was taking place between the monarch Elizabeth the Seventeenth and her first minister, Lord Cromwell.

"Your most gracious Majesty, it has been a continuous series of setbacks. One of every two new fighters are destroyed during their first test flights. Pilots are deserting, and a series of breakdowns are hampering our fighter manufacturing plants. Worst of all, the reinforcement convoy was ambushed. Half of the fighters were lost. I tell you, my noble queen, Gladstone is involved in this. If I can prove it, I want to hang him immediately."

The monarch was sitting on her throne and answered, "He must have at least the appearance of a trial. And I think it would pain him more to keep him alive long enough to see the destruction of the Hibernians. Think of it, Lord Cromwell, fifty to one hundred of the fighters carrying cameras transmitting the detailed extermination of the Irish race back to our planet. The attack broadcast live into every Brittanic household. And the Melbourne men's prison in the Australian quadrant. Then we can broadcast live the execution of Gladstone."

Lord Cromwell replied, "Your mind is as bright and cunning as my own, Your Grace. I have instructed my intelligence agents to shadow Gladstone everywhere he goes."

✧ ✧ ✧

The Brittanic monarch and her prime minister would not have been so pleased with themselves if they had known the chamber room had electronic listening devices all over it. In fact, the whole palace was wired. Every conversation was intercepted by a receiver in a dingy apartment across town.

The anti-royalist Underground had battled the government for decades and were a great assistance to the Hibernians. One of the reasons for the inferiority of the Boomerang fighter-bombers was the fact that several of the aeronautical engineers who designed it were in the Underground.

An electro-magnetic pulsar beam was used to transmit and receive communications with Hibernia. Patterns of varying frequency and amplitude were the code for the messages sent or received. During the previous war, when the Hibernian air fleet attacked London, an evacuation signal was sent. All of the Underground operatives left the city except a crew manning the post listening into the Crystal Palace. However, the Underground had received a message indicating that next attack on London would be so total that not only the entire Underground apparatus would have to evacuate from London, but in a radius of eighty kilometers.

The Underground would have been far more successful if it did not consist of disparate elements. These various groups battled each other more than they fought the common enemy. One group consisted of former members of Gladstone's Freedom Party. They were moderates desiring a republic as they had decided the monarchy was beyond hope of reform. Others were rigid socialists like the Sinn Feiners on Hibernia. There were Scottish and Welsh separatists. In the English sector, there was even the Fascist National Front, isolationalist and authoritarian but populist. The largest numbers of operatives were plain folk simply tired of being taxed into poverty to pay for the monarch's luxury.

It was two in the morning. W.E. Gladstone had walked into the industrial district at the edge of the city. He stopped at the gates of a warehouse, a cardboard plant. He approached the security guardhouse.

"Halt!" the officer commanded. Mr. Gladstone handed the guard a newspaper page. The guard read several words that were marked in blue ink. Without a word, he signaled the civilian into the gate. Gladstone walked right in the building, past racks of cardboard on wooden pallets. He was met by Candy, the girl he had met in Liverpool.

"Hi, love, We're going on a forklift." She led the man to a lift truck driven by a man in a uniform similar to that of the guard outside the building. The two stepped on a wooden pallet. The truck picked the pallet up and then it sped off down the long aisle. They reached the other end of the warehouse.

"Hold on tight, love," Candy said as the truck reached a very tall set of racks. The forks lifted the two people to the top of the rack, and they stepped on the pallets sitting on top. Several people were already on the pallets at the top of the rack, three men and another woman. The first man to speak was elderly and thin.

"I am Blue Goose. The girl is Nursie, and the other two are Plug and Socket. None of us knows each other's real names."

Candy then added, "This is the only time you will meet anyone else in the Underground but me, love."

"You must realize, she will be your contact anytime you have valuable material," said Plug, a corpulent, balding man.

Socket, a youth, with a mat of ratty-looking hair, added, "Also, you will understand that if you are discovered and arrested, we can do nothing to rescue you except destroy the informer who turned you in. If it were one of us, the traitor would be thrown right off this rack."

Blue Goose went on, "We will try to contact you if the Hibernians plan an attack on the city so you can evacuate your party members."

Nursie, a young woman in a nurse's outfit, said, "Mr. Gladstone, after we overthrow the queen, we'll need political leaders who can set up an assembly to create a commonwealth republic. But you must let the masses of people decide their government."

Gladstone answered, "The Freedom Party does not know I have contacted you. As much as they oppose the war, I do not feel they would join in an uprising. Being men of peace, they would not be able to oppose it."

After a few minutes of silence, Blue Goose signaled the fork lift to begin taking the operatives down. They came down two by two. Blue Goose said to Candy, "I feel you are getting too emotionally involved with him. If he is caught, he is dead."

"I know, love, but I think he'll be safe. You want to take me for the rest of the night?" Candy answered.

"Business as usual?" Blue Goose asked.

"No business, I just can't stand being alone after a night like this," she replied.

What none of the Underground realized was that a royal investigator was watching the warehouse. He was perched on the roof of a machine tool plant across the street. With a dual telescope, he watched every single operative come and go. The officer thought to himself, "So, the Jeremiah of Parliament is playing a Judas. Well, I don't have proof he has given them anything valuable, but we'll be so close to him, he'll think we're riding his back."

❖ ❖ ❖

"Cruds," Eugene O'Rourke muttered. "It's the third day in a row the traps have been raided. I'd bet a gram of gold Jack Hanly did it." Gene O'Rourke, with Cathal and Deirdre, was walking the trapline in a foggy morning. "Not a single mulquix, just a lousy halkinx," he muttered.

"What's a halkinx?" Deirdre asked.

"An animal whose fur in only good for fancy toilet paper. Flesh the taste of roofing tar and a scent gland that will stain, sting, and burn a man. Some are so allergic they nearly die!" Uncle Gene answered.

When they got back to the floating home, Gene slit the hind legs of the halkinx and hung it up. Taking the sharp knife he carried, he slit across the hind quarters. With a series of short, scraping cuts, he peeled its skin off the carcass inside out. Taking the fur inside out, he pulled it on a board carved to a smooth oval. Then, using a long, flat drawl blade, he scraped the flesh and fat from the inside of the skin. Eugene said, "When she's dry, I'll use a tin smith shears to cut her up into squares. The halkinx does make fine toilet paper."

Cathal and Deirdre had discussed what Uncle Gene said about the halkinx. "Uncle Gene, we've an idea. To catch old Jack Hanly, first cut off the scent glands from the carcass and put it in this old cloth. We'll squeeze 'em in this medicine bottle. Tonight we'll bait a trap with the scent glands and set a rock under the trap so it won't sink. He'll be faced with a live halkinx," Cathal said.

"He'll be zooped like a loaded cigar," Deirdre added.

That very night they went out to the trapline again and set two traps with the scent glands, one apiece. The next morning they found Jack Hanly vomiting over a trap where a live halkinx was shooting his scent. Game Warden Joe Harrigan came along, and after dispatching the animal with his pistol, he arrested the thief.

In the afternoon Joe Harrigan stopped off at the O'Rourke houseboat for tea. "He confessed to raiding traps all over the marshland. Just who was it who thought of booby-trapping him?"

"It was Deirdre and I," Cathal answered.

Deirdre added, "You see, to catch a gink, you must think just like a gink."

The officer said, "Did you see the oil slicks on the marshlands? I've known for years there's oil in the marshlands, but you know the people here are afraid of oil wells coming in and driving our people out. There is an intelligent way to get the oil. Drill a well outside the marshlands real deep, then strike it off at an angle into the marshland. That way we can get the oil without ruining the lives of the marshland settlers. Before the war, I went into a Brit village; they have wells out there."

Cathal went into shock. "Does the military know this? Does my father know?"

"Of course they know. It's a wonder they have not tried to knock out those oil wells. If there is a lot of oil in the quadrant, the border people would never be poor again," Gene answered.

After dinner, Cathal walked with Deirdre out across the plankway to the floating greenhouse. Behind the greenhouse the two kissed and embraced for awhile. Cathal began to make a cat's cradle with a piece of string. Deirdre lit a smoke and sat down beside her boy, who looked at her in a funny way. Deirdre looked at Cathal with as serious a look as she ever had.

"Cathal, do you really mind my smoking? If you mind, I'll try quitting."

The boy waited a minute in thought. "It's not that I mind, I was just surprised that the first time I saw you take a cigarette from Karen Quinncannon was the day before the attack on our hometown. I am used to it now. In fact, the last time smoke bothered me was at a military wedding our family went to when I was twelve; my eyes burned. I don't mind a bit," the boy answered.

"Then why are you looking at me in that way you are?" she asked.

"You are filling out, Dee," Cathal answered, raising his hands cupped up across his rib cage.

"Flatterer. I want to kiss you on the tongue," his girl answered. As he opened his mouth and puckered his lips, Deirdre took a very long, deep, fast, drag and tossed the butt in the water. Deirdre embraced her boy and kissed him. The braces on their teeth clicked as she exhaled a lung full of smoke in her boy's mouth. She held her mouth against his until she heard him cough as the smoke went down his lungs.

"Gee, I've never tasted it before." Cathal was a little shocked and dizzy.

"That was a trick your sister Shelley taught me, and she learned it from Brigid Hallohan," Deirdre answered.

Then her boy seized her and kissed her back hard. "Oh, your braces cut my lips, Dee."

"And yours hurt mine. Let's just kiss on the cheeks before we both bleed all over." Cathal and Deirdre embraced.

✦ ✦ ✦

It was the last week of July. All of the debris had been cleared from DeValera Park. Temporary flagpoles had been erected, and the flags of Hibernia and three free quadrants, Leinster, Munster, and Connaught, fluttered in the wind. Tables were set up for serving food. A bandstand was prepared for musicians. Instruments were brought to the park—harps, flutes, uilleann pipes, accordions, a concertina, and Irish bagpipes. It was the celebration of the Pan-Celtic festival. Back on Earth the festival was the meeting of the four Celtic peoples: the Irish, the Scots and Welsh of Britain, and the Bretons of northwest France. During peacetime in the Outer Solar System, the Bretons came from Franco-Italia and the Scots and Welsh from Brittania. But now only a small number of Bretons appeared.

Grandstands were erected in the park as the traditional Hibernian sports were to be played. The distaff side would take to the field first as Athlone's camogie team would face Dublin, then hurling, and finally, Gaelic football. The racetrack was open south of the city, admissions at half price. Housewives brought baked goods, soda bread and brambec, and giant stewpots of mutton stews and capons.

Shelley O'Rourke and Sean O'Connell came into the park and were surprised. They met Brigid Hallohan and Shelley's brother, Eamon. Brigid took Shelley aside and said, "He's been seeing me secretly for over a month. A week after the charity dance, he sent me a thank-you note and flowers. Then one evening I just stepped out on the stage and I saw him in a front row seat. He was wearing a civilian overcoat over his uniform. After the show was over for the night, he was waiting for me outside the backstage door. He took me to a late dinner."

Shelley was happy and excited. "Did you get him into the apartment yet?"

"No, but it's just a matter of time before I'll have him for the night. He is really a nice, shy, sensitive guy under his pilot's uniform," was Brigid's answer.

Meanwhile, Eamon and Sean were talking.

"Hi, Eamon, why hide the fact you finally found a girl you like? Have you and her got together yet?"

"No, I, I'm not ready to do that, but she is nice to me. I don't think she wants to hurt me. I guess I am afraid of losing the respect of the wing," was Eamon's answer.

"Lose the respect of your fellow pilots? Are you crazy? The other pilots will really be glad for you. You'd finally be a regular guy, especially the day that we can tell you've had her for a night. Every pilot will cheer," Sean answered.

The opening ceremony began with the Hibernian national anthem and patriotic songs. The Taoiseach sent a written message proclaiming: "The recognition of our heritage of the ancient Celts, a project of the day our Celtic race will be free and all alien oppression." This was a reference to the Scottish, Welsh, and Breton separatists who sought independence in space as well as back on Earth.

The very first event was the camogie match. Constance Fitzgibben, player-coach, took to the field herself. The Dublin team was determined to avenge the previous loss in May. In the first half the Athlone girls had a good wind against them. Connie Fitz and two other girls suffered bruises after a mass collision. After a short delay, they returned to the field. At the end of the first forty minutes, the Dubs led 1 goal 10 points to 1 goal, 3 points. Connie's discouragement stemmed partly by the fact she thought her parents and her younger sister, Sharrey, were absent. Sharrey's alleged absence was painful because, even though the sister was not athletic, Connie always hoped she'd be supportive. Then, just as the second half began, Connie saw her parents sit down in a grandstand. A short time later, Connie saw her sister Sharrey in another section of seats. The fact that she was sitting with Tigeress gang girls and smoking didn't lessen Connie's joy.

"Let's go at 'em, the wind is with us now," was her war cry. The Athlone team arose to the occasion, using speed and skill. They ignored the Dubs rough tactics. When the gun fired, Athlone had won by 2 goals, 15 points to 1 goal, 15 points. Connie was carried on her players' shoulders.

The next game was hurling. A team of pilots from the Athlone base faced a team of shirt factory and brewery workers. Sean O'Connell went into the newly erected field house and emerged with fellow pilots. The lieutenant had played since age ten. His friend Eamon had preferred boxing and hand-to-hand combat, but with some coaxing the flight captain was also suited up to play. Eamon O'Rourke was trying to rediscover hurling; he had not played since age thirteen.

As the girls' game before, the flat-bladed stick carried the ball to the net. Three points was a goal if the ball went into the net, while only one point was awarded for over the cross bar.

Eamon lacked the skills to score, so he acted as Sean's policeman. The game became a bit physical. Shelley and Brigid went wild cheering for their men. Shelley said, "I wish Cathal and Dee were here, but Uncle Gene is still on his traplines."

The pilots had played as a unit while the factory men were a collection of men, a pick-up team. As the game continued, the pilots gradually dominated, leading 1 and 15 to 0 and 17 by the end of the first half. After ten minutes of the second half, a sudden mass collision knocked both Eamon and Sean senseless. The girls screamed as they were carried off the field. After play resumed, the game became tepid and slow. The pilots won 2 and 20 to 1 and 21. Eamon and Sean emerged from the field house bruised, limping, but proud.

Sean slapped his captain on the back saying, "He has a potential to be a half good hurling player."

The football game was between two junior teams from primary schools. It was so orderly and skillful, it put their elders to shame. The team for No. 3 Primary School beat school No. 8 by 1 goal 3 points to 1 goal 2 points.

After the games were over, the four young people toured a handcrafts exhibit of leather goods, handwoven cloth, tin, silver, and copper smithies, and candle and barrel makers. A dance group performed traditional step dancing. Poets recalled tales of Hibernia's ancient past. Artworks over two thousand five hundred years old were publicly displayed, although under guard. Tables offering a banquet of foods were available, as were barrels of ale.

In the afternoon the Athlone racetrack opened. Eamon was coaxed by Shelley, Sean, and Brigid into coming along. They succeeded in getting him to put a couple grams of gold in with theirs to bet on the third race. As the horses came into the home stretch, the usually quiet flight captain joined his friends in cheering their horse to victory. Eamon said, "I never thought betting could be so exciting."

"Maybe a bit of Father is coming out," Shelley answered.

Then Sean added, "Settlers from planets Espanol and Oporto have opened a Jai Lai Fronton in Dublin. Let's plan to go there someday soon."

Chapter 6

It was the first day of August. The floor of the Brittanic parliament building was a din of yelling and cursing. The speaker pounded his gavel and directed the sergeants-at-arms to restore order.

W.E. Gladstone arose, his party behind him, "Mr. Speaker, I request the floor."

The Speaker's answer: "The Chairman gives the floor to the Opposition leader."

"Gentlemen of this hallowed chamber," was his initial salutation. "The government has yet to learn the folly of its course of action. Earlier this summer we lost a third of our fighter force. Must we continue this foolish conflict until our cities are leveled and our economy bankrupt? We must end this mad venture."

Suddenly the great doors of the entrance of the parliament opened. "Your Majesty, Mr. Prime Minister," the Speaker exclaimed. Elizabeth the Seventeenth and Lord Cromwell entered with the Beefeater guards and dismounted men of the Household Cavalry.

"Guards! Seize Mr. Gladstone immediately," the monarch ordered.

"At last, Gladstone, we have detected your alliance with the anti-royalists. You are a traitor. You will hang!" Cromwell yelled.

The entire parliament wen into an uproar. Additional soldiers came. The queen commanded, "The parliament is dissolved. All members of Gladstone's Freedom Party are under arrest until the war is over."

"We may have more necks to put into nooses," Cromwell exclaimed.

As handcuffs and leg irons were placed on him, Gladstone stood erect without fear. "Mr. Speaker, before I depart to Melbourne, I demand to deliver a final word of warning."

The Speaker defied the monarch. "In accordance with our ancient customs, Mr. Gladstone is allowed to finish his speech."

"Gentlemen, I must confess, I was very mistaken. I wrongly believed that the war was the evil genius of Cromwell and that Elizabeth the Seventeenth was a noble queen and woman led astray. However, I now realize that the monarchial form of government is the root of this war. To bring peace and save the country, the monarch must go!"

Lord Cromwell pointed his angry finger, saying, "This is proof of his treason. He has just signed his death warrant."

The news of Gladstone's arrest sent an electric shock through the country. An Underground operative was one of the Beefeaters. When he reported to his immediate contact, he said, "I could have thrown my ceremonial pike right through the royal bitch. I could have ended it right then and there."

The Underground pulled almost all of its operatives out of London. Only the crew listening in on the Crystal Palace remained. The passive sabotage operations ceased until they could be sure penetration of their cells had not occurred. Soon hundreds of Boomerang fighters were delivered.

✧ ✧ ✧

A week had passed after the news was reported of Gladstone's arrest on the enemy planet. The Hibernian Defense Ministry held another war room meeting. The defense minister was grim.

"Gentlemen, we have entered a period of maximum danger. The Underground's sabotage campaign had held up the build up of the enemy's fighter fleet; however, now they will be building their fleet at an increased rate of production. Is there anyone at this table who has any sort of idea to stall the enemy?"

When no answer came after five minutes. Defense Minister Flynn said, "Well, gentlemen, all that I can report is that our air fleet is up to 570 and pilots are available. We are building ten more Bullethead fighters and additional surface guns. Also, the Alpha-X-10 project team is going to try a force field experiment in Cashel later this month. Finally, we are experimenting with an electric arc weapon. A cathode and an anode as tall as a broadcast tower will turn on an electrical arc. If an enemy fighter flies between the towers, the arc will short out the fighter's electrical control system. The craft will then simply crash."

✧ ✧ ✧

During August the *Parnell* was a beehive of activity. The crewmen who were selected to be part of the landing party were put through an indoctrination program. The timetable for when their party reached Earth was repeated over and over. It was calculated that the bus trip from San

Francisco to Chicago would take ninety hours, not including layover times in Salt Lake City and Omaha. They also calculated the time for the trip from Shanghai to Hawaii and from Hawaii to San Francisco. Depending on the speed of the hydrofoil used from Shanghai to Hawaii, the time was estimated from thirty to sixty hours. The time of the trip from Hawaii to San Francisco was judged to be in a range of 110 to 275 hours. In total, it was believed it would be two to four weeks from reaching the surface in Shanghai to arriving in Chicago. Allowing for all other contingencies, the operation could take up to six weeks or more.

"Do they still play baseball in America?" Helmsman Conor Cosgrave was in the serviceman's room talking to the American refugees.

"Yes, but it is not the professional games like a thousand years ago," Sammy King said.

Roger Steck added, "There have been no professional sports since the early twenty-first century."

The lieutenant was in shock. "How could that happen to the most powerful nation on Earth? How did your country come to such a sorry state?"

Sammy King began, "It was in the last third of the twentieth century. The environmentalist movement started about 1970. As that decade progressed, we were in the middle of a shortage of accessible usable energy. It was becoming difficult to find oil in our own country. Coal was said to be too dirty to burn. We were attempting to expand nuclear fission energy."

Roger Steck then continued the chronicle. "In 1979, an accident occurred at an atomic electrical generating plant in Pennsylvania. The press, as usual, sacrificed accuracy for good headlines. The environmentalists gained enough political power in the next two decades to block solutions to our energy shortage problems. By the time they gained total power, around 2010, the country was already in a decline. At the dawn of the twenty-first century, we were plagued by an influx of illegal immigrants. By the 2050s, we had masses of illegal emigrants leaving the country."

Cosgrave protested, "But couldn't you have revolted against the environmentalists? Didn't you Americans have a virtual arsenal of firearms?"

Betty Ann answered. "In 2011 they passed a heavy tax on the alloy metals used in manufacturing firearms. Then they paid out bounties for turning in firearms. Many millions of rifles and pistols were turned in by people who needed money simply to buy food or other necessary items. The people who kept their guns were smart. Hunting became the only way to put meat on the table. People began to use bows and arrows. A personal property tax on firearms was passed in 2037, exempting single shot muzzle loaders. Wild animals, many with rabies or canine distemper, were everywhere biting people."

Sammy King pulled three paper bills from his shirt pocket. "Look at the faces. They are twentieth century environmentalists: Brown, Nader, and Commoner. They replaced our noble founding fathers: Washington, Jefferson, and Lincoln."

Betty Ann, now angry, blurted out, "We don't even fly our old red, white, and blue star-spangled banner anymore. We fly a flag the environmentalists designed, dark and light green stripes and a Greek letter like a flattened "O" meaning death. Every time I see it flying I cry inside."

Her father, Roger Steck, then added, "We don't use the scientific metric system of measure. When it was introduced in the 1970s, a xenophobic reactionary movement crushed it out. There were idiotic claims that the metric system was part of some conspiracy. Pure paranoia."

Sammy King then added a note of irony. "Many of the ecologists' strongest supporters were actors, actresses, professional athletes. They were so wealthy that at first they were not impoverished by a stagnant economy. With lodges in the resort areas of thousands of hectares of land, they could stand back and tell others to do with less and less and still less. But when the economy collapsed about 2050, the stage and cinema and sports organizations went broke. The high-living entertainers learned what it was really like to do without."

Roger Steck then said, "You know, sometimes I wonder if we should be doing what we are attempting. Many of the people back home are actually quite contented. We have gotten back enough power so there is nobody hungry or naked now. We rebuilt our railroads for freight. The buslines carry our people across country on repaved roads. Many of our farmers get by on their steam tractors and harvesters. However, I think again, and I remember people must be given a choice. Many of our people back on the North American continent will choose to stay with the simple life. But others of those must have the chance to reach out to those who live in the Outer Solar System."

Helmsman Cosgrave was sick with grief. Learning the details of America's condition was like learning of the loss of a friend. He ordered a double shot of poteen and a stout. He wondered what reaching the American land would mean to him—renewed joy or additional despair?

❖ ❖ ❖

It was the fifth day of the month, and again DeValera Park was the site for the erection of podiums and stages. The Interplanetary Volunteers were holding a cultural fair to compliment the Pan-Celtic festival of the previous month. Two dozen temporary flag poles were set up. The opening ceremony was the rising of each flag of the planet-nations and the playing of their anthems.

The first event was an early afternoon concert by musicians who were IPVs from planet Sovietia. They performed Tchaikovsky's *Overture 1812* with bells and carbide cannon. The second event, later that afternoon, was another concert. The Franco-Italians performed Verdi's *Aida*. A dance show was performed in the evening by IPVs from Polonia. The following day the park was a kaleidoscope of arts exhibits and booths with the national foods of various planet-nations.

Eamon and Shelley O'Rourke came to the park at mid-morning. Accompanying them were Brigid Hallohan and Sean O'Connell. Eamon walked arm in arm with Brigid while Shelley walked with Sean. At noon they went into a giant tent in which a dining room was set. A multiplanetary smorgasbord was arranged so the guests could sample many different dishes.

Eamon, who loved seafood but rarely got to the chance to have it, sampled Scandinavian lutefisk and Franco-Italian shrimp scampi. Shelley tried Balkan gyros and Turko-Persian falafel. Brigid had Peking duck, while Sean feasted on veal cordon bleu.

In the afternoon, dance groups from a dozen planet-nations performed a virtual collage of customs, movements, and sounds from the planets Balkan, Turko-Persia, and Arabia. A dozen belly dancers exhibited their ancient art. Two were from the Golden Peacock and recognized Brigid as she came by. That evening there were no performances on the stage as workmen built a backdrop for scenery. All the following day and night and the day after, work went on in that corner of the park.

On the night of the eighth, the curtain was raised. Colonel Becker addressed the audience. "Ladies and gentlemen, as our part of this interplanetary festival, the IPVs of Planet Deutsche have practiced and rehearsed for two months in our spare time, preparing both instrumental and vocal arrangements. Now we are ready. It is my supreme pleasure to announce this production of one of our ancestors' greatest operas, based on ancient Teutonic folklore. Our production is *Die Valkure* by the immortal Richard Wagner."

Many of Hibernians had never seen an opera performed, as most only knew the ancient Irish plays of Earth. These were performed at the Abbey Theater in Dublin, a total reproduction of the theater on Earth. However, Colonel Becker gave a clear explanation of each act.

After Act I, the audience applauded loudly. Shelley asked, "Why can't we make one of our great plays into an opera, like Liam O'Flahery's *The Informer?*"

Eamon answered, "First we'd have to teach them to sing in Gaelic. Of course, we still have to teach half our own people."

There was a standing ovation when the last curtain dropped. Eamon whispered over to his sister, "Tomorrow I'll tell the Colonel what you said."

The festival was only half over when another, and totally dissimilar, event took place. Apprentices Boy's Day was the one day other than the Twelfth of July on the border people's calendar. Again the mass of men in black suits and women in long plain dresses marched into Athlone. Again the four girl gangs acted as guards, although at a fraction of their number due to the short notice. With her five equals in Galway, Shelley O'Rourke was in total command. Brigid Hallohan and the Quinncannon sisters acted as lieutenants.

Again the girl in the black denim jacket met the sober James King McKerr. The Orange Lodge Grand Master was also a colonel of the border people's militia. His son, William King, was present in the uniform of a new light academy cadet.

"The only reason I was allowed off base for this event was to deliver an address to our young men. I was to urge them to try to become pilots. But, like their fathers, they prefer to fight as infantry."

His father added, "When we regain our homes, a banner of King William of Orange will lead the way."

Mrs. Ann McKerr was present in the usual modest dress of a border woman, but Agnes was wearing a quite modern blouse and a skirt cut so high it exposed her legs, which were heavily bandaged at the knee. As Agnes hobbled around on crutches, Shelley asked, "Was Agnes in an accident?"

James King McKerr replied, "No, she dressed to represent Mary Ann McInherny, the sole survivor of the Shankill massacre of 2002. A dozen Provisional Republican guerillas beat her for refusing to give up her English language."

"So?" a flippant Karen Quinncannon retorted. "Our people were tortured for centuries for speaking Gaelic."

Mr. McKerr continued, "The twelve men, all masked, forced her to watch the slaughter of the people in Shankill, including her parents. Then they violated her innocent body, three men at a time. She was so badly internally injured, she could never bear children. Then to finish her off, they shot her through the kneecaps of both legs so she would die of loss of blood and shock. But she lived for fifty years, although crippled for life. On every anniversary of the foul deed, she would walk on her crutches into West Belfast, Andersontown, and the Falls area. Her sight shamed the Green communities. It may have been one of them who assassinated three of the culprits by a car bomb in 2017."

Karen Quinncannon was almost in tears, as were Shelley, Clara, and Brigid. Karen shook James McKerr's hand, saying, "By Holy Mary, I will never mock your people again."

Then Shelley added, "When the war ends, a covenant of peace and friendship between our two peoples should be signed."

The final event of that day, by the light of torches and kerosene lanterns, was an association football or soccer match. The IPVs and settlers formed one team. The other was formed by the Orange border people, as they played soccer instead of the Gaelic games that the rest of Hibernia played. The visiting teams included several former players of the professional Interplanetary League, but the boys in Orange fought them to a 2-2 tie. Their goalkeeper was Cadet Billy King McKerr. The gun fired, ending the game. The crowd gave applause to both teams. The game was a tie, but the Orangemen had won something more important. The border people were now accepted by most of the rest of Hibernia for themselves.

The festival continued two more days and ended with a choral group of young singers from every planet-nation.

✧ ✧ ✧

The trial of W.E. Gladstone took place in Parliament. The verdict and sentence was in before the opening gavel. Elizabeth the Seventeenth and Lord Cromwell presided personally over the hearing, the monarch in her full robe and crown and her chief minister in a powdered wing. The defendant was in chains before his accusers, still unbroken despite a severe lashing.

"W.E. Gladstone," the monarch commanded, "you are found guilty of high treason against the government and nation off Brittania. It is our sentence that you are to be taken to the Melbourne prison in the Australian sector. There you will be hanged by the neck until dead, and then you will be beheaded."

"However," her chief minister added, "your execution will be delayed until the execution of the Hibernians is complete. The attack that will be the final solution to the Irish problem will be broadcast into every home of our planet and the Melbourne prison. Then, your mounting the gallows will be broadcast to the planet-nation."

"If you intend to postpone my execution until the destruction of Hibernia, then I know I will be alive long after the both of you are dead," Gladstone answered without fear.

The monarch commanded, "Take the prisoner away at once!"

Lord Cromwell turned to her, saying, "Your Majesty, may I suggest we send invitations to each and every member of the aristocracy. Think of it, the entire ruling class here at the Crystal Palace to celebrate the extermination of Hibernia."

"A most excellent suggestion, Lord Cromwell," the queen answered.

The queen and prime minister did not know that the court stenographer was in the Underground. Late that night, the young woman reached an Underground operative outside of the city. Candy was working at a pub. The stenographer sat down beside her at a table.

"Want a beer, sugar?" Candy answered, "Gee, it's not often a girl tries to date me. I don't come cheap."

"It's not that. I have to meet a man called Blue Goose," the stenographer whispered.

"Let's forget the beer and go," Candy answered, adding, "If you weren't an operative I'd ask you to spend the night with me anyway. Business is slow."

The next morning the two women arrived in Liverpool by bus. Blue Goose was waiting at the wheel of a milk truck. The girls got into the back of the truck. The stenographer spoke first.

"Gladstone is to hang, but only after Hibernia is destroyed."

Blue Goose answered, "In that case, we better reactive our operations. I will contact the overall command."

Candy said, "Drive us to a lodge; we're both tired. Alone or not, I need sleep. I'd get more sleep working at the bar."

✦ ✦ ✦

Two days later a unit train was traveling on a railway bridge over a deep valley near Liverpool. The train carried tank cars with the raw materials for ion plasma fuel. It also carried engine parts for Boomerang fighters. As the train reached the middle of the bridge, bombs went off. The bridge caved in and the train went with it. The explosion was heard the length of the valley.

The city gaol of London held the members of Gladstone's Freedom Party. The prisoners were demoralized by the news of their party leader's death sentence. Then, at midday, the prison was shook by a bomb. The outer gate and wall were breached. Two gun towers were hit by laser fire. The Underground launched an assault on the prison. They ran past the gate to the inner building. They broke the door and dropped the guards where they stood. They blasted open the outer cell block door, then opened the individual cells. In minutes the prison population was freed. The Freedom Party members were led out by the operatives. The rest of the prisoners ran in all directions.

The attacks on the prison and the train signaled the Underground's return to activity.

✦ ✦ ✦

Student Nurse Theresa Lynch had spent over a month trying to forget Kate MacBride and the other four girls transferred to Galway. Kate wrote an occasional letter telling Terri of everything they were doing. In one letter Terri read that the five girls were rotating their beds. Two pairs of beds were doubled up and two pairs of girls would sleep together. One girl would sleep alone. They rotated on a five-day cycle, each girl sleeping alone one day out of five. Terri put the letter down. She began to remember that first night. Kate, with her huge breasts pressing against her. The big girl's tongue as it penetrated Terri's slit. Kate's hands opening her own slit and guiding Terri down to eat her out. The one night all five of the girls came in the clothes closet. Terri remembered going down on her knees and eating out Kate, then Caroline, Mairead, Jamie, and Mary Plunkett. The big cigar loaded with canapec juice swiped from the medicine locker that Kate lit and passed around. Terri remembered coughing on her first puff, then the lightheadedness coming on as the cigar was passed around.

Terri walked to the edge of the nightroom. She looked out the window to the ground ten floors below. She opened the window and looked outward. She thought it would be so easy. Just crawl out the window and jump.

The hospital intercom interrupted: "Nurse Lynch, report to the emergency operating room."

Terri turned around and left the nightroom. The elevator took her to the fifth floor. The patient was suffering a pulmonary edema. The operation to save the man's life took hours, Terri's entire work shift plus several more hours. Colonel McCracken praised the young student nurse for her newly found skill.

After her shift ended, Terri went back up to the nightroom without dinner. She walked right up to the open window. Again she thought of jumping. Then she thought to herself, "If I had jumped this morning, the patient might have died on the operating table. I'd be guilty of murder."

Terri walked back to her bed. She looked at the nightstand. There were the pictures of her father, mother, and her brother, Garrett, whom she had worshipped. She looked at the medal for bravery by her brother's picture. "Garrett died a hero. If I jump, what does that make me?" she thought as she looked straight at his picture.

Minutes passed, and then Terri felt a celestial presence. Not words, but thoughts: "Private Lynch, this is Captain Lynch. Even though you are my sister, I will talk to you like any other who would disgrace the uniform of Hibernia's Defense Service. I did not die in a fighter just to see a student nurse turn coward. Bernadette O'Rourke was the wife of my base commander. She died manning a surface gun. She died a heroine. What you are going to do is more than cowardice; it is almost treason. Don't shame your parents."

Terri Lynch stood at attention and saluted her brother's picture. Her thought waves answered, "No, Garrett, I won't jump. I will become a full commissioned nurse. I will make you and our parents proud of me again." She walked back to the window and closed it. Then, checking her watch, she determined the mess hall was still open for a late supper.

✦ ✦ ✦

It was evening, and the weather had turned unseasonably chilly. Eamon, Brigid, Shelley, and Sean had spent the day at the racetrack and then had dinner at one of Athlone's best restaurants. As they walked away from the restaurant Brigid asked, "Eamon, could you escort me to my apartment? This weather is awful."

He answered, "Yes, I will," then turned to Shelley. "Sean can escort you home. Don't wait up for me, I'll be going back to base."

His sister answered, "We won't, I mean, I won't wait. Good night."

Eamon could sense that Shelley and Sean would probably spend the whole night together, but he did not attempt to prevent it.

After a slow walk, during which Brigid told a couple of risqué jokes, they reached her apartment building. They entered the hallway and went up the stairs. "Come in for a minute, Eamon. I've got some Schlivovtza to warm up your chilly bones."

"What's that?" he asked.

"Balkan plum brandy—fiery."

When Eamon entered the apartment, he failed to see Brigid lock the door on the inside.

She brought out a decanter of brandy and two glasses. "To the safe return of your father." She raised the glass in toast.

Eamon's first sip of brandy produced a pained look. "That's powerful," he said.

Brigid placed a cigarette in her long green jade holder and pointed to a matchbox on the end of the table, asking for a light. Eamon nervously struck a match, and then Brigid kissed him on the cheek.

The room was cozy, with a sofa beside the low table and a thick carpet. Brigid turned on an electro-victrola and a soft tune filled the room. A single orange-shaded lamp had been turned on when they first came in, and the room was still rather dark. Brigid rubbed Eamon's thigh and then reached over and kissed him hard on the mouth.

He responded by taking her hand and kissing it. "I think I am in love with you and have been in love with you since that evening in May before the attack," Eamon said slowly and cautiously.

Brigid raised her jade holder to her mouth and filled her lungs with smoke. Then she seized Eamon and kissed him. As her tongue darted into his mouth, she exhaled the smoke into his throat until he coughed. Then, kissing him on the cheek, she practically threw him on his back. He at first tried to break away but could not bring himself to become violent enough to do so. Then his arms circled her waist. Brigid was wearing a low-cut evening gown, like the one she used on the stage. Eamon's hands were on her bare back.

For over twenty minutes they lay on the sofa necking. Brigid then lit another cigarette and, kissing Eamon, emptied a lung full of smoke into his mouth. She got up off the sofa and put another record on the electro-victrola. Then she began to dance and slowly removed her dress. Soon she was only wearing a bra and panties. Eamon rose from the sofa and watched, partly with pleasure, partly in shock. At her suggestion, he copied her actions, and soon he had on only his jockey shorts and white socks. His outer dress uniform lay on the floor beside her clothes.

Brigid kissed him, "You say you love me—show it. Let's go into bed now."

Eamon began to tremble and a tear came down his cheek. "I've locked the door," Brigid said firmly.

"You don't understand what you are asking me to do. You are asking me to throw away everything I believe in." His words were weak, like a frightened boy.

Brigid put her arms around him and said, "Eamon, I know what you told me in May, but it will be all right. Just because you won't deserve a virgin bride doesn't mean you can't marry another girl, one who has been around. You're like my shy sweet father. My mother seduced him the night he proposed. It was his first time, while she had screwed dozens of men."

"I don't know what to do," he whined.

She replied, "I can show you a real good time."

Brigid led Eamon into her nightroom. "Just remove the rest of your clothes and lay on your back," she said, adding, "It's a big waterbed."

Eamon asked, "Aren't you worried something could happen?"

Brigid answered, "There's a box of condoms in the chest of drawers by the bed. I am putting in a diaphragm. When a girl screws as much as I have, she has to be careful."

After going into her bathroom for the diaphragm, she lit a cigarette, placing it in her jade holder. Totally nude, she climbed up on the bed and stood above Eamon. She lowered herself, took his erect rod, guided it deep into her, and began to slowly rock.

Eamon was soon breathing heavily, saying, "I never knew it could be so good. I love you. I want to be with you for all time, I. . . ."

Brigid flicked cigarette ashes onto Eamon's chest, then playfully brushed the hot end against the nipple of one of his breasts. She put his hands up to her breast, stopping her rocking to prolong the ecstasy. "I can be more than the hot showgirl you screwed on a cold night in August. We can be friends and lovers. Like my mom did, I hope to meet a nice guy and settle down. Maybe you are the guy."

After a few minutes she began to rock fast. Eamon soon yelled as he felt his glands fire into Brigid, "I love you, want to marry . . . ooh, ooh!"

The next morning when Eamon awoke, Brigid was holding his head in her lap. "I hope you enjoyed that. There are some ex-showgirls who charge up to twenty grams of gold for a night."

"Did you ever do that?"

"You mean, sell my body? Not exactly. Me and a dozen other girls inherited a big amount from a shirt factory executive. We took turns spending weekends with him. We didn't ask to be in his will, he just did it. And the plum brandy, that was pay for a favor I did for an IPV doctor. He was a Serbo-Croatian from planet Balkan. One of his patients was an elderly widower, a terminal case. I dressed up as a nurse and slipped into his hospital room for the whole night. He died three days later a happy man."

Eamon looked up at Brigid and, rising his head, began to suck on her breast. She said, "You know, the day before the attack, your little brother Cathal delivered flowers to our main dressing room. If he had gone in Pam O'Reilly's personal dressing room, she would have balled Cathal right then and there. In fact, if he came into my room, I'd have balled him myself."

Eamon was shocked. "Cathal is just a boy!"

She retorted, "You were just a boy last night, Eamon. Of course, he is with his girl Deirdre on your uncle's houseboat in the marshlands. They might have learned it by themselves."

The two arose from the bed, showered, and went out to breakfast. Afterward, Eamon walked Brigid back to her apartment. "Can I see you again?" he asked after kissing her on the cheek.

"Sure. You're my lover now." Brigid kissed him squarely on the mouth.

When Eamon reached the Athlone air base, he was met by Sean O'Connell.

"Sean, you look like you didn't get any sleep last night."

"Well, Eamon, you look no better."

"Were you with my sister Shelley all night?"

"Were you with Brigid?" The guilty look on both of the two men's faces was the silent answer.

The two men entered the pilot's locker room, and the other pilots began snickering. Lieutenant Ranier asked, "What have our wing captain and first lieutenant been doing last night?"

Lieutenant Antonio Soares added, "And with what two women were they with?"

Captain O'Rourke answered, "Attention; at ease, Sean. Apparently none of you understand that a gentleman does not talk about such things."

Lieutenant O'Connell added, "You don't say anything about the women you love behind her back."

Lieutenant Ranier asked, "In love with or made love to?"

"Either or both, it makes no difference," was Eamon's reply. Lieutenant Soares answered, "We understand, Captain. Congratulations to the both of you."

"At ease and as you were, gentlemen," the captain ordered. The rest of the day passed without another snicker.

❖ ❖ ❖

It was the last week of August. Cathal O'Rourke and his friend Deirdre O'Toole had returned to Athlone. Cathal returned to his home while Deirdre went to the Quinncannon sisters.

It was Sunday, August thirtieth. The O'Rourke children went to morning mass. Afterward they met their friends, Brigid, Sean, and Deirdre. They all went to the O'Rourke home for brunch. In the early afternoon Eamon and Cathal were playing chess in the parlor. On the front porch Sean sat with the three young girls. He took out a long thin cigar saying, "This is special, rum-flavored." He lit it then handed it to Shelley. She in turn passed it to Brigid, who handed it to Deirdre.

The phone rang in the kitchen. Eamon picked it up. On the other end a heavy accented voice spoke: "This is Major Miriam Eshkol, Abrahamite Embassy. I am at the Interplanetary shuttle base. A young Abrahamite woman has arrived and is attempting to contact you. She has a letter from a Captain Eamon O'Rourke. Are you that officer?"

"Yes, Major," he replied.

"The girl's name is Naomi Sennech. The letter says there is an infant girl in this city whose father was Naomi's late brother."

"Yes, I sent the letter. Can I talk to Miss Sennech?" Eamon asked.

"I am sorry, Captain, but she is a deaf girl. She does read a little English but cannot speak it. I will have to accompany her until the initial meeting of her with the parents of her niece."

Eamon answered, "I will try to meet you at the shuttle base, and I will contact the family as well." After he hung the phone, he called all the others into the kitchen and explained the phone call.

"Brigid," he asked, "Do you know their phone number? If so, call them. Tell them to wait at their home. We will pick them up and take them to the shuttle base."

After Brigid called the McLaughlins, all six went out to the driveway where two motorcycles, one with two side cars, sat. Eamon, Brigid, Cathal, and Deirdre climbed into one, Shelley and Sean on the other.

In ten minutes they reached the two-story frame house. Maureen Kelley and Theobald McLaughlin were waiting out front.

Mo spoke. "The children are asleep and Miss MacDevitt can take care of them."

Eamon asked, "Either of you ride a cycle?"

"No, we can use my father's old car," Theobald answered. Eamon and the McLaughlins got in the car.

"I will drive," Mo Kelley said as she got behind the wheel. "Theo never got a license. Now if this car can only start. I usually take a bus to work." The car coughed and wheezed its way to life and lumbered out of a creaking garage.

"Hope you aren't stopped for over-age plates," Jan MacDevitt said as the machine groaned down the street. Turning to the five who remained, she asked all of them in for tea.

The shuttle port had had only light business since the war. Major Eshkol and Naomi stood near the gate off the street leading into town. The major wore a light blue military uniform. When the car pulled up, parked, and its occupants got out, Major Eshkol saluted, saying, "Captain O'Rourke, I am Major Eshkol, and this is Naomi Sennech."

Naomi, in a plain grey dress and shawl, came up to hug the two civilians, almost by instinct. Her hands then asked, "Where is my baby niece?" as Major Eshkol translated. Theobald answered, "She is at home with her big brother and sitter, Miss MacDevitt."

The major then explained the details of the girl's visit. "Miss Sennech is on a ninety-day visa. It can be extended another ninety-days. Also, if there is a suitable school for her, she could receive a student visa good for one year and renewable. After that, well, that is too long to be determinable."

Eamon O'Rourke answered, "I read in the newspaper that the new O'Donovan Rossa School for the Deaf and Hearing Impaired will open in Kilkenny in November."

"Kilkenny!" Mo Kelley exclaimed. "My parent's farm is down there." The McLaughlins embraced the young girl.

The Major then added, "I will have to accompany her for a few days until I can be sure you can care for her."

The five people climbed into the old motorcar, which wheezed its way back to the McLaughlin home.

Miss Jan MacDevitt and the children were waiting at the gate of the house. Mo Kelley took the baby girl from the sitter.

"Here is your niece, Naomi," she handed the baby to her. For a minute the young girl looked at the little baby in her arms. Then, sitting down on a front porch step to free a hand, she signaled, "She is a beautiful girl. But, please, tell me, how did you meet my brother, Issac?" Major Eshkol translated Naomi's hand signs into words.

Maureen Kelley sighed and sat down beside Naomi, taking her hand. "It is a long story and not too pretty." Mo waited for the major to translate:

"I am a dancer, a tassel twirler. I work at the Golden Peacock Music Hall. Over five years ago, I worked at a place called the Cat's Paw. It was a dump. The girls who worked there were expected to mingle with the men and go out with them. For all purposes, I was a tart. I'm not ashamed of what I did. I always liked men. Well, one day I met a pilot named Captain Garrett Lynch. We became friends, and he said he wanted to marry me. Then he was killed during the last war. Half a year later, I gave birth to Barry, my young boy. I returned to work at the Cat's Paw and hustled every man I could to support myself and send money to my parents in Kilkenny. They took care of Barry after he was weaned from my breast. Until then I would nurse him in the dressing room until my turn to dance was up. Then after I finished dancing and feeding him, I'd start servicing the customers." Mo Kelley waited a couple of minutes for the story to sink in.

Naomi asked through the major, "How did you meet Issac?"

"It was over two years ago. It was peacetime, but pilots were still patrolling. Your brother Issac came in on a furlough. I met him first at the Cat's Paw, just like I met Garrett, but soon he was seeing me outside. He was even interested in Barry. He knew it was against the custom of his people to intermarry, but he said he loved me. Again, as with Garrett, I felt like a lady. Then he went off on a test flight of an experimental tracking system and crashed. I was pregnant again. The Cat's Paw burned down while I was in the hospital. I was determined to never cheapen myself again. I began dancing at the Golden Peacock, where the *only* thing I do is dance. I am paid three times more for just dancing than for all that I did at the Cat's Paw.

"I met Theo, my husband, in the cemetery. He was putting flowers on the tomb of his parents, whom he took care of for thirteen years, since he was ten. I was putting flowers on the graves of the pilots I loved and lost. He offered to sit for my babies so I could work. Soon it became a courtship. We married in March."

Naomi thought for a minute, then her hands spoke. "You could have given the children away, but you loved them enough to keep them. Thus, you are a good mother. I did not care when the rabbi back home described you as a Jezebel. I am proud to know you as the mother of my niece."

"Thank you, Naomi," Mo said. "I love Barry and Esther as much as any mother could ever love her children. I have their love and the love of my man-child, Theo McLaughlin. May Holy Mary help me if I ever lose him. Now, I welcome you to my family."

The entire assemblage of people gathered around the little Abrahamite visitor. Theo then counted the entire number, "Well, we have thirteen here instead of five; I will get out another big capon for the stewpot."

Jan MacDevitt then said, "I will brew more tea for now. Goodness sakes, we have a whole afternoon and evening to talk about near everything under the sun." The mass of people entered the house.

✤ ✤ ✤

A week later, at the Defense Ministry, another pre-dawn meeting was held. The Taoiseach, the defense minister, Colonels Becker and Kalminsky, and Commanders Donahue and MacMullen were present. Defense Minister Flynn opened the conversation:

"Gentlemen, our friends in the anti-royalist Underground of Brittania have sent us their most recent report. Within this week the enemy will send a reinforcement to the quadrant. No transports, but up to six hundred fighters. To divert our forces, their quadrant force will launch an attack with their current strength."

Commander Donahue of Dublin asked the defense minister, "Do we have an idea where they will hit? Dublin or Athlone? Or the bases ringing their quadrant Roscommon, the North Pole, or Connemarra?"

"The bases around the quadrant aren't large enough targets to be worth losing 250 fighters. The attack is, of course, of diversion, but they do want to damage us as much as possible. It will be Dublin or Athlone. I suggest that two squadrons be each ready at the South Pole Base and Roscommon to assist defending the cities."

Commander MacMullen then made a suggestion. "The fighters we send to assist should, after take-off, reach up to one hundred kilometers. Out of atmospheric friction they will save fuel, even at speeds up to forty thousand kilometers per hour. They will come right down on top of the enemy when it reaches either city."

Commander Donahue then offered two of his own Dublin squadrons to aid the defense of Athlone. Colonel Kalminsky accepted the offer and in reply pledged two squadrons of Athlone fighters to assist if Dublin were hit. The defense minister was pleased by the unanimity of the meeting.

Colonel Becker then rose a more distressing matter. "Herr Flynn, we still have fewer pilots than fighters and many of the new pilots are inexperienced.

We added the equivalent of two squadrons each of green pilots to both the Athlone and Dublin bases, working them into units of seasoned veterans. The two-man crews of ten new Bullethead fighters are right from academy."

Defense Minister Flynn commanded, "What is your recommendation, Becker?"

Becker's reply: "IPV veteran pilots, including men formerly of Peenemude are to be used at the South Pole as instructors. I suggest they be the squadrons sent up the line to Dublin or Athlone."

Joe Flynn approved Colonel Becker's proposal. "Gentlemen, I have another small surprise. The *Arthur Griffith* was moved north to Cashel two days ago to decrease its time to reach its station near Portlaoise. I sent workcrew up to mount a pair of laser batteries on board. It was hard work, but the old craft isn't a sitting duck like she was. Now the big question: will the enemy hit Dublin or Athlone?"

The Taoiseach had been silent through the meeting, listening carefully. Since the massacre of children at the Gaelic schools in Roscommon, he had studied every military report in detail. The man whose profession was peace was girding himself, mentally and emotionally, for the war.

"Gentlemen, I do not claim to tell you the business for which you are trained. But it is very clear to me that they will hit this city. The entire brain and nervous system of our defenses are here. They might even try to destroy this very building. I, therefore, instruct you to begin all alert procedures."

✦ ✦ ✦

It was a tearful moment at the evacuation train the following morning. Mo Kelley and her husband, Theo McLaughlin, gave instructions to Major Eshkol for the care of Barry and Esther. The major translated for Naomi. Mo said, "My parents will meet you at the Kilkenny station and you'll go to their big farm. I am sorry that Jan MacDevitt isn't coming with."

Theo added, "Yes, she just told us the other day she is going by bus to the Enniskillen Valley. You know, she has been in a courtship with Paddy Tully, an ex-postman. They hope to wed in a couple of months. He has friends and relatives in the valley. They'll be safe."

Major Eshkol, whose uniform and star of David emblem was as military as a Hibernian pilot, saluted and shook their hands. Naomi, tears running down her cheeks, hugged the mother and step-father of her niece. Her hands gave her parting, "May God protect you." Then with her voice she added, "Shalom."

✦ ✦ ✦

"I would rather spend ten hours in surgery than one hour with these forms and requisition papers," Colonel McCracken thought to herself. She put away the last form and closed her desk. A knock came at her office door.

After the colonel permitted the entrance, Nurse trainee Lynch came in with an envelope. The nurse private saluted and then reported, "Colonel, I have just received this letter from Captain Eamon O'Rourke of the Athlone base."

The colonel took the envelope from the young nurse and read. She looked at the photo of the young boy. Colonel McCracken read over the letter, then looked up at the young girl, whose eyes were filled with hope. "We are on a full alert with no leaves allowed until the danger is passed," the colonel firmly stated.

"But, isn't there some way I could at least contact the captain and that family? That little boy is all that is left, a remnant of Garrett." Terry Lynch was beginning to lose hope.

The colonel answered, "Let us go to the radio room." When they arrived, Colonel McCracken instructed the radio operator to signal the Athlone base.

✦ ✦ ✦

Captain O'Rourke had just finished addressing his squadron pilots when he was summoned to the radio room. He picked up the headphone, "This is Colonel Patricia McCracken, Kilkenny Base Hospital. I have a student nurse here, Private Theresa Lynch. She has received a letter from you informing her of a little boy, a nephew."

Captain O'Rourke answered, "Kilkenny Hospital! The children are probably on an evacuation train to there. The mother's parents have a huge farm there, the Kelley farm."

"The Kelley farm!" the colonel noted. "I have walked past that farm delivering medical reports."

The captain answered, "I can call the McLaughlin family here. They can contact the parents. Colonel, can any arrangement be made for a formal meeting?"

"Negative. All leaves are cancelled here, just like in Athlone," the colonel answered. Then, after ten seconds of looking at a tearful Nurse Lynch, "Wait a minute. Could they come to the civilian wing of the hospital? We have a visitor's room. Nurse Lynch finishes her duty shift at . . . 1900 hours. They could visit for an hour at least there, still technically on the post. After the alert is over, we could arrange for a pass, even a furlough. My records indicate she hasn't had time off since April."

Captain O'Rourke answered, "That is a brilliant idea. My full regards to the nurse."

The colonel hung the phone. Terri Lynch was in tears. "Thank you, Colonel. I haven't felt this happy since before the last war."

Colonel McCracken answered, "My daughter just had her third infant. Bald as an egg, red as a beet, wrinkled as a prune."

✦ ✦ ✦

The evacuation train pulled into Kilkenny. The McLaughlin children, the major, and Naomi came out. Michael and Ann Kelley came right up to them. "Grampy, baby sister has an aunt." Barry Lynch tugged at his grandfather's leg.

The Kelleys shook the major's hand and embraced Naomi. Michael Kelley announced, "Barry Lynch, you have an aunt too. A little nurse at Kilkenny Hospital."

The little boy began to ask, "Can I see her?"

Mrs. Kelley hugged Naomi saying, "We've got a big dinner for you, child. Roast mutton, potato soup, mixed vegetables, soda bread, and spice pie."

"Yessiree," her husband added, 'I'd bring out a ham, but they'd not been cured enough yet."

The major gasped. "It is a good thing, Mr. Kelley. It is against the customs of our people since seven thousand years ago to consume swine flesh. No offense meant—just a reminder who Naomi and I represent. Also, remember, Naomi is deaf. I must translate for her until she can learn to lip read English."

Michael Kelley answered, "And Gaelic. You must remember where you are! The O'Donovan Rossa School will open soon."

It was 7:30 when the McLaughlin car entered the gate on the surface of the Kilkenny Paramilitary Hospital. The security guard had been informed of their arrival. They parked over the civilian part of the complex, then they walked to the surface floor of the barracks building. They took the elevator straight to the bottom. Leaving the elevator, they walked down the slotted runway. Then they reached the ten-story building of the hospital itself, actually walking around backward under where they came. They walked into the entrance of the hospital, to the night desk. The clerk on duty directed the party to another elevator. Two floors up, they entered the waiting room. Major Eshkol recognized Colonel McCracken's rank insignia and saluted. Then, from below the colonel, Terri came up. She opened her arms wide and received all of her visitors. Michael Kelley said, "You're a pretty thing. Here is your nephew."

Barry Lynch leaped up into the arms of his aunt. Ann Kelley said, "This is truly worth a late supper. Let's sit down and cover the last few years."

"Auntie, here is baby Esther and my other aunt." Little Barry pulled on Terri's uniform to introduce her to Esther and Naomi. The quiet girl handed the baby girl to the nurse. Terri asked, "You are her aunt. Oh, it does say a little about Esther in the letter."

Naomi's hands made several signals. The major translated, "We have on planet Abraham a saying from our ancestors. It means congratulations and good luck." Naomi dropped her hands and spoke to the people looking toward her. "Mazel Tov."

✦ ✦ ✦

175

Chapter 7

Four hundred kilometers above the surface of Hibernia, the tanker *Arthur Griffith* orbited at the latitude of Tipperary sector. At the bridge, Captain Tomas O'Dwyer was watching the ship's scanners while deep in thought. The placing of two laser gun turrets on board his craft brought considerable pride to the captain and his crew. It had required the mid and aft sections of the ship to be depressurized during the period the platforms and electrical equipment were installed. This had required his crew to wear pressure suits for an entire week. The same thing had been required when the work of engine mountings had been performed on the *Parnell* earlier that year.

Captain O'Dwyer ordered two shuttle craft to have laser guns mounted on board. This, in addition to the twin turrets on the tanker and two escort fighters, was reassuring to the crew. The captain thought in a whimsy, "At least we won't be caught helpless when Her Brittanic Degeneracy's Boomerang pilots come in for tea and brambeck."

Tomas O'Dwyer was a career officer, a former Bullethead fighter pilot. Taking command of the *Griffith* was for him the fulfillment of ambitions. She was old and small, but she was his. He was proud of his crew. The thought of the *Griffith* being decommissioned and dismantled was a blow to the collective morale of the crew. The fact that he and his crew would be considered first to man the *McCracken* did not lessen the sense of bitterness.

The captain had finished a breakfast of black pudding, fresh soda bread, tea, and the ungodly powdered eggs. Just before his ship had moved from its South Pole station, he had purchased a large stock of fresh eggs. He had done this with his own money though a private supplier. The galley would serve real eggs the morning after the upcoming battle, if the ship survived.

As he sat in the captain's console, the scanner operator reported, "Captain, we are picking up a large number of craft. They are coming out of the enemy quadrant, heading southwest."

Captain O'Dwyer answered, "After a week, the Brits have finally made their move. Helmsman, pull us out of latitudinal orbit and steer us northwest in the direction of Athlone." Then he turned to the radio operator, "Radio Athlone war room. Tell them we are coming in, and signal our fighter escorts to follow."

✦ ✦ ✦

In Athlone the city had been quiet for a week. At the air base many pilots had remained out by their fighters for several days. Serving carts had been loaned from a vacant hotel to wheel food from the mess hall to the flight hangars. Infantry-type knapsacks were rolled out beside fighters, pilots taking their night's sleep just a jump away from a cockpit.

Around the city, most of the auxiliary gunners had made similar arrangements. The women ate and slept at their gun turrets. Around them a city half-dead held its breath. The shirt factories and synthetic gas plants still operated, but the workers had an eye on the pathway to the network of giant bomb shelters.

✦ ✦ ✦

In the war room, Taoiseach O'Hara, Defense Minister Flynn, and Colonels Becker and Kalminsky awaited the report of the scanner sighting that would be the opening of battle. The young colleen operating the scanners reported, "Colonel Kalminsky, we are picking up a force of fighters. Computer printout says that . . . they're Brittanic. A wave of fifty."

Then a minute later she added, "More waves of fighters following. Fifty and another fifty . . . two more waves. Print out, 250 craft, apparent target . . . Athlone!"

Joe Flynn announced, "Sound the alarms. Radio Dublin, Roscommon, South Pole, and the *Griffith*." The Nigerian IPV at the radio answered, "The *Griffith* is already pulling out of its Cashel station and coming in."

✦ ✦ ✦

The alarm rang throughout the city. The shirt factory workers marched straight to the shelter complex. At the other edge of town, the Corbett Flower Shop closed. Jim Corbett headed for his ambulance station, instructing two employees to go down into the deep basement where the mushrooms were raised. Cathal and Deirdre obeyed quietly.

✦ ✦ ✦

Within one minute of the alarm, Athlone squadron 1 was in the air with squadrons 2, 3, and 4 close behind. Captain O'Rourke signaled, "A-S-1 leader to base, we are on our way. Please advise the D, R, and SP squadrons to converge over city." As the Needlehead fighters roared down the airstrip and off, the Bullethead squadron fired straight up from their launchers.

✦ ✦ ✦

In the war room the defense minister and others could see the approaching enemy on the massive overhead screen. Colonel Becker spoke. "Our Athlone squadrons 1 to 4 will make the first contact, back tracking in a running fight until squadron 5 to 7 come up. When they drop back to the city, six extra squadrons will come in."

The scanner operator reported, "Sirs, the last two waves are merging as one and dropping fast. The first three are going to meet our squadrons head on." The radio operator turned her receiver to loud speaker. "This is Colonel Murphy, South Pole. Squadron 1 is airborne, heading up to one hundred kilometers, but squadron 2 is not ready. Their fighters were undergoing maintenance. Sudden breakdown of tracking scanners. Part of Squadron 3 is able to fly. It will be a delay of fifteen minutes to thirty minutes."

Defense Minister Flynn muttered, "Our plans go awry at the worst possible moment."

The scanner operator then reported, "The three waves of enemy fighters are merging into one."

Colonel Kalminsky answered, "Radio Major Hoffman's Bullethead squadron to shift their attack to the second wave. Give them their location, altitude, and speed."

✦ ✦ ✦

Two hundred kilometers over Athlone, ten Bulletheads continued their first climb. Major Ernst Hoffman radioed the other pilots, "*Achtung*, the enemy is forming two attack waves, the second is dropping low and fast. We are to intercept them. Use scanners. We will fire together." The Bullethead pilots saw the second wave of the enemy had overtaken the first. It was already ahead and dropping altitude to a level low enough to being strafing.

The still climbing fighters leveled off. Then they nose dived, heading almost straight down, diving so rapidly that in a minute they were almost on top of the. Major Hoffman ordered, "Fire, then pull up, Schnell!" The ten craft released a stream of plasma charges. Then as each pilot began to pull his craft off its dive, the tight attack phalanx came apart. Below the ten plasma bursts formed an elongated chain of lightning-like fire. Two dozen Boomerang fighters flew right into the ion cloud and disintegrated. The rest continued downward to begin strafing.

Major Hoffman radioed to the war room. "The enemy is now so low, we cannot use regular diving attack procedures. We will turn around and pursue." This meant his pilots would be firing the plasma guns like conventional lasers, at one target at a time. "What a waste," he muttered.

✦ ✦ ✦

Captain O'Rourke led squadrons 1 and 3 while Lieutenant O'Connell followed with 2 and 4. As their forward scanners picked up the approaching enemy, the squad merged into one long wave. Then, when visual sighting took place, they pulled into an attack phalanx, wings nearly touching.

The wave of Needlehead fighters fired pencil beams as one. A dozen Boomerang fighters vanished. Many of the Athlone fighters streamed through the holes made by the wreckage, others flew over or under the enemy fighters that remained, dodging return fire. Then the two opposing fighter wings broke off into individual dogfights as the mass of fighters still headed south.

✦ ✦ ✦

Over twenty-five minutes had passed. Colonel Becker was asking the radio operator to signal Roscommon and Dublin. The woman at the console replied, "I am sorry, there is only static."

"*Mein Gott*, they could be jamming our radio communications and/or scanners," the colonel answered. Colonel Kalminsky suggested the use of the electrophone.

Over the phones, Commanders Donahue and MacMullen reported jamming of electronic equipment. Defense Minister Flynn, after hanging up the phones, said sadly, "Their take-off was delayed by twenty minutes more. The enemy will reach us first."

As the running battle streamed south, Captain O'Rourke signaled his pilots to continue pursuit. As the fighting continued, three Needlehead fighters, piloted by green cadets, were destroyed. One pilot ejected from his craft in a safety pod. Then, before Eamon's horrified eyes, the pod was shot to atoms by a Brittanic fighter. "You murdering bastard!" the captain exclaimed over a radio frequency set so the enemy could hear it. Then Eamon rolled his ship over and around, back to the foe. Switching his laser to a pencil beam, he cut the Boomerang fighter in two.

For a moment he paused to reflect on an incident from the last war. It was the first air battle he was in after the death of his mother. A Brit pilot had bailed out of his fighter and was floating down, helpless. For a split second, Eamon's finger was ready to pull the trigger on his laser and kill the enemy pilot. Only the code of honor that his own father had personally instilled in him prevented him from committing cold-blooded murder.

Then Eamon's pause was broken by the voice of Sean O'Connell, "Eamon, you've one on your tail!" Captain O'Rourke pulled his craft leftward just in time to avoid the enemy's guns. Then, while firing his tail laser, he climbed up into an Immelmann roll. He came right down behind his helpless enemy and destroyed him with short fast laser bursts. "Captain O'Rourke, to all pilots, begin double teaming the enemy planes," he radioed his flight wing.

❖ ❖ ❖

Major Hoffman's Bullethead squadron was picking off one fighter after another. Then, using their secondary afterburners, the Boomerang craft began to try to run away. The major received a message: "This is the war room. Be careful entering the northward edge of the city. The new Electric Arc weapon and a laser battery group are set up for an ambush." Major Hoffman radioed the massacre to his pilots and then signaled back, "Our squadron will pull about to rejoin Captain O'Rourke's squadrons."

❖ ❖ ❖

On a road coming north of Athlone, a late tram of evacuees was sighted by a single Brit fighter. Diving, the fighter hit the vehicle with laser fire. The engine exploded. A handful of people fell out the emergency door. They ran down into a gully beside the road and into a culvert.

One of those climbing out was Pamela O'Reilly. As she began to head for safety, she heard a cry for help behind her. A small boy on crutches was trying to get out of the bus. She turned around and climbed back in the bus. Picking the boy up, she carried him out again. Then, running as fast as she could with the burden in her arms, she got into the large drain pipe just in time. The enemy fighter had come back and, strafing, finished off the tram. Several of the people who had fled now began to cry for the people who could not get out of the bus and were dead.

"What is your name?" Pam asked the little boy who was now on her lap.

"Timothy MacBride" was the answer. "My parents are still in town. Why did they send me up here? Did they want me to die? They sent my sister Kate to gaol, and they must want to be rid of me too."

"I'm Pam O'Reilly, little boy, and I wish you were about fifteen or older," the girl answered.

"I'm only nine, ma'am," Timothy said. "Why do you want me to be older?"

Pam was going into heat from the excitement. She replied, "So I could scr—oh, what the hell." Then she seized the innocent cripple in her arms and kissed him. She laid back on her side, pulling the boy tightly against her. "Let us just lay here. We'll be safe," she said as she began to hug the little boy in her arms. While they were laying together, the other survivors were trying to pull the charred bodies out of the burnt tram.

As the first wave of Boomerang fighters approached the city, they split into three groups. One veered eastward in a wide arc to come into the petroleum storage tank park east of Athlone. The second wave veered west and began to strafe the shirt factory district. The third wave headed straight south. As it reached the northern edge of town, the Electric Arc weapon was turned on. A half dozen enemy fighters came through the arc. With their controls shorted out, they spun out and crashed. Another wave of fighters climbed up over the electric arc, then descended right into the scanner range-finders of a six-turret laser battery. Three Boomerang fighters were destroyed at once.

With this ambush a large number of enemy craft were channeled into a laser crossfire, then a Boomerang pilot's gun destroyed one of the twin towers of the electrical arc. The surprise weapon was out of action.

✦ ✦ ✦

On the east side of Athlone, the wooden dummy storage tanks went up like kindling. Several held a mixture of water, vegetable oil, and a little amount of kerosene to burn like a real tank. Then the parts of the state refinery that were not yet underground were hit. A conflagration began. Firefighting units attached to the refinery attempted to fight the blaze. Several fire trucks came under laser fire. The surface batteries around the refinery put up a shower of fire at the strafing craft.

✦ ✦ ✦

On the other side of town, one shirt factory after another was hit. A single fighter zig-zagged down the street and would blast open the walls of the shirt factories. The fighters following would open into the exposed workrooms, destroying looms and spinning equipment.

In the deep bombshelter built for them, many of the women who worked the mills were crying, fearing not just for their jobs but for their lives and those of their families. Among them were the Quinncannon sisters. Karen screamed, "We're all going to die, I know it. We're going to die."

Then their shop foreman, a burly grey-haired man, shouted, "Quiet, all of youse! We've survived her Brittanic degeneracy's flying scumbags before, and we will survive this too. Now, all of youse, let's just say a rosary and pray for our brave boys doing battle with those Brit cutthroats."

✦ ✦ ✦

As the central group of the enemy entered the heart of town, surface laser bursts began to fill the sky. The Boomerang craft were using pencil beam to destroy every building in sight. Again the Brewery co-op was hit and the Fitzgibbon department store; the Islamic bank was hit again, as was the Hibernian Petroleum Institute building, barely finished. As the enemy came over the entertainment district, several music halls were set ablaze, including the Golden Peacock. As they watched the music hall burn, Brigid and Shelley muttered, "Lousy Brit vandals." Then they resumed firing their laser gun.

✦ ✦ ✦

In a working class neighborhood on the south side of the city stood the home of Joseph and Katherine Concannon. They were down in the basement of the red brick home. With them were Robert and Finola MacBride and Arthur Concannon, Joseph's brother. Despite the danger and its resulting need for harmony, an argument was reaching a climax.

Joseph yelled at his brother, "Don't try to fool me, Arthur! I know perfectly you have been writing to that—that wicked girl who brought disgrace to this house. It's my wife's idea to bring you here for shelter; I'd throw you out myself!"

"Joe, can't you forgive Mary P. after five years? She's your only child," the brother replied.

Robert MacBride interrupted, "You sound just like my wicked and ungrateful son, Timothy. We pampered him because of his crippled legs, but all the time he has been writing to his pagan sister. He even met her in July. Well, cripple or not, I hung him up by his arms on a meathook and laid my old razor strap into his evil hide. It was Finola who put him on the bus, without a proper guide as well."

Then Arthur Concannon, as gentle as any ten men, exploded, "You whipped a crippled boy like a horse! You bastard!" He threw a punch that flattened Robert to the floor. Joseph Concannon picked up a tire iron and said, "That does it. Out of this house. Never come back again."

Arthur climbed up the ladder and out of the basement. Then he walked out of the house and around to the backyard. He had just reached a toolshed when he heard a fighter's engine. He dove to the ground and, looking up, saw a Boomerang fighter. Its laser gun hit the house dead center. Then it was apparently damaged, for it crashed right into the remains of the house. Arthur Concannon thought, "My God, they're dead, all dead. M.P. is an orphan now. So are Kate and Timmy. What will become of them?"

✦ ✦ ✦

In the war room, panic was setting in. The Taoiseach cried out, "The city is becoming a bonfire. Where are the reserve squadrons?"

182

The radio operator switched again to a loudspeaker. "This is Lieutenant Ranier. Squadrons 5, 6, and 7 have sighted the enemy and Captain O'Rourke's wing. We are joining the battle now."

Another pilot radioed in. "Major Hoffman, we are ready to join Captain O'Rourke's squadrons in engaging the enemy."

The defense minister commented, "At least the second wave of enemy fighters won't reach us." Turning to the scanner operator, he asked for an estimate of the time before squadrons arrived from Dublin and Roscommon. "Still up to thirty more minutes," the colleen at the terminal replied. "They aren't coming fast enough."

The minister asked, "What is stopping them?"

✤ ✤ ✤

Brigid Hallohan and Shelley O'Rourke had hit several Brit craft and were still firing when a ricocheting laser burst hit the turret. "It's out of action, Shelley. We must head for an air-raid trench," Brigid said as she grabbed Shelley's hand to lead her.

The two girls ran, stooped low, until they reached a dugout, then jumped in. They thudded against hard-packed earth.

"Brigid, I think I broke my arm." Shelley was wincing in pain. "Brigid . . . Brig?" She turned around to see her friend holding her leg.

"It broke," was Brigid's reply. Then they heard a loud explosion. The two girls peeked up over the top of the dugout. "Look," Brigid yelled, pointing to the now destroyed turret.

"If we had remained there we'd be in little pieces. It's like how my mother died in the last war," Shelley exclaimed.

Then Brigid answered, "We better get down the tunnel. We're still exposed out here." The two girls helped each other down into the shelter.

✤ ✤ ✤

Theobald and Maureen McLaughlin were down in the root cellar in the backyard of their home. They had sat quietly hugging each other when a loud report came from outside. Theo got up and looked out through a simple periscope his father had built into the cellar years earlier. "The house, it's on fire!" he exclaimed. He started to climb up the stairs to the door.

His wife stopped him. "Theo, no! Don't go out there please!" she cried.

"But Mo, our house, my house, the one I grew up in, it's—"

"You'll be killed! Theo, I don't care about the house, so long as I have you. Theo, for God's sake listen to me." Mo Kelley was partly afraid and partly angry.

"Theo, I lost two wonderful men to this damn war. Before you came along I felt like trash. You've made me feel decent. If I lose you, I go back to what I was. Please, my husband, stay here until the all-clear."

Theo McLaughlin was crying, "Mo, our house, it's gone. What can we do?"

"Theo, we can go to my parents' farm until the war is over. Then we can rebuild. I'll have to continue dancing. There is a good place in Kilkenny—as respectable as the Golden Peacock." Maureen answered and kissed her husband.

They walked back down to the rear of the cellar. They kissed for a few minutes. "Theo," Mo whispered, "I want to please you right now. I want to do with you something I haven't done with you yet. It's what I did for men when I worked at the Cat's Paw." She gently disrobed and her husband did the same, until both were nude. She instructed her husband to lie on his back. She walked over to stand right over his head looking down to his groin.

As she lowered herself, she spread her anterior cheeks with her hands. She sat on his mouth and instructed him to push his tongue into her. She leaned forward until she lay flat on top of her husband. As she felt his lip sucking inside her, she grabbed his manly organ. She opened her mouth wide and swallowed the bulbous end of his erect tool. Her hands began to massage the sac below. Soon they were tasting each other's juices.

✦ ✦ ✦

Ensign William King McKerr had battled with a single enemy fighter since his unit met the enemy. Now he was nearing the city. The Brit pilot was just as green; neither had hit the other. Then the enemy got McKerr in his sights. The ensign turned in time to avoid a fatal hit, but the laser burst damaged his engine and a metal fragment entered his cockpit. As he felt the metal hit his ankle, he fired both his tail guns and retrojets. He barely had time to climb to avoid the enemy crashing into him. Then, what was estimated by computers as a 1000 to 1 chance, happened. The tail gun scored a direct hit; destroying the enemy fighter. Ensign McKerr had no time to celebrate. He radioed his wing commander.

"Captain O'Rourke, this is Ensign McKerr. My craft and I are shot up. I have to make an emergency landing." He dove and dropped his landing gear. "I am approaching a greenhouse. It has a sign, Corbett Florist. I am attempting to land in the field near it," the Ensign reported.

"I hear you, McKerr, just look out for civilians," the captain replied, not telling the pilot that his brother was down there.

Ensign McKerr guided his crippled ship to the field of flowers dying in the early autumn. He fired his retrojets and descended. His ship bounced twice, then came down flat. It plowed up the beds of dying flowers and strawberries. The fighter came to a halt one hundred meters from the greenhouse. He opened his cockpit and climbed out, then his wounded leg gave out from under him and he began to crawl. He thought, "My plane is going to blow itself and me to eternity."

In the basement among tables of mushrooms, Cathal and Deirdre had sat, playing spin-the-bottle and kissing. The loud noise startled both of them.

"That may be a fighter crashing," Cathal said. "We better go up to see."

"Why?"

He answered, "If it's on fire, we could be trapped down here." He took his girl's hand and led her up the stairs to the surface. As they emerged, Cathal exclaimed, "It's a Hibernian craft. It's burning and the pilot is wounded, crawling."

"What can we do?" Deirdre asked. Without answering, Cathal ran straight for the plane. Deirdre followed him until they reached the pilot. The two helped the pilot up and, half carrying him, they helped him to the greenhouse. Then the plane exploded in a ball of fire. They got the first-aid kit and went to the basement again.

Cathal first picked up the electrophone and dialed the fire-ambulance department. He reported the location and the pilot's wounds. After he hung up he said, "They'll be here as soon as possible. Let's get at that leg."

Deirdre gasped after pulling off the pilot's boot and cutting the pant leg off. "We have to set a pressure dressing on the leg to stop the bleeding," she said. Using garden tape and binding strips, they tied the dressing on the leg. Deirdre said, "I don't know if it's right, but it'll have to do."

The pilot finally removed his helmet. He exclaimed, "I remember the two of you. In May you saved my sister Agnes. I'm Billy King McKerr."

The two young people introduced themselves again.

"Did you get any Brits?" Deirdre asked.

"The one who shot up my plane. You two saved my life," he replied. The suddenly he asked Cathal, "You related to Captain O'Rourke?"

"He's my brother," the boy answered.

"I'll put you in for a medal, the both of you," McKerr exclaimed.

In a few minutes the siren of an ambulance was heard. The three came back up to the surface. Jim Corbett himself came out of the cab with two other medics. As they set the pilot into a stretcher, he told his employees, "You better go back down to the basement. The city is getting shot to hell. We might not even get the cab to the hospital; the Brits are shooting everything."

Cathal asked, "Will he be all right?"

"Well, he's lost some blood, but he's on an IV; he'll live."

Then, as they carried the stretcher into the ambulance, a pair of Needlehead fighters came overhead. Ensign McKerr sat up to salute. The ambulance pulled out of the driveway. Cathal and Deirdre returned to the basement.

Deirdre went through her purse, taking out a cigarette. "I'm nervous and, I'm scared—" she said as she lit it. Cathal embraced her and kissed her. They sat down by a milk bottle. Deirdre looked at Cathal, saying, "You look kind of nervous too." She spun the milk bottle and when it stopped, its mouth pointed to the boy. Deirdre took a deep drag on her smoke then kissed him to the teeth, exhaling into his throat. The Cathal spun the bottle and when it stopped, he kissed her.

✦ ✦ ✦

In the war room the state of panic had continued as reports began to come in on the damage to the city. Then an electro-phone call came in from the North Pole.

"This is Colonel Neils," the caller announced. "Our scanners have picked up a massive enemy convoy, five hundred maybe six hundred fighters. They are halfway across the space corridor to the Ulster quadrant. Please advise."

Colonel Becker answered, "We are under full attack; cannot intercept. I recommend purely defensive measures."

Colonel Neils answered, "Thank you. We will put one squadron up as a guard."

Then the radio operator reported, "Captain O'Rourke is reporting in."

At the Defense Minister's command the loudspeaker came up: "This is Squadron 1 leader. My squadron and also squads 2, 3, and 4 are low on fuel. We will have to pull out soon. Where is the *Griffith*?"

Colonel Kalminsky picked up the microphone, "The *Griffith* is at its station and ready. Signal Reserve Squadrons 5, 6, and 7 to continue action. What is your casualty report?"

"Bad," the captain replied. "It's the new pilots mainly. Twenty planes destroyed, another twenty forced to land. I count five pilots murdered in their ejection pods. If we don't get refueled, more fighters will have to ditch. Below me I see the city is on fire. Our pilots destroyed nearly fifty of the enemy in their second wave before they reached the city."

The colonel answered, "Our report indicates thirty-five to forty-five bandits brought down by surface fire. Get to the *Griffith* and return as quickly as possible.

✦ ✦ ✦

The *Arthur Griffith* had reached its battle station south of the city. It headed east at an altitude of forty kilometers. The two fighter escorts were larboard, north of the ship. The two armed shuttle craft starboard, southward. Captain O'Dwyer ordered the damage control and refueling crews to be ready.

The ship radio operator began to monitor communications to and from the city. He reported, "Captain, it's not good. The city is being shattered." Then the scanner operator cried out, "Enemy fighters, half a dozen coming in from the north, fast."

Captain O'Dwyer ordered, "Sound general quarter. Signal escorts and larboard battery to engage as they approached. The starboard battery is to fire with the shuttle craft."

As the six Boomerang fighters came in, two pulled off to meet the escort fighters. The other four came in straight across the tanker firing. As he passed on the other side, one fighter came into crossfire from the starboard gun and the shuttles. A cheer went from the crew when the scanners showed the destruction. Many of the *Griffith*'s crewmen had lost friends on the tankers destroyed in the last war. Then a second Brit fighter exploded, by an escort fighter's guns, bringing more cheers. The enemy fighters regrouped to strafe again. A shuttle was hit and damaged. Several hits struck the tanker. Then the crippled shuttle was destroyed. A crew voice came over the intercom to the bridges. "This is the No. 7 refuel pumping room. We're on fire and I'm dying, my legs are severed. I'm sealing off the room and depressurizing. Goodbye, all." A loud report shook the bridge itself.

An escort pilot radioed, "What is happening? A panel and a crewman are floating up from between the fuel tanks."

The scanner yelled, "There are more fighters coming, at least a squadron."

Captain O'Dwyer exclaimed, "We are finished!"

Then the radio operator shouted, "They're ours, it's Athlone's Squadron 1!"

Over the loudspeaker came a reassuring voice, "Captain O'Rourke here. We'll drive off those bandits, but then we need fuel." The four remaining Brittanic craft fled east.

Captain O'Dwyer then spoke directly to Captain O'Rourke, "I am concerned. We are only one tanker with only two fuel tanks. Our scanners are indicating three more squadrons are coming up behind you."

O'Rourke answered, "Many fighters have less than 10 percent of fuel left, others less than 5 percent."

O'Dwyer answered, "Could you take a partial filling, say 25 percent, just enough to avoid a forced landing until each is serviced and then back in until full?"

O'Rourke thought a moment, then said, "It could work. I'd not want to have some craft have to ditch while others fill up. We could even get back to Athlone and the battle on 50 percent."

The first fighters came up under craft. The refueling crews began the careful process of lowering the fuel hoses. The fighters still had two fully charged laser batteries, so recharging was unnecessary.

✤ ✤ ✤

Over Athlone the reserve squadrons continued the unequal battle. Lieutenant Ranier radioed in, "We are pairing one veteran pilot with one green pilot each, still we are barely holding up."

Another voice interrupted, "Captain Kesselring, South Pole Squadron 1, we are coming down fast. Part of Squadron 3 is right behind us. We are all IPV veterans!"

The incoming fresh craft caught part of the enemy fighters as they were regrouping south of the city. Without the usual attack phalanx, they brought down several Boomerang fighters. As they began to enter the city, cheers could be heard over the airwaves from the cockpits of reserve fighters.

Then the colleen operating the scanners shouted, "They're coming in! Dublin and Roscommon are coming in! They merged into one flight, sixty fighters. Slow but sure—we are saved!"

After a few minutes Lieutenant Ranier reported, "The Brits are leaving. One large group is headed northeast; the remainder is trying to act as rearguard. With the South Pole force, we will finish them."

The scanner operator confirmed Ranier's report. "About one hundred enemy craft are heading out, while about fifty are remaining."

Colonel Kalminsky took the mike, "To Captain Kesselring and Lieutenant Ranier, knock out their rear guard, then drive the rest into the Dublin-Roscommon group."

The scanner operator then reported, "A few enemy craft were headed east from the position of the *Griffith*. They have turned north and are heading to Orange Country. There is a village near called Shankill."

The defense minister asked, "What, in all that is holy, could be there to attack?"

The Taoiseach, who had been silent for nearly an hour, answered. "A school. A ghastly, above-ground school, probably still open."

Near the border of the enemy quadrant was the Shankill village. In an air-raid trench, James King McKerr was pondering the events of a whole month. Grand master of his Orange Lodge, colonel of the militia, he was the village leader. He was worried. His son, William King, was a pilot, against his father's wishes. His wife, Ann, was at home with a cold. At least she could go to the root cellar if the siren went off. It was his daughter, Agnes, whom he feared for most. She had ever so timidly disagreed with her father, defending her brother's being a pilot. After he had hided her with his razor strap, he had thrown her out of the house. Ann cried all night. James King McKerr worried, fearing literally for his girl's life. "If only I could control my temper," he thought. "If only I could tell her I love her."

At the McKerr house, Ann McKerr sat with her Bible and tea. A knock came at the door. When it was opened, Agnes appeared.

"My baby girl," the mother hugged her daughter as she came in the door. Then the air-read siren went up. The two women barely reached the root cellar when Ann screamed, "They're strafing the school!"

Four Boomerang fighter bombers came over the village and dived straight at the building constructed with rocks and bottles instead of bricks. Four laser pencil beams hit the building and one wall collapsed. After they passed over, they returned, turned about, and started again. Little children fleeing from the burning building were cremated as they ran by laser beams. Through his binoculars, Colonel McKerr watched in horror. After the fighters left, the militiamen ran to the school to identify their children. Then, on a dual bicycle, Ann McKerr, second grade teacher, and daughter Agnes arrived. Colonel McKerr embraced both of them, forgetting the past family feud. Ann ran to the bodies not yet covered. She broke down in tears.

Agnes took her father's hand, saying, "Father, it's too awful, so terrible. Hold me."

✦ ✦ ✦

The remaining Brittanic fighters had turned northward when the Dublin and Roscommon fighters arrived. Moving in a battle phalanx, the Hibernian fighters crossed the enemy formation firing pencil beams. The tight mass of fire brought down a random number of Brit fighters. After they passed over and through the enemy mass, the Hibernian force circled around. They went from going southwest to west, then straight north. Gaining speed, they moved past the enemy, then they circled around until going southeast. They passed again through the enemy firing as a group. The fleeing enemy continued north with only a few fighters breaking off to engage the Hibernian craft. Coming in fast, they succeeded in destroying a few Needlehead craft before being shot down by the mass of fighters. After circling one more time, the Dublin-Roscommon group made one phalanx attack. Before they could circle again, the Brittanic fighters finally reached their own air space.

✦ ✦ ✦

In the war room the radio operator spoke. "Captain McCarthy of the Dublin and Roscommon groups is reporting. Twenty-four enemy craft destroyed; they lost seven."

Defense Minister Flynn took the microphone, asking, "Explain the low number of enemy destroyed. Were your pilots unable to engage in singular combat?"

Captain McCarthy's reply, "Sirs, for most of my pilots, it is actually their first solo in a fighter. Many have had only simulator training. I and the few veterans kept them in a tight phalanx. It was the only way to keep them from crashing into each other or shooting each other down. The Brits did send a few fighters off to hit us. That accounts for our lost craft."

Then, on another frequency, the radio operator picked up another report. "Sirs, Captain Kesselring and Lieutenant Ranier report that the remaining enemy craft over the city are destroyed."

189

Colonel Becker, after calculating all reports, exclaimed, "We destroyed 175 enemy craft, losing between forty and sixty of our own craft. Reports indicate we have picked up most of the downed pilots."

Defense Minister Flynn answered, "But the city is a total wreck, fire everywhere. And the Brits succeeded in bringing in their convoy."

The staff orderly came in with a written report. The Taoiseach read it. "My God, it says Dublin, Roscommon, and the North Pole did not get the new radio frequency tables. They were still using Beta-Delta tables, instead of Gamma-Kappa tables. No wonder we have suffered this disaster."

✦ ✦ ✦

After they had returned to the Athlone landing field, Captain O'Rourke and Lieutenant O'Connell were summoned to the Defense Ministry building. They went down the war room and were soon joined by Major Hoffman, Captains McCarthy and Kesselring, and Lieutenant Ranier. Direct radio communications were reopened with Dublin, Roscommon, Connemara, and both poles. The fighter pilots gave complete reports on the day's battle.

The Defense Ministry then spoke to the assembled meeting. "Gentlemen, we came close to total defeat today. If the enemy had known of the breakdown of our radio communication system, that reinforcement convoy could have struck out at our other bases. Dublin, Roscommon, Connemara, and the North Pole could right now be under overwhelming attack. Then they could have brought up the remainder of their home fleet. In twenty-four hours we could have lost the war."

The Taoiseach then rose from his chair, his voice clear and definite. "If this assault had taken place a few days ago, tens of thousands of lives would have been lost instead of scores. I want an investigation to the reason for this breakdown of our communications. I'd hate to think that finally the enemy has succeeded in setting up an intelligence system inside of our planet. Also, I want a study of a plan to evacuate part of our civilian population to another planet-nation before the enemy launches an all-out assault. Perhaps another planet-nation could be contacted to send us a transport convoy. The Brits would not fire upon the craft of a neutral. Not yet, I think."

Colonel Becker was surprised at the Taoiseach's proposal. "Herr Taoiseach, this is a dangerous proposal. The other planet-nations may believe we are actually trying to get them into the war directly. I suggest, instead, that we try to find a series of counterstrokes to hold off the enemy until the *Parnell* can return. For example, we know the enemy has petroleum production east of the quadrant marshlands. A proper target! Also, we should assist the underground."

Commander MacMullen answered, "Colonel Becker has a very good idea. But it will take a carefully organized operation to hold losses to a minimum. I suggest that we wait for a couple of weeks as they might be expecting a reaction."

Commander Rafferty replied, "Our base at Connemara has been a quiet sector since the opening of the war. We could launch a surprise attack from there."

Captain O'Rourke spoke. "The phantom squadron craft could be the perfect weapon for this operation. Also, an amphibious assault across the marshlands would be the perfect compliment."

Defense Minister Flynn then spoke. "We must believe that the *Parnell* will return, but we must make all possible preparations for battle on the belief that it will not return. These operations must be based on the worst set of conditions, to be revised only when the *Parnell* returns."

Taoiseach Colm O'Hara again spoke. "If we fail to repel the enemy, every city of Hibernia will be leveled by laser fire. The surviving civilians will be shot or hanged, even children and infants. The IPVs and settlers will probably face torture first. The fact that other planet-nations have assisted as well will be Cromwell's excuse to conquer the entire Outer Solar System."

When the all-clear siren came, Cathal and Deirdre emerged from the basement of the florist shop. They climbed upon Cathal's pedicab and pedaled out the driveway. They went to the ambulance station where Mr. Corbett worked. When they arrived, they asked him where the pilot had been sent. Mr. Corbett answered, "St. Oliver Plunkett Hospital at the south edge of town." After thanking him, they pedaled off.

After a weary hour they reached the hospital and went to the patient's waiting room. They asked the clerk, "We are looking for a wounded pilot, Ensign McKerr."

After paging the emergency room the clerk answered, "The pilot is in the recovery room, asleep, but you could talk to Dr. Fitzhugh." In a few minutes a burly but gentle looking man came in. He still wore a surgeon's gown. "Are you Cathal O'Rourke and Deirdre O'Toole?" he asked. When they answered he said, "That dressing you two put on his leg saved his life and his leg, too. Have the two of you thought of entering the medical profession?"

Cathal answered, "Well, no, sir. You really think so?"

Then the doctor asked, "Do you have an older sister named Shelley? We put a cast on her arm."

"Shelley's hurt?" Cathal asked in shock.

The doctor added, "She will be here at least overnight, as will her friend, a Miss Hallohan, whose leg is in a cast."

Deirdre exclaimed, "Brigid's hurt too! Crud!"

Doctor Fitzhugh answered, "I believe you could go up to see them. Third floor down."

The two young people went down the stairway instead of taking the busy elevator. They walked down a long hall into a dual bedroom. Shelley was sitting in a chair beside Brigid, who was in bed with her leg hung in a strap.

"Hi, you two kids. Okay?" Shelley waved with one arm, the other in a sling.

Cathal replied, "We were here to see a pilot who ditched right by the floral shop."

Deirdre added, "It's the McKerr boy. You know, we saved his sister in May."

Shelley became grim. "If you see him, don't tell him about Shankill. The Brits destroyed the school there. His mother is a teacher and might be a casualty."

Deirdre looked hurt. "We pulled him away from his plane and now you tell us about that. I feel so helpless."

Then Captain O'Rourke and Lieutenant O'Connell came in. Eamon exclaimed, "Shelley, Brigid, you all right? We came to see Billy McKerr and then the doctor told us about the two of you."

Brigid replied, "I won't be dancing for awhile with my leg, and besides, the music hall got hit. I guess I will teach full-time this year."

Shelley asked Sean, "You got a smoke? The nurse offered us canapec in water. I told her canapec goes only in a good cigar."

Sean reached into his jacket pocket. "I've another rum-flavored one. Sorry, pilots keep off loaded cigars."

After lighting it he handed it to Shelley. She took a couple puffs and handed over to Brigid. Brigid said, "Umm, good. Sweet," then gave it to Deirdre who also enjoyed it.

Cathal turned to his brother Eamon. "I'll take Dee to the Quinncannons. I guess you two will return to your base. Did you see McKerr?"

Eamon answered, "Yes. He is awful worried. He heard about Shankill, the school there. I told him I will find out about his family. He thanks you for saving his life. He's asleep now; you can see him tomorrow."

✦ ✦ ✦

After an hour the two officers and the two young people left the hospital. Eamon and Sean took the big cycle back to their base. Cathal, pedaling, took his girl Deirdre across town. They reached an apartment building in an old neighborhood. They walked into the entrance hall. At the end was a set of mail boxes in the wall. Over the box reading C and K Quinncannon an envelope was taped. It read "To Dee." Deirdre read it. "After stopping here for dinner, we are going back to the plant. The work crews are going to work all night to clear away debris and start the machinery back in working order. We will spend the night in the air-raid shelter."

Deirdre put down the letter, "I don't have a key."

Cathal answered, "We can go to my home."

The two walked back to the pedicab. Deirdre got there first, saying, "I'll pedal awhile."

When they reached the O'Rourke house, Cathal said, "I think we have some bread and cheese for a dinner, and we can make tea."

After the evening meal, they sat down on the sofa in the parlor. Deirdre asked, "What do we do about tonight? I mean, sleeping."

Cathal answered, "You can use Shelley's room."

"Cathal, I thought you might want to take advantage of the opportunity and go into your father's room," the girl replied as she pulled close to him.

The boy answered, "Dee, I couldn't do that. I like you, respect you, too much to do such a thing, I. . . ."

Deirdre was smiling. Her teasing brought a painful look to the boy's face. He could not handle the feelings he was beginning to feel. His father had tried to explain the way a boy develops into a man.

Deirdre took his hand and in a serious voice began. "Cathal, the night I became a Tigeress girl, I slept with Brigid. You know, Shelley has had Brigid over here in your father's bed. In fact, she has had Sean O'Connell over too. Brigid told me she had Eamon one night in her bed in August. I'm ready, if you are ready."

Cathal was almost in shock. "Dee, we're just sixteen, both of us. I, I can't do that yet. I love you too much to try anything that could hurt you."

Deirdre looked into his sad, troubled face and answered, "Cathal, I understand you are like Eamon. Your time will come, and I will be ready." She kissed him, and then Cathal went over to the radio and turned it on.

It was past midnight. The two had sat on the sofa playing the electro-victrola and kissing. Cathal yawned and got off the sofa. After they went to the separate rooms to undress, Dee knocked on the door of Cathal's room. He was in a white night shirt; Deirdre in only her bra and panties. She stood before him a moment to make her offer. Then she kissed him.

He kissed her back, saying, "I am not ready yet, but good night."

Deirdre said, "Good night," then returned to Shelley's room.

Chapter 8

It was Monday, September 14. In the war room of the *Parnell* a planning session was held. Present were Commander O'Rourke, Colonel Kamzov, Lieutenant Cosgrave, Ensign O'Brien, Dr. McIntire, and the three Americans, Sammy King, Roger Steck, and Betty Ann Steck.

Commander O'Rourke spoke first. "In just a few days we will reach the old sonar system and Earth. Then a landing party will attempt to go to the Americans to obtain information on the force field project called ODIN. Colonel Kamzov will be in command of the ship in my absence. He will begin to retool the engines of the *Parnell* for additional speed."

Roger Steck of the American scientist underground then commented on the operation. "On May 23, Sammy, Betty, and I put a sealed message on one of the unmanned ultra-hyperlight factor mail shuttles. It probably reached Earth the first week of August. The message had a Shanghai address. There it was decoded so our operatives could set up arrangements for our arrival there.

The message was recoded and sent to the States. It probably went by aircraft across Eurasia to France. Then a hydrofoil took it to just off the New York coast. Then it would be taken by an old-fashioned steamer to the city. One of our cells picked it up."

Sammy King added, "One of our agents will be at the U.S. Embassy in Shanghai, where we will obtain our visas. As you know, fifteen other operatives were picked up from Sovietia when we took on Colonel Kamzov's technicians. Only the three of us will go with you to the States. The rest will remain in Shanghai."

Commander O'Rourke spoke. "There will be four Hibernians going with you, Dr. McIntire, Cosgrave, O'Brien, and myself. When we reach Chicago we will radio the ship. The radios will be put in the right boot. Colonel Kamzov, you are to have the laser gun mounted on our shuttle after we land in Shanghai. And a rescue party ready if we need it."

Colonel Kamzov replied, "Comrade Commander, we will have all arrangements ready. I have been studying the computer printout of the operations of the converted engines. With additional conversions we might surpass factor 100 on our return trip to Hibernia."

Then the navigator Ensign O'Brien spoke with pain in his eyes and voice. "It will be necessary to go over factor 100 if this time schedule I have charted is true. First we will have a stand-down time of two days in Shanghai. Then the trip to Hawaii. The distance is 9200 kilometers, with a hydrofoil doing 100 to 200 kilometers per hour. That part of our trip will be two to four days. Then it is 4400 kilometers to San Francisco. Those old steamers might not do thirty kilometers per hour, in fact, some are as slow as ten. That means six to eighteen days. With two days in San Francisco and one night each at Reno, Salt Lake City, Cheyenne, and Omaha, the bus trip to Chicago could take eight days. In short, a total of eighteen to thirty-two days."

Commander O'Rourke's jaw dropped in complete disbelief. "Up to a month? God help us!" He slammed his fast on the table.

The ensign answered, "Sorry, sir, it's as accurate as I could get. Now if we could get a hydrofoil straight to San Francisco, it would be only 10,000 kilometers; the ocean trip'll be two to four days instead of eight to twenty-two days. So the total trip could be twelve to fourteen days."

Sammy King shook his head, saying, "No hydrofoils come near the West Coast. The sight of a technologically advanced craft might make the people realize that the environmentalists have robbed us of prosperity. The government has prevented aircraft or any other high speed means of transportation."

Roger Steck added, "It took thirty years to get that bunch of fascist bastards to repair the railways for freight and the highways for buses. You know that back in the early twenty-first century they said people were to use buses or trains instead of motorcars. Then they let the highways and railways deteriorate. Highways designed for 110 kilometers per hour are set at forty! That is, twenty-five miles per hour instead of seventy. The bus trip could take three days if the roads were in top shape."

Commander O'Rourke turned to Colonel Kamzov, saying, "After evening's mess, report to my quarters. I have an important item to discuss with you."

✦ ✦ ✦

That evening Colonel Kamzov came to Commander O'Rourke quarters. The commander was sitting at his desk with his evening tea and invited the colonel to sit down in front and take a cup himself.

Kamzov asked, "Comrade Commander, what is it that you wish to discuss with me? Why is it so important to be kept from the rest of the landing party?"

O'Rourke answered, "As you may know, there is a wall safe in this quarter containing the ship records. I have a second safe containing a secret weapon project I have had at the back of my mind for several years. A contingency plan if we could not build a force field."

Seamus O'Rourke arose from his desk and walked to a bookcase on the wall. He moved several books from one shelf and revealed a small safe. He opened the safe and took out two models. They were models of the *Parnell* and the *Griffith*. He also took out a set of papers.

"Colonel Kamzov," the commander said, "on the wall behind the desk is a model of the *Parnell*. Here is a model showing her after the conversion is made. All four fuel tanks are removed, as well as the pumping apparatus on the underside. Laser gun turrets are mounted in their place, thirty-two two-gun turrets in all. Two rows of turrets, eight turrets to each row on the topside, two rows on the underside. The rows of turrets are staggered diagonally so both rows of turrets can all fire in one direction."

Colonel Kamzov asked, "Where do we obtain the gun turrets, and how will this be used in battle?"

The commander replied, "We will bring up turrets from the surface batteries. Their auxiliary crews will man the guns. Think of it as a final attack on the enemy quadrant. While our fighters engage the enemy's craft, we will be bombarding their bases and the frontier defenses. We can descent to thirty to forty kilometers. By banking the ship to 45 degrees, the guns on both top and bottom can fire. With these thirty-two turrets and the six already on board, we would have seventy-six guns, the firepower of five squadrons of fighters. I also believe the *Griffith* could carry twelve two-gun turrets."

Colonel Kamzov thought for a moment. Then he asked, "I can see the potential of such a weapon, but what does this have to do with me, Comrade Commander?"

The commander answered with a voice deep and solemn, with painful seriousness, "If the landing party is ambushed or otherwise prevented from obtaining what we seek, you are to present these plans to Defense Minister Flynn upon your return to Hibernia. Also, when you drop off the Soviet technicians at that planet, tell them to warn the Soviet government to arm for war."

Before Colonel Kamzov could reply, the commander picked up the microphone of the intercom on his desk: "This is Commander O'Rourke, to the crew of the *Parnell*. In a short time, we will reach Earth. A landing party, including myself, will go to the surface. Then we will head by oceanic transportation to America. Colonel Kamzov will be in command of the ship in my absence. He will have full authority. His orders are my orders. We have a deadline of October 31. If by that time the landing party has failed to radio its position or report a definite date for completion of the mission, Colonel Kamzov is directed to take this ship out of its stationary orbit and return to Hibernia."

Before O'Rourke could switch off the microphone, he could hear cries of "No!" from the crew.

He sharply replied, "These orders are to be obeyed."

Colonel Kamzov was in shock. "Comrade Commander, this is impossible. The men, they. . . . In the time I have been on board this ship, I have learned how they feel about you. They do not just respect you as an officer and fear your authority, they love you, sir, as a father. They would mutiny before allowing you to be left stranded in the armpit of the galaxy."

Commander O'Rourke answered in pain, "Do you think I would want to remain on Earth waiting, while knowing fifteen light years away my home planet could be destroyed? To know I may never see my family, that you could arrive to find the bloody Union Jack flying over all of Hibernia? My oldest son, Eamon, is a fighter pilot; my daughter, Shelley, is an auxiliary gunner. They would die fighting. But my youngest, Cathal, just a boy. . . . You know, in May I was talking just this way to your son, my orderly." After a pause he continued, "This is why you must obey that order and give these plans to Defense Minister Flynn. It will give us some additional firepower, the chance we will need to survive."

Colonel Kamzov arose and saluted. "I will carry out these orders. I will put these models in the strongbox in my quarters." Picking up the models, he departed.

Commander O'Rourke sat down at his desk. In a glass photoframe were the pictures of his family. He whispered, "Bernadette, my beloved departed wife, watch over our family, our children." Then he buried his head in his hands and the tears came.

✤ ✤ ✤

Three days had passed. It was evening, and Commander O'Rourke was at the bridge at his command console. The operator of the radar and sensor scanners exclaimed, "Commander, I am picking up readings of a planet, in fact, several, orbiting in parallel to each other."

The commander ordered the viewscreen transmission cameras activated. A large screen in the bridge projected the incoming images. Commander O'Rourke ordered, "Maximum magnification!"

The scanner operator then reported, "I have been feeding the information the scanner is picking up into the computer memory banks. The readout indicates it is the planet Pluto! The next planet is Neptune."

Commander O'Rourke shouted, "We have made it! Helmsman, begin deceleration to below light speed, down to forty thousand kilometers per hour when we reach Earth's moon. Have the computer estimate the time we will reach the planet. We will orbit Earth thrice before establishing stationary orbit over Shanghai. I will break the ship's radio silence. Contact each member of the landing party of our upcoming landing."

After a half-hour the scanner operator reported, "Commander, the computer estimates that even with their gradual deceleration of the ship, we will reach Earth by 1400 hours tomorrow."

✤ ✤ ✤

It was 1800 hours the following day when *Parnell* achieved stationary orbit. Commander O'Rourke told the ship's radio operator to select a broadcast frequency from the computer memory banks that was used on Earth. Then he picked up the microphone by the commander console: "This is Commander Seamus O'Rourke of the Hibernian space tanker, *Charles Stewart Parnell*. We are requesting permission to land a shuttle craft in Shanghai." After no immediate reply, he repeated his address.

Then an accented voice came over the air. "Greetings to our friends from the Outer Solar System. On behalf of our honorable chairman, Han Toadzu, we welcome our visitors. We will activate a guidance beam for your shuttle. We are containing the Consulate Complex of the Interplanetary Federation to arrange a formal reception."

The Commander replied, "Negative. We desire only contact with the Hibernian consul, no others. This is an absolute necessity."

The Eurasian replied, "We will comply with your request."

✤ ✤ ✤

The landing party that prepared to board a shuttle totaled twenty-three in all. The commander, Dr. McIntire, Lieutenant Cosgrave, Ensign O'Brien, the shuttle's pilot who would return to the tanker, and eighteen Americans. Each carried his own luggage, even the commander. Colonel Kamzov walked alongside the commander. Just before the commander boarded the shuttle, the last to climb on, he saluted. Then the two officers shook hands. O'Rourke said, "Be sure to make a record of this day, September 17, 3153. We'll radio when we reach Chicago. Bring the ship over then. Remember my instructions."

Colonel Kamzov answered, "Good luck, comrade," then departed the launch chamber.

After the shuttle was sealed tight, the pilot radioed the bridge. The launch chamber was depressurized; the giant door opened. Then the shuttle's engines came on and the ship pulled out and away. The shuttle was an asymmetrical oval like a cracked eggshell or a metallic prune.

The shuttle moved quickly downward to the surface. The pilot reported, "The guidance beam is on and we are heading straight and true. Altitude is now twenty kilometers. We are coming in to a cloud cover." The ship descended into a mist. Several minutes passed. "Our radar is showing a sudden object, like a sudden mountain." Then the ship dropped below the clouds. Ensign O'Brien looked out the window and yelled, "Look, it's a giant building like a skyscraper. It must be several kilometers high. How was it built?"

The landing party saw the massive building. The shuttle touched down on a huge landing strip at the top of the craft. The landing party disembarked, and then the shuttle immediately took off. The Hibernians saluted as it left. After a couple of minutes, the landing party was greeted by a number of men in Sun-Yat-Sen coats. The first man approaching was in white, the rest in blue.

The man in white spoke. "Greetings, Hibernians. We were puzzled by your request. I am Lee Kung, foreign service official of the Eurasian People's Co-prosperity Republic." Commander O'Rourke and the landing party introduced themselves. Then they were led to a large glass elevator. Lee Kung said, "If you are surprised by this building, you should be. It is two kilometers above ground level, one kilometer below the ground and one kilometer in diameter. It has 941 stories, a city in a single building. Over two million people live here. Many have never left the building or even traveled the distance of fifty floors above or below them. My own parents have only come above the ground level three times in their lives."

The elevator car was on the side of the building. Looking out and down, Lieutenant Cosgrave was part dizzy, part awed by science. It was still bright daylight out, so he asked, "What time is it here in Shanghai?"

Lee Kung replied, "10 A.M."

After ten minutes of gradual decline, it came to a halt at the surface. Lee Kung asked, "If you wish to reach the Interplanetary Consul Complex, a monorail will come by in a few minutes. The station is down this walkway. Follow me."

The monorail train pulled up on an overhanging rail above the station at the end of the walkway. Lee Kung used a governmental passcard to enter the station, leading the group of people into the building. They went up an escalator to the landing ramp. The doors of a passenger car opened, and the group of over thirty entered. After a minute the train took off.

The monorail moved straight east to the harbor of Shanghai. It went past several giant buildings like the one at which the landing party had arrived. Then the train turned south. Lee Kung said, "We are traveling at 120 kilometers per hour. We will reach the complex in fifteen minutes."

When the monorail came to a halt and the group of passengers disembarked, they immediately saw the complex. A walkway from the station led to a circle formed by twenty buildings. They were only a few stories tall. A flag flew atop each, designating which planet-nation they came from.

After going through the station, the Eurasians stopped. Lee Kung said, "I will continue with you. The other Eurasians will report to other duties."

Roger Steck spoke. "Of the twenty-two of us in this landing party, only seven will go the consulate. The other fifteen will stay in Shanghai. Only four of the twenty-two are Hibernians. The rest are Americans. Those seven of us will go to the Hibernian consulate." After Roger, Betty Ann, and Sammy gave final handshakes to the other Americans, the other ones left with the Eurasian escorts.

When the eight people reached the Hibernian consulate, a beaming red-headed man ran up to Commander O'Rourke. "Seamus, old man, it is a wonderment to see you. How did you get here so fast—and why?"

The commander's astonished answer: "Keith Sullivan, you old diplomat. I've not seen you in ten years. Let's get into the building before the enemy sees us."

Keith, puzzled, asked, "What enemy do you mean . . . oh, God, not again."

"Yes, Sullivan, since May."

"But I was talking to Ambassador Pembroke yesterday. He seems a good man for a Brit. In fact, he says he is a secret member of Gladstone's party."

"Cromwell's the Brit Premier now."

"Not the prince of darkness himself!"

When the party reached the building, complete introductions took place. O'Rourke spoke. "We must have travel visas to enter the United States. We will be on a cultural research project. Our real objective is to contact the Underground. We will obtain the technical means to create a force field."

Keith answered, "I will contact their consulate in Hangchow, southwest of here. You have to exchange our grams for their paper money."

✦ ✦ ✦

After three hours of processing, photographing for passports, and medical examinations, the landing was ready. They left the Hibernian consulate, getting back on the monorail on a southbound train. The train roared over fields of rice. Giant machines were harvesting the bountiful crop. The landing party was awed by the beauty of the landscape below them.

It was two in the afternoon when the train reached the Hangchow station. Lee Kung still led the visitors down the escalator. Hangchow consisted of regular buildings instead of the massive structures in Shanghai. It looked ultra-modern and yet in ways just like a Hibernian city. After going down a walkway across an iron gate, the party descended down a long flight of stairs. A dull roar came up. Lee Kung said, "This is our subway system. Not as modern as the monorail, but fast enough for the city." He used a government passcard to cover the fare for the entire party. Each of the seven visitors were carrying luggage that by now seemed very heavy. The subway crossed the length of the city in thirty minutes. After emerging from the subway station up to the surface, they walked down two more blocks. At the end of the street was a two-story building. A green flag fluttered in the breeze. Betty Ann Steck exclaimed, "It's the environmentalist flag. That is the American consulate."

✦ ✦ ✦

The American embassy was a shabby affair, a sad contrast to the facilities of the Interplanetary complex. There were no outside gates, only an oaken door. Roger Steck was the first to enter, saying, "If I am recognized and detained, you will have to enter the country without documents." The other six remained outside.

He was greeted by a corpulent balding man with an inane smile. "I am Joe Prescott, the United States Ambassador. The Hibernian consulate phoned saying you require entrance visas. We have not had any visitors to the States from the Outer Solar System in decades. I welcome you on behalf of my government."

Roger Steck replied, "There are four Hibernians in our party; two others and I are American. We visited Hibernia for three years as part of a research project. It was a study of American and Irish relations from the eighteenth to twenty-sixth centuries. Now, four Hibernians are making a visit here for the same purpose."

Joe Prescott was overjoyed. "You are the first Americans to have visited the Outer Solar System and returned. I just know Americans will not be happy for long. I read the reports that the Environmentalist Council sends us about what conditions are like on those other planets. Smog, polluted water, nuclear wastes. Why, it's just like we were in the twentieth century. And to think that scientist rebels want us to go back to that sorry state. You know those malcontents made the government spend 300 billion dollars just to repair those old expressways? People driving cars! Do they want to destroy the environment? It is great to meet an American who has come back to us. In a month you'll be back to a country with pure air and water and a lush forests."

Roger Steck smiled on the outside. Inside he thought, "You ass, you believe that pack of lies the government sends you. I'd like to take you to Hibernia or Sovietia or Deutsch. You would see that you don't have to wreck the environment to have progress."

Then, from the stairway, a second man appeared. He was young but stern, with a suspicious look on his face.

Joe Prescott introduced him. "This is Amos Ross, our security officer. We can't let people into America who might cause trouble."

Amos Ross was tall and powerfully built, and a pair of pistols hung on his belt. He told Roger, "I think I know you from some place before, but where I am not sure. Call the rest of your party in immediately."

Roger Steck's heart sank. "He is almost on to me. If I signal them away, it will tip him off for sure."

In a couple of minutes the other six persons were in the building. Commander O'Rourke and his other two officers were in dress uniform; Dr. McIntire in his black suit; the Americans in plain work clothes.

Amos Ross turned to his supervisor. "Mr. Ambassador, I suggest that another aide take the Hibernians to our guest quarters. I would like to talk to the Americans in private, in the basement debriefing room."

✦ ✦ ✦

Roger Steck, his daughter, Betty Ann, and Sammy King waited two hours in the debriefing room. Then Amos Ross came in. "I see that you are bored with your surroundings. Perhaps a game of chess might amuse you while waiting for the arrival of my personal interrogation unit." After there was no reply he added, "Perhaps you prefer a card game. Here is a deck." Roger Steck took the deck and shuffled through it. "There are only hearts and diamonds in this deck," he exclaimed.

Ross replied, "I am sure you have a deck of clubs and spades." After a gasp by the three Americans, he then said, "Sorry to have to scare you by this act. I have to deceive that old fart, Prescott." He then handed Sammy King a satchel, "It has visas, money, papers, and tickets on the hydrofoil *Canton*. It leaves for the Hawaiian islands tomorrow at noon. We will wait another hour and then go up to the guest room on the second floor. An adjacent room has a cot for the young women. And now, how about a game of five card stud?"

✦ ✦ ✦

It was dawn the following day. The seven members of the landing party left the U.S. Embassy. Amos Ross accompanied them. Commander O'Rourke, Lieutenant Cosgrave, and Ensign O'Brien had changed out of their Hibernian uniforms into civilian outfits. They were thus indistinguishable from the Americans, Roger Steck, Betty Ann, and Sammy King. Only Dr. McIntire, in his black suit, was the exception. Ross spoke. "You will have to take the train back to Shanghai. Your next contact will be in San Francisco. Prescott left last night for Peking, so we don't have to worry about him."

O'Rourke asked, "How did you know that we would arrive exactly in time to take that ship?"

202

Ross replied, "We received the message that you would arrive in late August. We booked the first ship for September 2, then rescheduled to September 5, then the ninth, the twelfth, and then sixteenth. If you arrived Monday you would have been on the *Calcutta*. You are going to have a great trip. You will reach Hawaii in one day, San Francisco in four to six."

Ensign O'Brien exclaimed, "That is impossible. I . . . I have the very time schedule here."

Ross read it. "Whoever put this together is a fool. Hawaii is only 8000 kilometers, not 9200. The distance from there to San Francisco is only 3850, not 4400. The *Canton* and most of the other hydrofoils can do three hundred per hour. And you might get a clipper from the Hawaiian islands. They do up to forty per hour. Who did this?"

O'Brien answered, "One of the other fifteen Americans, a tall man, about two meters. Handsome, but a might arrogant. He said his name was Calvin Kenner."

"Kenner!" Betty Ann Steck exclaimed and began to cry. Amos Ross commanded her to explain. "Back in Chicago, where I grew up, there were two men in my life. Calvin Kenner was a guy who believed he was God's gift to women. He played basketball—you know, there are professional sports in the western part of Eurasia. He returned to America and thought I would fall at his feet, but I was engaged to marry Stanislus Sowinski. Calvin came back the following year. He had quit basketball and had entered the Underground. He had no qualifications but became the right-hand man to Tate Sanderson, the Chicago leader. Then, then . . . " Betty Ann stopped for a minute.

Her father held her and said to Ross, "This is the painful part, Sowinski, her fiancée, was to be one of the operatives on our mission to the Outer Solar System. Then, one evening, he was talking to us over the phone. He was warning us of danger. The phone went dead. When we found him, he had been beaten nearly to death. He was in a coma when we left."

"And Calvin Kenner was his replacement on the mission. All the year you were en route he hounded me," Betty Ann finally answered.

Ross then commented, "I think we must run a check on Kenner. And Sanderson."

❖ ❖ ❖

The subway led back out to the edge of the city, then down the walkway to the monorail station. As the monorail left the city, it passed over a newly paved highway. It passed over a parked car. Outside the car two men discussed a common matter. One heavy, balding man chuckled, "Ross thinks I am going to Peking. Of course I am, but first, I have to complete business here. Here, Kenner, an envelope with a quarter of a million dollars, a numbered account in a Nanking branch of the State Bank system for two million dollars. After the complete destruction of the Underground, you will get another numbered account for ten million dollars."

The tall man smiled. "And on top of it all, I will get to go back to playing ball after a two-year absence. And revenge on that lousy dame, Steck's daughter. She actually turned me down. She was going to marry a pimply-faced blimp Polock! I broke his head just when he was going to turn me and Tate Sanderson in. Sanderson put me on this mission in place of the guy I killed."

Joe Prescott commented, "By acting like a complete ass, I am making an ass out of Ross."

Kenner asked, "Were you able to put a homing device in that brief case Ross gave to the Hibernians?"

Prescott answered, "No, it's not necessary. You and Sanderson will be sufficient to intercept them. You will, no doubt, take a hypersonic airplane to the Europe edge of Eurasia, then a hydrofoil to near New York."

Kenner then handed a small leather pouch to Prescott, "This had a list of the other fourteen operatives. You can round them up at your leisure."

Prescott opened the pouch and looked in. "A beautiful white lining, and here are the papers. I trust you will contact Sanderson as soon as you reach New York."

Kenner thought to himself, "You are a bigger fool than Ross thinks if you think I am going back to the armpit of the universe. I get back into pro ball in two weeks without waiting, and you won't be able to stop me."

Prescott thought to himself, "He will probably ditch in France to play ball again, but he is expendable."

Prescott then said, "We could have used a homing device, but we prefer the old-fashioned way of doing things."

Kenner asked, "The old-fashioned way?"

"Yes." Prescott pulled a .357 caliber derringer from his coat and fired. Kenner slumped to his knees as blood flowed from his side, out of a ghastly hole in his belt. Prescott said, "You didn't think we would pay twelve million dollars? Sanderson could have gone himself, but you were a perfect tool." Prescott fired the second shot into Kenner's head. He took the envelope with the money. He thought, "I have to ditch the body somewhere else." He dragged the body into the car and drove off.

The car drove along the coast up a hill, around tight hairpin curves. Then the white lining of the pouch Prescott carried exploded. It was a plastique explosive. The burning fragments of the car went over the cliff and into the pounding surf.

✦ ✦ ✦

From the Diary of Conor Evans Cosgrave

It is 2300 hours, Saturday, September 19, 3153. The last thirty-six hours have revealed many surprising things. We are currently in a passenger's cabin on board the hydrofoil *Canton*. Our ship left Shanghai at 1300 hours.

We who live in the Outer Solar System tend to believe all of Earth is technologically backward. The conditions in Shanghai disproved this belief. The massive buildings two kilometers high and one kilometer in diameter are self contained cities, each with at least a million people. Amos Ross explained to us that in Peking there are buildings even larger, up to three kilometers in diameter. The city of Hanchow was a more traditional city. Its subway system was quite adequate. Ross explained that hypersonic airliners are the major means of passenger transportation on the Eurasian land mass. Like our subterranean railway system, they are capable of speeds up to eight thousand kilometers per hour.

Our landing party was impressed by the *Canton*. It is 200 meters long, 60 meters wide, and rides 30 meters above the water. Our cabin is very spacious and comfortable.

The commander, Dr. McIntire, Ensign O'Brien, and myself are in one cabin, while our American friends are in an adjacent room. The commander suggested we use civilian titles, even our first names until we reach our objective, Chicago. I feel he is worried by the suspicion that Calvin Kenner, one of the fifteen Americans, is a double agent.

The biggest surprise to me was the hostess who greeted us when we boarded. She read our names and then greeted us in pure Gaelic! She was a classic colleen, red hair and blue eyes, a descendant of the handful of Irish people who remained on Earth during the Great Migration. Later, after dinner, I was walking on the after deck. I met her and a conversation began that lasted so long the commander had me paged by ship intercom. The girl was Kathleen Durim, of county Sligo, and she asked me a hundred questions about life in the Outer Solar System. The only thing I did not tell her about was the war. It would have hurt her to know Britain's hand was at our throat again.

Dinner time was a touchy event for us as Ensign O'Brien was along. Fortunately he had been able to bring bowl and spoon. Our dinner was an Asiatic feast of Nipponese, Siamese, and Hundustani cuisine. Much of it is hotter than anything we are used to in Hibernia. The tea put the fire out for sure.

The commander, Doc, and Liam are all asleep, and I will retire in a while. Liam asked me to check our time schedules.

❖ ❖ ❖

It is Monday, September 21. We reached the Hawaiian islands at 2300 hours yesterday. We are in a time zone seven hours later than Shanghai. We anchored on Oahu's north shore at Kawela Bay. A motor-launch from shore took off the majority of the passengers. Hawaii was their destination. Then at 0200 hours a sailing vessel arrived off our starboard ship. My memory of school history books came out with a shout. The ship was a clipper, long and tall, its bow sharp form cutting through waves. It was, of course, primitive, but had a beauty unlike anything I had ever seen before. The ship was wooden, like the fishing vessels on a few salt lakes on Hibernia. On the ship's stern was her nameplate, S.S. *Josiah Creesy*.

The ship's captain, Nathanial Hall, greeted us when we were brought on board by a rowboat. He was a bearded man in a uniform right out of the nineteenth century, with brass buttons. He explained proudly that our craft is named for one of the most famous clipper captains of the 1800s. He boasted that his ship will reach twenty-two knots by the time we get into the prevailing westerlies. We will make about half that speed sailing against the wind for the first day. At 0400 hours we weighed anchor and set sail. We are zig-zagging, sailing at a 45-degree angle to the wind. We are going at about thirteen knots, about twenty-four kilometers per hour. Our accommodations are smaller and more spartan than we had on the *Canton*. The four of us from the *Parnell* are bunking with part of the crew.

Liam wished we could have brought his accordion along, but he did bring a mouthorgan. I have a jewharp, and Doc has a flute. The off-duty crewman clapped hands to the tunes we played. Our dinner was late at 2100 hours. Coffee, which is new to us, a hearty stew, and biscuits. How different than the cuisine of the *Canton*. Breakfast today was biscuits, a canned sausage with a milk gravy, and more coffee.

✦ ✦ ✦

It is Wednesday, September 23. Yesterday at about 1900 hours, the wind shifted from east to west. In just a minute we could literally feel the ship pick up speed. We soon reached twenty knots, about thirty-seven kilometers per hour. In the thirty hours from the time we left Hawaii until the wind changed, we traveled over nine hundred kilometers. We have covered nearly that distance in just twenty-four hours.

The commander held a discussion with the Americans late last night. The Americans explained to him that when our party is in transit on ship or bus, we are relatively safe. However, during our layover periods, we are in danger of interception. The commander has instructed us to be cautious.

The weather these several past days has been clear and sunny. As I watch the crew of the *Josiah Creesy* work, I am reminded that Hibernia has few outlets for training in seamanship. There is a romantic atmosphere on board, history in the making.

I am anticipating what we will find when we reach San Francisco. If this beautiful but obsolete craft is an indication of America's technology, we will be entering the nineteenth century.

✦ ✦ ✦

We have arrived in the United States. At around 2400 hours, Friday, September 24, our ship entered the San Francisco Bay. The first thing I noticed was that the famous Golden Gate was gone. Sammy King, one of the American scientist underground operatives, explained the bridge was closed in 2317 as unsafe. In 2357 the bridge collapsed into the bay during a great earthquake. Many tall buildings dating back to the twentieth century were leveled. Many lives were lost, but less than what would have been lost if it had taken place three hundred years earlier. There is not a single building over two stories in the city. Log cabins right out of the frontier days are the majority of homes. Roger Steck said that a log cabin is the safest kind of building during an earthquake. There are even two-story log buildings. Conventional framework is set up on the inside so wallboard or plaster can be used. The use of wood increased the fire hazard, requiring every adult male to be a volunteer fireman. The whole bay area has a population of only one hundred thousand, a fraction of its former size.

Our ship docked at the Yerba Buena island, a former naval base. A ferry boat took us to the city proper at 0630 hours. The waterfront was full of sailing vessels like the one on which we had journeyed. After passing through customs, we walked to Third Street, where a city bus was being loaded. The bus went south to Geneva Avenue, past an area of open land. We got off and walked about one kilometer.

We reached an area surrounded by white fence. A plaque was inlaid on a block of carved stone. Sammy King said it was a historical monument. It had been the site of the Moscone-Milk convention center, also called the Cow Palace. The building was one of those lost during the quake of 2357. Its main significance was that in 2002, the environmentalists held a convention there. Sammy cursed the site where America's downfall was plotted. Then he jumped the fence and walked up to the marker. He took out a folding knife and with it dug into the ground at the foot of the marker. After a couple of minutes he pulled out what appeared to be a plastic envelope.

Roger Steck was very happy and indicated that the envelope was planted there a short time ago. Apparently when the Underground teams went to the Outer Solar System, this was a predetermined return station. The three Americans read the instructions indicating our next step. The commander asked if they were worried someone would see us. Betty Ann pointed out that the surrounding area was now isolated. Indeed, we had passed not a single building during our walk.

We walked west to Mission Street, and soon a northbound bus took us to Seventeenth Street. At the corner of Seventeenth and Mission was a two-story cabin-like building. A sign outside read: Mission Hotel.

We rented a single massive room on the second floor. It had electricity, but the lights would go off at 2200 hours. It had three double beds and a single. A shower house and lavoratory next door to the hotel were the sanitary facilities. Our breakfast and lunch was at a diner down the street. It was the same simple fare we had had on the *Josiah Creesy*. Roger Steck explained the once famous Chinatown disappeared during the Great Migration as most Asian-Americans returned to Asia.

In the early afternoon, Roger Steck went to a public electrophone to contact a cell leader. When he returned, he explained that we would take a bus the following morning. The cell leader had made the reservations the previous month. The reservations were updated on a weekly basis. Roger was pleased to report that the speed limit on the divided highway was increased from forty to fifty-five kilometers per hour. Reno, Nevada, could be reached in seven to eight hours. However, we should have our heavy winter coats ready, as the Sierra mountains will be cold. Sammy King noted that the buses were hundreds of years old and poorly heated.

As a precaution, we have stayed all day around the hotel. Roger Steck did, however, go out in the evening and brought a couple of newspapers. I could not believe the outrageous headline of the *San Francisco Tribune*: Nuclear Reactor Blows Up in Shanghai, Millions Dead.

The "accident" was to have taken place on the eighteenth, the very day we arrived. Sammy King told us the newspapers print fabricated reports like that all the time. If you were to believe the press, not a single week goes by in the Eurasian republic without a nuclear accident taking place. The gullible ignorant masses are never told that the reactors are fusion reactors. The press also print up sensationalistic reports of smog from burning coal. I remember reading Earth history. A nineteenth century Russian official, Pobiedonostov, wrote: "The press does not reflect public opinion, it creates public opinion."

It is 2200 hours, Monday, September 28. Yesterday at 0700 hours we left the Mission Hotel. A municipal bus picked us up at the corner of Seventeenth and Mission. We traveled north to the corner of Ninth Street and Pertolo Drive. Walking down Ninth Street, we entered the California-Nevada Bus Company station. Sammy King went to the ticket booth. He picked up an envelope that contained tickets for a bus trip to Wells, Nevada. He explained that there were many operatives in that bus company. It is at Wells that we will transfer to another company.

At 1000 hours an intercom announced that the next bus was to be off to Wells. Sacramento, Reno, and Winnemucca would be the stopover sights.

Our party walked out to the loading area. The buses were a collection of twentieth century motor vehicles. Each had a self-contained lavoratory. Old city buses, yellow buses, and streamlined with the names of two old bus lines of the twentieth century. Roger Steck explained that those companies collapsed with the rest of the economy. When the conditions revived, a company was formed and found buses from all over the West Coast. It took all of the firm's money to repair the motors; none was left for painting.

At 1030 the bus pulled out of the underground parking lot on to Ninth Street. Then it got on to the on-ramp of a divided highway labeled Interstate 80. After a short drive we reached a landing dock for a ferry boat. The boat carried all buses and a collection of cars, horse pull carts, and crafts around Yerba Buena Island and over to the city of Oakland. After the bus left the dock of the ferry, it got back on I-80.

Our trip to Sacramento took over three hours. We passed a region of hills where grapes were ripening on the vine. The twin southside lanes were for autos and buses. The two northside lanes were for other traffic. Our buses had one eastbound lane, and traffic came toward us on the lane beside us. The posted speed limit was thirty-five miles per hour, about fifty-five kilometers, but with the traffic, our real speed was about forty-four kilometers per hour. We had a rest stop for fifteen minutes at a station just east of Sacramento. When we traveled through the Sierra mountains, everyone on the bus opened their luggage to put on heavy coats. After another four and a half hours, we reached Reno and lunch.

Reno was once, I was told, a place people went to get divorces. Far to the southeast was the tourist city, Las Vegas, now a ghost town. Other than a bus station, the only large building left was the Gambler Hall of Fame. Sammy King explained that it has wax statutes of famous gamblers, entertainers, and courtesans of Las Vegas history.

As for Reno, there was the bus station and a few long cabins. There was only one slot machine in the dining area of the station. This was all that was left of a once entertainment city.

The passengers opened the bus windows as we traveled to Elko and then Winnemucca, a long twelve-hour ride. We all dozed off in our seats before reaching Elko. It was around 0830 hours that the outspeaker announced we were at the end of the line in Winnemucca.

We were too tired for breakfast. After leaving the bus we went into a lobby and all sat down on a long bench. Only the commander and Roger Steck resisted the need to doze off again. At 1100 hours an intercom announced a bus leaving for Salt Lake City at 1300 hours. After a lunch eaten in slow motion, we waited to board the bus. We pulled off at 1330. The bus ride took another seven hours. We put our watches ahead another hour, and it was 2130 hours.

The bus station had a large sleeping quarter behind the restrooms. The quarter consisted of cot beds and hammocks. The commander and Ensign O'Brien took hammocks so the Americans, Sammy King and Roger Steck, could take cots. However, they took hammocks. Betty Ann Steck went to the sleeping quarters behind the women's washroom. We are tired and sore all over. Sammy King believes we will have a contact tomorrow with an operative. He will phone a cell in the area tomorrow.

✦ ✦ ✦

Tuesday morning Sammy King made an electrophone call at a public booth. After he made the call our party picked up our luggage and left the station. We boarded a municipal bus that took us southward. After about an hour our bus arrived in the city of Provo. I was very impressed by the physical beauty of the area. Roger Steck told us that Salt Lake City is now the second largest city in the country. Over 90 percent of the population consists of Mormons and related sects. That unusual church spread its converts throughout America during the twentieth and twenty-first centuries. When the economy collapsed, most of its adherents migrated to this state. Salt Lake City had a population of 4 million out of the 11 million in the state.

We approached a red brick apartment building near the heart of the town, 1711 First Avenue. Sammy King knocked on the door and a tall robust man emerged. Three extremely beautiful women followed. The man's name was Alvin Kuhn. The three women's names were Diane, Susanne, and Millie. I asked if they wee his daughters, and he answered that they were his wives. Sammy explained that Alvin was a Danielite, a Mormon splinter group that had revived polygamy. It stunned the commander, but the women's politeness ended it quickly.

Alvin Kuhn explained that the New York cell had sent a message westward. Fourteen of the operatives that returned from space have reached New York, however, one was missing: Calvin Kenner. Roger Steck explained our suspicion of Kenner. Alvin also reported that Prescott, the U.S. Ambassador, is missing. Sammy replied by explaining that we are also wary of Chicago cell leader Tate Sanderson.

We entered the apartment building. It was quite modern. Alvin Kuhn explained that we will spend the day here and the next bus will head east tomorrow.

We were given a fine breakfast of eggs, sausage, toast, fried potatoes, a fruit bowl, and coffee. Then we retired to a parlor with a view screen receiver. They call it a television set. Broadcasting begins at 1300 hours. The biggest thing on the air this month is a pre-recorded national spelling bee championship. Diane Kuhn, a petite blond, explained that few people have T.V. sets. A number of giant receivers are in theaters. Propaganda films and slanted news are the main bill of fare.

Alvin Kuhn explained that the remainder of the bus trip will be particularly rough. There will be only short layovers on the way. He suggested we get as much rest as possible. The commander was very happy that we will get a good sleep tonight. Susanne Kuhn, a tall, buxom redhead, and Millie

Kuhn, a quiet brunette, entered the parlor. They announced they were preparing a baked ham for supper, yams, cornbread, a salad and two kinds of pies. Betty Ann offered to help them in the kitchen.

After the Kuhns left the parlor, the commander removed his left boot. He removed the heel and took out the radio inside it. He gave it to Roger Steck. If the Hibernians became separated from Steck's group, he could alert the *Parnell*. I am thinking of what pleasure we could have if this was tourist journey. We could stop for several days and visit throughout this entire area. I believe the commander's family would like this area. Indeed, with the ultra-hyperlight capacities now possible, travel between Earth and the Outer System will become commonplace. People from Outer System will make this North American continent the vacation spot of the galaxy.

The dinner was the best feast we have had since we left Shanghai. Betty Ann said she had discussed the life in this area with the Kuhn wives. Alvin Kuhn openly admitted he was violating federal law, but that law is now totally ignored here.

I plan to carry this volume in my coat instead of my luggage, as I might want to write while on the bus.

✧ ✧ ✧

It is 0900 hours, Friday, October 2. Our bus is rolling across the plains of the State of Illinois. We have been on the road almost constantly since 0730 hours, Wednesday.

At dawn Wednesday, we returned to the Salt Lake City bus terminal from Provo. Our next bus pulled out at 0730 hours. We entered the cove area of the Rocky Mountains. I had never seen such grandiose scenery in my life. The commander said he wished he had brought a camera along. Roger Steck replied by saying we could pick up picture postcards in Cheyenne. It was, at least for the moment, like we were on a vacation tour, not a military mission. At 1230 hours we had a half-hour lunch stop at Rock Springs, and then we were on the road at 1300 hours. In five hours we reached Rawlins for dinner.

It was not until midnight that we reached Cheyenne, and in fifteen minutes we headed for North Platte. It became chilly that night; good thing we had our heavy coats ready. Thursday morning, 0745 hours, we got into North Platte and breakfast.

After 0815 our bus pulled out to Kearney. We were now into Nebraska and set our watches up another hour. It is wheat country, and off the road steam-driven tractors or horses were pulling harvesting machines.

Sammy King explained that when the economy collapsed in the twenty-first century, many people returned to farming. Many readopted the ways of the Amish, a Mennonite sect that spurned autos, electricity, etc. Those people would, however, use air compressors for air-driven machinery. As a concession to the people, much of the idle land on both sides of the interstate roads was given back to farming.

Throughout Thursday, we went through Kearney, Lincoln, Omaha, and into Iowa. We reached Des Moines at midnight and Davenport at dawn. Illinois is corn country, but the simple means of harvesting is the same. Our bus passed a train of wagons on the other twin lanes. The men were dressed in black. These, Sammy King said, were the Amish. Their women were dressed head to foot.

By early afternoon we will reach Chicago. I can sense conflicting feelings in Commander O'Rourke. On one hand, he is no doubt happy that our tiresome journey is over. On the other hand, we will be far more vulnerable remaining in one area.

I feel I should close this diary until we are back on the *Parnell*.

✦ ✦ ✦

While it was 9:00 A.M. in Illinois, it was 11:00 P.M. in Shanghai. Amos Ross had been summoned in the Shanghai Medical Examiner's office. He went directly to the city morgue. There he met Lin Fong of the Eurasian Republic Secret Service.

"Good evening, Mr. Ross. I have sad news for you. We found a body washed up on shore. It resembles your Ambassador Prescott," Lin Fong said. He walked to a body vault and opened the door. He pulled the body rack out and pulled the sheet off. Ross confirmed it was the ambassador. Lin Fong added, "A second man was found with him in the wreckage of the car, apparently shot by the diplomat."

When Fong pulled the second body out, Ross exclaimed, "Kenner!"

Fong then asked for the explanation. Ross replied, "Apparently they double-crossed each other."

Fong said, "It is so. We took two bullets from this man you call Kenner. They match a gun in the ambassador's pocket. The ambassador also has an envelope with a large amount of money and the remains of a leather case. It must have contained a bomb. Also, here is a leather letter envelope from the State Department to Ambassador Prescott. Perhaps you wish to read it?"

Ross opened the letter and read:

To Ambassador Joe Prescott:

In 3151 a group of scientist subversives left America on a mission to the Outer Solar System. A contact we have inside the subversives explains that they are expected to return in early fall of 3153. One of these operatives, Calvin Kenner, is a paid informer. You are to contact this man. He will have a list of operatives for you. You are to pick up this list and pay him for this information. A quarter million in cash, a numbered bank account for two million, with a promise of another ten million if he continues back to the U.S. There he will con-

212

tact T.S. in Chicago. T.S. is a deep plant we put into the scientist movement. He will reveal the entire governing council of the rebel movement.

If, however, you suspect that Kenner will desert us, you are to dispose of him immediately. T.S. will continue the operation.

Amos Ross turned pale. Then, in a rush, he explained, "This letter reveals an assassination plot against the Environmental Department. I must wire this letter to the state immediately."

Lin Fong answered, "Of course, it is an internal matter to your country. However, please photocopy this for our records."

Ross took the envelope and left the medical examiner's office. He did not head back to the U.S. Embassy. He went to the radio-photo-copy service office. He made two copies of the letter. One he simply folded up and put in his pocket. He thought to himself, "I will mail this back to Fong after they reached Paris." Then he took the original letter to an electro-photo-copy-transmission screen. He put the letter into the slot; it went under a light rod. This picked up the print on the letter. In seconds, in an office in Paris, in the French province of Eurasia, the light beam was picked up. The letter was reproduced in Paris.

When the copying was finished, Ross used a keyboard to type out the address. Again he thought to himself, "It will go to our contact in LeHarve by delivery boy. He will put in on a hydrofoil to just off the New York coast. Then a streamer to New York, then to our New York cell."

After paying for the copying, Ross left the office. He took the subway north to the edge of Shanghai. There he entered the terminal of Shanghai People Airport. He booked himself on a hypersonic airliner to Paris. From there he would take a hydrofoil down the Siene River to LeHarve and out to sea. He thought to himself, "If I fail to contact Steck and his friends, the scientist movement and the Hibernians will be finished."

$\diamond$ $\blacktriangle$ $\diamond$ $\blacktriangle$ $\diamond$

Chapter 9

It was past noon Friday, October 2, when the Central Transport Bus No. 7911 pulled into the terminal in Chicago. Among the passengers were the four Hibernian military officials, Commander O'Rourke, Lieutenant Cosgrave, Ensign O'Brien, and Dr. McIntire. Accompanying them were three Americans, Sammy King, Roger Steck, and his daughter, Betty Ann.

The party entered the lobby, Sammy King leading. They stopped when Sammy King pointed to a man across the lobby. Sammy exclaimed, "Look, that is an Environmentalist secret police group-leader. He is the man wearing a light green uniform and Greek letter armband. Those boys play rough. I will go first. If he stops me, just let me go with him, then get out of here quick."

Sammy King walked into the center of the lobby to a row of seats. He sat down with his luggage right in front of the Environmentalist gendarme. After five minutes, Sammy gave the high sign, a widely stretched hand across the back of the neck. The rest of the party ran in and sat down alongside him. Then suddenly the gendarme walked up to Roger Steck. In a threatening voice he said, "Halt, you—the old man. Show your identification papers now."

Steck quietly produced his visa and identity card. "Roger Steck," the officer intimated, "you are a known scientist and your daughter and the other, King, isn't it? So, you have been in hiding. Let me warn you, we know your every move. Who are these ones?" The four Hibernians produced their diplomatic papers and visas. "Hibernia? You mean you are from out there? On a research project of American-Irish relations? That does not wash one moment. I recommend you leave these scientists before you get into trouble and not be allowed to return to where you came from."

✦ ✦ ✦

The gendarme walked away. Commander O'Rourke gave a sigh of relief. "That was too close."

Sammy King's reply, "That will happen again until we get to our operatives. I was amazed that we did not see gendarmes earlier on our trip. It is as though they deliberately set a man here."

The commander then answered, "We had better radio the *Parnell* now. You think a toilet booth in the mens' room could work?"

Roger Steck said, "You need a diversion. We have not shaved since Tuesday. We men could all go into the washroom, run water, and talk it up." Dr. McIntire volunteered the use of his shaving kit.

✦ ✦ ✦

The six men entered the men's washroom, where several men were washing and shaving. The two Americans, Ensign O'Brien, and the doctor all went to a row of sinks. They removed their outer coats and loosened their collars.

After running hot water, Dr. McIntire brought out a shaving soap mug and brush. After each man lathered his face, an old-fashioned straight razor was passed around. Roger Steck began conversation with "My brother has a vegetable farm in what was Richton Park. It'll be nice to see him."

✦ ✦ ✦

Commander O'Rourke entered one toilet booth, while Lieutenant Cosgrave took the adjacent booth. Cosgrave removed the left heel of his boot and slipped it under the booth to the commander.

The commander opened the compartment and turned on the transmitter. He began, "This is Commander O'Rourke to the bridge of the *Parnell*. O'Rourke to the *Parnell*. Come in Colonel Kamzov. Come in Colonel Kamzov. . . . This is Commander O'Rourke to Colonel Kamzov, come in Colonel Kamzov."

Then a Slavic accent came over the radio. "Commander O'Rourke, this is Colonel Kamzov."

O'Rourke announced, "We are in Chicago; we made it. We may have some difficulty—what was that?"

Kamzov replied, "The crew. I plugged you into the intercom." The *Parnell*'s crew were cheering; the long, painful wait was over.

Then the Commander spoke again. "Attention, listen carefully. We may have some difficulties. There is a double agent in the scientist movement. When we radio to be picked up, bring down the armed shuttles. And if you pick up our homing device, come in immediately."

Colonel Kamzov answered, "The landing party is ready at your order, Comrade Commander."

O'Rourke replied, "I am signing off for now." Then after he gave back the boot heel to Cosgrave, the lieutenant said, "Remember the pay electrophones in the sleeping quarters in Salt Lake City? Maybe they have phones here. Sammy or Roger could call their contact."

✦ ✦ ✦

When the men left the washroom, Betty Ann was still sitting by their luggage. Roger Steck gave a slip of paper to his daughter. Betty Steck took it and then went into the women's washroom. Roger said, "Betty can make the call."

When she came back she said, "Red Edie Cabot will be here in about an hour."

After a half hour passed, a dozen men in blue uniforms arrived. They were Chicago police. There were two officers in the lobby when the party had arrived earlier; however, regular police were not a concern of the Americans. Then the leading officer, a black man like Sammy King, came up to him. The officer, said, "You are Sammy King?" After an affirmative answer the officer declared, "You are under arrest on suspicion of robbery. Your friends are also under arrest." Before anyone could move, a dozen guns were drawn. The seven were thrown up against the wall and handcuffed. When Dr. McIntire protested he got a knee in the back. The two other officers approached to aid in the arrest. The head officer told them, "We have them cuffed, returned to your posts. We read 'em their rights when they get into the meat wagon."

The police led the seven civilians out the bus terminal to the windowless wagon marked CHICAGO POLICE. The seven were herded into the back of the wagon. After the door was closed it was totally dark.

Cosgrave asked, "Commander, shouldn't we use the homing device to signal Kamzov's rescue party?"

Sammy King answered, "Don't panic. I have a hunch we are in good hands. Chicago police would have read us our rights as soon as the cuffs went on."

✦ ✦ ✦

After an undetermined time, the wagon stopped. The door came open, and the seven were let out of the wagon. They were in front of a large building with the sign: CHICAGO ICE CO. They were walked through a door into a very cold room. There, by a table lit by a battery lamp, a man sat. He removed a black felt hat, revealing thinning red hair. "Sorry for the inconvenience, but I think our phone line is tapped. We had to come in early or other Chicago Police or Environmentalist gendarmes would have picked you

216

up. I'm Red Cabot." He pointed to the head officer. "Allan Jackson. He is real police, as are the others, but they were off duty and they are in the movement."

Another policeman apologized to Dr. McIntire, "Sorry for the knee to your back. It had to look like a real bust. Those two at the bus terminal are rookies, it fooled 'em good."

After the Hibernians introduced themselves, Sammy King asked on their behalf, "Are you the Chicago cell leader? What became of Tate Sanderson?"

Cabot replied, "He is on the High Council, which will meet in West Frankfurt soon."

Roger Steck gasped, "Sanderson! Not on the High Council?"

Cabot asked, "You don't believe those rumors that he is skimming off funds?"

Sammy King then explained the fears he and the others had. Cabot was in shock. "The High Council has not convened in seven years. The present members have never met face to face. He could turn the entire council over to the gendarmes. The movement would be charged with treason if they discussed the deal the Hibernians offer. This is, of course, if he is a traitor or a deep plant. Calvin Kenner was a bad egg, I felt all along. Too bad about Sowinski. The last I heard he was in our Knoxville base."

Betty Ann said, "You mean my Stash is still alive?"

"I don't know," was Cabot's answer. "Maybe you'll get down there after this is wrapped up."

Then Sammy King spoke. "Since we cannot prove Sanderson is a traitor, we should set a trap for him. We will probably go to Rantoul before down to Frankfurt. However, for a few days we can rest and think of something."

Ensign O'Brien asked, "Another bus trip?"

Cabot answered, "No, cars. You may go to Steck's relatives in Richton Park."

Steck then said, "My brother doesn't have a phone on his farm. At least not when we left Earth. We will have to use a public phone in the village."

Cabot then took a notebook out of his table, "We have an early evening ice truck making deliveries in Richton Park. Albert Steck is on the list. I suggest you put on company outfits and go down with the truck."

"Perfect!" was Roger Steck's reply.

Cabot led his seven guests into the warehouse. Giant blocks of ice were sitting in sawdust. Cabot said, "I was in the ice business long before I joined the movement. I figure people will still need ice, even after we have enough electricity to bring back refrigerators."

Roger Steck replied, "Before we left Earth, my brother gave us a going-away party with real homemade ice cream."

After putting white one-piece suits on, the seven were led to a large delivery truck. Cabot brought in a young man from the office. He instructed the man to drive the seven guests to Richton. "Be sure to make your regular deliveries first."

The commander, Lieutenant Cosgrave, and Ensign O'Brien climbed into the back of the truck where ice blocks were stacked. Dr. McIntire and Sammy King followed into the back, while Roger Steck and Betty Ann climbed into the cab. Before the truck's back door closed, Cabot called in, "You are riding with the best ice in Chicago, cut during winter from the clear water of Lake Superior."

✦ ✦ ✦

As the truck pulled out, Ensign O'Brien noticed windows on the back door and on the side of the truck. Sammy explained, "It is a one-way window; we can see light, but it won't let light in that could melt the ice. We will be able to see the road outside. Often an ice man rode back here. It was put in so he could see what amount of ice was available without opening the door."

The truck pulled away from the warehouse. A latch opened and a voice came in from the driver's cab. It was the driver. "It will be a while before we get to Richton, and then we will make deliveries first. The boss said to drop you off, and I'll get you there." Then the latch shut.

The Stecks listened to the driver. "Tom Bork's the name. I've worked for Cabot twelve years. Once in a while he has me makes a special delivery, like now. I don't ask questions, I just obey orders. He's a good man to work for, and he ain't never had me do anything to hurt nobody."

Roger Steck asked, "You mean you are not politically motivated?"

Bork's reply, "Hell no, and if you're one of the science people, don't tell me anything. The less I know, the better. Like when the boss has me deliver barrels and bottles to an establishment north of the city. I don't ask what is in them."

"An establishment? What kind?" Betty asked.

"It ain't the kind a proper lady even knows about," Bork replied. "I guess Cabot's in with your science people, but he is in business, and at times we must deliver ice and other things to places I'll not enter elsewise. Now mind you, I tip a bottle myself, but I don't wager my pay away or step out of me wife. This place north of here is, well, I should not describe it in front of a lady."

Inside the rig Sammy was explaining the city to the Hibernians. "Richton Park was one of the south suburbs. When the economy collapsed, many houses were torn down and old basements filled in. Albert Steck has a vegetable farm of about fifty acres, that is about twenty hectares. The farm is on the site of a twentieth century housing development. We will see the concrete rim of the basements in a few places. The last time we were here, he did not have electricity. Albert grew up in Chicago like Roger and myself. I guess he is a natural born farmboy."

The truck headed south on the old Dan Ryan to I-57; the four Hibernians looked out the window at the devastation. Commander O'Rourke commented that the areas of leveled buildings looked like the results of a war.

Sammy King replied, "The south side of Chicago was where my ancestors lived. Now out the backdoor window, in the distance, you will see the John Hancock Building National Landmark. It is the last skyscraper in Chicago. All the rest are gone—Marina Towers, the Prudential Building, Lakepoint Tower, all of them."

✦ ✦ ✦

It was nearly two hours before they reached Richton Park. It was a village of about a thousand people. The first stop the truck made was at a butcher shop. O'Rourke immediately volunteered his crew and himself to help Bork deliver ice. The huge blocks were carried on thin backs. Of the four, O'Brien was the least affected by the weight.

After the butcher shop, the next deliveries were to a grocer and then homes in the village. There was electric light in the homes in the town, but nothing else. When they drove out of town to farmhouses, electricity disappeared. They had kerosene lamps and wood-burning stoves. The commander thought of the farm in Munster quadrant of one of his grandparents. It had no power either.

✦ ✦ ✦

It was nearly dusk when they arrived at a huge vegetable farm. The mailbox read, MR. AND MRS. A. STECK. The seven passengers removed their work suits. Tom Bork carried the ice block up to the door and knocked. "Besides ice, ma'am, I've some visitors for ya," Bork said.

The farmer's wife, a giant blonde, exclaimed, "Paw, it's your brother Roger and a mess o' company."

A tall, robust man with weathered skin ran out and threw his arms around Roger and Betty. "By golly, you're back, and who is these folks? Sammy, I recognize, but who is the rest?"

The Hibernians introduced themselves without mentioning military rank. Seamus O'Rourke again volunteered his men to help Farmer Steck. Albert answered, "If you were here a couple of weeks ago, you could have helped in the harvest, but Alma needs help in the canning."

Alma answered, "Now Paw, that be enough till the morning. Come to the kitchen. I've a soup pot on the back burner. I bet you are starved."

Albert then took his brother aside. "If this is scientist business, the less you tell me, the better for both o' us."

✦ ✦ ✦

The next three days the four Hibernians aided the Steck's farm. The land had to be plowed under for the winter. Hay for draft horses was brought by wagon from a grain farmer several miles away. Doctor McIntire took soil samples, even though his field was nuclear physics rather than herbal chemistry. Betty Steck helped Alma can vegetables and fruit as well.

On the third day, a boy on a bicycle came up to the farm. Seamus thought, "He resembles my boy Cathal."

The boy announced, "We got a call at the drug store for a Roger Steck. He is to come in to the store. The man will call back." Albert Steck got the buckboard and a team of horses from the barn. Roger climbed on the wagon and they headed to town.

About a half-hour later they reached the drug store. Roger Steck went into the store and right into the public phone booth. He waited for another half hour before the phone finally rang. A familiar voice came on. "Roger, good God, I had to call the operator and information until I learned the druggist was the message service. I've got news from Rantoul. You can head there in a couple more days. The computer data on Odin will be there. However, I also have a bad report as well. Amos Ross just came into New York. He phoned by indirect means. He has proof Sanderson is a double agent. Prescott and Kenner killed each other. We have to alert the High Council or that bastard Sanderson will turn them in."

Roger Steck replied, "In that case, we head off to Rantoul as soon as I can get a car or truck."

Red Cabot answered, "I can't send an ice truck down there, but I'll try to find something at this end."

❖ ❖ ❖

Several hundred kilometers southwest, it was still hot weather in Carbondale. Hundreds of years ago it was the site of Southern Illinois University, but it was now another tiny farm village in the southern Illinois Ozarks. The campus of the old school had collapsed into ruins. Buildings with no windows, walls missing, wild foliage taking over. In the midst of this ruin a singular man came carrying a backpack. He was a plainly dressed man, of average height. His only distinguishing feature, aside from the knapsack, was his hair. It was greasy and unwashed. He sat down on a sidewalk. He looked at a watch, anticipating the arrival of someone else. The roar of a motorcycle broke the quiet stillness. The approaching machine had huge tires to allow it to go into the rough terrain. Two gendarmes were on board. Both wore black jackboots, trousers and ties, and a light greenshirt with Environmentalist armband. After stopping, they walked up to the backpacker, saluting with out-stretched right arms, which he returned.

"Sanderson," one gendarme, wearing an officer's cap, said, "we had a bad report today. Joe Prescott is dead in Shanghai, and with Kenner, the man we planted in their outerspace expedition."

The backpacker exclaimed, "That jock! I knew he would try to walk out of the deal. I had instructions sent to Prescott to kill that beanpole if he tried to desert, but he must have thought out his escape."

The second gendarme, who wore a steel helmet, asked, "We may have to arrest the council in Frankfurt before those Hibernians arrive there."

Sanderson answered in rage, "Fools! We could not charge the council with treason if they are arrested now. The charge of conspiracy to commit Environmental sabotage carries only a two-year sentence. We want the council dead, all of them!"

The first officer replied, "We can still torture them into revealing their entire network. Even a conspiracy charge would be sufficient to destroy the movement once and for all."

Sanderson answered, "You are right, but what about the Hibernians? If we arrest them it could cause an attack by that spaceship they are from."

"Nonsense," the helmeted gendarme said. "That planet is already in a war with its neighbor, Brittania. When the landing party fails to return by some prefixed date, they will go back where they came from."

The first officer then said, "We have only a few gendarmes down here. We may have to use regular police, even bring some down from Chicago. When the regular police take the prisoners back north, then we can take over."

Sanderson finally conceded. "I will be over in Frankfurt. You will be ready to arrest the council in about two weeks, whether the Hibernians are there or not. We will be meeting in an abandoned mine operation. I will simply walk out of the mineshaft and signal you to come on in."

The two gendarmes saluted and then, climbing back on their motorcycle, rode off.

✦ ✦ ✦

When Roger Steck returned to his brother's farm, he explained the situation to Commander O'Rourke and the rest. Albert Steck then said, "There is a moving van company that has an office in Park Forest, east of here. They often take on day labor. Maybe you can get on a van going south."

Sammy King said, "It's worth a chance. Let's get packed."

In half an hour the seven guests of the Steck family were ready to go. Their luggage was put on the wagon and Albert took the reins. In an hour going on Route 30 they reached the village of Park Forest.

It was late in the afternoon. The wagon pulled up to a converted barn on a lot that held a number of trucks. A sign outside read; COOK-WILL MOVERS. WE MOVE ANYWHERE IN ILLINOIS. DAY LABOR AVAILABLE.

The two Steck brothers got off the wagon. Albert hitched the wagon to a post, then followed Roger into the office. Inside a burly, jolly looking man sat at an oaken desk, a cigar in his mouth jutting up in the air. "Hi, guys. What is your needs?" the man greeted them.

Albert spoke, "My brother and his friends need a truck to take them to Rantoul. They will deliver whatever you may be sending downside in return for a ride."

"I see," the man answered. "I'm Seth Thorton. I will check my schedule to see if we have any job assignments headed to Rantoul or abouts." He got up from the desk and went to a file drawer to search through a log book. "You are in luck. Tomorrow we have a delivery. We are moving a family from the village of Blue Island to Urbana in the morning. It'll take two trips or two trucks. How many of your friends are there?"

Roger replied, "Seven, counting myself," then he produced an identification card.

Thorton's eyes lit up. "I recognize you," he said, pointing to Albert. "You got that big truck farm west of here. If this is your brother, your friends are all right by me. I will need an identity card from all of 'em. Also, do they got any experience? I'll assign a couple of my regular employees. Since you're getting a free ride, you'll be paid just meals and mileage instead of the day pay. Finally, each of you will have to pay two dollars each. My regulars are Teamsters, Local 750. It's the only way I can hire temporary. Be here 7:30 in the morning—7:00 will be better."

Roger stepped out of the office and waved to the others to come in. When the Commander and his men showed Thorton their visas, he did a double take, "What in the world are you doing here? On a cultural exchange? I don't know what culture you'll pick up driving a moving van, but be here tomorrow morning."

The following morning the Steck farmhouse awoke at 5:00. Alma cooked up a huge breakfast for the departing guests. At the breakfast Albert asked his brother where he was going. Roger answered, "I can't give the details, but if we succeed, America will be free again."

Commander added, "And so will our home, Hibernia!"

Then Alma said, "I just remembered, Roger, your wife, Evie, wrote us from Knoxville. And Sammy, Ophelia wrote in the same letter. Here it is."

Roger then took the letter and he and Betty Ann read it. Betty screamed, "He's alive! My Stash, he is alive. He, he still has a memory loss, but he is alive!"

Then Sammy King read the letter and said, "When this is over, Betty Ann, you will be transferred south. In fact, we may all get down to Knoxville."

At a little past 7:00, the wagon pulled up to the truck lot of the moving company. Seth Thorton was outside the office with two workmen. One was quite tall and very lank with a bland, almost blank face. The other was a man with a muscular body but short legs. His face was ragged and virile. Thorton greeted the new workers. "These are my regular moving men, Bill

222

Engles, we call him Beanpole, and Mitch Higgin, Bulldog. You follow their instructions. They are veterans in this business."

Thorton went into his office. Bulldog walked up to Seamus O'Rourke. After introductions, Bulldog eyed them all, then said, "You don't look like any of the usual day laborers we get. You look sober, like you had a real working man's breakfast, not a bottle in a brown paper bag. And we ain't never had a girl in a moving van. She might even know how to pack ladies' dainties. Hey, Beanpole, get over here."

The two trucks were identical, numbered 134 and 213. Bulldog Higgins muttered, "Two-thirteen has a faulty transmission. The damn gendarmes have the boss put so much noise control equipment on, he don't have enough money for regular maintenance. I don't mind regular cops, the blue boys, but those green shirt gendarmes will ruin a man's business faster than a pot-hole in the road. The boss would try to bribe the bastards, but those creeps are paid five times a regular copper. Their only interest is kicking people in the face. They even boss the regular cops as though they were nothing." He climbed into the 213 truck while Beanpole went into the 134.

Beanpole Engles, in a voice like a small child, said, "Perhaps the young woman should ride in this truck?"

Bulldog's reply, "Yeah, I get kinda vulgar talking too much for a dame to hear."

As the two trucks drove on west on Route 30, O'Rourke asked Higgins, "How did he get that voice?"

Bulldog explained, "His father was a science advocate. When he was five years old, gendarmes beat his father to a bloody pulp. Then they kicked the little boy in the crotch and ruptured his balls. He's what they call a eunuch."

Dr. McIntire's mouth fell to the floor. "That is inexcusable!"

Bulldog's retort: "It is lucky he and his dad weren't killed."

✦ ✦ ✦

In about an hour they reached Blue Island. They pulled up to an ancient ranch-style home. Sammy King told the commander that it was the type of house built over one thousand years before.

The two drivers walked up to the front door and knocked. When the door opened, an elderly couple emerged. The wife walked up to the trucks while her husband talked to the drivers.

The woman said, "I am Prudence Jones; that's my husband, Otto. We ask you to be particularly careful. We packed some fine china that my grand-parents gave me when we married forty-two years ago. We are willing it to our boy and wife. They are in Urbana. Please be careful."

Bulldog was happy when he went into the house, saying, "You have already packed your dainties. They'll go into the 134 truck. The heavy stuff will go into the 213 rig."

The commander was amazed with Higgins's strength. The stocky man lifted a sofa on one end while O'Brien was on the other. Engles, like a boy following his mother, obeyed every one of Prudence Jones's instructions. The seven temporaries helped load the furniture into the rigs, even bundles of old newspapers and magazines.

Otto asked Conor Cosgrave, "You folks are farmers? Where are ya from?"

Cosgrave replied, "We are Hibernians on a cultural tour of Earth."

After about two hours of careful loading, shifting, tying down, and setting, as Higgins called it, the trucks were off. Seamus and Cosgrave rode with Bulldog, the doctor and O'Brien with Beanpole. The Stecks and Sammy King rode with the Joneses in a small ancient car. Otto Jones said with pride, "It is a 1955 Chevy. Think, it's twelve hundred years old and she still runs. O' course, I had thirty-five years restoring it. I worked for the postal office in the city. Fixin' up this here car on weekends was something we all shared. Prudence would put a pot of soup on in the morning, then join my boy Emil and me on the car. Even Emil's bride, Suzie Kay, helped. Emil and his wife, Suzie, moved to Urbana twenty years ago."

They had been on the road two hours when suddenly the 213 truck came to a halt. The 134 truck and the car had to slam up their brakes.

Higgins climbed out of his cab swearing. "That transmission—it's shot to hell! I'd like to grab one of those gendarmes and break his damn neck! Beanpole, get over here. We got to figure how we're gonna get this fixed."

Engle's answered, "Gilman is east of here. I saw the sign. Maybe we'd get help there." He thought a moment. "Bulldog, we got the tow bar in my rig. We could tow 'er down."

Bulldog thought it over. "It could work, but we better go slow, not more than ten or fifteen mph."

Otto Jones then walked up to the two truck drivers. "Could some of the lighter stuff be put into the Chevy? I know we got a lot of light stuff in 'er now, but it could help you tow."

It took a half hour transferring the load of newspapers and other things to the car. Cosgrave waved a red danger flag to the oncoming traffic, which, fortunately, was little. Then the towbar was put on the front of the 213 truck. The 134 pulled past it, then backed up to the 213. A double clamp was inserted. Finally Bulldog shifted into low gear and the two trucks rolled as one. Beanpole steered the second truck to follow. The Chevy followed behind with three warning flags.

✦ ✦ ✦

It took four hours for the moving vans to reach Urbana. When they pulled up to a white frame house at the proper address, a dozen people were waiting. Otto Jones said, "It's Emil, Suzie Kay, and some of their neighbors.

I know you boys want to get back to your company. You just unload your trucks and go on. We'll put everything in the house."

Bulldog Higgins said, "Thanks. My records say you made a 50 percent down payment. The boss will mail you the bill for the rest." Then he turned to his partner Beanpole and the seven temporaries, "Let's get you back up to Rantoul as soon as we're unloaded. We'll be able to do thirty miles per hour empty."

A half hour later they were off again north. Roger Steck told them to go to the site of the ancient Chanute Air Base.

Bulldog then turned around and looked straight into Steck's eyes. "You—you're scientists. I shoulda know'd that people who aren't derelicts taking day labor to go out to the middle of nowhere just had to be fleeing the law. Well, the Beanpole and our boss hates those gendarmes' guts. You will be there for sure."

✦ ✦ ✦

In a quarter of an hour they reached the broken down hurricane fence at the air base site. Before Beanpole and Bulldog drove off they climbed out of their cabs. They shook each one's hand. Roger Steck, Betty Ann, Sammy King, O'Rourke, O'Brien, Cosgrave and McIntire. Bulldog went back into his cab and opened a strong box and took out an envelope. He said, "Here is your pay, divide it amongst yahs. Here is the receipt book; each sign a slip."

When it was done, Beanpole said, "My father was a believer in science and was beat up bad for it. I don't know what you are doing, but I hope you succeed." Then the two truckmen climbed back into their trucks. In a minute they were gone.

Roger Steck and Sammy King led the party across what was once a landing strip. Roger commented, "Over eleven hundred years ago this was a U.S. Air Force base, when we had an air force. There hasn't been an aircraft in the states for over seven hundred years."

Sammy King added, "We found this base decades ago. We repaired the buildings and brought computers in from one of our other centers. In a few days the ODIN file will be available." At the other end of the strip several aircraft hangars and a large building with a round tower were standing. The passage of time was evident only by the grass growing up through the cement, covering it like a mat. The buildings were weathered and worn with time.

They reached the tower and Roger knocked on the door. A man carrying a rifle came out. Roger presented identification papers and then signaled the others to follow.

Sammy King explained, "We dug down into the ground underneath these buildings. We were under observation as soon as we came into the fence. Gendarmes would have been met with rifle fire before we would escape by a tunnel."

The party went down several flights of stairs, then they reached another heavy door. After the door opened a terribly old man stood waiting. He wore a completely white outfit. Roger and Sammy stopped in almost total shock. The old man bowed and said, "Greetings, come on, you must introduce our guests from the outer system."

Roger brought in the Hibernians. Betty Ann was gasping, "This is the governor-general of our movement, Anton Durnning. He is here for the council meeting, but we thought. . . ."

"That I would remain in hiding until the meeting, then appear like out of a mist?" Durnning answered.

"This is too important," Roger told his daughter, "for romantic theatrics. This could be the decisive turn of fortune in this struggle."

Durnning was introduced to the Hibernians. He said, "Commander, I have been in the Underground longer than you have been alive. Your arrival brings a ray of hope to a country that has suffered in darkness."

Commander O'Rourke answered, "And you have the information we seek. You will save our home planet from destruction."

"The ODIN project. Is that what you seek? It will be available in a few days. The computer data is being brought in."

Commander O'Rourke then asked, "I am still surprised that such an important official of this underground movement would expose himself at such an isolated place."

"And why not here? Remember the council meeting is to be in West Frankfurt one day's journey south. This is just a pawn on this chessboard, not one of the major pieces. It is here we have computer data on all various sciences. It also is one of our universities. It isn't an operations base like Frankfurt or Chicago. A pawn, not a king or queen."

O'Rourke answered, "I play chess myself, I understand that. And if I may ask, how are you passing the time?"

"By teaching. In fact, I am lecturing some of our younger operatives on nuclear physics," Durnning answered.

Doctor McIntire stepped forward. "That is my discipline. Could I sit in your lecture?"

Durnning replied, "I'd be honored if you would give a lecture yourself. You probably have more updated material."

Roger Steck came up to Durnning and, getting his attention, explained the security leak.

Durnning answered, "Sanderson! The council knew he was a poisoned berry for some time. Just right now he is in one of two places. Talking to a gendarme over in Carbondale or up north of Chicago at a place called the Leopard's Den. There a man can study the laws of probability, the effects of hard alcohol on human organs or female anatomy, even physical therapy. Rather boring, I feel. He was never a true scientist."

Betty Steck exploded, "He is responsible for the near-fatal beating of Stanilus Sowinski, a loyal operative and my fiancée. How could you allow that monster to run loose?" Betty Ann was in tears.

Durnning answered her in a voice so calm it chilled her. "My child, we didn't know or suspect him until after that incident. I can assure you, Stash Sowinski is alive and well. He lacks a bit of memory. The question is, how to set a trap for a rat?"

Commander O'Rourke replied, "Perhaps he could be caught in the trap he is setting for us, like in the Bible. Haman was hanged on the gallows he had built for Mordecai."

Durnning answered, "I see the commander is a man of the humanities instead of science."

"I prefer to feel I am a man of both the humanities and science," Seamus replied.

Four days passed, during which the Hibernians assisted the underground education program. Durnning pointing out the full facilities of the base. He told the commander, "We have everything necessary for the operation of this base, even enough electricity to run our computer facilities. The coal comes from old mine shafts around West Frankfurt. Many of the younger cooperatives know the value of hard work."

The commander asked, "Wouldn't the smoke of a coal-fired boiler attract attention to this base?"

Durnning answered, "We have a means of crushing the coal to a powder fine as talc. The fire is in a bed of crushed limestone. The technology existed at the end of the twentieth century. Of course, the Environmentalists still objected to it."

"Do you have other facilities like this?" Seamus asked.

"Yes, in fact we have some facilities on the surface that operate as business fronts bringing in needed revenue. Near the old city of Detroit, Michigan, we took over an abandoned automobile plant. We manufacture spare parts. There are many old cars, trucks, and buses hundreds of years old, all needing replacement parts. We make enough parts to assemble a complete car. However, 99 percent of the gasoline used in America is imported."

"So that's how we rode to Rantoul in a 1955 Chevy sedan," the commander answered.

Then, as they continued to walk to the computer, O'Rourke asked, "With all these facilities, why haven't you succeeded in overthrowing the government?"

Durnning answered, "We are scientists, not professional revolutionaries. Thoughts of having to bomb and shoot people are distasteful to us. We have

227

studied every revolution in the twentieth century. Not a single one failed to create a tyranny worse than its predecessor. We are afraid we will be corrupted by power. We have a fundamental axiom: You cannot liberate a man by killing him. That is part of the reason why we don't know how to get rid of Sanderson. Except for the guards, few of us know anything about firearms. The rifles we have are smuggled in from Eurasia. Otherwise, we would only have muzzle loaders."

"Then how could you possibly overthrow the Environmentalists?" O'Rourke asked.

Durnning answered, "We hoped we could educate a large number of operatives and then slowly infiltrate into the highest government levels. Bring down the enemy from inside. However, they keep penetrating our own ranks."

✦ ✦ ✦

When they reached the computer room, Cosgrave, O'Brien, and McIntire were watching the printout terminal. McIntire said, "We are waiting for the printed technical summary of the ODIN project."

When the printout came and the machine stopped, McIntire tore off the sheet and readout. In a minute he looked up. "It's just what I suspected. It involves the entire family of atomic particles and is carried in a medium of microwaves. However, without technicians who have an immediate operational knowledge, it would take some time to set a successful test projector."

Durnning answered, "There are several council members who know the ODIN project by heart. I am sure they would be willing to go to your planet to assist in setting up the force field."

Then Commander O'Rourke said, "I feel this computer material should be sent up to the *Parnell* at once. If the council meeting is ambushed, at least Kamzov can take the technical information back to Hibernia."

"I agree, it would be wise to do that," said Durnning.

The computer discs were removed from the computer and put in a hand wagon. It was brought to the surface and then wheeled out to the far end of an ancient landing strip. Anton Durnning accompanied the Hibernians to the end of the field. Cosgrave took the radio from his boot. The commander radioed the *Parnell*, "Commander O'Rourke to the *Parnell*, O'Rourke to the *Parnell*."

Colonel Kamzov's voice came back, "Yes, Comrade, are you ready to be brought up?"

"No, but we are sending computer material up to the *Parnell*. Send down one shuttle. I am activating a homing device," O'Rourke answered.

It was about five minutes until the shuttle landed. Durnning was awed by the craft. In a minute a hatch was opened and the computer discs were put on board. Then O'Rourke talked to the pilot.

228

"We are going to keep a homing device on continuously. If a second homing signal comes on or the first one goes out, come in at once with all three craft." The pilot answered, "I'll pass the instruction to Colonel Kamzov. He has a message for you, sir. The work on the *Parnell*'s engines is completed. He believes she'll do factor 120."

When the shuttle left, Durnning then proclaimed, "This does call for a celebration." After they went back down to the underground center, Durnning declared, "A dairy farmer who sympathizes with our cause has donated milk, cream, and eggs. Tonight we will have homemade ice cream! You know, Commander, many of us in the Underground lead simple, spartan lives. This is a luxury more treasured than a weekend at a boring fleshpot like the Leopold's Den."

❖ ❖ ❖

The following day Amos Ross arrived in Rantoul and was joined by Red Cabot and Allan Jackson. They reported to Governor-General Durnning, who was holding a conference with Commander O'Rourke and Roger Steck. Amos Ross spoke first. "We know now for certain that Sanderson is an Environmentalist spy. The High Council will meet in West Frankfurt in two weeks. How can we keep him out of the meeting until the council has departed?"

Durnning answered, "We should exploit his one weakness, his frequent visits to the Leopold's Den. If he was arrested during a police raid there, just before the council meeting, he would be locked up until after we are finished."

Allan Jackson shook his head. "That place is outside of Chicago. I can't take them up there. Also, we would have to know when he intends to go there. He may even go to a local tartshop in Carbondale, if they have any here."

Red Cabot answered, "My ice company makes deliveries at the Leopold's Den; ice blocks, clean cubes, and some other things. Jackson would be intercepting if this were normal conditions."

Jackson then said, "Yes, I could pass the information of your bootleg liquor to a local police department up there. Then I could lead the locals right to the place."

Cabot answered, "I will make that delivery. My regular driver, Tom Bork, would go crazy if he got arrested up there. He is devoted to his wife. It makes him sick delivering up there. I don't blame him; the perfume and heavy makeup those tarts wear made me puke a couple of times when I use to deliver there myself."

Then Durnning asked, "However, I remind you, we must know—when is the next time he will go there?"

Jackson answered, "I will have a couple of my men enter his apartment in Chicago. We might find a record indicating the day of his usual trip up there."

Three days had passed. Allan Jackson and several of his officers had obtained a general search warrant. They drove west on ancient Fullerton Avenue to the edge of town. In an area of vacant lots stood a single old brownstone apartment, a two flat. After parking their patrol car across the street, they walked into the building and up the stairwell. It was old and dull-looking inside, in need of paint.

They came to apartment 3, and using a pair of steel pin rods unlocked the door. Allan Jackson blinked in disbelief. A thick carpet, bright red; walls painted in orange; a plush sofa. The furniture included a television receiver, which was rare in Chicago, and an incense burner. Into the bedroom Jackson walked. "Good God, a mirror on the ceiling—a water bed!"

Jackson's man, wearing gloves, went through each drawer and closet carefully, taking each item of clothing out and putting it back in place. He found several magazines featuring nudes, boxes of condoms, and an envelope containing a white powder. Finally a diary was found. Jackson, who was trained in speed reading, went through the pages. After about five minutes he exclaimed, "He's usually up to the Leopold Den around the third week of the month. He will probably go there this Friday or Saturday."

One of Jackson's men then commented, "Looks like he brings them down here. Maybe we should keep a watch on this place." Jackson replied, "We don't even know if he is back in town. He might not come back."

✧ ✧ ✧

Two days later Tate Sanderson was spotted pulling up to his apartment on a motorcycle. Through binoculars a police officer watched him enter the building. It was noon. A chilly drizzle was coming down, the sky threatening a full storm. The officer phoned into Allan Jackson, who immediately left police headquarters. Soon Jackson arrived at the officer's car. Hours passed until dusk closed over the city.

Sanderson left his apartment and took off again on Route 43. Immediately the police followed, but at a distance. When they reached the north edge of the city, they were joined by the sheriff's police and village units.

Red Cabot had told his number one driver, Bork, to take the day off. He drove north on I-94 until he reached Narragansett Avenue. Then, after a zigzag of turns on Narragansett to Route 14, turned onto Route 43.

Red Cabot drove north into Lake County to what was left of the city of Lake Forest. He pulled up into the parking lot of a two-story building. A huge sign read: LEOPOLD'S DEN ROADHOUSE, DANCERS TOPLESS, BOTTOMLESS, CASINO, NO COVER CHARGE. As the semi-tractor pulled around the building, Cabot saw the motorcycle that had Sanderson's license plates. After reaching the rear of the building, he backed the rig into the loading dock. He left the cab and walked to a back door.

He rang a buzzer and announced his arrival. A huge door opened upward, while two loading planks were pulled from the underside of the rig and the door opened. Inside the rig large ice blocks sat on wooden pallets. A pallet jack was rolled up into the rig and then took a pallet out. The pallet was wheeled down into the giant cold storage room. The insulated door opened, revealing ice blocks, cases of liquor, and some food.

Several bus boys, using tongs, carried ice blocks into the storage room. The pallet jack was removed from the pallet. The jack was wheeled back to the truck for another load. Cabot, meanwhile, took a two-wheeled cart, loaded cases of liquor, and wheeled it out of the truck to the storage room.

After five minutes the unloading was finished. A buy boy signed a receipt and then Cabot walked back to his truck. He closed his truck, then walked toward the center of the building, past the bar, where customers were drinking untaxed liquor he had delivered, and past gambling tables. Past a stairway leading up to the second floor. There were little booths where the dancers would privately service the male customers on water beds.

He walked into the main office of the establishment. At a desk sat a black man in a bright orange suit, yellow tie, and broad brim hat. Behind him were two blond women. One, obviously trying to hide her age with makeup, wore a red formal gown. The second girl was quite young, in a gossamer nightie revealing her breasts. The young girl stepped forward. "Hi, sugar, want a drink?"

The older blonde cut her short. "Don't try it girl; he's a dead one."

The black man rose to greet Cabot with a handshake. "Cabot, my man. It's been three years since you've delivered here yourself. Where's your boy, Tom Bork?"

Cabot replied, "I gave him the night off so he could be with his family."

The elder woman shot back, "Bork is a square family man. I understand why he is a dead one, but you're not married but dead. What is wrong with you anyway?"

Cabot answered, "I am married to a cause that I am devoted to as much as Bork is devoted to his sweet innocent wife."

The madam turned red and shouted, "Damn it, I'd like to tie Bork spread-eagle to a waterbed, tie his wife to a chain, and have one of my girls hump him right in front of the housefrau." Her male partner answered, "Hey, baby, lighten up. Cabot delivers good ice and booze. Let's not worry about his private life or that of his boy."

Then he opened a desk drawer and took out an envelope and gave it to Cabot. Cabot fingered the bills, then put it in his coat pocket. The procurer then said, "Come on, why not celebrate a bit? Take a chance on the roulette wheel or blackjack?"

The younger blonde then added, "Honey, I can be a conversationalist if all you can do is talk."

Cabot thought a minute. "I have to stall until Jackson's police come in, but not give in too quickly." Then out loud: "I must be going, but maybe a beer. After all, it's my own stock."

The madam told the young girl to go with him to the bar. Cabot walked to the bar, the girl on his arm. As he walked past the gambling tables, he noticed many gendarmes of various rank.

He sat down on a bar stool, the girl beside him. He told the barkeep, "A snowshoe and a pair of beers." When the barkeep blinked, he explained, "Blackberry brandy and peppermint schnapps."

The blonde told him, "I am Jackie Weems. I've heard of you. What are you like?"

Cabot answered, "I am a man devoted to something you could not imagine." Then suddenly he saw a familiar greasy-haired man coming down a stairway and then up to the bar. He turned to the approaching man, saying, "Sanderson, good friend, long time no see."

Jackie whispered to Cabot, "He's a regular here, a creep."

Sanderson was startled. "Cabot, what are you doing here? Don't you see the gendarmes?"

"Easy, Tate, let's not get too loud. We could attract attention," Cabot answered.

Jackie tapped Cabot on the knee, saying, "There is a hallway to a linen supply room where we could talk in private if you have something you don't want others to hear. I can wait outside."

Sanderson replied, "That's a good idea, but first, I must go to the men's room." Cabot sensed that Sanderson would tell the gendarmes to make an arrest.

In a minute Tate returned. Jackie led them to a door with a glass window. Behind it was a hallway leading to another door marked LINEN ROOM. A single wall mirror was the only fixture. The two men walked into the hallway.

Sanderson placed his hand against his right coat pocket. There was a bulge in the pocket, probably a pistol. The greaser muttered, "Are you checking up on me? I am a high council member. You could be in trouble."

Cabot turned toward the door, looking into the mirror at Sanderson's right hand. He saw through the glass window several gendarmes coming toward the hallway. Then he said, "Tate, it's all over for you."

As he saw Sanderson reach into his pocket, he flung the door open and dived to the floor yelling, "Help! Robber!"

Sanderson fired a pistol. The bullet hit a gendarme in the arm. Two other gendarmes pulled out guns and returned fire. Sanderson fell with several holes in his chest. Jackie, screaming, ran out to the bar.

The gendarmes surrounded Cabot. Thinking fast, he exclaimed, "He was trying to rob me! I deliver ice here, and he was after my pay. He tried to kill me."

One gendarme exclaimed, "This one's dead. Probably the environmental saboteur we were to arrest. The other may go."

Cabot, whimpering, answered, "Thank you, sirs. I owe you my life." He walked out to the bar and sat back down.

Jackie, nervous came up to him. "You're into something I'd rather not know about."

Cabot answered, "Just sit down beside me and wait. This little play will be over soon."

Jackie asked him to buy her a pack of cigarettes. After lighting one, she kissed him on the cheek and rubbed his thigh. "Please take me upstairs. I could love you so. I never saw a man die before. Hold me." Jackie was nervous.

Cabot thought, "We could go upstairs, but just to talk."

Then Cabot heard the welcome sound of the front door being knocked down. Police came in a swarm, Allan Jackson at the head. "This is a raid!"

Jackson ran up to Cabot. He hit Cabot across the back with a baton, then handcuffed him after he hit the floor. Kneeling down he whispered, "Where's the traitor?"

Cabot answered, "Dead. Get me into a patrol car, not a paddy wagon. The gendarmes might still recognize me." Then raising his voice, he added, "Not so hard! Pig!"

Jackson pulled him up by the neck. "Pig is it! as he kneed Cabot in the back. He told two officers, "That's the turkey. Take him to my own patrol car. I want to interrogate him personally." Then seeing Jackie trying to flee, he brought her down with a flying tackle. "Take her with the iceman," Jackson said.

In a few minutes the Leopold's Den was a shambles. The gambling tables and slot machines smashed. Liquor bottles broken, thick carpeting torn up. The working girls and their clients were rousted out of their beds, many of them naked. When two in one bed refused to unlock their legs, the bed was overturned. The tart and her man were carried down the stairway by a dozen policemen, still locked in intercourse. The pimp and madam were handcuffed to each other. They were cursing and screaming as they went into the paddy wagon. A fire broke out during the raid. When the arrests were complete, the police simply let the Leopold's den burn to the ground.

The following morning in Rantoul, Commander O'Rourke and his men were in the mess hall with Governor-General Durnning. Durnning was watching in puzzlement as Ensign O'Brien mixed his cooked steel-cut oats and scrambled eggs together with his wooden bowl and spoon. Commander O'Rourke then explained to Durnning the Ensign's unusual table manners.

A young girl operative came up to the governor-general and presented a message. After reading it, he arose and exclaimed, "It's a call from Allan

Jackson. Sanderson is dead! Now we can proceed with the High Council meeting without fear."

The commander lifted his coffee cup and gave a toast to the success of the raid that eliminated the double agent. Dr. McIntire and Lieutenant Cosgrave joined him in his toast, but Ensign O'Brien shook his head. Durnning then asked, "Why are you negative, young man? This has been very good news we have received."

Ensign O'Brien then explained his doubts. "This man Sanderson could have already told the gendarmes the exact or approximate location of where the meeting is to be held."

Commander O'Rourke added, "O'Brien is correct. They could comb the entire West Frankfurt area with a large force of men until the mining site is located."

Governor-General Durnning shook his head. "You have ruined my day young man; but you may have saved us from walking into a trap. What can we do now? A call from down there last night said half the council members have already arrived. The rest will arrive about the time we will, tomorrow evening."

Commander O'Rourke then answered quickly, "I suggest we leave this very morning for Frankfurt. Then you can begin the council meeting as soon as we arrive with the members already present."

Durnning asked, "What about the other members?"

O'Rourke's reply, "You can give each of the late arrivals a written summary of the minutes. What is necessary is that you end the council meeting before the time it was to start. Then you should evacuate that area completely."

Durnning thought a moment, then announced, "I agree. Gentlemen, let us pack our baggage. First we must phone Frankfurt to inform them of our plans. We have several motorcars ready."

✦ ✦ ✦

In a half-hour the commander's men were packed and ready. Governor-General Durnning, Sammy King, and the Stecks took a little longer. Two motorcars of indeterminate make were waiting outside the tower building with two armed guards who would accompany them. After loading up the baggage, the passengers embarked. Durnning took the wheel of one car; Sammy King drove the other. The two machines drove down across the pocketed ancient air strip, then across a field to Route 45. The cars drove to Rantoul proper to get on to I-57, then turned south. Sammy King told his Hibernian passengers, "It is around 170 miles to West Frankfurt. At the speed we are going, we will be about seven hours or more to reach there. It'll be around dinner time."

Commander O'Rourke thought to himself. "The homing device might not work down in a mine shaft. We might have to radio the *Parnell*. It might even be necessary to bring one of the armed shuttles to circle the area." Then he turned to his subordinate officers and explained his plans.

Cosgrave suggested, "Why not take their council meeting up to the ship."

The commander answered, "If these men were captured later, they could be tortured, revealing our technological capabilities and our plans to aid the Underground."

As the cars traveled south, the terrain changed gradually. From an area of wide flat countryside they entered hill country. The guard with the Hibernians said, "This is the Illinois Ozarks. We still have peach orchards and strawberry fields down here. Many people moved here after the economy collapsed hundreds of years ago. Most people still live off the land."

Sammy King then said, "This was also a region of oil production. Why, there were oil wells in the parking lots of shopping centers and even in public parks."

"You could actually smell the aroma of crude oil in the air," the guard said.

Several rest stops were made along the way. The Hibernians actually enjoyed the scenery. Ensign O'Brien commented, "These up and down hills remind me of Kerry sector over in Munster quadrant."

For Commander O'Rourke it was a reminder that they were far from home.

✦ ✦ ✦

At the last rest stop Lieutenant Cosgrave and Ensign O'Brien walked out to the edge of the rest area. O'Brien asked, "What are those weeds growing out on that hill over to the west?"

Governor-General Durnning, who had ridden in the second car, walked up to them and explained, "That weed, the one with the thin leaves, is marijuana. It was smoked as a recreational drug during the twentieth and twenty-first centuries. The Environmentalist Party legalized its use at the same time they outlawed nuclear power."

Sammy King, who had walked up to Cosgrave added, "It was part of the whole sinister plan. Make the American people so intoxicated and lethargic that they wouldn't mind having no electricity or jobs."

Durnning continued, "By the end of the twenty-first century economic conditions were so poor, people could no longer afford the luxury of drugs. The weed grows wild now across the countryside. The Environmentalist Party still tries to promote its use, as it is a tax revenue item. They probably own that tartshop where Sanderson was killed. That is why real policemen like Allan Jackson support our cause. They know the gendarmes and the Environmentalists are involved in vice, gambling, and drug traffic."

✦ ✦ ✦

It was late in the afternoon when the cars reached West Frankfurt. Just east of the village a mining elevator shaft building sat atop a slag covered hill. The two cars entered a parking lot surrounded by a broken chain link fence. At the end of the lot a wooden cabin with a guardhouse sat. Durnning explained, "This is an operating coal mine. We will have to put worksuits on and enter with the second shift."

When the group reached the cabin they were greeted by a tall man in a grimy worksuit. His face was covered with coal dust. Durnning greeted him loudly, "Hank McKay, old friend, it is good to see you. How has it been ten years you've been in the mine?"

The man answered, "Yes, ten years since I broke the heads of a couple of gendarmes with an axe handle down in Texas. I hear my face is still on wanted posters."

Governor-General Durnning then explained the mining complex. "This is mine No. 1. The miners are local people, descendants of people who worked these mines hundreds of years ago. Most have no interest in science but appreciate our reopening the mines." Hank McKay then added, "This mine and mine No. 5 way to the east are worked by locals. Mines 2 and 4 are worked by operatives, most on a tour of duty here, others, like me, are permanently stationed here. Mine No. 3 is where the meeting will be held."

The four Hibernians and their American hosts put on dark blue one-piece worksuits and steel work helmets. Then they walked up the hill, Hank McKay leading. At the top of the hill they entered the elevator shaft building.

Commander O'Rourke took out the homing device from his boot and placed it on a window sill by the doorway. He explained its purpose. Hank McKay then said, "I'll keep an eye on it."

The elevator moved slowly down into the darkness below. The lamps on the helmets were turned on. Durnning said, "We will soon be over a thousand feet down."

Hank McKay then told his superior, "As a security measure, Mines No. 1 and No. 5 will close at midnight. The workers were given notice and a layoff bonus for the week."

"Good," Durnning answered, "At least these simple folk won't be caught if a force of gendarmes comes in. Tate Sanderson was our big worry, but he's dead."

Then McKay answered, "The boys over in 3 were scared he'd walk some of the bully boys right in the shaft entrance. We put in explosives ready to collapse if necessary."

After reaching the bottom of Mine No. 1, the group got off the elevator, then they climbed on board a railed personnel carrier. It moved slowly down the track, northward, as indicated by a map floor plan on the console by the driver's seat. After traveling about half a mile by the odometer, it stopped by a locked door. The group got off and McKay went up to the door. One hand worked a combination lock, the other worked a lock and key. He explained this bottom shaft wasn't a producing one, so none of the locals got down here. Also, only operatives had the key and combination for this door. The door revealed a narrow but lighted tunnel. In the distance another locked door was visible. The visiting group walked through the tunnel and then through the second door.

As soon as they entered the second mine a number of miners applauded. Hank McKay said, "They were expecting you, Governor Durnning. It is the highest honor for an operative to meet our leader."

One of the miners came up to Durnning, a slender worker. A feminine voice said, "Governor Durnning, all of the council members have arrived. The last members arrived earlier today. A couple even put in a few hours of work in the shaft."

McKay answered, "Thank you, Ellen Turner."

Durnning also thanked the young girl, adding, "I put in several tours of duty in the mines over thirty years ago."

Hank McKay then said, "Ellen Turner has been down here for three years. She wasn't an operative of the movement but a fugitive from the gendarmes."

The young girl who was walking alongside cut in, "I was sixteen in East Kentucky. The government seized my family's tree farm for the National Forest Service. When my parents resisted, a squad of gendarmes machine gunned them. I had walked home from school when I saw my parents being shot. I found out the gendarme officer who led the death squad. I got my father's old muzzle-loader and put a minie ball right between his eyes. I've heard of that guy Sanderson. If he came here, I'd drop him the same way."

After taking another elevator up three levels, the group walked to a guarded tunnel door, then through the tunnel into a comfortable room with powder blue paneled walls, electric lights, and furniture. From a door at the other end entered a group of people. The leading person was a boyish looking man. *"Bon jour, Monsieur Durnning,"* was his greeting as he extended his hand.

Durnning shook the hand hardily. "Pierre Buchamp, how is the weather in Quebec? This gentleman is the deputy governor of the council."

After everyone was seated at a long table, introductions were made. The governor-general announced, "At this side of the first table, Charlie Littlefeather of the Navaho reservation, Arizona; Renaldo Vegas of Juarez; Karen Woods, Los Angeles; Joe Andre, New Orleans; and Tommy Burns, Plaines, Georgia. At the other side, Irving Leibermann, New York; Tony Rossi, Philadelphia; Dennis Bilandic, Cleveland; Pat Doyle, St. Paul; and Emil Rogers, Portland.

Then Buchamp spoke from the second table. "Here is Jill Clarke, Edmonton; Sherry Tillstrom, Denver; Mike Devlin, Kansas City; and Marie Banks, Halifax."

After Durnning introduced the Hibernians, Commander O'Rourke made his presentation, "Ladies and gentlemen, my men and I have come from our planet to make an offer to assist your movement in return for you helping us in our struggle."

Tommy Burns, a grey, wrinkled man, asked, "What kind of exchange are you suggesting?"

Governor-General Durnning answered. "They offer to provide weapons and manpower for an uprising. In return, we would provide technical assistance in setting up a force field, the ODIN project."

Immediately several council members shot up out of their seats. Karen Woods, a black woman with bleached hair spoke. "My discipline was advanced physics. I wrote the teaching manual on the ODIN project used in our underground universities."

Emil Rogers, another black, thin and lisping, added, "I teach the ODIN project. I could construct the particle beam projector blindfolded; so could Rossi and Bilandic." The two nodded their heads. Both had dark hair and eyes. Rossi had olive skin and was the heavier of the two.

Dr. Joseph McIntire then explained the state of Hibernia's force field project. "We already have projectors, but we did not know what particles were to be used."

Durnning added, "The computer printout of the technical nature of the project was sent up to their ship. However, they will need the assistance of our technicians to put the force field into immediate operation."

Then Irving Leibermann, small, dark, and worried asked, "What would we get in return for the ODIN project? How do we know it could bring that conflict to a conclusion? What relevance is the conflict out there to our problems? We could wait for years for this war to end."

Commander O'Rourke rose from his chair. In a voice strong enough to project the urgency of the situation, but calm enough not to threaten, he explained his country's plight.

"I am coming from a nation literally fighting a war of survival. The Brittanians deliberately plan to exterminate the population of my planet-nation. Then they intend to begin a plan to conquer the entire Outer Solar System. Lord Cromwell intends to put the Union Jack on every one of the twenty-one planet-nations of the system; a Brittanic empire. Then they will come across the corridor of space to here. I have read the entire history of Anglo-American relations. In the nineteenth century Lord Palmerstone openly talked of invading and reconquering the United States. Britain supported the Civil War attempt to break up your country. The imperialist Cecil Rhodes attempted to conquer your country by scholarship and diplomacy. In fact, in the late twentieth century the British royal family supported the environmentalist movement—the very movement that has ruined your country."

Leibermann then replied, "You have convinced me that we should help each other. However, can we help each other? I can see how you will be able to use the ODIN project."

Governor Durnning walked up to a wall map of the Western Hemisphere. He pointed to the area north of the forty-ninth parallel. "Back in the twenty-sixth century, Alaska, the forty-ninth state, succeeded from the union and became a protectorate of the Eurasians. They have a small but relatively well-equipped army, fighter planes, winterized tanks, etc. The U.S. army has none of these and has fewer automatic weapons than the gendarmes. After the migration ended, the death zones at the forty-ninth parallel and the Rio Grande were removed. People moved into stretches of land where only a fraction of the original population remained. The Yukon and the Northwest territory area is uninhabited." Then Durnning pointed south of the Yucatan area of what was Mexico. "Central America and South America are both almost devoid of people. Here is where landings of troops and equipment could be made."

Commander O'Rourke then joined Durnning at the wall map, saying, "We can return to Earth after the war is over. We will bring a convoy of transports with the *Parnell*. They will carry volunteer soldiers and disassembled fighters and land tanks, laser equipped. While the forces are organized into an attacking army, laser rifles could be smuggled into your country and to your cells. We would be two armies. One coming north across the Rio Grande, while the second comes down from northern Canada."

Durnning replied, "Excellent. Our cells could launch an uprising in the central states area. Using radio equipment you would signal your armies to come in."

✦ ✦ ✦

While Commander O'Rourke and Dr. McIntire remained at the high council meeting, Lieutenant Cosgrave and Ensign O'Brien left. They went with Roger and Betty Steck and Sammy King to a lunchroom two levels up. Hank McKay was there and announced, "Hey, King and Steck, here are your relatives from Knoxville." Behind him were three people. One was a buxom, attractive black woman; the second person was a grey-haired woman with steel-blue eyes. In back of them was a heavy set young man. His face was pitted from acne that had developed into cysts.

"Evie, Ophelia, Stash!" was the collective yell of three operatives. Roger threw his arms around Evie while Sammy began kissing Ophelia. Betty Ann began to cry. "Stash, my Stash." The young man ran to her and kissed her. "I'm all right now, Betty."

Hank McKay said, "After the council meeting is completed, you are all to be reassigned to Knoxville after a two week leave."

Cosgrave and O'Brien introduced themselves, then Ellen Turner came into the dining room. They all sat down at a long table after going up to a soup and bread line. Ellen Turner removed her helmet, revealing blond hair matted with coal dust. She asked the Hibernian officers, "Could you tell me

239

about your home? People where I live don't even know about the Outer Solar System."

Cosgrave started, "Hibernia's a beautiful planet; green hills and forests; lakes that look like silver; and the mountains of Mourne in Connaught. When the mist rises from the plateau of Athlone, it's like taking the veil off the bride's face." Ellen Turner was spellbound by the Lieutenant's description of his homeland.

Ensign O'Brien asked, "Could you tell us something about yourself?"

Ellen Turner began, "I lived way over in east Kentucky, Harlan County. It use to be coal country until the gendarmes closed everything down. They never paid my folks no mind until father had planted pine trees on fifty acres. Then they came." A tear came down her cheek as she continued, "I will remember that day to the end of my life. The gendarme commandant wore a dark green overcoat, almost black it was. His men in light green shirts, black pants, and jackboots. They put my parents up against the wall of our cabin. Paw went for his musket, and he and mom were cut to pieces. I had my hand over my mouth, else they'd a catch'd me and killed me too. The gendarmes set fire to the cabin with my parents remains laying against it."

Cosgrave tried to comfort the girl and asked, "What happened then?"

Ellen answered, "Paw's musket was on the ground by the cabin. I took it after the gendarmes had left and the fire was out. I swore to God Almighty I'd get the man who ordered their deaths. I went up to Wheeling, West Virginia. I found him coming out of a roadhouse with a fancy lady on his arm. I waited until she was a few feet away, then I shot him dead. Two gendarmes fired at me but missed. I fled to Ohio, where I heard of the Underground. I've been in this mine for three years."

✧ ✧ ✧

The High Council meeting continued until past 11 P.M. After a lively debate, the council voted eleven to six to accept the Hibernians' offer. Karen Woods, Emil Rogers, Dennis Bilandic, and Tony Rossi were given the assignment of going to Hibernia. After the vote, Governor-General Durnning said, "Ladies and gentlemen, I suggest that our guests and the assigned council members leave tomorrow. I feel that the gendarmes will attempt to locate our council in another area in two weeks." After a voice vote he announced, "The council meeting is ended. I suggest we all leave tomorrow. Buchamp will contact all of you as to the location of the next meeting."

✧ ✧ ✧

After a huge breakfast, Commander O'Rourke and his men took the elevator to the surface of Mine No. 3. The four American scientist council members accompanied them. Also with them were Governor Durnning, the

Stecks, the Kings, and Stash Sowinski. Commander O'Rourke and his men shook the hands of Roger Steck, Betty Ann, and Sammy King.

O'Rourke said, "We will be back soon."

Then Hank McKay came up to the surface by the elevator yelling, "Gendarmes are over in Carbondale—ten troop trucks, fifty men each with tommy guns. They'll be here in an hour."

Governor Durnning turned to the Commander, saying, "You were right about the gendarmes." Then turning to McKay, "Sound the evacuation alarm; get the miners on our trucks. We can be out of here before they arrive."

Commander O'Rourke then offered to bring down his armed shuttles to defend the mining sight. Durnning turned him down, saying, "That would tip our hand to the assistance you plan to give us. We'll be all right."

Commander O'Rourke said to Roger Steck, "Remember the radio I gave to you when we were in Salt Lake City? Use it to radio the *Parnell* in five hours after we go up. If you are in trouble, we will send down our armed shuttles. Ensign O'Brien will give you a homing device."

"Thank you," Steck replied.

It was about five minutes after the Commander radioed the *Parnell* that the shuttle arrived. After another round of handshakes, the four Hibernians and four Americans climbed on board. Governor Durnning said, "May God protect you during your journey," as the shuttle took off. Those on the ground waved until it disappeared.

✦ ✦ ✦

When Commander O'Rourke got off the shuttle he was greeted by Colonel Kamzov.

"Comrade Commander, we are ready to put out of stationary orbit," the Colonel said.

Commander O'Rourke replied, "We are going to wait five hours for a radio report from the surface."

"In that case, I will give you a summary of the technical modification of the ship's engines."

✦ ✦ ✦

Commander O'Rourke and Colonel Kamzov were on the bridge of the *Parnell*. Five hours had passed since the landing party had come on board. The ship radio operator reported, "Commander, we are receiving a transmission from the surface. I'll put it on the intercom."

A familiar voice came over the air. "Roger Steck here. We are over in Eldorado, heading for Evansville, Indiana. No casualties. We got out before they arrived. We booby trapped mines 2, 3, and 4 with explosives. The gendarmes are going to get a surprise."

The commander replied, "Good luck, Steck. We will return."

Roger Steck then said, "I am signing off. Good luck."

With that, Commander O'Rourke gave the order, "Helmsman Cosgrave, pull the ship out of stationary orbit and begin acceleration up to factor 40."

In just minutes the ship began to pick up speed. Helmsman Cosgrave read off the pace. "Factor 0.7, factor 1.1, 1.9, 2, factor 5, factor 10, 20, 27, 33 . . . factor 40 reached, sir."

The commander then said, "Colonel Kamzov, you take the helm until the crucial stage is passed." The officer obeyed quickly.

A quarter of an hour passed; the crew on the bridge on edge. Then Kamzov said, "We have reached factor 52 and I will begin acceleration. Factor 60 . . . 70 . . . 80 . . . factor 90 . . . factor 100 . . . 107 . . . 111 . . . 117 . . . factor 124. That is the maximum."

Commander O'Rourke then said, "Good work, Colonel. Return the helm to Cosgrave. Navigator O'Brien, plot our course for Hibernia. After the work shift is over, we can all celebrate in the servicemen's room."

Chapter 10

The first rays of dawn broke over Athlone. Three days had passed since the Brittanic attack. A rainstorm the previous night had put out the last fires and cleared the air. It was a bright September morning, Thursday the seventeenth. The damage to the city was revealed in all its ugliness. The burned out buildings, blocks of houses leveled, the shattered DeValera Park, the cries of people who had lost their homes, jobs, or worse, loved ones.

A subterranean railway train pulled into the Athlone station. The doors of a passenger car opened and five young women got off. All were wearing the black denim jackets of Limerick prison with Hibernian auxiliary service armbands. Two of the girls wore black veils on their heads and walked ahead of the other three. Kate MacBride and Mary Plunkett Concannon had come to Athlone to attend memorial services for their parents. Caroline Quinn, Mairead McNutt, and Jamie Feeny also came along.

The girls were met by their friends, Shelley O'Rourke and Brigid Hallohan. Also present were Karen and Clara Quinncannon, Deirdre O'Toole, and members of the four girl gangs. Shelley ran up to Kate, throwing one arm around her, the other in a sling.

"Kate, I know it hurts; I didn't think we'd meet again and under this sad occasion."

Kate, holding back tears, answered, "I remember when you lost your mother."

M.P. Concannon also came up, embracing the other two. "It was my Uncle Arthur who sent us the electrogram. He will be at the cemetery."

The group of young girls went up the upstairs from the station to the street and climbed on board a bus. Their presence scared other passengers, even though they did not make any gestures of a threatening nature.

✦ ✦ ✦

At the southwestern edge of the city was the Marie Drumn Memorial Park. The girls got off a bus, went down the street, and walked into the burial grounds. Up and down a number of hills they walked until they reached a mass grave being filled with body bags.

"Mary P!" the grey-haired man yelled as he noticed his niece approaching.

The thin brunette was crying loudly. "Uncle Arthur, I can't stand it. They never wrote me, but I still loved them."

Kate MacBride went up to a burial official and asked for a list of names of people being buried. "I read my parents' names, but what of my little brother Timmy? Is he alive?" Kate asked in horror. The thought that her little brother was dead too cut her insides like a knife.

An Athlone constable came up to her and said, "Are you Kate MacBride? A small boy and a young woman are over at the precinct station on the other side of the park."

The constable escorted the group of girls over to the station. Sitting on a bench outside the small building, an attractive woman held a little boy on her lap. Kate MacBride ran up to her, Brigid Hallohan, hobbling on crutches, just behind. Kate picked the little boy up.

"Timmy, you're alive, my little baby brother."

Brigid asked, "Pam O'Reilly, where did you find the little guy?"

Pam answered, "We were on an evacuation tram that got hit."

Timmy looking up at his sister, "Mommy and Dad are gone, sis; that lady was nice to me. She saved my life."

Pam answered, "I'd a been very special nice to him if he was about five years older."

Brigid kidded her saying, "You were always the one to rob the cradle. Of course, I've done it myself."

The girls all returned to the grave site. An official led Kate and Mary P. to a row of body bags. They opened four of them, revealing the slain parents. The two girls began to cry again, joined by the others. The bags were closed again. Then they were put on a hoist and lowered into the grave.

After watching the grave being filled for an hour, the girls walked away. They went over a pair of hills to another mass grave. It was the burial site for those who had died in May. On a massive granite tombstone were names of the victims, including Mr. and Mrs. Joseph O'Toole. Now Deirdre began to cry, saying, "I told Cathal I felt responsible for their deaths. They were in the living room, waving to me through our picture window when they were hit."

Shelley put her arms around her and said, "Don't blame yourself; it was the fault of the Brits."

Later, the girl gang members walked to the military part of the cemetery. The green, white, and orange Hibernian tricolor few above small markers. Shelley O'Rourke walked up to one marker that read:

BERNADETTE O'ROURKE, 3103–3149. She knelt beside the marker, said the rosary, then placed a small flower cup in the ground by the marker.

✦ ✦ ✦

In the war room of the Hibernian Defense Ministry, a meeting was being held on the aftermath of the attack. Present were Taoiseach Colm O'Hara, Defense Minister Joe Flynn, Commanders Donahue, MacMullen, and Rafferty, and Colonels Becker, Kalminsky, Neils, and Murphy.

Joe Flynn spoke first. "Gentlemen, I believe it imperative we prepare a number of countermeasures. However, we must do something about these undertrained pilots."

Colonel Becker agreed wholeheartedly. "If that Brittanic force was attacking fresh into battle, instead of withdrawing, low on fuel and laser battery charges, those young pilots' first mission would have been their last."

Commander Donahue announced, "I could order Captain McCarthy to have his pilots ferried by shuttles to the South Pole for an intensive retraining program."

Colonel Murphy answered Donahue, saying, "Captain Kesselring's pilots are veteran IPVs. They were perfect instructors for these green pilots."

Colonel Kalminsky then added, "I will send Major Hoffman to the South Pole. He can detect if some of these young pilots would make better co-pilots on Bullethead craft."

Then Defense Minister Flynn spoke again, "The next agenda is a counter attack. The target I propose is the petroleum fields in Ulster quadrant, east of the marshlands. I believe the phantom squadron craft could be used to strike the oil rigs. Then pilots would land inside the quadrant and work their way back to link up with an amphibious assault group."

Commander MacMullen then asked, "How could this operation take place through the marshlands? Also, aren't these craft out of laser battery charges?"

Colonel Becker signaled a guard to open a door and three officers came in. The colonel announced, "This is Colonel Skorzeny, IPV. He is an expert on commando tactics and the use of laser-land tanks. He launched the assault on the enemy quadrant during the last war. The other two officers are Captain O'Rourke and Lieutenant O'Connell."

Colonel Skorzeny, a tough, athletic man in a black sheepskin overcoat, spoke first. "Since the last war he have put our land forces under a training program in the latest methods. However, we will need a guide for moving through the marshlands."

Captain O'Rourke answered, "Sirs, I know a man who lives in the marshlands. He can show the colonel's men how to use swampboats and set a path across the marshland."

Colonels Becker and Skorzeny simultaneously asked, "Who is this man?"

Captain O'Rourke replied, "My uncle, Eugene O'Rourke. He has had a floating home in the quadrant marshlands for years."

Colonel Skorzeny was skeptical. "He is a civilian. What does he know about military affairs?"

"He knows the marshlands, Colonel, sir; and that is what counts in this operation," Captain O'Rourke answered.

Then Lieutenant O'Connell spoke. "I'll have some distressing news for you. Of the twenty-four Boomerang fighter-bombers we have in the phantom squadron only five have any charge left in their laser batteries. We would have difficulty recharging the batteries on these craft. Unless we can have aerial bombs mounted on these craft, the fighters would be ineffective."

Colonel Skorzeny then suggested, "Perhaps we should use regular fighter craft to cover a land assault on the oil fields instead of using commandos to rescue the pilots."

Colonel Becker answered, "I believe we have a stockpile of explosives at Peenemude, near Kilkenny; they could be designed into aerial bombs."

Defense Minister Flynn then cautioned the staff meeting, "I suggest we hold off this counterattack for a few weeks. The enemy is expecting some kind of response. A delay will develop their overconfidence."

Then a messenger boy came to the conference room with a large envelope. Joe Flynn opened it and read the contents.

"It is a communiqué from the anti-royalist underground in Brittania. They have located the site where the parts of the Boomerang fighters are assembled." He read it out loud.

Colonel Becker then took the message and read further. The colonel commented, "The parts for several hundred enemy craft are warehoused in the Liverpool sector. If we could hit that assembling center, we could delay their production by two months."

Joe Flynn commented, "This operation could be in tandem with the marshland operation."

Then Becker read a second page of the report, "What are they thinking of? This letter says they want us to escort a transport of Scottish and Welsh refugees crossing the corridor between the planets. This is a program that will only result in disaster."

❖ ❖ ❖

A Drive-It-Yur-Self hauling trailer was hitched to the rear bumper of the old McLaughlin auto. The garage had not been hit. Theo McLaughlin and

Maureen Kelley had spent the previous two nights in there. Now they began to load their remaining belongings into the trailer.

"Theo, what is that clock you have there?" Mo Kelley asked.

Theo answered, "It is a grandmother clock. My mother got it from her parents. It was in the garage back of a pile of oil cans. It needs to be cleaned, but it can run again."

Jan MacDevitt and her husband-to-be, Paddy Tully, arrived by a city tram and greeted their friends. Jan cried, "Mercy sakes, what a sad end to a beautiful house!"

"Yes," answered Theo, "but we still have each other."

Paddy Tully said, "Jan and myself can drive the auto for awhile so the two of you can rest for a bit. Is Mo's parents coming up here to help?"

Mo Kelley answered, "No, they are cleaning up the room I used to sleep in as a kid. They are taking care of our children, Barry and Esther."

Then Theo walked to the auto with a metal strong box. He opened the box with a key. He said, "This contains the photos, legal papers, and other papers of my parents. Here, Mo, this is the wedding picture of my parents. You would have loved them as much as I did."

Mo Kelley answered, "Your mother was a beautiful woman."

Then Jan noticed a gleaming object in the bottom of the box and pointed it out to Theo. He picked it up out of the box and exclaimed, "It is a medal, the Order of St. Patrick. Here is a paper commendation:

> To Shuttle Pilot First Class, Patrick Keane McLaughlin, for heroic service during the Brittanic war of 3124. As a shuttle pilot he destroyed several troop transports sent against the sacred soil of Hibernia.

Theobald McLaughlin began to cry. "My father was a hero. He told me he was in the war, but he never said anything about a medal."

Maureen Kelley then reached into the box and pulled out a photo of Pat McLaughlin in his uniform. She commented, "He's a handsome man."

Theo stood up erect, still trembling, at attention. He raised his hand to his forehead to salute his father's memory. His wife, Mo, and their friends joined in the salute. Theo, his voice breaking, said, "Mother, Father, your son loved you, still loves you, and will always love you."

✦ ✦ ✦

Eyebrows were raised when an Orange border family entered St. Olivier Plunkett Hospital. The man in the lead walked up to the receptionist desk.

"I am James King McKerr and this is my wife and daughter. We are asking when is the time to visit patients? My son is a patient here, a pilot, Ensign William King McKerr."

The receptionist turned to a file listing of patients, then said, "He is in room 311. Visiting time is beginning just now. He can be wheeled into the visiting room on the second floor."

James King McKerr thanked the receptionist, then led his family to the elevator.

When the elevator door opened, several nurses and a nun emerged. The nun shook her head in shock at the sight of a man in a black suit, bowler, and orange tie. The nurses were also surprised. The McKerr family shrugged off the hostile reception and entered the elevator.

"Father! Mother! Agnes! You're alive!" Billy King McKerr exclaimed. He wheeled his chair up to them. "When I heard the Shankill school was hit I thought I had lost all of you."

Ann McKerr answered, "My son, we lost many of our innocent children. Murderers, pure murderers."

James asked his son, "Are you all right? I wish you would return to the militia."

Billy King told his father, "I am a pilot of the Hibernian Air-Space Defense Service. If I cannot be a Needlehead pilot, they might assign me as a Bullethead co-pilot or in the repair branch."

Then Agnes said, "My father, I am glad Billy King is here to back me up. I intend to join the Auxiliary Service to be a surface gunner."

James King shouted, "Don't you know what the people of Shankill are saying? They think the government deliberately left our village undefended to get our people killed off. I ought to forbid you to do that, my daughter, but . . . but, go ahead." James and Ann McKerr embraced their daughter and their son pulled his wheelchair up close.

"Father," he said, "I hope you are all proud of me. I got the Brit fighter that hit my ship."

✦ ✦ ✦

After a break for lunch, the Defense Ministry conference meeting resumed.

Commander Rafferty spoke. "Commanders Donahue, MacMullen, and I have discussed the risks of these proposed operations. We believe that the attack on the Ulster petroleum fields should be carried out first. Then, after we have analyzed any errors made during the operation, we can prepare for the Liverpool attack."

Commander Donahue added, "We should all remember what happened during the raid on the enemy planet during the last war. We lost three of our tankers and our repair ship. We now have only one tanker available."

Commander MacMullen then added, "I admit my personal feelings affect my beliefs. Many fine pilots and crewmen were lost on those tankers. One of them was my . . . my son, on the *John Redmond*."

Colonel Murphy rose and answered them. "The comments we have heard are valid. I lost a brother on the *Michael Collins*, and I know Donahue and Rafferty lost sons on the *Daniel O'Connell*. The loss of the *Arthur Griffith* would be too great."

Defense Minister Flynn sighed, then said, "I am convinced; we will postpone the Liverpool operation."

Then Colonel Becker arose from the conference table and walked to a wall map of the Ulster quadrant. "Gentlemen," he announced, "here, two hundred kilometers northeast of the marshland, are the oil fields. Straight northeast, three hundred kilometers up, is the refinery complex. A number of parallel pipelines run from the oil fields to the refinery."

Colonel Kalminsky then suggested the attack route. "The phantom squadron should fly due north to the marshlands and turn northeast. First hit the oil fields, then the pipelines, then the refinery. Then turn around to land at the edge of the marshland."

Lieutenant O'Connell then answered, "Begging the colonel's pardon, the refinery should be hit first. Intelligence reports show storage capacity capable of keeping the refining of crude oil running for several weeks with the shipment of new oil."

Major Hoffman agreed with the junior officer. "A more important factor should be considered. The enemy's nearest fighter base is five hundred kilometers north of the refinery. By hitting the refinery first, the phantom squadron will be moving away from the enemy base before their fighters can respond. The squadron should fly north of the marshlands, then turn due east straight to the refinery, then, turning southwest, go down to the oil fields."

Colonel Becker then answered the two pilots. "Your alternative is correct. I recommend that the Bullethead squadron be at a high altitude station, say one thousand kilometers over the marshlands, to run interference to intercept any fighters that the Brits send up against the phantom squadron. Thus, Major, you are to remain in Athlone. After the operation, you will be then transferred to the South Pole."

Major Hoffman replied, *"Danke, Mein Herr."*

Lieutenant O'Connell was pleased at hearing that the Bullethead squadron was to run interference. He said, "Thank you for the backup, Colonel. With only five of the phantom craft having any laser charges, they'd be cut to pieces if caught by the enemy. Also, I feel the aerial bombs should be only mounted on the fighters that have no laser charges. The other five could act as guards."

Defense Minister Flynn then arose from his table seat. "Gentlemen, it is obvious we have the operation set up. I suggest we adjourn this meeting. Colonel Skorzeny and Captain O'Rourke are to be directed to the quadrant marshlands. Lieutenant O'Connell is to go to Pennemude; Colonel Becker is to accompany the lieutenant as most of the IPVs there are Becker's countrymen. The rest of us should return to regular duties."

After the meeting broke up, Colonels Becker and Skorzeny discussed the upcoming operation with Captain O'Rourke and Lieutenant O'Connell. The captain spoke. "I will have to make a pair of phone calls before we leave. First, I will call my Uncle Eugene. He will meet us in the village at the south edge of the marsh. Colonel Skorzeny, I think you will actually enjoy swampboats; they're very fast. The second call will be to our next door neighbor to leave a message for my family. My sister is attending a memorial service. My brother's at work."

Colonel Becker then asked, "How is your family, Captain?"

Captain O'Rourke answered, "Shelley broke her arm mounting a gun during the attack; Cadet Hallohan broke a leg along with her."

Colonel Becker commented, "They are a couple of spirited young women, particularly Cadet Hallohan. She has other talents besides manning a surface laser."

Lieutenant O'Connell answered, "The captain and myself both know Brigid's many charms."

Colonel Becker asked, "And how is your youngest one? Do you know, your uncle and I taught him to play the concertina?"

Captain O'Rourke answered, "Cathal is once again a busy delivery boy, always at work. During the attack one of our pilots landed outside of the greenhouse. Cathal and his friend Deirdre O'Toole administered the first aid. He's a fine lad."

Colonel Becker then replied, "Your little brother is working to battle loneliness. Loneliness is a difficult thing for a man to fight, but for a mere boy it is very painful. Captain, I hope you and your father, Commander O'Rourke, realize and appreciate just how really brave that little boy actually is."

Across the corridor of space to Brittania, at the Crystal Palace, Queen Elizabeth the Seventeenth was holding a conference. "Your most noble majesty," Lord Cromwell announced, "The results of our recent operation were most favorable. We have ferried six hundred of our fighter craft to the Ulster quadrant without loss."

The monarch's answer was hardly that of celebration. "However, Lord Cromwell, we did lose 170 of the 250 fighters we had in the quadrant, with some of our best pilots. This loss of trained personnel is unbearable."

The Prime Minister replied, "The Ulster quadrant fighter command carried out a successful mission, decoying the Hibernian fighter force from intercepting the convoy. They inflected heavy damage on the enemy capital city, massive damage, demoralizing their population."

The Brittanic monarch leaned back against her throne and sighed, "Perhaps you are right; I feel we should move to the next agenda. What is the current status of the build-up of our home airfleet?"

Her first minister smiled and presented a production report. "We have one thousand fighters completely assembled, with pilots in training; four hundred shuttle craft with pilots trained in strafing tactics; eight hundred to one thousand fighters in a state of partial assembly in Liverpool. We estimate that in two months these fighters will be totally assembled and with trained pilots. We could launch our final offensive just before or after the end of the year."

The Brittanic monarch was joyous. "Cromwell, think of it! Hibernia exterminated! What a gift to present the Brittanic people at the building of the New Year! I will have a royal proclamation prepared to announce the death warrant of Hibernia."

Lord Cromwell bowed, saying, "You have my total obedience, your grace." The queen and her first minister would not have been so happy if they knew the chamber room was electronically tapped and that the anti-royalist Underground knew their every word.

A panel truck a short distance from the Crystal Palace picked up the conversation. In an hour cells of the Underground received the information and began to develop counter measures.

✦ ✦ ✦

It was after dusk when Cathal O'Rourke returned to his home. The last three days after the attack on the city, the floral shop was swamped with orders. A second two-wheeled cart was hitched to his pedicab. Pedaling was extremely hard, and the little delivery boy's legs were knotted with pain from his hips to his toes.

He read two notes in the little notebox by the front door. His brother was going up to the marshlands. His sister and friends had gone to the Quinncannons for a dinner reception after the memorial services. Cathal sighed and said to himself, "I bet they're having a wild party. It's just as well they're not here; I'd be out of place. I do wish I could see Deirdre. I've seen her just a couple times at the shop. I haven't been this alone since before the May attack."

He went to the kitchen and took out the smallest of three teapots. He made himself tea, and with soda bread and cheese had a supper. He read the family mail and wondered how to tell his sister and brother about several overdue bills. Then he thought of the evening after the attack, when Deirdre O'Toole had been over for the night. He thought to himself, "Most boys would have taken Dee into Father's double bed for the night. I couldn't do it. I wonder if Deirdre told Shelley that I did nothing. And what Deirdre said. Her with Miss Brigid when she joined the Tigeress Gang. Shelley having Lieutenant O'Connell in Father's room. And my brother Eamon with

251

Miss Brigid. I remember in May when I delivered flowers. She had my brother, my noble brother. She asked me what was wrong with him; asked me if he didn't like girls. After the other night, I wonder, is something wrong with me? Deirdre said she'd be ready when I want to have her. I can't do it; I don't want to hurt her."

He turned on the family's big radio. After the evening newscast, a program of music and poetry came on. The poems reminded him that school would be starting soon. He said to himself, "I can patch things up with Dee." Finally he turned off the radio and lights, then went to his room and bed, hugging a stuffed toy mulquix.

✦ ✦ ✦

The following morning Colonel Becker and Lieutenant O'Connell arrived at the air strip near Peenemude. They were met by Major Bauer and Dr. Scheer, who were respectively in charge of the military and technical operations. The two Teutonic IPVs saluted the colonel.

"It is a honor to have your presence. We are already beginning to disassemble and reassemble plasma explosive into aerial bombs."

Dr. Scheer then noted, "One of the captured enemy fighters was sent here last month for examination. We believe the fighter can carry four one-thousand-kilogram bombs, two on each wing. I remember the report that the enemy convoy in June carried aerial bombs to be mounted on fighters."

Colonel Becker answered, "Correct; however, they were old-fashioned chemical explosives. The bombs we will use will be up to ten times more powerful. We have nineteen fighters to have bombs mounted on their wings, a total of seventy-six metric tons of plasma explosive."

Major Bauer asked, "I thought we had twenty-four of the enemy craft?"

Lieutenant O'Connell explained, "The other five fighters still can operate their lasers. They will act as escorts."

Dr. Scheer then answered, "An excellent decision. I will make one strict instruction to your pilots. They should drop the two outboard bombs one wing at a time before dropping the bombs near the fuselage; otherwise the fighters will bank to one side or the other."

Major Bauer then asked, "I understand an amphibious assault will be planned in conjunction with the serial attack. Is that for rescue of the pilots?"

"Correct, Major," Colonel Becker replied.

When the four officers reached the Peenemude rocket base, the entire unit was assembled for inspection. The flags of planets Hibernia and Deutsch flew side by side. Major Bauer explained, "We have prepared ourselves for your personal examination, Colonel Becker."

"A perfect display of discipline, Major. After inspection, I intend to address them on the seriousness of the operation they are undertaking," the colonel replied.

A convoy of troop trucks rolled north toward the marshlands. Infantry troops, both green-clad Hibernian regulars and Colonel Skorzeny's commandos in black, were in the trucks. In a troop truck at the head of the convoy, Colonel Skorzeny rode with a platoon of his men and with Captain O'Rourke. The pilot spoke. "When I phoned my uncle he said he would ask his neighbors to loan us their swampboats."

The colonel answered, "I hope he did not tell his neighbors our objectives. One word to the wrong person could endanger this operation."

Captain O'Rourke answered, "He would have had to give some explanation to satisfy their curiosity."

The troop convoy came into the village and the town people and the people from the marshland had gathered. Eugene O'Rourke was at the docks at the edge of the marshland.

"Sorry, nephew of mine," he said in an apologetic voice, "but rumors of soldiers coming here spread like wildfire after the attack on the city. We have thirteen boats by the docks and about another ten back in the marshlands."

Colonel Skorzeny was upset. "This is not good at all; everyone in this village knows what we are doing."

Eugene O'Rourke said to his nephew, "Your Aunt Beth has a rich mutton stew for dinner for all of us and we've fixed the guest room for the two of you."

Colonel Skorzeny replied sharply, "The captain and myself will bivouac with my men."

Eugene answered, "Well, sirs, I've a big map of the marshlands you'll need. If you at least take dinner with us, you can get an idea of the area."

The colonel was surprised by the answer he received and said, "I usually make it a point to endure the same conditions that my men will go through, but we will take up your offer for dinner."

Captain O'Rourke explained to his uncle, "Colonel Skorzeny believes an officer should set an example for his men."

✦ ✦ ✦

Three weeks passed in the marshlands and Peenemude. In Peenemude the IPV workers assembled proton-positron plasma into aerial bombs. The phantom squadron fighters were ferried down to the fighter base at nearby Kilkenny. Racks for holding the bombs were attached to the wings and a self-destruct timer built into the cockpit. In the marshlands, Colonel Skorzeny's men received instructions on how to run the swampboats. Several paths were set in the marshes toward the enemy quadrant. A trapping stake would be driven into the wet ground and several traps set atop the stake. This was how the paths were set up.

Outside of a small village halfway between Athlone and the marshlands, a final staff meeting was held. Defense Minister Flynn, Commander MacMullen, Colonels Becker, Kalminsky, and Skorzeny, Major Hoffman, Captain O'Rourke, and Lieutenant O'Connell were all present. Defense Minister Flynn announced, "The offensive will be called Operation Mulquix-Red-Bird. Mulquix is the amphibious part of the operation; Red Bird the aerial operation. The phantom squadron will take off from Kilkenny and pass right over Athlone and the marshlands. When they reach the latter, they are to radio Athlone and the village by the marshlands. Major Hoffman's Bullethead squadron will be launched from Athlone and will reach up to fifteen hundred kilometers over the Ulster quadrant with their scanner reaching the enemy bases north of the refinery area. At the same time the amphibious group is to hit the Brit village at the east end of the quadrant."

Colonel Becker completed the scenario. "The Phantom squadron will head north of the marshland, then turn east right to the refinery complex. After destroying the refinery, they are to head southwest, hitting the pipelines and finally the oil fields. The fighters are to land, set the self-destruction timers, then the pilots are to head to the village captured by Colonel Skorzeny's men. Major Hoffman's Bullethead craft will be called Bluebird and will shield the phantom fighters as they head southwest from the refinery area."

Colonel Skorzeny commented, "The weather is getting worse. Rain, on one hand, could shield our landings, but it could also sink our landing craft. I have ordered Captain O'Rourke to tell the people in the marshlands and the village to head to the western end of the marshlands."

❖ ❖ ❖

Three days of rainstorms came down upon Athlone and the marshlands. It became miserably cold. The swampboats were put under a covered dock landing. Colonel Skorzeny read the upcoming weather reports and declared, "When the rain ends this area will be blanketed with fog. Our boats will be unable to move at top speed. This could be a critical delay for our amphibious assault. Captain O'Rourke, did your uncle make a map of the path to the enemy village?"

Captain O'Rourke replied, "Yes, I went out with my uncle and two of your junior officers into the marshland to make the map. My uncle can check the trapline again if necessary."

Colonel Skorzeny answered, "Good. As soon as this rain stops our swampboats will go into the center of the marshland. That will make up for the delay of moving at reduced speed."

❖ ❖ ❖

Before dawn in Athlone, the rains stopped; the sun broke through the clouds and it cleared away the sky. A radio message came down for the marsh. "This is Colonel Skorzeny. We are in the middle of the marshland, ready for Mulquix." The alarm rang into the fighter hangar at the Athlone base. The pilots of the phantom climbed into the captured Brit fighter craft. In minutes the Boomerang fighter-bombers with the question mark in place of the Union Jack were in the sky heading north. Ten minutes later the Bullethead fighter-bombers were fired out of their vertical launch tubes and soon were over one thousand kilometers above the surface of the planet.

✦ ✦ ✦

In the war room the Taoiseach, the defense minister, and Colonels Becker and Kalminsky waited for the reports to come in.

The voice of Lieutenant O'Connell came over the air. "Redbird leader to Mulquix. We are over the marshlands heading north; come in Mulquix."

The voice of Captain O'Rourke came in reply, "This is Mulquix. We are moving now, headed east."

✦ ✦ ✦

The phantom squadron headed north in three waves. Lieutenant O'Connell led the five laser-armed fighters while the bomb-carrying craft followed in two waves. Lieutenant Ranier led a wave of ten fighters while the remaining nine craft were led by Lieutenant Soares. Nearly 350 kilometers north of the marshland they turned east, then after going another 350 kilometers, they discovered the refinery complex. The squadron had flown into the quadrant at a very low altitude, under the enemy scanners. Lieutenant O'Connell gave orders to his pilots.

"Ranier, your wave will hit the refinery; Soares's wave will hit the storage tanks. We'll hit the surface guns."

The phantom fighters came down to the complex where Brittanic soldiers were actually waving up at them. The first wave of fighters opened laser fire with pencil beams. Several surface guns were hit before they could be manned to fire back.

The second wave of Boomerang fighters swooped over the refinery; each craft dropping one bomb. The bombs fell in a small cluster in the center of the refinery. A massive ion fireball arose, disintegrating the refinery, and thick black smoke came up. The third wave of phantom craft dropped one bomb each into the storage tanks. The tanks vanished, and the oil inside went up in flames.

Lieutenant O'Connell was strafing the remaining guns when he heard the accented voice of Lieutenant Soares, "O'Farrell, Branigan, you're too low, pull up."

255

O'Connell steered his fighter around to witness the ghastly sight. Two fighters released their bombs into storage tanks while too low. The crafts were caught in the uprising ion fireball and vanished. Then Lieutenant Ranier's voice came over the air.

"McElhone, you're heading into the laser fire; turn!"

A single remaining surface gun hit the oncoming fighter, sheering a wing off. The fatally damaged craft nose-dived into the still firing gun. O'Connell looked around the area, then radioed, "We're finished here; let's head south. Red-bird to Mulquix, Red-bird to Mulquix, first objective scratched. Heading southwest. We lost three."

✦ ✦ ✦

Fifteen hundred kilometers above the planet the scanners of the Bullethead fighters picked up the blips of a Brittanic fighter force taking off from the base north of the refinery. Major Hoffman radioed, "Bluebird to Redbird, Bluebird to Redbird, an intercepting squad is coming south. We will move in to block for you."

The Bullethead squadron came over the Ulster quadrant and then down by scanners right above the oncoming enemy. A wave of twenty enemy craft appeared. Major Hoffman ordered his wing, "Open fire," then a chain of ten ion plasma fireballs burst in front of the enemy. Most of the enemy craft disintegrated. The Bulletheads dived straight down then climbed back up. A second wave of enemy craft appeared. A Bullethead fighter flown by a rookie crew collided with one of the enemy craft. A second Bullethead pulled up too slowly and was hit by laser crossfire from several enemy craft. Major Hoffman watched in horror at the loss of two of his craft. Then, angered, he ordered his remaining craft to open fire as soon as they had turned about into the enemy. The plasma bursts hit the enemy craft in ones and twos. Major Hoffman's Bullethead battled its way out of the enemy force.

After ten minutes, the enemy craft pulled away, fleeing eastward. Major Hoffman led his fighters south, continuing to guard the phantom squadron. He radioed, "Bluebird to Redbird, Bluebird to Mulquix, Bluebird to Redbird, Bluebird to Mulquix, we have intercepted the enemy. Two of our craft were lost, but we brought down twenty-nine of the enemy. We are continuing south. We will veer southwest when we reach the first objective of Redbird."

✦ ✦ ✦

The phantom squadron headed southwest. Lieutenant O'Connell thought to himself, "Three good men lost. O'Farrell was married back in April. McElhone's wife just had their third baby. I owed Branigan ten grams silver. Three good men and Hoffman's wing lost four others. Good crickin' galls!"

Lieutenant Soares radioed, "There, just north of us, a pumping station and the pipelines above ground."

O'Connell answered, "We'll hit the pipelines with lasers. One of you bomb the pumps."

The Boomerang craft that had lasers opened up with pencil beams. The beams cut into the three parallel pipelines like a knife through butter. The fighters flew just above the pipes, cutting them in half until the pipes went back underground. An oil slick several kilometers long was formed. When a bomb wrecked the pumping station, the oil caught fire along the length of the pipeline.

✦ ✦ ✦

The fog still covered the marshes, and the flotilla of swampboats slowly headed east. Colonel Skorzeny looked over the map at the pathway and said, "The path divides into two branches. One heads right to the village, the other to a landing south of the village. That is good. We will trap any fleeing enemy."

The flotilla split into two columns and headed east. Colonel Skorzeny and Captain O'Rourke led the column that entered the village. They stopped their motors and drifted up near a dock landing. Several commandos slipped overboard and swam up to the docks. Two unsuspecting guards were dropped silently, and a flashlight signaled the other boats to come in. In two minutes the commandos were heading into the village. The people in the settlement were caught while opening their shops and offices. The people surrendered in shock; several women fainting and children crying.

The other column went up to an abandoned landing and disembarked. They moved north through the fog, arms ready for battle. They came up to the village and joined the first column.

The village mayor, hands raised in terror, pleaded for the lives of his townspeople. Colonel Skorzeny, in a voice just harsh enough to threaten, said, "There were two guards at the landing. Where is the garrison? Tell us now!"

The terrified mayor replied, "Two kilometers east of here. The guards are sent here every eight hours, without supervision."

Colonel Skorzeny ordered the people of the village to be taken back to the dock landing. Then he said, "Now we will destroy the garrison." He ordered three small laser guns brought from the boats. Each was small enough to be carried by two men. The commando force then moved out of the village and into the fog. An advance line of skirmishes reconnoitered around the Brittanic garrison, then returned to present their findings. A squad leader reported, "It is a small base, above-ground barracks, a hurricane fence topped with barbed wire. Two machine gun towers and guards outside the fence."

Colonel Skorzeny ordered his force spread wide to hit the enemy on three sides. He instructed the laser gun to be deployed, one aimed at the gates, the other two to hit the gun towers.

The commando squads slipped back into the fog close to the garrison and dropped the guards. Units of commando and regular Hibernian infantry moved closer to encircle the base. Colonel Skorzeny ordered a laser gun to fire at the gates. A laser burst flattened the gates while the other two lasers hit the machine gun towers.

The laser gunshot hit the hurricane fence repeatedly. The commandos and regulars stormed into the base, firing on hastily assembling Brit soldiers. Some tried to surrender but were shot from behind by superior officers. A group of men ran to a thick stone blockhouse. From there they again tried to fire back with laser rifles and automatic weapons. The commandos threw grenades in the wooden barracks to set them afire.

The remaining Brittanic soldiers continued to fire from the blockhouse. The casualties mounted, and it appeared the commando operation would have to withdraw. Then Colonel Skorzeny ordered the three lasers to be put side-by-side and fired at the blockhouse. The laser bursts pounded the stone walls until they began to crumble. Then the three guns converged at a weakened point and broke through. A loud explosion shattered the blockhouse. Captain O'Rourke exclaimed, "It must have hit an ammunition magazine." In a few minutes the last Brits surrendered.

Captain O'Rourke then took a field radio and signaled, "Mulquix to Redbird, Mulquix to Redbird, landing area secured. Come on in."

The voice of Lieutenant O'Connell answered. "We're coming."

The phantom squadron fighters continued southwest, hitting the pipeline whenever it came to the surface. Lieutenant O'Connell ordered his pilots to report their weapons status and afterwards noted, "Two of the five craft in the first wave are out of laser charges. Of the sixteen bomb carriers, five have no bombs left at all, two have three bombs each, seven have two each, and two had one apiece. That's only twenty-two bombs. We'll have to use our lasers." The downward scanners picked up the oil fields. There were many pumping rigs, several drilling rigs, a warehouse of equipment, but no defenses. Lieutenant O'Connell ordered, "Let's go to work!"

The fighter bombers swooped over the oil fields, firing lasers and dropping bombs. The pumping and drilling rigs disintegrated, setting oil on fire. Clouds of black smoke rolled up into the sky. The warehouse of equipment literally melted. After the last bombs were released and the lasers went out, the pilots pulled up and headed southwest. Lieutenant O'Connell radioed, "This is Redbird to Mulquix; we're coming home. All objectives scratched. We're low on fuel. Have the medics ready; we might have to ditch."

✥ ✥ ✥

At the burnt-out garrison, Colonel Skorzeny and Captain O'Rourke waited with the commando forces for the phantom squadron. The sun rose, burning off the fog. Minutes seemed like hours, and the Colonel commented, "They may run out of fuel."

Then, after a horrible wait, the Boomerang craft appeared. The voice of Lieutenant O'Connell came over the radio. "We're coming in; got the tea on?"

The twenty-one Brit craft landed; the pilots set the destruction timers and ran. The fighter craft exploded one after the other.

The pilots were greeted with cheers. O'Rourke and O'Connell shook hands and bear-hugged, saying, "Well, Colonel, it's time for a boat ride again."

Colonel Skorzeny ordered the commando and the pilots to withdraw.

The force returned to the village and the people were released. Electrophone lines were cut and the village radio transmitter wrecked. The colonel said, "These people will not be able to contact anyone for a few days."

The mass of soldiers got back on the swampboats. The fog had finally lifted, and the swampboats raced across the marshland to the village on the southside. The village folks cheered the heroic victors, Eugene O'Rourke leading the cheers.

"Eamon, my nephew, and Sean, your friend, I knew you'd be back safe," the uncle said smiling. Then he added, "Bethie's prepared a big dinner for you if your Colonel could let you off. In fact, we'd be honored if he joins us."

Colonel Skorzeny looked around and saw some of his men fraternizing with the young winsome colleens of the village. After thinking a minute, he told Eugene, "First, I must see that our wounded are sent to a field hospital and the prisoners we have are processed; but I will join you for dinner." Then after a pause, "Normally I disapprove of my men having casual acquaintances with women in an area like this. However, they have fought hard and successfully defeated the enemy. I feel they could be allowed to celebrate for the day."

✦ ✦ ✦

In the war room of the Defense Ministry a wave of relief came over the Taoiseach. Colm O'Hara sighed, saying, "They have done it. The amphibious group has returned with our pilots."

Colonel Becker noted, "After we examine the completed reports by Colonel Skorzeny, Captain O'Rourke, and Lieutenant O'Connell, we will begin preparations on the second counter-offensive against Liverpool."

Colonel Kalminsky answered, "Yes, Becker, I will order my two pilots to file full reports when they arrive in Athlone. I will also order Major Hoffman to file a report as well."

The Taoiseach then asked, "Becker, do you remember that request from the Underground of Brittania to escort their convoy? What are we to do about that request?"

Colonel Becker's reply was sharp as well as shocked, "It is out of the question, Herr Taoiseach. What they are asking could result in the loss of our last remaining tanker, several squadrons of fighters, and, of course, their convoy. Thousands of innocents would be blown to atoms."

Colm O'Hara then answered again. "Well, gentlemen, perhaps we should discuss this at the next meeting of all base commanders. For now, we can relax. A press release should be readied for the public. It will rebuild our people's morale. I still have some poteen in my office to toast this victory."

As the officials walked out of the war room, Defense Minster Flynn stumbled and fell. The Taoiseach and Colonel Becker helped him. Joe Flynn assured his comrades, "I've just a case of stumbles." He kept to himself the feeling that something was seriously wrong. When the officials went into the office he dropped the glass of poteen offered him by the Taoiseach. He thought to himself, "I will undergo a complete physical examination. If this is what I suspect, I may have to retire."

✦ ✦ ✦

That evening in the O'Rourke floating home, Colonel Skorzeny was commenting on the meal that Beth O'Rourke had served. While holding a forkful of meat he said, "This is an unusual dish. What is it?"

Beth's answer, "Mulquix, young man, the animal that is caught here in the marshes. I soak it in salt water for twenty-four hours, then roast it with mushrooms and primrose wine."

Captain O'Rourke then commented, "My aunt is a fine cook, as fine as my mother was."

Aunt Beth put her hand on her nephew's shoulder, saying, "Yes, Eamon, Bernie, your mother, taught me to make the potato spice pie we have for dessert."

Lieutenant O'Connell then said, "Eamon, I helped her make the rum sauce."

After dinner the three guests gave Beth O'Rourke a break by washing the dishes. Then Eugene O'Rourke led his guests outside of the house. He took out his old pipe and tobacco pouch. Lieutenant O'Connell took out a pair of cigars, giving one to Colonel Skorzeny. The three men were quietly smoking for a few minutes. Eugene O'Rourke turned to his nephew, Eamon, saying, "Back in summer that colleen, Deirdre, lit my pipe a number of times."

"Yes, Uncle Gene," Eamon replied, "Miss O'Toole is kind of wild—like Shelley was at that age."

Eugene answered saying, "Yes, she is a girl full of mischief, but she is sweet on Cathal. It's a good thing that shy boy has a girl who loves him."

Then Lieutenant O'Connell entered the discussion, saying, "Apparently Eamon hasn't told you yet he got lucky. His girl's none other than Brigid Hallohan!"

Eugene O'Rourke blinked, saying, "The dancer, you mean, this young boy. . . ."

Sean O'Connell answered, "Eamon is a man now, not a boy; he got lucky!"

Colonel Skorzeny smiled, "Fraternizing? What would your father say?"

Eamon answered, "I am not sure."

The colonel then told Eugene, "Thank you for your hospitality, but soon I must to back to my men."

Gene answered, "I hope you will allow my nephew and his friend the use of the guest room for the night." The Colonel answered, "The operation is completed; it will not be necessary for them to bivouac with my men; however, tomorrow morning they must be ready for the return to Athlone. We will have prepared a full report for the Defense Ministry."

The two pilots thanked the Colonel and saluted him before he got aboard a small speedboat and left. Uncle Gene then asked Eamon, "What will the two of you do when you return to town?"

Eamon answered, "After we file our full reports, we will try to get a few days leave. Brigid and I and Sean, here, and my sister Shelley might rent a cabin down by Big Bog Lake for a few days."

Sean then added, "If it weren't for school, Cathal and Deirdre could come along. Then again, if they did come up, it could be part of their education."

Thousands of kilometers southeast of the quadrant marsh, a big event was taking place in Kilkenny. The Beehive was a small, clean, but lively music hall. The barker, dressed in a bowler and vest, walked out on the stage to announce, "Ladies and gentlemen, we have a special event for tonight. A local girl who made good up in Athlone and Dublin has returned to our stage. Here she is, the girl with jet-propelled tassels, Miss Maureen Kelley!"

The tall redhead came out on the stage. She wore a brief black outfit, tassels hanging from her pasties and one more on her G string. The drum roll and clarinet accompanied as she started to dance, slowly at first, then faster until the tassels seemed to vanish. She wiggled her hips side to side and kicked a few high steps. She blew kisses to the audience, which was on its feet. She reached the end of the runway and, turning sharply, let her rear tassel flip up to the crowd. She did a hand spring and then the splits, leaning on her back to raise her legs up in the air. Rising to her feet again, she rocked side to side, her tassels going so fast a man shouted, "They will pull the pasties off."

As she concluded her act, she blew another kiss to the audience and waved. In the midst of the now wildly cheering audience, a party that Mo Kelley had personally invited sat, beaming with pride. Her husband Theobald McLaughlin, her parents, Michael and Ann Kelley, the aunts of her children, Nurse Terri Lynch and Naomi Sennech, and Naomi's translator, Major Eshkol. The Major asked, "Is this type of entertainment native to Hibernia?"

Theo replied, "No, the music halls came about from the settlers from other planets." He added, "Never is my wife more lovely than when she's up there. The night we were married, it was performed in the main dressing room before the show started. She started the show and I watched from backstage. We had the reception in the main dressing room. Then, when the show ended for the night, the theater management let us spend the night alone in the dressing room."

Mike Kelley then told the Major, "When Mo told us she wanted to be a dancer, we were a bit shocked, but we never rejected her, even when she had troubles. Now she has a fine man for a husband. You know, they married in March, and it weren't until they came down last month we met him."

Then Terri Lynch spoke, "Mr. McLaughlin, because of the war I lost my family and so did Naomi. Because of you and your beautiful wife and children, we both have a family again. I thank you very much."

After Major Eshkol translated for Naomi, the young girl replied, "I also thank you. Neither Terri nor I will ever be lonely again. We learned about each other, and our lives were about the same."

Theo McLaughlin answered, "Mo Kelley is the most wonderful thing to happen in my life."

The evening performance continued with a chorus line, a lady magician in a plastic leotard and a comic act. After it finished and Mo Kelley put on a more modest dress, the party went to a local diner. Mo Kelley greeted her husband with a kiss on the cheek, then said, "I wish Jan MacDevitt and her fiancée, Paddy Tully, could have stayed down here, but they had to return to Athlone to complete their wedding plans. We have an invitation."

❖ ❖ ❖

"Thank you, Cathal," Deirdre said.

"Thanks, too," said Sharrey.

Cathal had struck a match from the matchbook on the table to light the girls' cigarettes. They were sitting at a table in a tea room. It was early evening after school. Deirdre kissed her boy on the cheek while Sharrey caressed his hand. Sharrey Fitzgibbon said, "Dee, you're lucky you have a great boy for a friend."

Deirdre answered, "Yes, he is wonderful. Say, Cathal, did you know Sharrey's going to become a Tigeress?"

Cathal answered, "That is nice. I wish Eamon was home. I wish Father were home."

Deirdre answered, "Yes, Cathal. Shelley told me about what your father's mission is."

Cathal answered, "Did she explain to you that if Father doesn't return we could lose the war? We could all die!"

Dee then told him, "Don't worry. Shelley is sure he'll be back."

Sharrey Fitzgibbon looked at her cigarette, then said, "If Connie were here she'd groan, saying I'll never have the lungs to play camogie. Then I'd tell her that I am not an athlete and that she's not my mother."

Deirdre then asked, "How will your parents react if you become a Tigeress?"

Sharrey frowned and replied, "My parents really don't care much what I do. They are all consumed with their department store. When Connie was a child they doted on her and her prowess in camogie. When I came it was an afterthought. As soon as I was old enough for school they kind of decided to pretend I didn't exist. They put me into public instead of church school to save money, I guess."

Cathal and Deirdre, both shocked, asked, "Do you resent your older sister's getting all your parents' attention?"

Sharrey's answer came after a minute of thought. "I used to resent her, but she has tried to make up for our parents by paying some attention to me. I guess this is why she is disappointed by the fact I am not like her."

A waiter came up to the table. He announced, "We have fresh baked soda bread and cheese. And a special tea, spiced and sweetened with honey." The three gave their orders, then the waiter tapped Cathal and in a whisper, said, "Slip me a silver gram and I can get a drop of rum into it. Good for the cold weather." The two girls nodded approval and Cathal handed a gram of silver to the waiter.

Just after the waiter left, Shelley and Brigid came up to the table. Shelley announced, "I have news. All five secondary schools will hold a dance to raise money to help the people of Shankill rebuild their school."

Brigid added, "The girls will go on auction to the boys just like at the Golden Peacock. And there will be a dance contest with a prize!"

Shelley declared, "One of the girls of the Tigeress or the other gangs must win. We can't have it go to a gink girl who has parents on the commission."

Deirdre and Sharrey were pleased, but Cathal frowned. Shelley asked her brother, "Don't you want to help the border people? They helped our people to rebuild the Gaelic schools in Roscommon."

Her brother replied, "I don't know how to dance, and I guess Dee doesn't know either."

Shelley gave out a laugh, then said, "Well, we will teach the both of you. Sean, Eamon, Brigid, and I! You'll be the hit of the dance!"

Chapter 11

Dawn came to London like the lifting of a curtain. The sunlight gradually bathed the city in light. The sun's light came up a jewel-like dome, a steel umbrella holding panes of thick glass, setting atop a creme-colored marblite wall. The reflection of light from the dome could blind anyone who looked toward it. This was the Crystal Palace, the residence of Her Majesty, Elizabeth the Seventeenth. Inside the dome was a lush garden-like estate covering over fifty hectares. In one corner was a flower garden. Red and white roses and blue violets formed the Union Jack. In the opposite corner of the estate was a massive colored water fountain and the statue of King George the Thirtieth. The monarch was astride a horse, running a sword into a rebellious peasant, presumably Hibernian.

The castle itself consisted of a glass and steel bubble, with a simple red brick building inside. The Palace was comfortably warm, even though outside winter was setting in already.

In the chamberoom on her golden throne, the monarch awaited the arrival of her ministers. When a guard announced their arrival, she ordered a detachment of guards to bring them to her throne. She arose from her throne, announcing, "We are not amused."

Prime Minister Cromwell asked, "Your Grace, what had displeased you?"

The queen bellowed, "Those treacherous Hibernians have attacked our quadrant. Our petroleum fields are burning, a garrison wiped out, and a village captured. Don't you read the reports radioed here from our quadrant?"

Behind Cromwell a trembling, sickly man spoke up. "My most gracious monarch, Lord Cromwell has been inspecting the fighter manufacturing complex in Liverpool. He was not informed of the enemy's sneak attack."

Then Lord Cromwell spoke himself. "My secretary is correct. I am certain it is the desperate act of cowed and frightened people."

The monarch was noticing the other ministers in the entourage. She pointed to a military officer, khaki-clad and holding a cropstick. She shouted, "Lord Kitson, as the defense minister, you are in charge of defending the quadrant. How did this happen?"

Lord Kitson answered, unnerved, "The village was at the edge of the quadrant marshes. The garrison was east of the village instead of being a fortified shoreline. The enemy must have landed from the marsh, seized the village, and then overran the garrison. The oil fields were attacked by fighters. I don't believe the reports that they were our own craft, unless the enemy captured some of our craft, or. . . ."

The monarch interrupted, "Traitors, deserters, cowards. No doubt the villagers aided the enemy. Lord Kitson, I order you to radio our quadrant. A regiment of troops is to seize every adult male of that village; they are to be hanged publicly!"

Lord Kitson answered in horror, "That would be murder of your own subjects."

"Do not contradict me or you will be removed from your position," the queen answered. Lord Kitson saluted and departed. Then the monarch turned to Lord Cromwell, "Do you believe we could launch our final attack in December instead of early January? I am thinking of a Christmas present to the nation. . . ."

Lord Cromwell then made a suggestion. "Your Grace. I suggest that if any of the top Hibernian officials survive our attack, they be brought here alive. We could publicly hang them with Gladstone."

The monarch smiled. "A most brilliant suggestion. I can think immediately of the two Hibernians I would love to see hanged. That cowardly head of state, Colm O'Hara, and the most dangerous military man of Hibernia, Commander Seamus O'Rourke! The man who launched the attack on our planet in 3149."

Lord Cromwell thought for a minute, then said, "I just remembered an intelligence report from mid-summer. The enemy's tanker, the *Parnell*, has been missing from the planet since June. That is O'Rourke's ship. Maybe he's a coward as well as a Hibernian terrorist."

✦ ✦ ✦

Dawn came to Connemara in the Galway sector of Hibernia's Connaught quadrant. On a plateau south of Clifden was a small military base. It consisted of a fighter base, a military hospital, and the second level test site for the Alpha project. Nearby was the village itself, down into an area of rocky hills and tiny lakes. The road to the village was a series of hairpin turns. A small military staff car came down the road carrying a load of mail and documents. At the wheel was the head nurse of the hospital,

Captain Molly O'Garvey. At age thirty-seven she could look and act twenty at one time and fifty at another.

She muttered to herself, "Why didn't the colonel have an orderly deliver this mail? We've got surgery later this morning and I intend to have my nurses observe it. Here I am a messenger boy. Damn!" The car pulled into the town, where the postal office was just opening. She muttered, "We don't even have postal facilities on base. It doesn't make sense."

She had just delivered the load of mail to the post office and was about to return to the car and drive back to base when she recognized several young women. Five of the orderlies assigned to the hospital were helping an old man carry furniture into a stone house with a sod roof.

"Attention!" the captain ordered. Immediately the five girls stopped their actions.

"What are you orderlies doing here? You auxiliary privates? Quinn, explain!" the captain ordered.

Caroline Quinn replied, "Captain, we do have proper leave," as each girl presented a twenty-four hour pass.

Captain O'Garvey then asked, "Why here? Most nurses or orderlies would go to Galway and chase men. Are you moonlighting as a moving company?"

Mairead McNutt then replied, "This man is Mary P. Concannon's uncle, Arthur. He has moved here." Caroline then picked up the little boy still asleep in an old motorcar.

"This is Kate MacBride's brother Timothy. M.P.'s uncle is going to care for him. You see, Captain, Kate and Mary P. both lost their parents. Timmy is all by himself."

Jamie Feeny, lisping through her missing teeth, added, "Every time we go on leave we'll be here. All five of us will put in to pay for this home."

Captain O'Garvey then said, "You have my admiration. I was wary of you being transferred here, as I read the reports from Kilkenny. This, however, totally changes things. I hope your uncle and your little brother are comfortable here in Dunleer. I must return to base. Be sure to get back on time, and that's an order."

The five orderlies saluted stiffly and the captain returned the salute. Then as she walked away she turned around a moment and smiled.

❖ ❖ ❖

Repairs were taking place at the Golden Peacock music hall, leading to a reopening. Pamela Fuchida O'Reilly was now the reigning star of the show. Maureen Kelley had moved to Kilkenny and Brigid Hallohan was out with a broken leg, so Pam O'Reilly was now the star. The reopening was still a week away, but the stage was set for a celebration. A bridal shower was held that chilly October evening for a woman who had never performed on stage. Jan MacDevitt was being toasted by the showgirls of the music hall. Pam O'Reilly led the toast with Nipponese sake.

"To Jan MacDevitt, the little sister of the most generous sugar daddy ever to name a showgirl in a will."

Brigid Hallohan, still wearing the cast on her leg and the modest dress of a teacher, added, "She has been like a mother confessor to all of us. I wish Mo Kelley was up here, but I hear her family's doing fine down in Kilkenny."

Jan MacDevitt blushed and said, "You are all a wonder. You know my fiancée Paddy Tully and I have just barely kissed occasionally, even when we went over to the Enniskillen during the evacuation. He has sworn to me on the Holy Mother he is as innocent as I am. Maybe you could kind of tell me about what to expect on my wedding night."

Pam O'Reilly laughed out loud, saying, "If he's as innocent as you, he'll have to get some pointers from some man, maybe a pilot from the fighter base."

Brigid Hallohan then added, "I'll talk to Captain O'Rourke and Lieutenant O'Connell to explain to him what to do."

Pam O'Reilly turned and asked, "You mean you got stoneface?"

Brigid replied, "Yes, back in August. In fact, I might have a bridal shower someday."

Another showgirl, her French accent coming through, asked, "Did you have to lead him like a schoolboy?"

Brigid answered, "Yes, he was scared at first. I didn't realize that there are men that afraid of intimacy. It was like defrocking a priest, but he is really a fine man. Remember, Pam, back in May? I told you that if a girl screwed the hell out of him he'd become normal. I think he might propose, and I am thinking of someday settling down. He might just be the man."

The bridal shower continued until the wee hours of the morning. The showgirls imparted the romantic facts of life to the elder woman who was to wed. Jan MacDevitt thanked the girls, saying, "Paddy Tully and I are both old and we will be spending our retirement years together. We both led lives of solitary labor with little joy. I met Paddy after his retirement and after you girls set me up in the apartment you gave me. To think of it, if you showgirls weren't involved with my late brother, I would have never met Paddy and become his bride. God bless you all."

✦ ✦ ✦

Another strategy meeting was held in the war room. The Taoiseach, the defense minister and Base Commanders Donahue, Kalminsky, MacMullen, Murphy, Neils, and Rafferty. Also present were Colonel Becker, Major Bauer, and Dr. Scheer.

The defense minister spoke out first, "The main item on our agenda is how to knock the fighter assembly plant in Liverpool. We just received a communiqué from the Underground. The enemy will plan to launch their attack in mid-December. It is therefore imperative to knock out that complex by the end of November. However, there are two other items to be dealt with."

Colonel Kalminsky then reported, "During the attack on Athlone a number of our pilots ejected and their ejection pods were destroyed by the enemy fire. I believe we should pair off our fighter pilots. When one pilot must bail out, the other pilot is to cover the ejection pod floating to the surface." After the other base commanders agreed, the second problem was examined. It was Colonel Becker who opened the discussion.

"We have to explain to the anti-royalist Underground that it is impossible to escort a civilian convoy from the Scotch and Welsh sector of their planet to ours. It would simply be a disaster."

Defense Minister Flynn then noted, "A brief radio message could not detail the reasons why we cannot do this. I do have an idea though. The Underground has a supporting cell in Hindustan. Our embassy could contact them with a detailed message. It might be possible to have that convoy go to Hindustan, and then neutral Hindustan craft could bring the Scotch-Welsh settlers over here."

Colonel Becker then asked, "What if the Underground does not accept this? They might not cooperate with our attack on Liverpool. What if they simply send the transports out?"

Joe Flynn answered, "In that case, we will have to send the *Arthur Griffith* and fighters out to escort it. I am afraid, however, we would not get to her in time."

Colonel Murphy exclaimed, "That is madness! Do they want to get thousands of defenseless people killed? What is the reason for the Underground's irrational acts?"

The Taoiseach answered, "First, the idea of moving the Celtic peoples of Brittania, the Scots and Welsh, here has been discussed ever since the migration here in the twenty-fifth century. We even attempted a treaty with the Brittanians before the last war. Then, a bungled attempt by the Underground to assassinate George the Thirtieth took place. Three different groups tried to kill him but only succeeded in killing about twenty of each other's men. We tried to send a mail shuttle to London to explain we were not involved in the plot. The shuttle was lost somehow, and the war resulted. You see, the Underground consists of several factions that have battled each other more than they have battled the monarchy."

Colonel Becker reported on the attack on Liverpool. "I have some unappealing news. After studying the reports on the size of the enemy target, I estimate that it would take up to ten squadrons to destroy the base. That is far more than the *Griffith* could refuel during the trip across the corridor."

Joe Flynn then asked, "Does anyone have a suggestion on how to deal with this?"

Major Bauer spoke. "We still have a sufficient supply of proton-positron plasma as an explosive. All we need is a delivery system."

Commander Rafferty then noted, "We do not have any interplanetary missiles that could outrun the enemy fighters. The delivery system must have a speed of at least factor 5, even factor 10. The only spacecraft available here or in the entire Outer Solar System are the factor 70 class unmanned mail shuttles."

Colonel Neils, puzzled, asked, "You mean send a number of mail shuttles to the enemy planet? Do you mean to bomb Liverpool with Christmas greetings?"

"No!" Colonel Becker answered. "Mail shuttles carrying the ion plasma, an explosive present for the enemy monarch! Of course, they would have to be targeted."

Dr. Scheer then spoke. "It could be done. We could reprogram the shuttle's computer guidance system. They could be launched at a nominal speed, factor 2, and be guided across the corridor by radio beacons on the *Griffith*."

The Defense Minister Flynn then exclaimed, "Then when they are about three-quarters of the way across the corridor, the beacon would signal the computers on the shuttles to accelerate to factor 70. The underground could set up a beacon to direct the shuttles to the target!"

Colonel Neils then said, "It would take only a pair of fighter squadrons to escort the *Griffith*. Do we have any shuttles that could be used for this operation?"

The Taoiseach answered, "The postal minister reported that five shuttles are undergoing repairs in Dublin. They could be sent to Peenemude."

Colonel Becker then added, "Each shuttle can carry fifteen metric tons of the plasma. Think of it, that is as much as the phantom squadron used in the raid against the enemy quadrant. With one hundred shuttles, we could destroy any major city in the enemy planet. With five hundred shuttles, we could totally annihilate them!"

The Taoiseach, shocked, replied, "That isn't necessary, Becker. Gentlemen, I believe that we are fortunate in that the Brit's aristocracy is hostile to scientists or anyone else capable of thinking. It is also fortunate that most of the scientists there are secretly in the Underground. Otherwise these scientific super-weapons would be coming down on top of us, instead of them."

❖ ❖ ❖

It was a moonlit night, cold and clear. Eamon O'Rourke and Brigid Hallohan walked from their cabin to the glistening shore of Big Bog Lake. Sean O'Connell and Shelley O'Rourke followed close behind. The first couple sat down on large flat granite boulders close to the small beach. The second couple settled under a parklewood tree further back. Sean put his arms around Shelley and whispered, "Shelley, I have something to talk to you about, something that goes back to before the last war when you were still in school and I was a pilot recruit."

Shelley smiled and answered, "I have waited for this for over five years, including my years in gaol."

Sean took out a small ring box and opened it. The ring was a silver band with a red-violet stone. Sean apologized, saying, "It's a silver alloy and the stone is quapolite, but if you say yes, with a gold and diamond band I will thee wed."

As he slipped the band on her finger she kissed him on the cheek. Then she became serious. "You will have to ask Father's permission, and you know what he will say."

Sean groaned. "He will say to wait until the war's over. It is difficult enough to ask a father for his daughter's hand, but it's a nightmare when the father is your commanding officer."

Shelley answered, "We'll have to wait until he returns from Earth."

Sean answered, "If he doesn't return, we won't be around to get married anyway."

"Sean, for once, I really am scared he'll never return or be too late. It'll be harder for him to come back to find all of us dead."

Sean embraced her, saying, "I know, kitten. It would be the worst fate for an officer of a tanker to be the survivor of a dead planet."

About thirty meters away, Eamon was alone with Brigid. He said to her, "Brigid, since we first met in May, I am not the same man I was before. You have made me feel the joy of life. I would like to know if Sean and Shelley set me up that night back in August, when. . . ."

Brigid answered, "When I seduced you. Of course, they were quite happy to know I had you. You were so scared; I never had to lead a man before that way. You know, Eamon, I love you. You're like my father. Under that pilot's uniform is just a boy of a man."

Eamon got down on his knees and asked, "Brigid, I want to make the rest of my life with you. I want to marry you."

"Eamon!" Brigid took his hands and pulled him up to her. "You know when the cast is off this leg I intend to start back on the stage. My mother danced for several years after marriage; it helped get us a house."

Eamon sighed. "I just wish I knew if Father will permit the marriage."

Brigid answered, "Eamon, back in June, during the charity dance auction when you won the bid for me, Pam O'Reilly warned your father of my intentions. He confronted me later and he seemed to accept what I planned to do. I am sure he isn't the kind of hypocrite who would balk at a wedding."

Eamon took out a ring box and presented an engagement band. "It's silver and quapolite. Sean is probably putting a similar one on Shelley. Gold and diamond rings are a bit high for a pilot's salary."

As the two couples returned to the cabin, the girls each raised the hand that had the engagement ring.

"Sean," Shelley asked, "could you and Eamon help us? We have to teach Cathal and Deirdre how to dance for the benefit all the secondary schools are holding soon."

Sean answered, "That will be fine with me."

After the four young people sat down to evening tea, Shelley turned to Brigid. Her voice became serious and uncertain, "Brigid, we had better tell them now, otherwise it will mess things up later."

Brigid put her arms around Shelley and spoke to Eamon. "During the summer there were nights Shelley and I slept together. Some nights in my apartment, other times in your home, in your father's bed."

The two pilots shook their heads in disbelief. Shelley explained, "It goes back to when we were still in school. Father and you, Eamon, were on base. Mother was at a training session for auxiliaries and Cathal was up at Uncle Gene's houseboat. That evening Brigid and I got into the ale in the ice box and got kind of drunk. We were talking about boyfriends and began to hug and kiss each other. We went into that big double bed in our parents' room and spent over an hour. We were back out before Mother returned to the house, and we went into my room for the whole night. Until my trial in '48, our parents didn't know about us."

Brigid then added, "A woman has certain feelings only another woman can satisfy. If you remember the trial, that is the act of initiation of the Tigeress and the other girl gangs. In fact, I initiated Deirdre O'Toole in May, the night before the attack."

Shelley continued, "All during my term in gaol, I slept with Kate MacBride, and I'd be with her today if we were still behind bars."

Eamon was in shock. "Brigid, you mean, Sean and I could come home and find you and my sister in bed?"

Brigid threw her arms around the trembling man, "Yes, Eamon, we lick each other's boxes out. It wouldn't be like I was with another man. When we are married, you'll be my only man and you will be the father of the babies I'll have."

Sean then said to Shelley. "I don't understand it at all."

Shelley said, "Sean, you are the only man in my life, even though I've had women."

Brigid then said, "It's getting late, I can think of one way to forget hurt feelings." She took Eamon's hand and walked him to a large feather bed in one corner of the cabin. Sean then walked with Shelley to the other big bed. Shelley said, "Let's celebrate our engagements now."

✤ ✤ ✤

It was evening at the Athlone fighter base. The young airmen had been put through a severe training drill by Major Hoffman and Captain Kesselring. Many had been reevaluated to be the copilots of Bullethead fighters. After evening's mess, the young men were outside their barracks.

Major Hoffman was giving his recruits an informal talk when a number of new women auxiliaries came past. Ensign William King McKerr looked up and recognized one of the women walking by. He yelled, "Agnes, what are you doing here?"

Major Hoffman interrupted, "You know that auxiliary cadet?"

"My sister, Major" was the Ensign's reply. The sergeant leading the auxiliaries stopped his squad. "Quiet in the ranks." Then the Major asked the girl, "Do you know this young pilot? Remember, fraternizing is against regulations."

Agnes McKerr answered, "It is my older brother, Billy King."

The major signaled the pilot to come over to the squad of auxiliaries, then said, "Sergeant, I want a word with these two, to make the rules clear."

The sergeant answered, "I can wait a couple of minutes. Young girls, don't try to fool the major, he knows every ruse recruits try." He then led the other women away.

Major Hoffman then looked straight into the eyes of the two young people in front of them. "I want a straight answer from the both of you. Are you in fact related?"

Billy McKerr answered, "It is my fault, sir. Agnes is my sister, sir. Our father is Colonel James King McKerr of the border militia in Shankill."

The major then noted, "You are the only two recruits in the Hibernian Air Service from that sector. Could you explain the apparent disinterest of your   community?"

Agnes McKerr answered, "Major, it is traditional for our people to serve as ground troops. Our father is very influential in the village. I doubt if others will join the air service."

The major was upset. "Yes, the military during the last war tried to breach the fortifications of the enemy quadrant. They were cut to pieces. What is the reason for the disunity between your people and the rest of the population? I have only been on this planet a comparatively few years."

Ensign Billy McKerr gave a summarized history of the ill feelings between the Orangemen and the other Hibernians. The major shook his head saying, "It is no wonder you have nearly lost this war several times. You have my sympathy for what happened to your village last month. Remember, you are new recruits and under regulations. Perhaps next month, when you complete your training, you might get a leave. Auxiliary, you are to rejoin the sergeants and your detail."

After Agnes left, the major then turned to the ensign, "Return to your squad. Oh, yes, she is an attractive girl."

The ensign answered, "Father disapproves of us being here." Then he saluted and returned to the other pilots. A couple of the other recruits began to ridicule him, but the stern-faced Teuton cut them off.

✦ ✦ ✦

At the Athlone base hospital, Defense Minister Joseph Flynn had checked in a couple days earlier for a complete examination. Major Andrew MacIvor came into his private room carrying a report of the findings. "We have examined your muscle reflexes and the results of the brain wave test. You have a problem; degeneracy of the muscles and the central nervous system. You are losing coordination. It will be increasingly uncomfortable for you, and. . . ."

After waiting for about a minute, Joe Flynn ordered, "Give me the straight answer, the worst!"

The physician looked straight at him. "It is Amyotrophic Lateral Sclerosis. If it weakens your resistance to bacteria or weakens your heart, it could be a matter of months, otherwise, you eventually will be bedridden."

Joe Flynn was ashened faced. "Me, a vegetable, no. No! I have faced death in battle many times over thirty years. This is no way for a pilot to die."

"I am sorry, sir," the doctor was almost crying. "There is no cure for this. We've been out in space for hundreds of years, but we still don't know how to arrest this, not at all."

After he dressed and prepared to leave the hospital, he thought to himself, "God, a Brit firing squad would be better death. I want to live long enough to see this war won!" He mulled after his affliction. Then he thought to himself, "Perhaps there is a way to cut my suffering short and still win this war."

He drove to the Defense Ministry building and walked to the personnel department. A young ensign manned a computer terminal. "Ensign, I want a complete printout of the officers and crew of the tanker *Griffith*. I also want a printout of retired servicemen, former base commanders, fighter pilots, shuttle pilots, surface gunners, infantry, repairmen, etc. They are to have two criteria. One, they are to have technical abilities matching that of the *Griffith*'s crew. Second, they must all be under medical treatment for illnesses of a terminal nature."

The ensign blinked. "A ship of terminally ill men, sir? What the—?"

The defense minister answered, "That is a direct order, soldier!"

The ensign answered, "Yes, sir."

Joe Flynn thought to himself, "We'll ram the *Griffith* right down Queen Lizzy's throat!"

✦ ✦ ✦

The night of Friday, October 30, 3153, was bitterly cold. However, it did not cut down the number of young people who filled the Hibernian Veterans Legion Hall for an interscholastic charity dance. The students of the church schools, St. Michael's, St. Gregory's, and St. John Vianney's, came in neat uniforms. The boys wore white shirts and ties; the girls modest dresses. Several nuns were on hand to oversee their young ward's behavior. The students of the public schools, Thomas Ashe High and Roger Casement

Technical High, were in sharp contrast. A number of girls were wearing stylish gowns and their boys evening jackets. They were definitely the children of members of the school commission. Most of the boys were in rather plain work clothes, some coming off their part-time jobs. Many of the public school girls came in the familiar gang sweaters. Several teachers were on hand to chaperone the affair. This prevented a bottle of poteen from going into the punch. The ashtrays were also removed from the dance hall floor.

At least one nun had commented, "I wish another way had been thought of to raise money for Shankill. Of course, we are forever raising money for the Brit lovers anyway." This brought a cold steely-eyed glare from a public school teacher, a blonde whose leg was in a cast.

Another teacher exclaimed, "Miss Hallohan, I didn't know you were a bilingual instructor. I didn't recognize you in a full dress."

She replied, "Once this cast comes off, so will the dress."

The nun asked, "What are you talking about?"

The second teacher said, "Don't you know? This is Brigid Hallohan, queen of the Golden Peacock!" The nun retreated in horror.

After a formal opening ceremony, each of the girls stood up for auction bids in alphabetical order. The girls who had arrived with known boyfriends were bid upon almost solely by their boyfriends. The money paid went into a copper stew pot. Then some of the other girls came up for bid. To the surprise of the teachers and nuns, the girl gang members got many more bids and larger bids than the other girls.

After the auction was over, a traditional Irish folk band set up on the stage. With harp and flute, accordion and concertina, whistle and uillean pipes, they began to play traditional Irish step dancing music. Among the couples on the dance floor was Cathal O'Rourke and Deirdre O'Toole. Deirdre said to her nervous boy, "Let's just do what your brother and sister taught us."

They began to dance slowly at first. Then, as Cathal gained some confidence, he picked up the pace. A teacher announced that the dance contest would be in two parts. The dancing continued for nearly an hour, and then the band broke for a rest.

Sharrey Fitzgibbon came up to Deirdre, "Hi. Enjoying yourself?"

Deirdre answered, "It's great. Cathal is really good. I need a smoke."

Sharrey replied, "No way. They have a nun and a teacher in each washroom and outside the doors."

Deirdre sighed, "Well, let's get some punch."

Then Brigid Hallohan came up. "Sorry about the bathroom guards. I did manage to spike the punch though."

"Thanks," was Sharrey's reply.

When the band returned, a teacher announced that a dance contest would begin. The lights were cut and a large flashlight would cut the dancers. In two minutes the first couples were cut from the dance floor. It continued for twenty minutes before Cathal and Deirdre were dropped.

Deirdre sat down and Cathal got a couple of cups of punch. Sharrey came up with her dance partner, a boy from St. Michaels who was rather quiet.

"Kevin Burkitt is my name. When I bid on Miss Fitzgibbon, the nun who teaches my geometry class looked at me like I was committing a cardinal sin. I guess she doesn't think an altar boy should dance with a, a. . . ."

Sharrey answered, "A Tigeress girl? Poo on her."

Then a girl in a red Imperial gang sweater came up. She said to Sharrey and Deirdre, "When the dance is over all the gang girls will go into the alley behind the building and light up. We'll blow smoke right into the Mother Superior's face." Kevin Burkitt shook his head, shocked.

The first half of the dance contest was won by a blushing pair from St. Gregory's school. A blue ribbon was presented to them. Then the band left the stage and an electro-victrola was set up in its place. The brass records played modern Hibernian ballroom dance music. A popular music critic called it "A cross between Irish folk music and twentieth century American popular music which was neither fish nor fowl nor game."

After a half hour the lights dimmed again and the second dance contest began. After a few minutes the flashlight began to cut couples off the dance floor. As the dance continued more couples sat down. Most of those cut were from the church schools as the modern dancing was considered too lewd to be acceptable to teach by the church school authorities. Also soon cut were the children of members of the public school commission. Soon most of the remaining dancers were gang girls and their boyfriends. Cathal and Deirdre were finally cut, as were Kevin and Sharrey. The last dance couple, then one that won the contest, was a blue sweatered Girl Knight and her boyfriend. After the ribbon was awarded the dance continued for another hour. When the midnight bell rang the dance ended and the couples slowly departed. Suddenly a group of nuns ran back into the dance hall, fleeing a cloud of smoke. One nun cried, "They are trying to smother us." From outside was heard the loud laughter of the gang girls.

✦ ✦ ✦

The following evening, Brigid Hallohan and Shelley O'Rourke sat in a pew of St. Stephen's Catholic Church, just west of Athlone. Also sitting with them were Pam O'Reilly and other showgirls of the Golden Peacock. Sitting in the row ahead was Mo Kelley and Theo McLaughlin. Up at the altar Jan MacDevitt and Paddy Tully. Father Paul Joyce performed the wedding. Brigid asked Maureen, "How is your family?"

Mo Kelley replied, "My parents are taking good care of Barry and Esther. Their Aunt Terri is back on base, while Aunt Naomi will enter the O'Donovan Rossa school in a few days."

As the groom kissed the bride, the audience applauded. After they walked out of the church, Jan and Paddy were given the keys to the old

McLaughlin motorcar. A JUST MARRIED sign and a string of flowers ran from behind it. Paddy said, "We've leased a lodge on Robert Emmet Reservoir for the honeymoon.

As they drove away, Brigid and Pam both began to cry. Pam said, "You know, Jan is old enough to be our grandmother, but she is more like a baby sister."

✦ ✦ ✦

Cardiff was in the southeast quadrant of Brittania, in the Welsh sector. It was past midnight in the locker room of a rugby stadium. Blue Goose, Underground leader, awaited his comrades. He was worried and thinking, "Plug and Socket won't take this news at all." He heard the sound of footsteps and he turned around, a pistol in his hand.

"Oh! You startled me, love," it was the voice of Candy.

He bid her to keep quiet, and they waited for the other members. Nursie arrived soon, and finally Plug and Socket. Blue Goose said, "We have received a communiqué from the Hibernians. First I will tell you the good news. They are going to destroy the fighter assembly plant in Liverpool. They are sending mail shuttles filled with explosives. We must place a homing beacon to bring in the missiles."

Nursie asked, "What about our operatives who work in the plant? They are scientists, and if they die the new ones might not be in sympathy with us."

Blue Goose answered, "We will contact each scientist in the plant who is involved in the Underground. Some of them will get transferred out before the attack. Others will call in sick that very day. The shuttle will be escorted by a space tanker and will radio to us when they are coming. We will be able to get all of our people out of Liverpool."

Candy then said, "Well, love, Nursie and I will get a panel truck. It can be an electrician's truck or an office supply store van. It will be driven into the center of the plant. Then we can plant the homing device somewhere on the plant grounds. We could do it several days before the attack."

After discussing the details of the operation with the other operatives, Blue Goose then brought up disturbing news. "The Hibernians indicate it is impossible to escort a convoy of civilian craft across the space corridor. They proposed an indirect route. First, take the convoy to Hindustan, then come over on a Hindustan craft."

Plug and Socket both rose in anger. Plug, his Scottish accent thick and harsh, shouted, "That is a betrayal! After all we have done for the Hibernians, they can't escort a single ship across to move our people to their planet."

Socket, a Welshman, added, "The Scottish and Welsh autonomy council have paid good money to commission a civilian ship. The *Glasgow* is one kilometer long and a quarter kilometer in diameter. It can carry thirty thousand people."

Plug said, "We have thirteen thousand Scotch and nine thousand Welsh men, women, and children ready to settle on the Irish planet. Now they want us to go to the turbanheads. Aren't we good enough for them?"

Nursie answered with a sneer, "You should stay here and help us build a strong country after we topple the queen. Of course, only we in the English sector have a program to build our country. We don't need foreigners, Hibernians, Hindus, or separatists."

Plug screamed, "Don't give m any of your national front drivel. You English chauvinists are as bad as the queen. If it weren't for the war the Celtic Brittanians, Scots, and Welsh would already be in Hibernia."

After the three argued for a minute, Blue Goose shouted, "Quiet! Remember who is the real enemy. Now, Plug, Socket, you must explain to your council that the Hibernians can't escort the *Glasgow*. They can go to Hindustan. It will be sufficient."

Plug answered, "I don't know if they will accept it. They might send the ship out by itself."

Candy gasped. "Those people will be killed."

Then Blue Goose turned to Nursie, saying, "The National Front can put forth its proposals when we organize a constitutional convention after we defeat the monarchy."

When the others left, Candy said to Blue Goose, "I'm scared, love. Not for meself, but those poor people on that space freighter."

Blue Goose answered, "I know, but the Scotch-Welsh separatists are determined to have their way. They will probably be blown to bits in space."

It was Monday, November 9, and the first big snowfall had arrived in Kilkenny. The Kelley family motorcar pulled up and through the entrance gates of the new O'Donovan Rossa School for the Deaf and the Hearing Impaired. The motorcar pulled into a parking stall and then the occupants emptied out. Michael and Ann Kelley, Theobald and Maureen Kelley-McLaughlin, Major Eshkol, and Naomi Sennech walked to the admissions building, an old structure formerly the entire school itself. They entered the building and walked into a lobby. There, other people awaited with their children, who would also be admitted to the school. They went to the intake desk and told the receptionist they had arrived. The receptionist looked through a name sheet then said, "Oh, yes, the McLaughlin child. Dr. Kennelly and Father Harrigan would like to talk to you."

Two men approached, one a priest. The first man, a tall man whose red hair was graying, said, "I am Dr. Kennelly, director of the education program. This is Father Harrigan, our chaplain. Who is the head of this family?"

Mike Kelley spoke, "This is me wife, that is me daughter and her husband. The little girl is the aunt of one of my grandchildren."

Dr. Kennelly said, "I read the paper of admission you filled out."

"This is the girl?" Father Harrigan asked. "She is almost full grown."

"Yes," Major Eshkol explained, "I filled the form for the child. She has studied at the Herzel and Weizmann Schools for the Deaf on planet Abraham. She understands hand signals and reads lips and speaks. She must learn English to settle here."

Dr. Kennelly explained, "We have a complete program at our school. I think she will master English."

Father Harrigan added, "If she is as trained as you say, she can be a teacher's assistant to reduce her tuition."

Then Major Eshkol said, "I hope you remember, she is an Abrahamite. I must request you respect the faith of our people."

Father Harrigan answered, "Of course, Major, we do have children from other planet-nations, even Abraham, I think."

Then Dr. Kennelly said, "If you have the child's baggage and supplies, we can find a room quickly." He told the receptionist to phone for an orderly to come to the desk.

Mike Kelley and Theo McLaughlin went back to the motorcar to bring Naomi's baggage. They gave the baggage to the orderly. Dr. Kennelly said, "We will have a two-week vacation at New Years."

Naomi Sennech had tears in her eyes. She hugged all five adults with her and kissed them, then the orderly led her away. The Kelley family went back to their car and drove home.

Major Eshkol packed her bags and then was driven to the underground railway station. As she waited for the train back to Athlone, she turned to Theo and Mo McLaughlin and Mo Kelley's parents. She said, "It has been an unusual two months for me. I have never been assigned escort duty before. My regular duties will seem rather dull. Naomi is a bright girl. She will probably become a Hibernian citizen. My planet's loss is your planet's gain. I am sure her parents would have been proud of her."

Maureen Kelley said, "So would her brother Issac, the father of Esther. Someday I will tell Esther about him." Major Eshkol saluted and then boarded her train.

✦ ✦ ✦

Sadness had come to the quadrant marshlands. While a freezing rain pelted outside, the people of the marshes gathered in a public chapel to pay their last respects to Aidan Ronan McCluskey, who had passed away a few days before. The eulogy was delivered by Eugene O'Rourke.

"Today we say goodbye to Aidan McCluskey, age eighty. He was born here in the quadrant in 3073. At the time of his birth, the Union Jack flew across the quadrant. At his death, it flew only in the northeast corner. His wife, Darlene, told me that before he died he said that he'd live to see our banner, the Hibernian tricolor, fly over the quadrant. He died in his bed, with his wife, children, and grandchildren with him. I think that is the way any good man should die, peacefully, with little terror or pain. He was twelve when the rebellion of 3085 took place, so he was too young to fight. By the war of 3124 he was fifty-one, too old to fight. He was one of the few people fortunate to have lived in peace without ever feeling the barbarism that is war. When you consider the number of people who this year died violent, senseless deaths—the children of the Roscommon and Shankill schools and the men of the Brit village at the east edge of the marsh whose hanged and shot bodies have floated our way—I feel that in a way we should celebrate the life of Aidan McCluskey. For his life was allowed by the gentle hand of God to run its full course, uninterrupted by the acts of petty and foolish men."

After the memorial service was over, the darklewood coffin was carried to a truck. The truck would carry it to an above-ground mausoleum.

Gray, tiny Darlene McCluskey came to Eugene O'Rourke. She kissed him and said, "Young man, you have given a great comfort to me and my family. Aidan always said you were a fine young man."

Eugene answered, "When Bethie and I set up our floating home, it was he who taught me the ways of the marshes. How to fish and trap. My brother Seamus admired him too."

✦ ✦ ✦

When the letter from his uncle Eugene came telling about the funeral, Cathal read it and became melancholy. His brother, Eamon, had been transferred to the South Pole to train new pilot recruits. His sister, Shelley, was at the Athlone base to train auxiliary recruits. Once again, he was by himself. It was the end of the week, after school and work at the flower shop. He turned to Deirdre, saying, "Could you walk with me? I want to go up to the cemetery."

She answered, "Yes, the Quinncannons are working a double shift. I've been by myself for a few weeks."

The young couple bundled up warm against the cold and walked to a bus stop. They took the bus that headed to the southwest edge of the city and got off before the Marie Drumn Cemetery.

Cathal and Deirdre walked past the gates. Then they walked to the snowcapped hill leading to the military part of the burial grounds. They walked past rows of flag-topped tombstones to the one reading, BERNADETTE O'ROURKE, 3103–3149.

Cathal knelt to the marker, saying "Mom, I wish you were still here. Father is far away in space and I don't know if he'll get back. Eamon and Shelley are away, too. I am all alone. I remember you treating the boils on my back when I was nine. And when I came home crying because kids made fun of my glasses, you set me down in the big chair and hugged me until the tears went away. I love you, Mother. God knows how I need you."

Deirdre put her arms around the boy and they left. They walked to another part of the burial sites, to the tombstone of a mass grave. Deirdre read one of the names: Mr. and Mrs. Joseph O'Toole. She started to cry, saying, "I was happy that morning. One moment I was about to enter our front yard in a new sweater. The next moment I hit the sidewalk and saw them. They were burning, flying through the air."

Cathal then told her, "You know, Dee, I was watching the house from behind the stone fence across the street. I had been hurt when you told me you would join the Tigeress. I was going to walk away from you forever. Then, when I saw your house explode, I thought you were dead. It is lousy that people have to lose someone they love to realize how people need each other. I don't even know what this crummy war is about."

Deirdre answered, "I know, Cathal. I did a term paper on the Anglo-Irish wars. What did we ever do to the Brits that they should hate us enough to want to kill us off?"

After taking the return bus from the cemetery, they walked to the O'Rourke home. It was already dark, and when they entered the parlor Cathal turned on a light. Deirdre asked, "What is that chair over near the sofa?"

"It's a love seat. We brought it out of the attic and cleaned it up for guests. My mother comforted me there whenever I came home from school crying."

The two young people went to the kitchen. While Deirdre put on a teapot on the stove, Cathal took food out of the icebox. He said, "Here is cold mutton, left over turnip soup, and bread."

After having dinner, Deirdre went to the icebox and exclaimed, "Here is a bucket of ale. Let's have a mug."

Cathal was doubtful, but she added, "Come on now, Eamon, Shelley won't know or mind at all."

After some coaxing, Cathal got out a pair of mugs. They went to the parlor and turned on the radio. Deirdre said, "Sit down in that big chair, Cathal." When he sat down in the love seat, she pulled up on his lap. They toasted with the ale.

Going through her purse, she took out a red lipstick, then rouged her lips. Then she kissed him on the mouth. She said, "Let's just sit here for the rest of the night." They sat together, hugging and kissing, until the lipstick was smeared all over Cathal's face.

She picked up her purse, took out a cigarette and a matchbook, and handed the matchbook to her boyfriend. She looked at him, saying, "I want to share this cig with you while we neck."

He struck a match and lit her smoke. Deirdre inhaled deeply and, after taking the cigarette from her mouth, she kissed Cathal right to his teeth. She held her lips to his mouth and exhaled the lungful of smoke into his mouth until he took it down into his lungs. As the smoke came back out of his mouth, she asked, "Like that? Let's do it again."

Then she took another deep drag, kissed him to the teeth and blew the smoke down his throat. She continued with every drag she took until she crushed the butt in a glass ashtray. Then she rouged her lips again and the young people locked in a tight embrace.

After a while, Deirdre said to Cathal, "Let's spend the whole night together in this chair."

Cathal was worried, but she added, "Look, we will keep our clothes on and I am just sitting on your lap. That won't knock me up."

They got off the chair and Cathal went to a linen closet. "Here is a quilt. Mother made it before the last war. It's got our country's flag, the shields of all four quadrants, and two shamrocks, one orange and the other green." He then sighed, "She made this for me before the war, before she...."

Deirdre hugged him, "I know. My mother knitted my stocking cap last winter for me."

They went back to the chair. Cathal sat down and Deirdre pulled up on his lap. They pulled the quilt tight around them and she turned off the lights. She rested her head against his shoulder, saying, "If the war lasts long enough, your father might face a triple instead of a double wedding."

✦ ✦ ✦

From mid-October into late November, the rocket base at Peenemude was a beehive of activity. Five unmanned mail shuttles, sleek pod-shaped craft, were brought down from Athlone. The computer guidance systems were reprogrammed and a loan of ion plasma explosive loaded into each craft. The men of the rocket base, almost wholly Deutscher IPVs, worked a month of fourteen-hour days. A marching band was brought to the base by Dr. Scheer and performed for the men during and after the evening's mess. The music of Bach, Beethoven, and Wagner filled the air, lifting the men's spirits. During the daytime, many of the work crews sang ancient Teutonic war songs as they worked. Teutonic emblems appeared on each shuttle.

At the South Pole fighter base, similar intense activity took place. Veteran pilots, including Major Hoffman, Captains Kesselring and O'Rourke, and Lieutenants O'Connell, Ranier, and Soares, drilled new recruits. For thirteen hours daily and six on Sundays, the recruits went through every aspect of fighter training. Soon green recruits were transformed into skilled fighter pilots. After their half-day on Sunday, many pilots went as a unit by bus to an entirely enclosed underground race track. As it was the only diversion available to the pilots, the senior officers did not object to these pilots going to the betting window.

On board the *Arthur Griffith*, Captain O'Dwyer received a private conference with the defense minister. He was informed of a plan to replace the *Griffith*'s crew with a special squad for a mission of no return. The Captain accepted the fact that he would soon lose his ship. Then, without explaining to his crew, he ordered the ship retooled up to a speed capability of factor 5.

On the enemy planet, the Underground succeeded in placing a homing device inside the fighter assembly plant. A van for a stationery store came into the plant grounds past the guards. It drove to the research lab, where two scientific technicals, both in the resistance movement, received a number of boxes of printed forms. Two odd-shaped boxes were included in the shipments. One was put on the top shelf of a storage room by the lab. The other was taken to a custodian's room at the other end of the plant complex. Both could be activated on just a few hours notice.

The Underground learned from an operative in London that the defense minister, Lord Kitson, would visit the Liverpool plant on Thursday, December 3. They radioed to Hibernia that it would be the perfect day to attack.

✦ ✦ ✦

That fateful morning in Peenemude, the five shuttles were mounted on the rail launchers used for the Werewolf rockets. The base then radioed the South Pole fighter base and the *Griffith*. The engines came on and the shuttles went down the launch track, then off into the sky. At the South Pole, pilots who had waited by their craft for two weeks climbed into the cockpits. In a few minutes, four squadrons were off. Soon they reached the *Griffith*, which was at its latitudinal orbit. When the shuttles came up, the radio beacon pulled the craft to the tanker and they came underneath it. Then the force pulled out of orbit and headed across the corridor. Several hours would pass before the assault force reached the point where the shuttles would be released.

✦ ✦ ✦

At the enemy plant in Liverpool, Lord Kitson was disturbed by the absence of most of the top technicians from the plant. As he walked into an assembly room, an aide came up to him in panic.

"Your Lordship, our scanners have detected an enemy force approaching—the tanker *Arthur Griffith* and about sixty fighters," the young aide said. "Also, we have a report a renegade passenger fighter, the *Glasgow*, is about to leave from our South Pole. Reportedly, Scot and Welsh people are aboard, thousands!"

The Brittanic Defense Minister slapped his cropstick against the leg of the aide. "Radio Manchester to send up a fighter force, five squadrons. Have them hold the Hibernians off. Those micks are trying to help separatists escape. Radio the South Pole to prevent the *Glasgow* from taking off. If it leaves toward the micks, send out a fighter force to stop the *Glasgow*."

The boy asked, "Force the *Glasgow* to land again?"

"No!" Kitson yelled, hitting the boy again with the cropstick, "Destroy the *Glasgow*!"

❖ ❖ ❖

As the *Griffith* and its fighter escort reached three-quarters of the distance across the corridor, Captain O'Dwyer ordered the radio operator to signal the Underground in code. In a few minutes, the operator answered, "The Underground says their homing beacons have been activated."

The ship's scanner operator interrupted. "Sir, we are picking up a Brit fighter force, about fifty craft."

Captain O'Dwyer answered, "Signal Captain Kesselring to put his fighters out to engage the enemy. Helmsman, pull us up and away from the fighters." Turning to the operator of the tractor beam guiding the shuttles, he said, "Switch on the acceleration signal and deactivate the tractor beam."

As the tanker pulled up and away, the mail shuttles suddenly pulled away at an accelerating rate. The scanner operator said, "The shuttles have reached factor 5, 10, 20, 30. . . ."

❖ ❖ ❖

A Brittanic fighter pilot radioed to Manchester, "This is squadron 1 leader. We have several enemy craft approaching at unbelievable speed." As the five shuttles zipped right past the Brit fighters, the pilot added, "My God, they are going at factor 50 and increasing."

The pilot's report was relayed from the Manchester base to Liverpool. The young aide ran up to Lord Kitson, yelling, "My Lord, five enemy craft are heading here at ultrahyperlight-speed."

A second aide reported, "Our scanners report five craft headed for Liverpool."

Lord Kitson stepped out of the assembly plant, looked up and screamed, "There they are, coming straight at us. No!" The five shuttles crashed into the fighter assembly plant. An ion plasma fireball arose and the plant disappeared. Hundreds of newly assembled fighters and shuttles disintegrated. The plant buildings and machinery vanished. The ion fireball spread, and part of the city of Liverpool began to disintegrate. It would be hours before the fires ended.

❖ ❖ ❖

The Brittanic pilot radioed to his base and led his fighters to attack the *Griffith*. The Hibernian fighters, under Captain Kesselring, engaged them, and a dogfight began.

❖ ❖ ❖

Queen Elizabeth and Lord Cromwell were enjoying a command performance of chamber music. They were interrupted by the news of the destruction

284

of the Liverpool plant. The monarch cried, "Lord Kitson and our new fighters gone! Lord Cromwell, order a flight of fighters out to destroy the enemy tanker!" When she received the news of the *Glasgow*, she screamed, "Destroy it!"

✦ ✦ ✦

The scanner operator on the *Griffith* reported to Captain O'Dwyer. "Another group of Brit fighters are leaving the planet, another fifty." The Brit fighters slowly advanced toward the tanker. The Hibernian fighters, backtracking, had succeeded in keeping the enemy fighters off the tanker for awhile. Soon, however, Boomerang fighters began to strafe the *Griffith*. The tanker shot back with its pair of guns. The tanker began to take hits, and the second wave of Brit fighters were about joined in the battle.

The scanner operator called out, "Captain, we have picked up a large craft approaching at, over factor 100. The computer printout indicates it is. . . ."

The radio operator switched on the intercom and a familiar, long missing voice came up. "This is Commander O'Rourke of the *Parnell*. We will pull our ship about to intercept the enemy from behind." The crew of the *Griffith* rose in a cheer, and the fighter pilots are cheered as the big ship came into sight.

The *Parnell* pulled about behind the second wave of Brit fighters. The enemy craft was caught in a crossfire. The *Griffith* and its fighter escort were affront of the enemy, while the *Parnell* was behind.

The Brit pilot radioed, "This is Manchester squadron 1 leader. A second tanker, the *Parnell*, has arrived. We are in a crossfire. Our fighters are being cut to pieces." When he received an order to break off, he led the enemy fighters back toward their home planet.

✦ ✦ ✦

Commander O'Rourke then spoke to Captains O'Dwyer and Kesselring. "We can begin the refueling of the fighter force now."

The *Parnell*'s radio operator spoke to the commander. "We are picking up a distress signal from a craft from the Brit South Pole." When the intercom came on, a frightened voice was heard.

"This is Captain Douglas Campbell of the civilian freighter, *Glasgow*. We are under attack by Brittanic fighters. Please help us. We have nearly thirty thousand people on board."

Captain O'Dwyer gasped. "The Scotch-Welsh separatists. We told them we couldn't escort the craft."

Commander O'Rourke said, "Turn all about. We are all going in to save the *Glasgow*.

✦ ✦ ✦

The two tankers and four squadrons of fighters turned about and headed toward Brittania. The *Parnell*, with its faster engines, pulled away from the rest. Closer and closer they came to the helpless craft. The *Glasgow* was adrift in space and on fire. It began to break up. Then the crew of the *Parnell* gasped at the terrifying sight. The *Glasgow* vanished in a massive explosion.

"My God Almighty!" the commander exclaimed. "Radio the *Griffith* and the fighters. We're too late. We are to pull about and begin refueling the fighters." Then to Helmsman Cosgrave: "Set our course for the Hibernian South Pole." He picked up a microphone linked to the ship's intercom, "This is Commander O'Rourke. I am instructing the ship's chaplains to prepare a memorial service at 2000 hours for those lost on the *Glasgow*. Attendance, though not required, will be appreciated."

The commander left the bridge and headed for his quarters. He met Colonel Kamzov and the colonel's son, Corporal Kamzov. The colonel spoke, "We are trying to control our grief."

"Those poor, defenseless people," the teary corporal added. The commander told his orderly, "Corporal, you are relieved of your duties for the rest of the day. Get yourself together. I know how it hurts, I know." Then to the colonel he said, "I have some poteen in my quarters. I think we could both use a drink."

Part III
Final Battle

✧ ▲ ✧ ▲ ✧

Chapter 12

The tanker *Parnell* achieved its latitudinal orbit at eight hundred kilometers over the Antarctic Circle. The *Griffith* was orbiting over the circle too, at four hundred kilometers. The smaller ship set its orbit at a rate to be a half rotation away from the *Parnell*. As the larger ship reached the intersect of the Antarctic Circle with the Prime Meridian leading north to Athlone, the marshlands, and Roscommon, the smaller ship reached the Anti-Primal Meridian leading to Connemara.

Commander O'Rourke ordered the radio operator to signal the South Pole base. The voice of Colonel Murphy came on, "Commander, it's a great thing for us that you have returned. I have phoned the Defense Ministry of your arrival. Oh yes, most of Athlone's pilots are here training recruits. Your son is included, and I can inform him of your return."

The Commander replied, "Thank you, Colonel Murphy. Signal the Defense Ministry. I am taking the shuttle to Cashel with the scientist in charge of the Alpha project. I suggest the entire war council meet us there in a couple of days. I am sending Colonel Kamzov to Athlone with special conversion plans for the *Parnell*. Colonel, are the landing-launching platforms for tankers still in operating order at your base?"

Colonel Murphy was puzzled, but replied, "Yes, sir. All five are kept in perfect maintenance. The largest one, which was your ship's berth, was to be the berth for the *McCracken*."

The commander then issued direct orders, "Colonel, you are to prepare the largest platform to receive a landing. Keep emergency crews on hand, on standby alert."

Colonel Murphy gasped. "Land the *Parnell*? I don't. . . ."

The commander then said, "I will explain during the war council meeting."

After signing off, the commander left the bridge and headed for the shuttle craft station. Awaiting him was Dr. Joseph McIntire and the four American scientist Underground members brought from Earth: Karen Woods, Emil Rogers, Dennis Bilandic, and Tony Rossi. The shuttle craft room operator said, "Colonel Kamzov has already left for Athlone, Commander."

"Good," was O'Rourke's reply. After he and the scientists boarded the shuttle, the launch chamber was depressurized and the craft took off.

✦ ✦ ✦

In just twenty minutes the craft touched down at the experimental base at Cashel. As they disembarked from the shuttle, the Americans were awed. Karen Woods said, "I can hardly believe it has happened. Back in October we were on Earth inside an ancient coal mine. Now we are out in space on a distant planet."

Emil Rogers added, "You know, Commander, even after we overthrow the government, it may take decades to get America back on its feet. Most of our people are so ignorant of science they think we engage in witchcraft."

In a few minutes, a bus pulled up. Out of the bus three civilian technicians came to greet the arrival party. Dr. McIntire introduced them.

"These are my assistants, Dr. Patrick Foggarty, Dr. Millard Clarke, and Dr. Jan Masaryk, IPV of Bohemia."

After formal introductions were completed, the entire entourage climbed on the bus. They rode north of the village to the four hills. After disembarking, they entered a building atop the west hill and took an elevator down into the hill.

When they arrived at a computer terminal room, computer discs brought from Earth were mounted on the computers. The information was fed into the memory banks, then a printout was presented. Dr. McIntire presented the printout to his assistants. Dr. Foggarty exclaimed, "I see! A microwave medium using all subparticles, neutrons, mesons, protons, and gluons."

Dr. Masaryk asked, "With the assistance of these Americans, we could test the shield in twenty-four to forty-eight hours. Our atomic accelerator can produce the subparticles."

Dr. Clarke also noted, "We can convert a radar scanner into the necessary microwave beam projector on short notice."

Dr. McIntire then summed up his feelings. "This was staring us in the face; we simply failed to notice it. We could have set this up months ago."

Tony Rossi replied, "However, Doctor, we would not have been able to get the assistance we need for our struggle."

✦ ✦ ✦

Two extremely busy days passed at Cashel. Under the direction of the Americans, the force field project was set up for a first-level test. At the same time, the technical data was transmitted to the Connemara base for the second-level test. The commander and Dr. McIntire again went to the top of the   southern hill, accompanied by Emil Rogers and Dennis Bilandic. The doctor pointed north. "You see that jagged plateau to the north? It was once a rounded hill like these other three. When the shield failed in May, the test target shattered the hill completely."

Dennis Bilandic answered, "I am sure it will work. We are all sure."

Then a radiophone rang and the doctor picked it up. The voice on the other end said, "Pat Foggarty here. We are ready to activate the projector." When McIntire replied, in a half minute the beam shot across the valley to the parabolic mirror on the east hill. The beam reflected back and a milk-ish shield formed between the two hills.

Commander O'Rourke ordered, "Fire the laser!" and a cannon's beam hit the shield. The beam spread against the shield and was seemed to be absorbed into the shield.

Dr. McIntire exclaimed, "I believe that the energy of the laser is being added to that of the shield. The more heavily it is bombarded, the stronger it will become."

Commander O'Rourke ordered, "Continue firing and maintain the shield."

Five minutes passed and became ten minutes, and the shield held. Then the phone rang again. "Foggarty here. The coolant system is giving away. We'll have to shut her off." In a few seconds the shield vanished and the laser beam struck its target, a pile of rusted out motorcars.

A complete computer printout of the results for the test was analyzed. Connemara base was signaled to begin the second level. It was right there. A viewscreen transmission tower monitored the test.

Dr. Robert Gilligan, director of the Connemara test site, described the operation. He began, "We have activated our linear accelerator and are about to activate the projector beam up the radio broadcast tower . . . now!"

The milkish shield blinded the tower from the viewers. Then Dr. Gilligan said, "Here are two unmanned shuttles coming in by radio beam." The camera swung around, and two lights appeared in the starlit sky. The shuttles dived against the shield and exploded in two red fireballs. The shield held for two more minutes. Then Dr. Gilligan called out, "Our coolant is failing. We will have to shut off." The shield disappeared, and then the doctor reported, "I will send the printout."

In a few minutes, a teletype printout came in to Cashel. Dr. McIntire said, "Apparently the shield could last several times longer under laser bom-bardment than if the waves of fighters came in. Therefore, we must activate the shield just before they reach the eight hundred kilometer level. We must also improve the coolant systems. I do know we have each one of our pro-jectors ready to operate, thus the problem will be with the coolant."

The following day in Cashel a war council meeting was held. The Taoiseach, the defense minister, and all the base commanders attended. Commander O'Rourke presented the four American scientists.

For a half hour a discussion was held on the arrangements for the Underground. The Taoiseach read the proposals and commented, "We believe that we should assist these people. They have helped us immensely. The force shield will make it possible for our nation to survive."

Colonel Becker then reported, "We have five space transports, similar to the type used in the Migration. They can carry volunteer troops, fuel, laser photon charges, and disassembled fighters. Of course, the *Parnell* would lead the convoy."

Also present was Foreign Minister Ted Sheenan, who spoke. "I believe, gentlemen, we might have to approve this operation with the Interplanetary Federation. However, I also believe the Eurasian and African republics could provide the technological aid that would bring America back to modern prosperity."

Commander O'Rourke then presented a report of his observations. "Here is my logbook of the landing party during our four weeks in America. I saw a primitive land in the chains of oppression, as our planet suffered during ninety-one years of Brit rule. They have helped us; now we must assist them. I will lead the *Parnell* back to Earth."

After a fast lunch, the war council resumed their meeting. The Americans had left. The defense minister spoke first. "Commander O'Rourke, Colonel Kamzov presented to me your plan to convert the tankers *Parnell* and *Griffith* into attack craft. First let me say that the *Griffith* is going to be used in a totally different matter. That I'll explain later. As for the *Parnell*, it would take two to three months to convert the craft. We would have to depressurize the entire ship. The only way it could be accomplished in a few weeks would be for the ship to land back on its platform at the South Pole."

Commander O'Rourke answered, "Yes, I informed Colonel Murphy to prepare the platform for a landing." The council was stunned.

Then Colonel Becker reported an update on fighter production. "I have very excellent news, gentlemen. We will have eight hundred new fighters instead of only six hundred. Of these new craft, one hundred and fifty are an advanced model with two forward lasers. As late as September we had only twenty-five squadrons present. Seven in Athlone, six in Dublin, and three each at both poles, Roscommon, and Connemara. We will soon have twelve squadrons in Athlone, ten in Dublin, and eight each in the others. Also, we will have two whole Bullethead squadrons. I have prepared a plan to set a number of auxiliary bases for refueling near the three borders."

Commander O'Rourke rose from his chair. "The colonel has planned a perfect device to implement my plan. Joe Flynn, I have the model for the conversion of the *Parnell*." The defense minister brought out the model from a case and handed it to the commander. He continued, "Gentlemen, as you can see in this model of the *Parnell*, we have removed all four fuel tanks and pumping equipment. Laser gun turrets are to be mounted in place. A total of thirty-two turrets, sixteen topside, sixteen underside in two rows of eight. The rows are staggered so all sixteen turrets can fire one side or the other."

Commander Donahue then asked, "Where do you obtain the laser gun turrets and their crews?"

Commander O'Rourke replied, "We will use the surface laser guns of the auxiliaries. We will separate the turrets from the control panel by a two-meter wall, like the six turrets we already have."

Defense Minister Flynn then asked the Commander to explain the purpose of the conversion.

Commander O'Rourke walked up to a map of the enemy quadrant. He began, "While our fighter forces engage the enemy quadrant force several hundred kilometers up, I will move the *Parnell* down to thirty to forty kilometers. We will pull alongside the Ulster-Leinster frontier. We will bank the ship to a 45 degree angle and open fire. We will destroy the frontier defenses, cutting a five hundred to one thousand kilometer hole in the enemy's southward defense line so our ground forces can enter the quadrant. Then we will pull into the quadrant and destroy their fighter bases and the nuclear fusion reactor generating complex at the center of the quadrant. It will produce a thermonuclear explosion of up to thirty to forty megatons. When the enemy fighters try to withdraw to refuel, they will have no bases at which to land."

Colonel Becker then asked, "Who will man these laser guns?"

Commander O'Rourke replied, "The auxiliary surface gunners. I know that runs against our traditions, but we have no choice. We would have to take 120 men from the fighter force elsewise. There are also two very positive reasons to use the women gunners. First, each two-man crew was assigned to a particular gun and are used to the particular characteristics of that particular gun. Also, many of the surface gunners are women who lost children during the massacre of the Gaelic schools in Roscommon. I intend to give them a chance to avenge their children."

The defense minister then said, "Seamus, you have convinced me that your idea would work. Now, Becker, do you have a list of available ground forces?"

Colonel Becker then went to the map and pointed out the dispositions. "We have Colonel Skorzeny's commandos and some Hibernian regulars south of the marshlands. It would drive into Cavan sector. Far to the east at Louth sector is a Hibernian regular force under Colonel Costello, with laser land tanks. They would hit the Armagh sector. In between, up at Meath sector, is the Orange Militia facing Monaghan sector. More ground troops could be moved in from Roscommon and Connemara."

Commander O'Rourke then asked Defense Minister Flynn, "I presented your plans for *Griffith*. It could carry 12 turrets. I felt it could go north of the marshlands and destroy the Ulster-Connaught defense line. What is this alternative use you have for the *Griffith*?"

Joe Flynn arose and in a deathly solemn voice began. "We have reprogrammed the ship's self-destruct sequence to destruct on impact. We will use the *Griffith* to draw off the enemy home fleet. We will go across the corridor at sub-light speed. When we pick up the enemy fighters, we will accelerate to factor 5; we have up-tooled the engines. We will head for London and dive right into the enemy palace. We may produce the blast of a one hundred megaton bomb."

After a minute of silence, Commander O'Rourke protested: "You will be sending Captain O'Dwyer and his men to their deaths needlessly."

Joe Flynn replied, "The *Griffith*'s crew will be replaced with a special volunteer crew. All of the men on this list are retired veterans of Hibernia's Defense Service. Each is in a veteran's hospital, terminally ill. Included on this list are: Jimmy O'Kane and Arthur O'Doherty, two armed shuttle pilot heroes of the 3124 war; Tomas McConnell, who designed the Needlehead fighter just a few short years ago; Colonel Maxwell Feldstein, the IPV who designed our tanker fleet; and Commander Padraig J. MacSwiney."

Commander O'Rourke was stunned, "Joe MacSwiney was our first commanding officer after we left flight academy, yours and mine, back in 3124."

"Yes, Seamus, MacSwiney is in an electronic lung. He will operate the ship's radio on his back with an overhead mirror. And I will be at the command console."

The war council was now again silenced, and Joe Flynn continued, "Gentlemen, as some of you have noticed, these last three months I have constantly tripped and stumbled everywhere. The doctor says it is a degeneration of the nervous system. Soon I will be bedridden. That is not the way for an old fighter pilot to die. Don't grieve for me, gentlemen. This is a much better, faster way to die. My wife has been gone for ten years, my children are all grown. There is actually only one thing I regret. I won't see the look on that bitch Lizzy's face when we crash right atop the Crystal Palace. Mr. Prime Minister, I recommend you name Colonel Becker as my successor."

After the war council meeting ended, each base commander saluted and shook hands with Joe Flynn. Soon only O'Rourke remained alone with him. Seamus O'Rourke looked at the man who had been his comrade, friend, and rival for three decades of military service. He shook Flynn's hand and gave him a manly bear hug.

"Joe, I can hardly believe it. We have fought the Brits and each other for thirty years. Now it's over."

Joe Flynn replied, You will be a hero when this war is over; you could run for public office."

Seamus replied, "And become a gutless wonder like Colm O'Hara? Never!"

Joe said, "You know, Seamus, there is an irony in the fact you went to America on Earth. This thing I have was nicknamed for an American athlete. It's called Lou Gehrig's Disease."

"Joe," Seamus asked, "could you do one thing for me? After you crash, say hello to Bernadette for me. Tell her I'm coming."

After a few puzzled seconds, Joe Flynn said, "I will, Seamus, I will."

Just two hours after the war council meeting ended, Commander O'Rourke had returned to the bridge of the *Parnell*. He ordered the radio operator to signal the South Pole. Colonel Murphy, who had just arrived, took the microphone for a subordinate.

"Commander, our crew has prepared the landing platform and fire crews are ready."

Commander O'Rourke ordered all off duty crew to shuttle to the surface. Another hour passed, and O'Rourke ordered the landing to begin.

"Helmsman Cosgrave, begin descent to one hundred kilometers. We will signal the *Griffith* to climb to six hundred."

In a few minutes the giant tanker achieved its lower altitude, then the Commander ordered a descent to forty kilometers. The ship's gradual descent prevented any dangerous temperature build-up.

The commander gave the most critical order. "Descend to twenty-five kilometers, then reverse the engines as we reach the coordinates of the base. Set the ship's scanners to lock on the platform."

The massive tanker slowed to a halt as it reached the targeted base. Then the commander ordered, "Fire the steering jets. Pull the nose up vertical. All crew fasten seat harnesses. Fire reversing engines and forward engines to brake." The ship halted. Its nose arose until the ship was straight up, then it began to descend. O'Rourke ordered, "Helmsman, activate automatic steering lock on to the scanners."

The ship began to descend faster and faster. The operator of the outer temperature sensor reported a dangerous increase in heat. The ship's breaking engines slowed the descent, and the temperature leveled off. The scanner operator recorded the descent. "Twenty kilometers, seventeen . . . fourteen . . . twelve . . . nine . . . seven." The ship was slowing, its engines flames and massive hull was now visible in the darkness. The ship was hovering before its final descent. The scanner operator announced, "Three kilometers . . . two . . . one . . . nine hundred meters . . . seven hundred . . . five hundred . . . three hundred."

As the massive ship descended, the tip end reached the top of the platform. Then, slowly, the stern of the ship reached the top of the launch tube. Now the ship seemed to crawl downward a few meters at a time. The scanner operator continued, "Fifty meters, forty, thirty, twenty, ten, nine, eight, seven, six, five, four, three, two, one."

The commander ordered, "Cut all engines."

After several seconds of after-thrust, silence. For a few seconds, it was deathly quiet, then the entire crew broke out in cheers. When the hatches were opened and the crew came out, they were met by a cheering ground crew. The commander went directly to Colonel Murphy, saying, "Colonel, I entrust this conversion to your work crews for a few days. I am returning to Athlone. I probably have a half-year's reports to read and clear."

Colonel Murphy answered, "Yes, sir. I believe your son, Captain O'Rourke, has returned to there. He has a pair of battle reports for you: the defense of the capitol in September and a raid on Ulster in October."

❖ ❖ ❖

When Commander O'Rourke returned to Athlone, it was past midnight. He retired to his quarters on the base. During the following day, he studied the reports of the months of his absence. It was late in the afternoon; he had finished most of the reports when his intercom came on.

His receptionist spoke. "Captain O'Rourke and Lieutenant O'Connell wish to speak to you, sir."

The commander thought to himself, "I have studied their battle reports. What could they be here for?"

The receptionist explained, "They want to speak to you on personal matters. Each wishes to speak separately."

The commander then said, "Send in the captain first."

Captain O'Rourke entered the office and saluted. "Commander, I am here to make a request of permission, under Article 17, Section 22, Subsection B, a junior officer must obtain permission for marriage from his commanding officer."

The commander was stunned. "Captain, you are requesting permission for . . . Eamon, my boy."

Captain answered, "Commander, I am, I am—Father, I'm asking your permission to marry, sir."

"Who is your intended bride, Captain, er Eamon?"

Eamon's voice was breaking. "She is an auxiliary cadet. I know that is practically breaking the rules. It's Miss Hallohan."

"Miss Hallohan?" the father asked. "The dancer Brigid Hallohan? I remember the dance in June. One of her friends said she had designs on your innocence."

Eamon was almost in tears. "Father, it was back in August. Shelley and Sean, they set me up and she, she. . . ."

His father said, "She did the rest."

"Father, I was unable to resist. She's so wonderful, I. . . ."

"Eamon, don't feel ashamed. You love her and want to marry her. Has she accepted your proposal?"

His boy nodded, and then the father said, "A lesser man would have had a cheap fling with her then turned his nose up in the air and took a blushing bride. Eamon, you are doing the right thing—the thing a real man would do."

After the two men bear-hugged each other, the commander ordered, "Attention. Captain, send in Lieutenant O'Connell, then go to the outer office."

The lieutenant came in and saluted. "Commander, under Article 17, Section 22, subsection B, I am asking—"

The commander cut him off. "Lieutenant, this conversation should have taken place at least five years ago. Now you are going to address me as a young man would address the father of a girl still in school. Now, you were saying, Sean O'Connell?"

The lieutenant gasped. "Commander, oh, Mr. O'Rourke, I want to marry your daughter, sir, I. . . ."

Seamus O'Rourke smiled. "Sean O'Connell, were you physically involved with Shelley?" The terrified, guilty look on the Lieutenant's face gave the answer. The father of the bride then asked, "Is my daughter. . . ?"

"No, sir, she isn't, sir. I know, she can explain how we prevented, ah—I will accept all legal responsibility for my actions."

"Lieutenant, is it true that you and my daughter helped to set up the loss of my son's innocence?"

Again a guilty look gave the answer. The Commander's face became stern. "Attention! Send in the Captain," he ordered over the intercom.

The two pilots stood rigid, their commanding officer had his back to them. He walked up to a bookshelf where a painting of a beautiful woman sat. The commander took out a handkerchief from his back pocket, wiped his face, and blew his nose. He turned around, saying, "At ease. Eamon, Sean . . . Eamon, if only your mother was here. She would be making Shelley's wedding gown. You know, my son, before the last war Bernadette and I were terrified. During Shelley's trial we were afraid we were going to lose her to the gallows. Of course, marriage will be delayed until after the war. Gentlemen, this day is over. Let's go home."

❖ ❖ ❖

"As you were," the commander ordered. The two auxiliaries were standing by a pair of motorcycles, one with a sidecar. He came up to Shelley, saying, "Kitten, I see you gave your arm in battle. Your man, O'Connell, has asked for your hand." Then turning to the other woman, he said,

"Congratulations, Miss Hallohan, you have a fine young man for a future groom."

Eamon opened the motorcycle sidecar door and his father climbed in and sat down. Eamon mounted the saddle seat at the handle bars; Brigid Hallohan sat behind him. Sean O'Connell and Shelley O'Rourke got on the other cycle. Together they sped off.

✦ ✦ ✦

When the motorcycles pulled up in front of the O'Rourke home, Cathal and his friend Deirdre were sitting on the front stoop. Seamus O'Rourke jumped out of the sidecar and ran up the walk. He picked his son off the stoop like he was less than ten. He said, "Cathal, my boy, my dear boy. You are the only one I was worried about. Eamon and Shelley are both in the service and could take care of themselves."

His young boy said, "Father, Dee and I put a big pork roast on for dinner. Not a sausage, a fresh ham."

Deirdre added, "We got potatoes, peas, mushrooms, and fresh soda bread."

After dinner Seamus O'Rourke led his family and guests into the parlor. He described Earth and America to his family. Cathal asked, "Does this mean, Father, that when we win the war you'll retire from the service and never leave home again?"

The commander answered sadly, "No, my son. We made a deal with the Americans. They have helped us develop a means to win the war. In return, we are going to help them overthrow the tyranny that has oppressed their country for a millenium. I will be taking the *Parnell* back to Earth. Maybe, with the aid of God, I will be back to Earth next December. And then, Cathal, I can retire from service."

Deirdre O'Toole then spoke. "Mr. O'Rourke, your oldest son, Eamon, and your daughter will both be married after the war. Maybe when you return to Earth you will have another son about to marry."

Seamus answered, "Miss O'Toole, I thought it would be you and Cathal marrying before Eamon, but things have a way of changing."

Deirdre replied, "Mr. O'Rourke, since my parents died, I don't know how I could have endured without your son, Cathal. He is a gentleman."

Cathal answered, "Well, Father, I couldn't have endured the last few years in school if I didn't know Dee. She has always been nice to me when everyone else in school teased me about my glasses and braces."

The commander then went to the family pump organ. Eamon and Sean manned the bellows while Cathal got out his concertina. The girls began to sing. The O'Rourke family and guests sang for several hours before the guests had to leave.

✦ ✦ ✦

Several weeks passed, and the Hibernians were busy preparing the final measures for battle. The new fighters and their pilots were brought to the forward bases. Several auxiliary bases were constructed near the frontiers of the enemy quadrant. The retired veterans reserve, including ninety-year-old men who had fought in 3085, drilled with hand rifles. Families were evacuated far to the south end of the planet.

✦ ✦ ✦

Toward the end of the month, the special volunteer crew came on board the *Arthur Griffith*. Just before he got on board a shuttle to the surface, Captain O'Dwyer spoke to Defense Minister Flynn.

"For the record, I don't like losing my ship. However, I do feel better about it going out in a final death blow to the enemy than being dismantled. Good luck, sir."

✦ ✦ ✦

Back in Athlone, Seamus O'Rourke took his son, Cathal, and his son's friend, Deirdre, to the bus station. Just before they got on a bus for the marshlands he told them, "You are going to stay there until the war is over. It is ironic. The marshlands are just outside the enemy quadrant, but it is the safest spot on the planet now." He hugged both of the children and bid them off.

✦ ✦ ✦

Christmas and the New Year brought no joy to the Hibernian population. Instead there was only gloom. At the South Pole the conversion work was   completed on the *Parnell*. Over a hundred auxiliary surface gunners were brought down to the base.

Colonel Murphy was talking to Commander O'Rourke. "Sir, we are short one two-man crew for a gun turret. Two of the auxiliaries that arrived are injured. Cadets Hallohan and O'Rourke. Your daughter, sir?"

The commander ordered the two auxiliaries into the Colonel's office. He asked them, "Which one of you operates the firing mechanism and which operates the guidance stick?"

Cadet Hallohan answered, "I fire the gun; Cadet O'Rourke aims it."

The commander then said, "Hallohan's leg is broken, but her hands can fire. As for my daughter, it takes only one hand to move the joystick."

Before leaving the office Cadet Hallohan said, "Cadet Rankin, my former aiming operator, has been assigned a gun with a new auxiliary, Cadet McKerr."

The commander said, "Yes, her father is in the border militia and her brother is a Bullethead co-pilot. Dismissed."

❖ ❖ ❖

A war council meeting was held by radio viewscreen transmission. Colonel Murphy said, "The eight squadrons assigned to my base should be moved to the northward bases, leaving only the *Parnell*."

Colonel Becker, now the defacto defense minister, spoke, "We have intelligence reports. The enemy has fifteen hundred fighters, four hundred shuttles, and ten transports at home, with six hundred fifty fighters here. They could launch an attack at any time. We do have one bit of very good news. Assuming that our fighters remain above one hundred kilometers and at speeds of no more than twenty-five thousand kilometers, they will be able to remain aloft for over twelve hours without refueling."

As the meeting continued, it was decided to hold off the attack until just before the enemy moved. Dr. McIntire reported, "I have reports from each projector we have set up around the planet. We are ready to activate the generators with one hour's notice. However, even with an advanced coolant, the projectors could last just a few minutes. We must activate the shield projector just as the enemy reaches 850 kilometers.

❖ ❖ ❖

At the Crystal Palace of Brittania, Queen Elizabeth the Seventeenth held a final meeting with her military staff. Lord Cromwell was present, as was Lord Allerton, the new defense minister, and several generals. The monarch spoke. "I have signed the proclamation for the execution of the Hibernian population. I now would like a complete report of the status of our attack force."

Lord Allerton, a frail man, spoke. "We have six hundred fifty craft in our quadrant, they will attack the enemy's fighter force and engage the enemy until our home force arrives. We have fifteen hundred fighters, four hundred armed shuttles, and ten troop transporters. We will have one thousand of our fighters come down over the North Pole and finish off the enemy fighters that by then will be out of laser charges. The remaining five hundred fighters and the shuttles will come down the South Pole and bombard their cities. Then our transports will shuttle ground troops to the surface. Of course, ground troops will come out of our quadrant."

Lord Cromwell stated, "I read an unbelievable report. The enemy tanker, *Parnell*, returned to their planet at a speed of over factor 100. That is impossible, unless they have learned that new technology the Soviets are developing."

The monarch asked, "Where was the enemy craft for over five months? If it could move at that speed, it could have reached Earth."

Lord Allerton answered, "Could they have gone to Earth to learn to build the force shield it was reported that the Hibernians have been attempting to build for over ten years?"

299

Lord Cromwell replied, "That is nonsense—ridiculous, rubbish." But inside, the prime minister was not so sure.

✦ ✦ ✦

In Melbourne Prison in the Australian quadrant of Brittania, W.E. Gladstone remained in a death row cell. He had lost weight and was under constant harassment from the guards and other prisoners. However, he did not lose hope, and one day a clergyman came to visit him. He recognized the balding, heavyset man from a meeting during the summer. He addressed him as a minister until they got into his cell. Plug said, "We have pulled everyone out of London. We even got all of the members of your party out. We received a message from the Hibernians. They will level the city, taking the entire nobility with it."

Gladstone at first gasped, then said, "It will be the loss of many innocent lives, but Cromwell and the queen have brought this on our nation with their folly."

Plug said, "I know. Many people I personally know are in London. I am sorry; we will not be able to save them. Well, I had better leave now." Then they resumed their deception.

Gladstone said, "When the day of my execution takes place, I wish that you attend to me that morning and perform my funeral, Reverend McTeagle."

He replied, "Yes, my son, I will perform the services."

As the year 3154 dawned, the people of both planet-nations held their breath as the fate of both hung in the balance.

✦ ✦ ✦

It was mid-morning, Monday, January 11, 3154. The cities of Athlone and Dublin were now almost deserted. Only a few remaining auxiliary gunners and civilians were left. At each fighter base the pilots were eating and sleeping by their craft. At Cashel and at fourteen other sites, scientific teams worked, putting the final touches to the force shield projectors. In the war room of the Defense Ministry, the Taoiseach, his aide, Colonel Becker, and Lieutenant Colonel Kalminsky waited for news of the impending enemy attack.

It was 10:30 A.M. Athlone time. A messenger came into the war room with a decoded message. Colonel Becker read it, "A report from the Underground. The Brittanic home fighter force will launch at noon our time." At the command of Taoiseach Colm O'Hara, the attack signal was activated.

At the Athlone fighter base, pilots climbed into their craft and started up their engines. In a minute the first of fourteen squadrons took off out of the underground hangars, up to the surface landing strips, and then aloft. After becoming airborne, the fighters climbed almost straight up to an altitude of three hundred kilometers. Then they leveled off, and soon the other squadrons joined them.

✦ ✦ ✦

At the other end of the fighter base, the Bullethead fighters shot up out of their launching tubes, straight up to over one thousand kilometers before beginning a gradual descent. At the Dublin base similar actions took place. In both cities the remaining auxiliaries manned their lasers while civilians took to the air raid shelters. At the North Pole, Roscommon, and Connemara only Needlehead craft took off.

✦ ✦ ✦

At the South Pole there were no fighters as they had been moved north. However, at a massive landing platform the *Parnell* prepared to launch. Commander O'Rourke ordered his crew to put on their safety harnesses. He then radioed Colonel Murphy and ordered all the ground crews to leave the platform. The mighty ship's engines came on and the *Parnell* lifted up straight out of the platform. It was no longer a space tanker but a heavily armed attack ship. On board were thirty-eight two-gun laser turrets. Of these, six were manned by the *Parnell*'s regular gun crews. The other thirty-two were manned by women auxiliaries determined to avenge the children slaughtered in schools in Roscommon and Shankill. After the massive flying battery reached three hundred kilometers in altitude, it leveled off. Commander O'Rourke ordered the shuttle craft room, "Prepare all three shuttles; they are to be launched just before we reach the enemy quadrant. They are to go up to two thousand kilometers to be out of the battle. When they received the signals from the projection bases, they are to drop to eight hundred kilometers and take up their assigned positions.

✦ ✦ ✦

On board the *Griffith*, Defense Minister Flynn ordered his ship out of latitudinal orbit. As the tanker started across the space corridor, he radioed to Athlone, "We have some difficulty reaching the maximum hyperlight speed. We might not be able to draw off the enemy home fleet. However, we will hit London. I will radio back just before we reach our target. Good luck to all of you."

✦ ✦ ✦

In the war room, the Taoiseach and Colonels Becker and Kalminsky awaited news of the coming battle. The minutes passed like hours, then the scanner operator reported sighting of the enemy. The young colleen said,

"Our over-the-horizon scanners report the entire enemy quadrant fighter fleet is launching. A computer printout indicates six hundred to seven hundred Boomerang fighters. They are heading out to the frontiers of the quadrant with those of Leinster and Connaught."

Colonel Becker then said, "Apparently the enemy intends to launch their quadrant force first to wear down our fighters." He walked up to the Nigerian IPV who operated the radio. He took the microphone. "*Achtung*, this is Colonel Becker to all fighter squadrons. Engage enemy fighter force as soon as you make contact. You must achieve total destruction. Also remember our pairing system. If one pilot must eject, his partner must guard the pod until it lands safely."

✦ ✦ ✦

From Athlone some 210 fighters crossed over the quadrant marshlands. As the Brittanic fighters came in sight, the Hibernian squadron closed into an attack phalanx. Laser pencil beams were fired and a mass of enemy craft disappeared. Further to the northeast, the Bullethead fired down on an oncoming wave of Brit fighters. The enemy craft disintegrated in ion fireballs To the east the Dublin squadron had made contact. Captain O'Rourke radioed to Athlone, "This is Athlone Squadron 1 leader. We have engaged the enemy. The Brits are putting up heavy resistance, but we are wearing them down gradually."

✦ ✦ ✦

The enemy fighter craft were outnumbered four to three. With this numerical inferiority, their technical inferiority was a double disadvantage to the Brittanic fighters. On top of this, the Brittanic craft would run out of laser photon charges while the Hibernian craft had spare batteries. Despite this, the enemy put up a courageous resistance.

After an hour reports began to come in to the war room. Colonel Becker announced, "We have lost about seventy-five craft, but only a few pilots. Most ejected safely. We have brought down nearly two hundred enemy craft."

Then the colleen operating the scanners reported, "Sirs, our cross-corridor scanners have picked up the enemy home fleet. It has made it about one-tenth of the way across the corridor in two groups coming in echelon. The first group is Boomerang fighters, about one thousand. The second a mixed group, around five hundred fighters, about an equal number of shuttles and ten transports. The second group is turning away from the path of the first. The computer printout indicates destinations—the first group, the North Pole. The second group is headed to the South Pole. The *Griffith* will not make contact with either group if it keeps on its course."

Colonel Becker commented, "It is apparent they will have the second group attack our cities while the first group engages our fighters."

302

Colonel Kalminsky then ordered the radio operator, "Signal the *Parnell*, the South Pole, and Bullethead squadrons. When they have finished the enemy fighters, they are to head to the South Pole. All other fighters are to take positions over the North Pole."

✦ ✦ ✦

It was a festive atmosphere at the Brittanic Crystal Palace. Thousands of members of the nobility had gathered into the steel and glass dome. Thousands more were lodged in giant heated tents outside the structure. Others were lodged in the city, filling up all the hotels. In fact, even the homes of the townspeople were requisitioned by royal decree, and many townspeople left the city. This would be fortunate for them.

Just outside the brick castle that sat in the center of the dome, numerous tables had been set up. The throne of the queen had been set out before the throng. The monarch arose and said, "Ladies and gentlemen, it is our great pleasure to present our First Minister Lord Cromwell."

The premier arose and viewed the audience. The members of the nobility were dining on caviar from Turk-Persia, paté made by a Bohemian chef, and Franco-Italian champagne. Lord Cromwell spoke, his voice full of confidence and pride. As he raised his champagne glass, he declared, "First, I propose a toast to our most gracious monarch, Elizabeth the Seventeenth. And our next toast to our noble attack force. On board a number of the fighters, shuttles, and transports, cameras have been mounted. We will be able to see live the destruction of the enemy's cities and, afterwards, the execution of the top Hibernian leaders."

At the monarch's command, a curtain topped canopy opened, revealing a giant viewscreen receiver with a twenty-meter screen. A second receiver was brought into the garden in one corner of the complex. A third was set in one of the large tents. The queen explained, "Each receiver is set to a different frequency and will receive transmissions from different cameras. We will witness the assault from different sectors."

Lord Cromwell again raised his glass. "I propose another toast. To the sunset of the Outer Solar System, the eclipse, the eradication of the vermin known as the Irish race, and the dawn of the Brittanic Imperial Solar System."

The nobility raised their glasses with a hardy, "Here, here."

The only sad face in the crowd of happy people was a petite matron still dressed in black. Though only in her forties, her hair had turned white. She curtsied before the queen. The monarch, smiling, asked, "Lady Margaret Paisley, why are you so sad? This is the day we destroy Hibernia once and for all."

The woman answered, "I lost my husband in May and my sons are on board two of our transports, the *Invincible* and the *Indefeatible*. I have an uneasy feeling about all of this."

Lord Cromwell reassured her, saying, "My dear, I promise you, today we will honor your husband's noble sacrifice by destroying those responsible for his death."

Then a messenger arrived with news the queen and her premier could not have welcomed. His voice was trembling. "Your Gracious Majesty, distressing news. When the fighters of our quadrant force took off to engage the enemy, they were met by a Hibernian force larger than their own. They are suffering heavy losses. It is impossible. Our quadrant fighters could be destroyed, and the enemy could refit their fighters before the home fleet arrives."

Lady Paisley said, "Please, your majesty, consider calling off this attack. Many of the lives of our young men could be spared."

Lord Cromwell again tried to encourage her. "Lady Paisley, the enemy is playing right into our hands. Their fighters will be out of laser charges when our home fleet hits them." Cromwell's boasting hid his sudden inner doubts.

❖ ❖ ❖

The attack ship *Charles Steward Parnell* was moving straight north along the Leinster-Munster frontier. Commander O'Rourke ordered, "Helmsman, descend to forty kilometers. As we reach Athlone, steer to northwest until we approach the equators. Then steer the ship due east and bank the ship at a 45-degree angle to the larboard side." Then he ordered the ship's shuttles to be launched. By intercom he ordered, "To all gun crews, prepare to fire on my command."

The massive ship swung around eastward as it neared the equatorial line. As it banked over to one side, thirty-five gun turrets turned about to aim downward and northward. The commander gave a second command to the gun crews. "The underside turrets are to aim just at and above the border The topside and sidemount guns are to aim further northward."

The scanner operator reported, "Sir, we are beginning to give ground readings of the enemy border defenses."

With that the commander ordered, "Commence firing."

The massive ship seemed to vanish in a glow of light as the lasers fired. Of the thirty-five turrets, the three sidemounted ones were manned by the ship's regular guncrews. The others were manned by auxiliaries. Their voices sounded with battle cries. "This is for my children who died in Roscommon," came from Maria Soares and many others.

"For my mother," said Shelley O'Rourke.

Agnes McKerr uttered, "For the children of Shankill."

❖ ❖ ❖

During their occupation of Ulster quadrant, the Brittanians had built up massive defense lines on each corner of their quadrant. At the frontier itself was a deep mine field, of both small anti-personal mines and larger anti-tank mines. Behind that was a fence of finger-thick barbed wire, an anti-tank ditch, and another barbed wire fence. Beyond that lay a lightly manned zone of camouflaged machine gun nests. Behind that stood a single continuous trench for infantry armed with laser rifles backed by small laser cannon. Beyond that was a zone of three interlocking trenches for riflemen and pits for machine gun and larger laser guns. A zone of ammo dumps, a park for several hundred laser armed tanks and the communications system followed.

A few sentries still paced at the frontier, as in peace time. The guard was about to change. Trucks with armed men traversed the secretly marked road through the defenses to the sentry boxes. The two shifts of soldiers were just exchanging places when a rainstorm of laser fire fell on them. The soldiers died where they stood; the guard houses and trucks disintegrated. As the ground heated up from laser fire the mines went off, gratering the ground. The fences of barbed wire melted and the anti-tank ditch was filled in by falling debris.

Further north the rifle pits and machine guns and cannon emplacements shattered. Ammo dumps went off and the tanks melted in ruins. Infantry men were buried alive as their dugouts collapsed on top of them. Others out in the rifle pits or running were cremated instantly.

✦ ✦ ✦

As the massive ship continued east, the scanner operator reported, "Commander, our sensor detects explosions along the frontier." The commander replied, "Yes, the minefields. Continue firing. Report when we have passed fifteen hundred kilometers and prepare to radio our ground forces."

✦ ✦ ✦

"Ensign, you are jerking the trigger; squeeze it slowly, gently" was Captain O'Dwyer's order to his co-pilot. Billy King McKerr had been wasting his plasma gunshots. They were hitting one Brit fighter directly instead of exploding in a fireball in front of several enemy craft.

As the young co-pilot took a deep breath and reaimed his gun, a voice came over the radio. "This is Cosgrave. You've got a Brit on your tail, Captain," the voice warned.

Captain O'Dwyer managed to pull away from a direct hit. Lieutenant Cosgrave then said, "We'll take him off." The Bullethead craft swung behind the Brit fighter, then Ensign O'Brien sent a plasma burst right atop the Boomerang fighter. It shattered and the pursuing Bullethead rocket climbed to avoid collision.

Major Hoffman radioed in. "To all Bulletheads, we are going to reform our standard attack procedures to avoid this one-on-one combat." At his command, the Bullethead craft climbed up several hundred kilometers. Then, as they dove down again, their plasma guns fired. Another mass of enemy craft disintegrated.

✦ ✦ ✦

"This is Lieutenant Soares," a pilot came over the air. "My craft is shot up. I will take her back over our territory to land." As he pulled away another Needlehead fighter covered him.

Lieutenant Ranier said, "I will follow you until you are safe."

The crippled fighter passed back over the marshlands toward Athlone. As he descended below ten kilometers, the craft began to spin out. The ejection pod came out and then again to float downward.

Soares said, "You can return to battle, Ranier."

The other pilot replied, "No, I will follow you until you land." After a few more minutes he saw the ejection pod settle to Earth. When he saw the pilot climb out and wave, he turned around and returned to battle.

✦ ✦ ✦

Captain O'Rourke and Lieutenant O'Connell radioed battle reports to the war room. The captain reported, "We are beginning to break up the enemy craft. It appears many of the enemy craft are out of laser photon charges."

Lieutenant O'Connell added, "As they are fleeing, some are being shot down by other Brit craft."

Back in the war room, Colonel Becker noted, "The enemy will try to return to their fighter bases." He turned to the Nigerian IPV radio operator and ordered, "Signal the *Parnell*; after they are finished destroying about one thousand kilometers of their defense line, they are to hit their fighter bases!"

✦ ✦ ✦

The scanner operator reported to Commander O'Rourke. "Sir, we will reach fifteen hundred kilometers in a couple of minutes." The commander picked up the microphone linked to the ship's intercom. "Standby to cease fire on my order." When the scanner operator reported the fifteen hundred kilometer mark was achieved, he ordered, "Cease fire." He ordered the radio operator to signal the surface, and switching his microphone to the radio, he announced, "This is the *Parnell*. We have destroyed a fifteen hundred kilometer span of the enemy defense line. You can launch your ground assault. Good luck." Then he ordered, "Helmsman, pull the ship around northward and pull the ship level again. When we approach our second target, you are to bank the ship at 45-degrees to starboard. When we reach the third target, you are to bank to larboard."

The massive ship turned northward into the enemy quadrant toward the fighter bases. When the commander announced to the gun crews what they had accomplished, the crews cheered loudly.

❖ ❖ ❖

On the ground three columns moved slowly into the shattered defenses. Mine detectors found a few landmines and detonated them. Supported by autogiro gunships, the infantry and tank units moved over badly shattered ground, encountering scattered resistance. After an advance of about ten kilometers, they reached open country and rolled forward, picking up speed.

On the right, at Louth sector, the divisions of Colonel Costello's Hibernian regulars advanced into Armagh. A double wave of laser land tanks formed both a shield and spearhead. Behind this, infantry came back with laser cannons. In the afternoon, the Brittanians launched a counterattack, using land tanks and infantry stripped from the defense lines eastward. The Hibernian advance stalled and recoiled. After they formed a defense line for an hour, the Hibernians began to push back their enemy. Then they swung due east moving down along the enemy defense line. The Brittanic troops remaining in the fortified lines were trapped and forced to surrender. Still, pockets of Brittanic forces still fought savagely until wiped out to a man.

❖ ❖ ❖

Far to the left at the marshlands, Colonel Skorzeny's commandos slipped surprisingly fast through the defenses. Going into Cavan sector, they outran more heavily equipped Hibernian regular forces. As they moved along the shore of the marshes, they reached the village site of their October operation.

The young Teutons were shocked by what they found. A towheaded Lieutenant reported, "Colonel, the people of the village are all dead. Many women and girls are apparently dead of starvation. There is a massive gibbet in the village; men and boys are hanging from it. The bodies are bloated and rotting." The young officer was nearly in tears, as were his men.

After the colonel viewed the atrocity, he took a radiophone to call rearwards. "This is Colonel Skorzeny; send up a number of chaplains to perform Last Rites." His voice was strangled by his own grief. Then he ordered a platoon to gather all the bodies into a wooden building. He ordered a pair of laser cannons to aim at the building. He ordered, "After the priests have finished blessing these victims, you are to fire the building."

A startled gunner protested, "Sir, cremation is against church law."

The Colonel replied firmly but gently. "I know that, but there is nowhere around here for a decent burial."

After the commandos left the village, they streamed northward and collided with a counterattack. Brittanic tanks and infantry stripped from the Ulster-Connaught defense north of the marshes came southward. Skorzeny's commandos, skillfully using laser rifles in volleys like small cannon, stopped the tank assault. Then, when Hibernian regular forces came forward with tanks and large cannon, the Brittanians began to fall back.

✦ ✦ ✦

Between the two outreaching flanks, the Orange border militia entered Monaghan sector. They moved in skirmish lines of men with laser rifles and broadswords. Rearwards came small laser cannon and a few tanks. The small amount of armor provided the militia caused complaints.

During scattered resistance going through the wrecked defenses, Colonel McKerr took a wound in the hand. He refused a painkiller and instead read his Bible while the medic treated his arm. A junior officer came up to the medic truck and reported, "Colonel, we have found an enemy tank park. They found twenty enemy tanks undamaged by laser fire."

The colonel answered, "If they can be started, have them moved to the head of the attack line. When the enemy comes into close range, run up our quadrant flags and open fire."

The captured tanks moved northward and met a Brittanic force coming south. The Brittanic soldiers were cheering at the sight of the tanks coming to greet them. Then the Ulster flags were raised on the captured tanks and they opened fire. The skirmish lines came around from behind the captured tanks. After a savage battle, the Brittanians fled.

After an hour the militia reached Aughrim on the river Bann. The large bridge across the river had been blown up. The militia deployed along the south shore. Then, under covering fire from their tanks, the engineering units began to build a number of platoon bridges across the river.

✦ ✦ ✦

On board the *Parnell* the scanner operator reported, "We are approaching a fighter base, sir."

Commander O'Rourke ordered, "Bank our ship to starboard. Prepare the gun crews to commence firing." As the scanner reported they would be coming over the target, the commander ordered, "Open fire!"

The enemy base was a beehive of activity. A squadron of Boomerang fighters had landed to refuel. A Brit pilot climbed out of his craft after it pulled into a hangar. He ran to his commanding officer who was at the other end of the hangar. He gasped, "Sir, we are doing badly. At least half our craft are lost. Many craft are crashing. Also, before we landed our scanners were picking up a large craft; we can't quite believe—" Just then the hangar was hit by a rainfall of laser fire and collapsed. The fighters on the landing strip exploded and the strip itself was torn up. Tanks of fuel and ammo dumps exploded. The fighter base was undefended, and it was destroyed in a few minutes.

After the *Parnell* pulled away from the enemy base, it steered north again. While it approached another base, it banked to larboard and resumed firing. As the hours passed the *Parnell* destroyed one fighter base to another.

✦ ✦ ✦

"Sean, look out!" was Captain O'Rourke's warning. The lieutenant pulled his fighter out of the path of two Brit craft. The Boomerang fighters collided and vanished.

Sean O'Connell said, "Thanks, Eamon. Let's keep tabs on each other. We don't want Brigid and Shelley to become widows before they have been wives."

Then Lieutenant Ranier's craft came alongside the other two. Captain O'Rourke radioed, "To all Athlone squadrons, pull out of action to re-form."

The mass of nearly one hundred fifty fighters pulled around from the aerospace combat. Then they formed the formal tight attack phalanx. Firing laser pencil beams they cut through a mass of enemy craft, destroying a large number. Then the fighters separated again into individual combat.

✦ ✦ ✦

In the war room more reports were coming in by radio. Colonel Becker announced, "Over three-quarter of the enemy craft are destroyed."

The scanner operator then reported, "The enemy home fleet is halfway across the corridor. The division of the enemy into two units is definite."

Colonel Becker took the radio-microphone. "To Dr. McIntire in Cashel; what is the progress on the projectors?"

Dr. McIntire answered, "The Cashel projector and all other projectors will need more electrical power, but we have launched the shuttles."

Lieutenant Colonel Kalminsky phoned the generating complexes in Portlaoise and the Enniskillen. The Enniskillen hydroelectric dams opened their penstocks to maximum volume of waterfall. The coal and nuclear plants at Portlaoise opened up all reactors. In Dublin and Athlone a special siren signaled the population to shut off all but strictly necessary power.

In a few minutes Dr. McIntire phoned to Athlone. He reported, "We are now able to receive the necessary electricity to operate the projectors. We have a computer printout indicating that our coolant can maintain the projector for three to five minutes."

The scanner operator reported again, "The enemy force headed to the North Pole is dividing into three waves. The first wave is two hundred fighters, and the second wave is six hundred fighters, just behind the first. The third wave is two hundred fighters and is some distance behind the other two." After the scanner operator turned to the southern scanners she reported, "Like the northern force, the force heading to the South Pole is dividing into three waves. The first wave consists of two hundred fifty fighters, following behind by the second wave of one hundred fifty fighters and two hundred shuttles. The third wave consists of one hundred fighters and two hundred shuttles, escorting ten transports. They are some distance in back of the first and second waves."

Colonel Becker smiled. "This is good news. The enemy's advanced waves are so closely bunched together they will crash right into the shield before they can pull up."

✦ ✦ ✦

At the Crystal Palace the festive mood ended as the news came in from the quadrant. A messenger's report was unnerving.

"We have lost half of our quadrant fighter force. Also, the enemy tanker *Parnell* has by some way become an attack craft. It has bombarded our quadrant border defenses. Hibernian ground troops are sweeping into the quadrant. They are now wrecking our fighter bases."

Lady Paisley pleaded, "Your Gracious Majesty, call of this attack before it is too late."

Lord Cromwell, trying to convince himself as much as the matron, said, "Don't you understand? The enemy will dissipate its strength. We will overwhelm them!"

Lady Paisley asked, "What of the *Parnell*? It could attack the nuclear fusion complex at the center of our quadrant."

Lord Cromwell tried to defend his decisions by bluster. "The *Parnell*! That is Commander O'Rourke's ship. Your Majesty, I will present to you the head of that Irish pig."

The applause of the nobility in the audience brought a smile to the monarch. Lord Cromwell smiled too, but his smile was hollow.

✦ ✦ ✦

After the platoon bridges were completed across the river Bann, the Orange militia crossed. The Brittanic forces began to withdraw. Inside his command truck, Colonel McKerr received a radio message.

"This is Colonel Skorzeny. My advance units have linked up with Hibernian troops from Louth."

Colonel McKerr replied, "The enemy is trapped. We will advance to close the pinchers."

The border militia continued forward through heavy fighting. Just before sunset they reached Dungannon. A skirmish line of riflemen was about to fire on an approaching line of men, then one of the Orangemen shouted, "They're singing in German. It's Skorzeny's commandos." The two groups of men shook hands and bear-hugged each other. Stalheim helmets and black bowler hats were exchanged. Colonel McKerr's van pulled up to the

310

advance line. At his order a silk banner was unfurled. It was a banner of King Williams of Orange, the father of the Orange people. The Colonel was about to order the advance to continue. Suddenly an earthquake threw his men to the ground. Without even receiving a radio message, he knew what had happened.

✦ ✦ ✦

On board the *Parnell* the scanner operator announced, "We are coming up to the enemy generating complex."

Commander O'Rourke ordered the ship to bank to larboard and the guns to prepare to fire.

During the settlement of Hibernia in the twenty-fifth century, a source of deuterium was found in Ulster. An underground spring of saltwater with the chemical composition of seawater was located in the center of the quadrant. Deuterium was extracted from the seawater and nuclear fusion was made practical. A complex of reactors had been constructed. Destroyed during a Brittanic attack in 2994, the enemy rebuilt the complex for its own use. It consisted of ten nuclear fusion reactors.

The tanker *Parnell* pulled near the enemy complex. Commander O'Rourke ordered, "Lock in the sensors to the ship's automatic pilot. Have the computer program the ship to climb sharply to two hundred kilometers as soon as the sensors detect the exploding reactors." As the ship reached the target, the commander ordered, "Fire." The ship seemed to disappear as the lasers opened up.

The laser fire hit the complex by total surprise. The transmitters, power lines, and administration buildings melted. Then the laser guns began to hit a number of the reactors. The ferro-concrete buildings began to collapse. The reactors were hit and then exploded. First two reactors went off, then the others followed by chain reaction.

The blast shot up and outward. The entire sky lit up like a thousand suns. On board the *Parnell*, a sensor indicated the force of the explosion to be at least sixty megatons. The massive ship was shaken bow to stern. It climbed upward on automatic pilot. After the ship ceased its vibrating, the commander asked for a damage report.

From the engineering department a yeoman reported, "Some electrical panels have come out. A number of small fires. We are putting them out."

The ship's sick bay reported, "We have concussions and bloody noses, one broken arm; nothing more serious."

After the ship righted itself, the commander radioed to the surface. "This is the *Parnell*," he announced. "To all Hibernian ground forces, we have destroyed the enemy reactor complex. I recommend you cease your forward advance and take cover in case of radioactivity."

Then a radio message came in from Athlone. "This is Colonel Becker. Commander O'Rourke, you are to direct your craft to cover the South Pole.

The squadrons of Major Hoffman and Captain Kesselring will join you. We have just received a report that the last enemy fighter was destroyed."

As the warship moved southward, the ship's crew was cheering. The commander quietly reminded his men, "The next battle is the most important one."

As the *Parnell* headed south, it left a huge crater. It was twenty kilometers in diameter and five kilometers deep, a monument to Brittanian folly.

✦ ✦ ✦

In the war room, reports of the continuing land battle were coming in. The Nigerian IPV radio operator announced, "Colonel Becker, Colonel Costello has a report for you."

A Gaelic accent came over the radio. "This is Colonel Costello. Colonels McKerr and Skorzeny are here with me. Brittanic ground forces are surrendering unit by unit. A Brit staff officer has presented a map of a few abandoned underground railway tunnels. Our forces could bivouac inside until the radioactive fallout is over."

Colonel Becker answered, "Very good. Complete your operations and take necessary cover." He turned to Colm O'Hara and added, "It is fortunate those were hydrogen fusion reactors with no uranium leaving long term radioactivity." Then he ordered the radio operator to contact all fighter squadrons. He ordered, "They are to report remaining fuel supply and estimated flight time remaining."

After several minutes the radio operator reported, "Colonel, each wing captain reports fuel supplies will allow another five to six hours flight time."

Colonel Becker was pleased, "Excellent." By remaining above two hundred kilometers, the lack of atmospheric friction reduced fuel loss."

The colonel radioed to the Bullethead and Athlone squadrons to follow the *Parnell* to the South Pole. All other fighters were to remain over the North Pole.

After the squadrons reached their positions, they radioed the total number of available fighters. The radio operator announced, "The squadrons over the North Pole have about 540 out of an original 690 fighters in the air." Then a few minutes later she added, "South Pole reports 100 out of what was 120 fighters. Also, they have 27 out of 30 Bullethead craft and the *Parnell*."

Colonel Becker was very confident now. "The *Parnell* and the Bullethead fighters are equal to another 150 Needlehead craft. We do have enough power to defeat the enemy."

Taoiseach Colm O'Hara, less sure of the outcome, noted, "That is, if the shield works."

✦ ✦ ✦

312

In the Crystal Palace the mood was now one of shock. The report of the quadrant reactor complex being destroyed ended the confidence of the nobility assembled. Then a giant television screen came on and young nobleman began to speak.

"Viscount Paisley here, on the transport H.M.S. *Invincible*. We are nearing the enemy's South Pole. Our ten transports are moving in two parallel lines. One line is led by the H.M.S. *Hood*, followed by the *Repluse*, the *Renown*, the *Prince of Wales*, and the H.M.S. *Victory*. The second line is led by H.M.S. *Indefeatible*, followed by the *Inflexible*, the *Indominitible*, and *Irrestible*, and the *Invincible*. Our first wave of fighters are decelerating and are only five thousand miles from the enemy's surface."

Lord Cromwell raised his champagne glass, saying, "We are on the verge of victory. Goodbye, Hibernia, and goodbye, Gladstone."

✦ ✦ ✦

The colleen operating the scanners in the war room announced. "The first waves of Brittanic fighters are approaching the poles. Approximately eight thousand kilometers away."

After Cashel was radioed, Dr. McIntire reported, "All projectors ready."

The Taoiseach ordered a viewscreen camera turned on. On a screen it showed the sky over Athlone. The sun had set and the sky was pitch dark. Colm O'Hara said, "If the shield works, the sky will turn light gray, then orange-red as the enemy hits it."

Minutes passed and sweat came down the brows of many men. In the war room, on board the *Parnell*, in the cockpits of fighters, and at the projector stations, men held their breath. The scanner operator read off the decreasing altitude of the descending foe, "6000 kilometers, 3000 . . . 2500 . . . 2000 . . . 1500 . . . 1000. . . ."

At Cashel and at fourteen other locations, charges of atomic particles were radioed to track into the projectors. Transformers bringing in massive charges of electricity started the amplifiers. The radio from Athlone announced the remaining distance. "950 kilometers, 920 . . . 900 . . . 880 . . . 870 . . . 850. . . ."

Dr. McIntire ordered, "Activate projectors," over a radio to fourteen other bases while three of his assistants threw the switch in Cashel.

✦ ✦ ✦

The colleen read of the final distance. "840 kilometers, 830 . . . 820 . . . 810 . . . 809 . . . 808 . . . 807. . . ."

The Taoiseach and Colonel Becker watched the viewscreen. The pitch black sky slowly lightened to a solid cloudy gray. The colleen announced," 806 . . . 805 . . . 804 . . . 803 . . . 802 . . . 801. . . ."

✦ ✦ ✦

At the Crystal Palace the two other screens came on. On one screen was the view inside the cockpit of a Boomerang craft descending over the North Pole. The other was inside a shuttle at the South Pole. The fighter pilot spoke, "Manchester Squadron 1 leader here. We outnumber the Hibernians two to one. We are diving for the final attack. Here we go. . . ."

Then the screen went silent. The voice from the screen screamed, "Our fighters and shuttles, we can't pull out, no. . . ." then silence.

✦ ✦ ✦

As the Hibernian pilots two hundred kilometers below watched, waves of Brit fighters smashed into the shield. Some trying to pull up literally skidded on the shield and slowly disintegrated. In the war room, the viewscreen showed Athlone skies red with fire in the northern and southern horizons. Two minutes passed. Dr. McIntire radioed, "Coolant failing, we will have to shut down the shield."

In a few seconds the red-grey sky turned black again. The scanner operator announced, "Over the North Pole, there are about two hundred enemy left. At the South Pole about one hundred fighters and two hundred shuttles."

Colonel Becker took the microphone. "*Achtung!* This is Colonel Becker to all units. Attack all remaining Brittanic forces. Let none escape." The Taoiseach asked, "Couldn't they spare a few survivors as an act of mercy?"

Colonel Becker replied, "Did the enemy have mercy for the school children of Roscommon or Shankill or the people on board the *Glasgow?*"

The Taoiseach shook his head.

✦ ✦ ✦

Over the North Pole the fighters under Captains McCarthy and O'Rourke climbed to over one thousand kilometers. They overtook the demoralized enemy and surrounded them. Some of the Brittanic pilots tried to flee but were shot to atoms by their own comrades. Others tried to resist but soon were overwhelmed.

✦ ✦ ✦

Over the South Pole Major Hoffman led his Bullethead fighters first into the remaining Brittanic fighters. Captain Kesselring's Needlehead squadrons followed, and together they attacked the fighters and shuttles. Although actually outnumbered, they soon were destroying enemy craft by the score.

314

The *Parnell*, using its greater speed, passed the dogfight, then it pulled up to face the twin lines of transports. The commander ordered, "Helmsman, we are going right up between them. Gun crews, prepare to fire broadside as we pull up to the first two transports."

The *Parnell* moved up to the enemy. The *Hood* was on the larboard side, the *Indefeatible* to starboard. Commander O'Rourke ordered, "Fire." The laser turrets opened up, nineteen of them hitting the *Hood*. The other nineteen firing on the *Indefeatible*. The two Brittanic transports were hit by wave after wave of laser fire. The *Hood* broke up and then exploded in an ion fireball. The other craft veered away, drifting.

The scanner operator reported, "Commander, our sensors indicate it is burning inside, out of control." As the *Parnell* pulled away, the transport vanished.

The remaining Brittanic transports turned about in an attempt to flee. The *Parnell* and the Hibernian fighters overtook them. One by one they were destroyed.

✦ ✦ ✦

On one screen in the Crystal Palace Viscount Paisley was crying for assistance. He screamed, "This is H.M.S. *Invincible*. We are the last remaining transport. All the rest are destroyed. The *Parnell* is attacking. It must have the power of one hundred fighters. We have thirty thousand men on board. Save us. . . ."

The screen went silent.

✦ ✦ ✦

Commander O'Rourke radioed to Athlone. "Enemy attack force totally finished. We are returning to base."

A minute later Captains McCarthy and O'Rourke reported from the North Pole that the enemy was destroyed. Then, over the radio, a familiar voice was heard for the last time.

"This is Defense Minister Joseph Flynn. We, the men of the *Arthur Griffith*, who are about to die, salute the people of Hibernia."

Taoiseach Colm O'Hara, taking the microphone, ordered all units, "We, the people of Hibernia, salute the men of the *Arthur Griffith*."

The voice of Joe Flynn came on again. He and his crew began to sing Hibernia's anthem, *The Soldier Song*.

> We'll sing a song, a soldier's song
> With cheering, rousing chorus,
> As round our blazing fires we throng,
> To starry heavens o'er us;
> Impatient for the coming fight,

And as we wait the morning's light,
Here in the silence of the night,
We'll chant a soldier's song.

In the war room on the *Parnell*, and in the fighters, all Hibernian servicemen gave a farewell salute to the men on the *Arthur Griffith* as the last words came over the radio:

Soldiers are we, whose lives are pledged to Ireland;
Some have come from a land beyond the wave
Sworn to be free, no more our ancient sireland
Shall shelter the despot or the slave.
To-night we man the bearna baoghail
In Erin's cause, come woe or weal
'Mid cannons' roar and rifles' peal
We'll chant a soldier's song.

In valley green, on towering crag
Our fathers fought before us,
And conquered 'neath the same old flag
That's proudly floating o'er us,
We're children of a fighting race
That never yet has known disgrace,
And as we march, the foe to face,
We'll chant a soldier's song.

The Taoiseach radioed back, "Your gallantry will forever live in the hearts of our people."

❖ ❖ ❖

Lady Margaret Paisley grabbed a sharp knife and lunged at Lord Cromwell. As she was wrestled to the floor, she screamed, "You ass! My sons are dead. The entire fleet gone!"

Another member of the nobility turned to Queen Elizabeth, saying, "We are in mortal peril now. It was reported the *Parnell* is now an attack ship of tremendous power. It could attack our planet at will."

A frightened messenger came up to the queen. "Your grace, a Hibernian tanker identified as the *Griffith* has been discovered approaching our planet. It is headed here, to London."

The monarch commanded, "Shoot it down."

The messenger answered, "We have no fighters or surface guns. It seems to be diving like an armed missile."

The mass of nobility panicked and began trying to flee out of the castle. Through the darkened sky over London they could see a bright object

316

moving down toward them. The Queen screamed, "It will crash into the Crystal Palace!"

The *Arthur Griffith* came in at a rate and angle calculated to pass through the atmosphere without burning up. It hit the Crystal Palace like a missile, then an unbelievably bright explosion went off. The mushroom went tens of kilometers into the air. It would be days before the fallout settled. The Brittanic queen, the royal family, and the entire Brittanic aristocracy vanished into radioactive waste.

✦ ✦ ✦

In the war room of Athlone an electrophone call came in. The Taoiseach answered it and said, "That was the Sligo sector Astronomical Observatory. An explosion was detected on the northern pole of Brittania, estimated to be at least two hundred megatons.

After the all-clear sirens were rung, normal radio and viewscreen transmission resumed. The Taoiseach went on the air. "This is Taoiseach Colm O'Hara. Today, January 11, 3154, Hibernian forces launched an all-out assault on the Brittanic quadrant forces. Before noon Athlone time, our entire fighter force engaged the enemy fighters over the Ulster quadrant. At the same time the tanker *Parnell*, which has been converted into a powerful attack craft, destroyed a fifteen hundred kilometer stretch of the enemy border defenses. Our ground forces then entered the quadrant and forced the Brittanic army to surrender. The *Parnell* destroyed the reactor complex in the center of Ulster. Then our forces took defensive positions over the North and South Poles of our planet. When the enemy home fighter force attacked, they were destroyed by an atomic sub-particle force shield, the Alpha X-10 project weapon. Over 80 percent of the enemy home fleet was destroyed by the shield. Our forces totally destroyed the remainder. Then the tanker *Arthur Griffith*, with a volunteer crew comprised of all terminally ill men, including Defense Minister Flynn, crashed into the Crystal Palace of Brittania.

"The entire war lord class of the enemy planet perished in the explosion. It is believed that the enemy will be unable to threaten our nation for the next fifty to one hundred years. We have regained Ulster quadrant, and we have totally defeated the enemy. As Taoiseach, I am proclaiming a ten-day period of thanksgiving and celebration."

Colonel Becker then produced a bottle of Schepps from his homeland, and victory was toasted.

✦ ✦ ✦

In Athlone and Dublin crowds of people poured out of shelters. In a couple of days many returned from evacuation centers. The shirt factories proclaimed a week off. Showgirls and shirt factory girls danced in the streets with returning pilots. The Quinncannon sisters drank a toast of ale with Pam O'Reilly and the girls of the Golden Peacock.

✦ ✦ ✦

On the *Parnell*, the servicemen's room was opened. The crew and the auxiliaries had a big dance. The commander himself danced with his daughter and his future daughter-in-law.

✦ ✦ ✦

At the Kelley farm in Kilkenny, the children, Barry and Esther, were asleep. Michael and Ann Kelley, Theo and Maureen McLaughlin, and Naomi Sennech prepared to celebrate. Terri Lynch arrived as passes were issued as soon as the alert ended. Naomi wrote a note in English, saying, "I have a bottle of wine, kosher Abahamite wine, to toast our day of deliverance." When the glasses were raised she said, "*Mazel Tov! Shalom!*"

In Connemara the five orderlies went to Arthur Conncannon's house in Clifden. While Kate MacBride hugged her brother Timmy, Mary P. Conncannon kissed her uncle. Jamie Feeny said, "We are going to ask our boyfriends to move here in Clifden. It will be a beautiful place to live and start life all over again." Caroline Quinn and Mairead McNutt prepared tea and brambeck. The little family celebrated a new life for all.

✦ ✦ ✦

Inside an underground railway tunnel, Colonel McKerr led his men in prayer. His voice carried down the tunnel to all of them. He spoke:

"Our heavenly father, thou hast delivered us from the hands of thine enemies. Thou hast freed the oppressed from the oppressor. We thank thee in the name of thy son, Jesus Christ. Amen."

✦ ✦ ✦

In the houseboat in the quadrant marshes, Eugene, Beth and Cathal O'Rourke, and Deirdre O'Toole listened to the announcement of victory. Eugene O'Rourke said, "Bethie, could you make us a pot of tea, sweetened with honey?"

His wife said, "Yes, and I've been saving some brambeck for this day."

Eugene walked out of the parlor and into the cold night air. He walked into a smoking gazebo he had built. Deirdre followed behind him, and Cathal came behind her. Eugene filled his pipe and struck a match, while Deirdre took out a cigarette. He gave the girl a light, then began to light his pipe.

Deirdre kissed Cathal on the cheek and sat beside him. He placed his arm around her, saying, "I know Father has to go back to Earth."

Deirdre answered, "Yes, but he will be back. Then we will celebrate the third wedding in his family."

✦ ✦ ✦

The Hibernians celebrated for days. There would be a massive collective hangover afterwards. However, for now, death had taken a holiday, and after 160 years Hibernia was united and free once again.

Epilogue

Three weeks had passed since the explosion that had destroyed London. Masses of Brittanians fled into the southern hemisphere. In Melbourne, in the Australian quadrant, a provisional government had been set up. It was attempting to call a constitutional convention to establish a new government.

The assembly was held inside an auditorium. Former members of the old Parliament mixed with operatives of the Underground. After the chairman called the meeting to order, a number of spoke on how the government should operate. Then a middle-aged housewife, not an official member, began yelling at the speaker. She screamed, "What are you talking about? Who will take care of us? Our queen is gone. The royal family is gone. Without the aristocracy, who will reign over us? You traitors, who is going to govern our planet?"

"We will govern ourselves!" A familiar voice spoke from a side door. All eyes turned to the bearded man who entered the assembly, still in prisoner's uniform but recognizable.

The astonished speaker announced, "It's Mr. Gladstone. I immediately give to him the floor."

The elderly statesman took the podium and the audience began to applaud.

The housewife screamed, "Are you trying to be crowned Gladstone the First?"

The audience joined her, yelling, "Hail King Gladstone! Hail the new king."

The speaker exploded, "No! No, you fools. I will accept no crown. That was our country's downfall in the first place. The monarchy and aristocracy misled the Brittanic nation, both here and on Earth, for nearly three millenium. We must establish a commonwealth, a republic with no titled nobility. A state and society where all citizens are equal. I will not accept a crown.

I am willing to serve as counselor and minister for a few years. Afterward, you are on your own."

The previous chairman announced, "Here is the first Prime Minister of the Commonwealth of Brittania, W.F. Gladstone."

The audience was applauding and chanting, "Gladstone, Gladstone, Gladstone, Gladstone."

For W.F. Gladstone it would be the twilight of a long and distinguished career as a public servant. For Brittania, it would be the dawn of a new era of freedom and dignity.

He raised his hands to silence the crowd and then spoke. "If our new government rules wisely, perhaps in a few years we can establish normal relations, not just with our Hibernian neighbors but with the entire Outer Solar System. Perhaps again Brittania will be an honored and respected planet."

Again the audience applauded, yelling, "Gladstone, Gladstone, Gladstone." He gave a prayer of thanks.

It was mid-February. At St. Stephen's church in Athlone every pew was packed. The double wedding had become a major social event. The two brides came down the aisle, one after the other, Shelley O'Rourke in a pink gown, Brigid Hallohan in bright red. The grooms, on furlough from military service, were in tuxedos. The grooms came alongside their brides, and Father Paul Joyce began to perform the wedding.

Commander O'Rourke sat in the front pew with the parents of Brigid Hallohan and those of Sean O'Connell. Brigid's mother said to him, "I understand my daughter met your boy the same way I met my man." The commander nodded.

Among the guests at the wedding were the Taoiseach, the new defense minister, and the other base commanders and their wives. The Quinncannons, the Fitzgibbons and many showgirls, Kate and Timmy MacBride, Arthur and Mary Conncannon, Jamie Feeny, Caroline Quinn, and Mairead McNutt were present. The Kelley-McLaughlin family was there, with Terri Lynch, Naomi Sennech, and the McKerr family. Many Athlone pilots were also present. Lieutenant Cosgrave and Ensign O'Brien were the best men. Pam O'Reilly and Deirdre O'Toole were the maids of honor, and Cathal O'Rourke brought the four golden rings. Uncle Eugene and Aunt Beth sat in the rear.

When the newlywed couples left the church, the brides threw their bouquets. Brigid's was caught by Pam O'Reilly, while Deirdre O'Toole caught Shelley's. Colonel Becker told Commander O'Rourke, "You may have another wedding."

The reception was in a legion hall and the commander was talking to Colonel Kalminsky. He said, "It looks like many of our pilots will be leaving the service in a few days." He then noticed Ensign O'Brien eating a piece of wedding cake. While the others used a proper knife and fork, the ensign stuffed it whole into his mouth by hand.

The commander then said to Colonel Kalminsky, "Discharge time is always at noon. At fifteen minutes to noon of the ensign's discharge day, you are to summon him to your office and promote him to lieutenant. He could not be court-martialed for his table manners in that short a time. That way, when he reaches retirement age, his military pension will be on the pay scale of a fully commissioned officer."

The colonel answered, "A gracious action, Commander."

After two wedded couples drove off to their honeymoon, the commander turned to his brother, sister-in-law, and son. He said, "Eugene, take care of my boy Cathal and his friend Miss O'Toole in my absence." Then he hugged his son, "Cathal, obey your Uncle Gene. When I return from this mission I will retire from the service. We'll go to the reservoir behind Robert Emmet Dam for fishing."

Cathal, trying to hide tears, said, "Goodbye, Father."

❖ ❖ ❖

Commander O'Rourke entered the bridge of the *Parnell*. Colonel Kamzov and the colonel's son, Corporal Kamzov, were present. The colonel spoke. "Comrade Commander, we believe the ship and the five transports can do at least factor 60."

The commander replied, as he took the control console, "Good. Let's be off." He ordered the helmsman to pull out of latitudinal orbit and personally radioed the transport to follow.

In a few minutes the helmsman reported, "We have reached factor 67. The transports are just behind."

The commander then told the navigator to plot the course to Earth.

He turned to the Kamzovs. He said to his orderly, "Corporal, you can prepare a large tea for me and the colonel. Set it in my quarters, then you are finished for the night." He turned to the colonel, "I have my chessboard ready for a game, but first I am going to take a walk."

Commander Seamus O'Rourke walked out of the bridge, then up a stairway to his private walkroom. He opened a double layered metal dome door, revealing a transparent dome in between the two metal doors. He looked out the transparency to the starlit mass of space.

The *Parnell* and five transports were heading to Earth. Their mission: to assist the American scientist Underground to overthrow the Environmentalist dictatorship that had oppressed America for twelve hundred years. One epoch struggle has ended; a new one was about to begin.

As the commander watched as the stars passed his ship, he began to whisper, "Bernadette, my beloved wife, wait for me. I will be coming soon. We have won the war. Eamon and Shelley are grown and married, and

Cathal is going to be a fine young man." As he continued to watch the stars pass he felt a celestial presence. Then he head the voice of his wife.

"Seamus, my dearest husband, I am waiting for you. I have been watching over our family. I have acted in intercession on the behalf of our family and our planet-nation. I have prepared our home for us beyond the stars when you finally tire of life's work. I am waiting for you, Seamus, my love."

The space gunship *Charles Stewart Parnell* and five Hibernian transports raced across the vast mass of space. Ahead lay the planet Earth and enslaved America. Behind them was their home planet.

Hibernia, so long a province, was a nation once again.

67°30"

Sligo Derry Tyrone 45

60

22°30'

Roscommon St Columbas • St Agnes Fermanagh Cavan
Gaeltacht St Athanasius • St Basil

30

St Benedicts Ireland

0

Tipperary Longford West Meath

• Cashel • Alpine 22th

Offaly • Port Leois Laois 45

30

Waterford

Limerick Kilkenny • Kilkenny Carlow
Peenemunde

67°30"

Mayo

10

Galway
Clifden

Clare

0

30

081

0

Cavan

Monaghan 45 Armagh

Carrickacross

Shantill
Orange
refugee/1948

Meath

Louth

Dublin Cork
Dublin

WGST
Meath

223

Port Laois

Kildare
Laois

45

Northern Hemisphere

Northwest
Quadrant
(Connaught)

Galway
Mayo
Roscommon
Leitrim
Sligo
North Pole
Antrim
Donegal
Derry
Armagh
Down
Tyrone
Fermanagh
Equator
0°
Monaghan
Cavan
Tyrone
35°
45°

Northeast
Quadrant
(Ulster)

Southern Hemisphere

90°

Clare
Limerick
Tipperary
Cork
Kerry
Waterford
Dublin
Wexford
Kilkenny
Carlow
Wicklow
Louth
Kildare
Meath
Laois
West Longford
Longford
Equator
35°
90°

Southwest quadrant
(Munster)

Southeast quadrant
(Leinster)

Western Hemisphere

Cities
1. Dublin
2. Athlone
3. Clifden
4. Port Laois
5. Carrickmacross
6. Shanhill
7. Kilkenny
8. Cashel

North Pole

Leitrim Manor Hamilton

Connaught quadrant

60°

Mayo   Sligo

30°

Galway   Roscommon   Equator

Clare   Tipperary

30°

Corr   Limerick   Waterford

60°

Kerry   Killarney   Munster quadrant

South Pole

Ulster Quadrant

67°30'   Donegal

45°   Derry   Antrim

Tyrone   Down

22°30'   Fermanagh   Cavan   Monaghan   Armagh

Longford   Westmeath   Meath   Louth

45°   Offaly   Laois   Kildare   Dublin

67°30'   Kilkenny   Carlow   Wicklow

Wexford

Leinster quadrant